Chapter 1...Gui arrives a

Nine days after leaving Nantes, and two (d'Angély, Gui and Sir Richard brought th... whole command down to the teeming city of Bordeaux at last.

Dust covered and bone weary on exhausted mounts, they were all pleased to have arrived safely. Lancers, bowmen, heavy foot and spearmen, their gisarmes over their shoulders, long swords by their sides; their two tilt carts, laden with their gear and their wounded, Father Matthew in close attendance, all worn down and saddle sore. And at the back, behind Gui's and Sir Richard's chargers, now on leading reins, rode the two Vernaille brothers on their own destriers but under close arrest.

Twice they had tried to escape by falling off their mounts and once by running away at night. But each time they had been re-captured swiftly, the last by one of their own men. So on entering Bordeaux, Gui had ordered them to be tied to their saddles, with two men on either side of them with orders to strike them down if they tried anything further!

And in all truth, with their moaning and whining about discomfort, sparse food and being 'belted knights', Gui and Sir Richard had had enough of both of them, and were delighted to bring them, still bound, to the High Constable's Officer of the Guard and his men in their tough mailed hauberks and nasal helmets.

With simple bindings of cord now replaced by chains, and preceded by Gui and Sir Richard, Father Matthew close behind them with his big leather scrip, they were brought before the High Constable of Bordeaux himself, Guard Commander and overall military ruler of the greatest city on the western seaboard of France, where the Golden Leopards of England bravely flew from every gatehouse...the Lord Baron, Sir Hugh Willoughby.

A man of enormous presence, a former Commander of the North during Gui's time on the Borders before his knighthood, and now King Richard's High Seneschal of all Aquitaine, he was the most powerful man in this whole region of France. As they were ushered into the great man's Chamber of Office, ahead of his prisoners, Gui knew they would be amongst friends for the next few nights at least.

Sir Hugh, square faced and of medium height, with great strength in his broad shoulders as you would expect in so practised a fighter, rose to greet them with a smile as they were ushered into the room.

Steel-blue eyed, as befitted his Norman ancestry, clean shaven and with a fine head of dark brown hair, he had broad hands but fine tapering fingers; more those of an artist than the great swordsman he truly was. He greeted Gui warmly - this young warrior whom he remembered with affection from their days together on the Scottish borders, when Gui was still only a squire learning his knightly ways.

Both had served under the fierce auspices of Baron John de Methley, that bold knight whom Old King Henry, Richard's father, had put in charge of England's northern borders under the Lord Earl Percy of Alnwick, the great Earl of Northumbria, the King's Warden of the Marches and plenipotentiary in the north. Who ruled over those bleak, misted lands where Scotland marched beside England along the wild Cheviot hills, from Northumbria to the lakes and mountains of the west. It had been the great Earl himself whose sword had knighted Gui before the young man had returned to his estates around the King's New Forest in Hampshire. And Sir Hugh was delighted to see him again...though not the two Vernailles, and especially not Sir Bernard whom it was quite clear had lied to him from the outset...*And I will make him rue the day he ever did so!*

Coming from behind the massive desk that filled one corner of his great room, where three monks were seated amidst a pile of parchments, heads down, their quills busily scratching away, he came and stood before the two disgraced chevaliers and glared at them, hands on hips, his long bliaut of red and green wool, belted with golden leather, swirling as he moved.

"On their knees!" he growled with a sharp gesture to the burly escorts who had followed Gui and Sir Richard into his high ceilinged chamber. "*On their knees!*"

Lit by tall lancet windows that threw brilliant shafts of golden light across the polished oak floor, with beautifully crafted stone work in the corners, the chamber was in stark contrast to the dishevelled figures forced down before King Richard's Chief Justiciar and Seneschal of all Aquitaine. He now stood over them, the very harbinger of death itself. His flowing robes and clean cut mien, his athletic movement around his chamber and the strong aura of power that emanated from him made the two men at his feet seem no more than the strutting popinjays they truly were.

"I have heard, and read, all I need about your wicked attempt on the lives of these worthy knights," he said quietly, holding up the detailed parchments that Matthew had sent forward from the abbey at Saint Jean d'Angély. "One of whom, Sir Gui de Malwood, is King Richard's chosen man...and of those who follow him," he added, his voice deadly in its soft intensity, every syllable clipped and perfectly delivered. "And of your close liaison with the Lord of

Narbonne, the Lord Baron, Sir Roger de Brocas, the King's declared enemy, and whose warrant for arrest for High Treason, with the King's Great Seal upon it, Sir Gui carries with him."

"Sir Geoffrey and I did not know..." Bernard de Vernaille tried to say, any arrogance he might have displayed stripped from him, his face now pale with fear, sweating, his voice trembling.

"*Do not lie to me!*" Sir Hugh rasped, in a voice of iron. "I have had enough of your dissembling and your lies, you miserable wretch! This time it is not a 'pass' out of the city that is at question...it is your very lives!" he went on remorselessly, as they both gasped with horror.

"Do not mumble to me that: '*You did not know!*'" he seethed at them with biting scorn. "I am my Lord King's Chief Justiciar and Seneschal in all Aquitaine...a fact which seems to have eluded you completely in your planning. I see and hear *everything!* I hold the power of life and death over every soul within these Marches...*Of course you knew!*

"Do not attempt to lie to me. Of course you had full cognizance of whom you were attempting to kill. And why, you fools? For greed...and Philip Capet's royal favour? For hollow promises that never would have been kept? And that your father, whom you so disparaged in your ignorance and folly, never would have entertained for one single moment...how he must be spinning in his grave over your venal stupidity. Least of all would he have accepted promises from a vile mountebank, whose hands are thick with the blood of others; in whom 'honour' is a foul joke for the simple minded, and whose word means *nothing!*

"Yet it is with this man-of-blood, Sir Roger of Narbonne and Gruissan, whom you have chosen to ally yourselves! This ignoble, deceitful robber baron," he went on relentlessly, "who has murdered Sir Gui's family, slain his soldiers, burned his home and kidnapped his betrothed Lady, Alicia de Burley, King Richard's own Ward...the penalty for all of which treachery is death...as it should be!"

"*But we did not do those things!...*" Sir Bernard pleaded, bringing his hands together with a rattle of chain.

"No! You *snake!*" Sir High snarled at him, his voice rising as he spoke. "You didn't! But...you cretin, you chose to ally yourself to the one man who *did!* And have since carried out his orders to make a further attempt on Sir Gui's life, which has now failed. And tomorrow, at dawn, you will both pay the ultimate penalty for your stupidity..."

"*No!*" Both men cried out in terror.

"*Yes!*" Sir Hugh shouted, his face twisted in disgust for their behaviour. "You will pay in full for your greed and for your treason to your King...to whom you swore allegiance for your lands before me in these very chambers after your noble father had died, and whose honour you befoul...*at dawn tomorrow beneath my headman's axe!*" he added in ringing tones of utter finality:

"*No!*" They both cried out desperately again; Geoffrey de Vernaille scrabbling across the polished oak floor to grovel at Sir Hugh's feet.

"And, as declared traitors," he snarled down at them, spurning the wretched man's appeal with his foot, "henceforth *all* your lands will return to the crown. *No appeal!* Sergeant," he called out to his own officer standing nearby. "Take them down!"

And as their escort dragged them off their knees, still pleading their innocence and begging for his mercy, and hauled them to the door with tears in their eyes and faces grey with shock and terror, he turned his back on them with a chilling lack of remorse.

Then they were gone...their cries and struggles fading as they were marched away, while Sir Hugh turned to his secretaries and ordered them to draw up the necessary documents for his signature and his seal, before ushering them out of his room, requesting his guards by the door to send in two of the castle varlets to wait on him as he did so..

"In truth, Hugh? Their execution?" Gui questioned him after the door had finally been closed, surprised at the swift ruthlessness of his decision.

"Yes, Gui. *In very truth!*...But it does not please me to do so," he sighed. "The fact is that those two have been on the edge of such disgrace ever since their father, Rupert de Vernaille, died a few months ago. He was a man of great integrity and honour; served the Old King all his days and was always known as the 'Old Lord'. He was a true leal man to the crown, and one of the first of the Poitevin barons to swear his allegiance to Richard Lionheart after King Henry died at Chinon last July. He would have hated what his sons have done. He was a fierce old man and would have sent them to the block himself! "But those two?" He gestured at the closed door with disgust. "They are prime articles of malice and treachery. Bernard far worse than Geoffrey, but both weak, dissolute and greedy.

"I have had my eye on them for some time. I was certain that they were bound in with de Brocas...but could find no proof of it! But this," he went on, smacking the message Gui had sent ahead of his arrival with the back of his hand. "This is exactly what I have been waiting for. And they are one tentacle of that foul octopus in Gruissan that I shall lop off!"

And banging his hands together for a job well done, he ushered both men across the room towards where a number of great padded armed chairs stood loosely scattered around a fine oval table of polished walnut, beneath a pair of tall windows overlooking the city and the great Garonne river that wound its way through it.

"Now…you young cockerel," he said with a shake of his shoulders and the broadest of smiles, after Gui had properly introduced him to Sir Richard L'Eveque, and to Father Matthew, whose hands he warmly clasped. "The last I heard of you, before this *débâcle* with de Brocas, you were high in King Richard's esteem and off to seek your fortune with him in the Holy Land. I saw your name on the lists of knights who had signed up to travel with the King to Marseilles…heard you had done well at the Christmas joust in London too? Knocked our good Lord and Master clean out of his saddle and onto his royal backside no less!" he added with a great guffaw of good humour. "My boy, you are famous!"

And shouting for wine and food to the two tabarded servants who had quietly entered just at that moment, he flung himself down into a chair, gesturing for Gui and his companions to join him; and in a moment they were all settled comfortably in four of the huge padded chairs that graced his apartment, their long legs stretched out at ease for the first time since leaving Southampton.

*

"So, Hugh," Gui said sometime later, looking around him delightedly: "High Constable of Bordeaux, eh? You have done well for yourself, old friend. Different from the last set of bivouacs we shared along the Scottish borders?"

"Dear God, I should say so," Hugh replied, ordering wine to be poured from a tall pitcher into beautiful gilded goblets of chased silver, while his servants handed round dishes of simple savouries and smoked meats and cheeses. "Those awful quarters just south of the old Roman Wall at Haydon Bridge…burning cow dung for warmth? Brrrrrr!" And he shivered in bitter remembrance.

"Not like these, that's for certain." Sir Richard threw in lazily, looking around him. "I've been up there too in my time. Not a jolly experience I agree!"

"So?" Gui said, leaning back in his chair. "How did you manage all this without a massive bribe? For you've never had more money to spend than you could shake a stick at!"

"John de Methley recommended me to our Royal and Noble Suzerain, when he heard Richard was looking for a good man to run things here.

Richard's Commissioners considered my papers; and the King approved my appointment personally."

"Without any payment?" Gui asked incredulously. "I had heard these fat plums were only going to the highest bidders. You know how hard the King has been at work raising money for this Crusade?"

"It seems our good Baron John was owed a favour by the Old Queen, Eleanor, Richard's doting mama...and chose to call it in on my behalf in thanks for saving his worthless hide that day those Borderers attacked us at Kielder."

"How was that?" L'Eveque asked, with interest.

"A very nasty business, Richard," Gui said, turning to his friend. "It was winter: cold wet and miserable…real bleak, starving weather. The high fells can be bad places at those times anyway, but when the clouds tipple over them, and the wind's in the north-east full of sleet, they're plain, bloody frightening! We'd had a message that something was up. Left at daybreak in sleeting rain, two dozen men-at-arms and two knights. It should have been easy. Then the mist came down, and the sleet turned to snow. Couldn't see fifty yards, and suddenly we had arrows all about our ears, followed by a wild hand-to-hand assault.

"They were cattle rievers, of course! Thirty well-armed men and over a hundred head of fine black cattle. De Methley's horse was killed beneath him, took three in the chest poor boy, and went down in a welter of legs and flying hooves. Pinned the Baron as he fell, and the bastards made for him like rats up a pipe! Half a dozen of them, big, bad buggers I can tell you. Hugh was the first to reach them. Leaped off his charger and laid about him. Desperate cut and thrust, wild bloody *mêlée*, while Baron John struggled to get free. By the time we all got there Hugh was in a bad way. Bleeding like a stuck pig and shouting defiance at the devil himself! De Methley was unmarked; and the six would-be killers were all dead. Blood and brains everywhere: Hugh's armour was running with it!"

"Took me damned near two months to recover from those wounds," Hugh broke in with a grin, lifting his sleeves to show the scars. "After which any damp weather makes every joint groan. So, when this post came up I jumped at it. Baron John put the word in…and I got it!"

"Oustanding!" Gui exclaimed, with a broad smile. "It couldn't have happened to a better man. Where is Sir John now?"

"On his way to Messina. Which reminds me, you young varmint! I had him through here a week ago seeking news of you from Longchamps, no less; our good King's Royal Chancellor of England! And mighty mysterious he was about it all too. He's gone on now to join Richard at Marseilles. Apparently he arrived at Malwood with a strong escort just after you had gone, having left his ship at Southampton, and he's been chasing after you ever since I expect."

"Did he leave a message for me, Sir Hugh?"

"Yes. I have it on my desk somewhere. Said If I saw you to give it to you straightaway," he added, getting up and rootling amongst the papers and parchments all over his desk. "Yes! Here it is. Hope it helps." And he handed Gui a small folded square of parchment.

"What does it say?" Sir Richard asked a moment later, as Sir Hugh looked on silently.

"…'I hear the 'Man Eater' is loose. Look to yourself, and keep her close. That 'Tiger' still wants your Lady. Richard needs to know!'…" And he paused to look up and then out of the window, his eyes suddenly unfocused, his mind miles away…*And so King Richard bloody well should do by now! But where are you, my Alicia? France? Spain? Morocco? In that fucking bastard's castle? Where are you?*…And he ground his teeth in silent fury, while his friends watched him anxiously.

Then he sighed and blinked his eyes, and smiled at their concern. "Don't you worry about me. It's that fucking bastard who needs to worry!" He swore violently. "I'm fine…just thoroughly *irritated*," he growled angrily, "not knowing anything, and this," he added, smacking the parchment with his fingertips. "This doesn't help much! Did Baron John say anything else?"

"I told you. It was all very mysterious. He didn't stay for more than an evening meal and was then away on the first tide in the morning. Who's the 'Man Eater' and who's the 'Lady'? And does our Lord King know?"

"Well, he should do, Hugh. Father Matthew wrote to the King both at Vézelay and at Marseilles, long before we actually set out. And then again from St Jean after our recent struggle there, so he should know everything that has happened to both us and the Lady Alicia. And the 'Man Eater' is the noble Lord Baron of Narbonne and Gruissan, Sir Roger de Brocas!"

Chapter 2...How Sir Gui acquired a company of Welsh Bowmen.

Sir Hugh Willoughby looked at Gui from beneath his eyebrows and his breath hissed over his teeth: "So…that Man-of-Blood eh? He and Count Raymond together are the bane of my life, and with Richard off Outremer to whack the bloody infidels, they have become ever more dangerous.

"Richard and Philip have the County of Toulouse between them like two dogs with a juicy bone. It is only this crusade they have both signed up for, and exchanged the Kiss of Peace over, that is now keeping them apart…and Count Raymond and Roger de Brocas are just looking for any excuse to bring war to the region to set the ball rolling to suit themselves. The King would do well to sort out that bugger, de Brocas, once and for all."

"That, Sir Hugh," Father Matthew said, looking grave, "in large part is exactly what we are here for. It is all in the papers I have with me in my scrip," he added, patting his large leather satchel as he spoke. "And very much to do with the 'Lady' in Longchamps' message"

"Ahh! Your Lady Alicia, eh?" he asked Gui with a grin. "The White Rose of Malwood, I understand. The 'Lady' in the note...not Rochine de Brocas?"

"No, Sir Hugh!" Father Matthew exclaimed. "Definitely not Rochine de Brocas!"

"In all truth, Hugh," Gui said after a pause, spinning the stem of his wine goblet in his hands. "It is on *my* Lady's behalf we are on a desperate quest."

"Ah, that makes more sense," Sir Hugh added, looking at him over his wine.

"You know of the fair Lady Alicia, Sir Hugh?" Father Matthew asked in his liquid, Spanish voice.

"Who does not, who knows this boy here? She is the little beauty he told me of when we were last together on the borders. In that vile peel tower near Otterburn, with the rain pelting down and nothing but mouldy cheese and stale bannocks to eat for days and days. How could I forget," he said, poking his finger at Gui. "You went on and on about her 'til we could bear no more." And they all laughed.

"Well, Hugh," Gui paused, looking at the tall Benedictine in his black robe, his eyebrows raised, his head cocked inquisitively to one side…*Here we go again, like Niort! Someone else to tell. If Philip doesn't hear of all this it'll be a bloody miracle*…but receiving a slight tilt of Father Matthew's head in return he took a deep breath and said: "There are things I think you need to know, Sir Hugh, before I can explain any further, but without any tall pitchers with long handles," he ended enigmatically.

"What?" Hugh asked, startled, then looking around he suddenly grunted: "Oh!...yes…I see!! Quite right!" And swiftly dismissed the two varlets who had come in earlier, ordering his door keepers to let no one in unless it was their Guard Commander himself, and even then only if the castle were on fire!

"Right, Gui," he said tersely after the men had all left the room, "we are as secure here as we can be anywhere in this city. So…tell me all!"

And, with Father Matthew's help, and the documents they had brought with them both from the Holy Father, whose personal seal he had never seen…and Richard Lionheart's which of course he had, they told him all that had happened: about the attack on the *Mary* and how Alicia had been stolen and abducted by El Nazir on de Brocas's orders, and about the fierce battle at Saint Jean d'Angély…that made the air whistle through his teeth. About de Brocas's involvement with King Philip and Prince John…which made him growl and smack his fist into his hand. And about Lord Roger and Prince John's dealings with the Assassins and King Philip's duplicity…which made him throw his hat on the floor and stamp on it, he was so enraged.

"*That fiend!*" he roared out at the end. "So he's the 'Tiger' in that message! That murderous, two-faced, black-hearted piece of fucking French *shite!* Thank God I am an Englishman! That miserable bastard is just too evil to live!" And he drank deeply of his wine, draining his goblet, while pacing his chamber.

"So…young Gui," he said after a few deep breaths to calm himself further, and before half the guard turned up to see what all the shouting and banging had been about. "You'd like some help, I suppose?"

"Yes, Hugh. Please. We have lost about a third of our strength, one way and another. Both dead and wounded. And though we have picked up some good men along the way, de Forz's lancers have been superb, and his Gisarmiers are truly courageous…what I could *really* do with is a good company of longbow archers, if you have any, and a score or so of heavy foot!"

"God's Bones, Gui!" He exclaimed, looking down at him, still seated. "Why not half the bloody Crusader army, while you're at it?" And he laughed, throwing up his hands. "Heavy foot I can possibly lay my hands on…but longbow archers, out here? They are as hard to find as chicken's teeth. The French don't use 'em, and even Richard prefers the crossbow, easier to train raw troops to use. So…I don't know."

Then, after a pause while he paced up and down some more, with Gui and Richard studying his face and Father Matthew putting everything back in his scrip, Sir Hugh suddenly stopped, looked out through the windows for a few moments…*Oh, I don't know though. Maybe I just might!*...then turning, he looked across at them with a wicked grin and said: "Unless, of course, you'd fancy a few wild Welshmen out of Gwent? Can't speak the lingo, can't understand a word they say and look as if they've spent their lives in a hedgerow…but my city guard have had more trouble with them fighting everybody they can lay their hands on than any other troops under my command. They are a right royal pain in the arse, and my Captain of the Guard would just *love* to get rid of the whole scaff-raff of 'em!"

"How many?"

"You did say a whole company?"

"Yes."

"Hmmm. How would three hundred and fifty suit you?"

"*What!*" Gui and Sir Richard said together, astonished.

"Three hundred and fifty of 'em, lad! All mad, as only a true Welshman can be! But great fighting spirit, Gui!" Sir Hugh said with a laugh. "*Great fighting spirit*…anyone and everyone! Your Master-at-Arms will just love 'em."

"Do we have any Welsh speakers amongst our merry crew, Gui?" Father Matthew asked a moment later, amused at Gui's dismay.

"Oh my God, no!" Gui moaned bitterly, his face an almost comic mask of concern. "Don't tell me…they don't speak English!"

"Actually, dear boy, I expect most will do!" Sir Richard drawled. "And we have Welsh speakers anyway. There's Fitzurse's number two, Johnny Goodrich, and…two of Allan's lads I think? Peter Clwyd and Davy Appleyard…he's from Abergavenny; and young Jamie Grosmont."

"In all truth, Gui," Hugh said then seriously, as he came across to him. "Language is less of a problem than you might think. Gwent has been more Normanised than many other parts of Wales, and many of the Welsh princes and chiefs have married into Marcher families. No…it's not their language that's the problem, Gui," he said seriously, with a wicked grin through sly eyes at Sir Richard sitting opposite, and a swift wink behind Gui's back: "…it's their sheep!"

"*Their sheep?*" Gui queried, completely bemused, his eyes on stalks, mesmerised by Sir Hugh's words…while Richard had to get up and walk away, his hand over his mouth and Matthew behind him rolled about silently clutching his belly. "They have flocks of sheep with them?"

"Yes, Gui. Sheep!" Sir Hugh went on matter-of-factly, looking at Gui with a straight face, putting his hand confidingly on the younger man's shoulders "You can't have a Welshman without his sheep! Everyone knows that, laddie," he continued in a wholly mundane, matter-of-fact voice, while behind Gui's back silent tears ran down Matthew's cheeks. "They need the sheep to keep their legs in trim! If they don't have their sheep…especially with one leg always shorter than the other…

"What do you mean?" he queried, amazed. "Welshmen? One leg shorter than the other? Are you mad?"

"No, Gui. It's a real problem the boyos have. No…truly!" Sir Hugh exclaimed earnestly. "It's all those Welsh hills, Gui, don't you know?" he added then, his face finally betraying him.

"*Without the sheep they all run round in circles!*" Richard and Matthew both shouted out together as all three of them collapsed in howls of laughter.

There was a short strangled pause then, while Gui looked at them all astonished. Then, as realisation dawned, his face changed and with a sudden roar he shouted: "You *buggers!*" Hurling cushions at them, laughter spilling out of him at last. "You rotten, bloody *buggers!* You really had me then, you bastards! Bloody sheep! It'll be their damn leeks next I suppose?" he added with a wide grin. "And always having to leave their line of march to take one!" And there was a further moment of laughter and hoots of derision for his awful pun.

"Thank God for that," Matthew said a moment later, throwing his arm across Gui's shoulders. "I was beginning to think you'd never crack the paint!" And he ruffled Gui's head with great affection, before sitting down near where he had thrown himself, while they all collected themselves and more wine was poured out.

"So, Hugh?" Gui grimaced, putting his linked hands across the back of his head, while Father Matthew still chuckled beside him. "*Three hundred and fifty Welshmen?* Dear God Almighty. I must be mad! Stark, raving mad! Bloody 'sheep' indeed," he muttered darkly, looking round at their grinning faces as he reached for his wine goblet. "I will get you back for that, I swear it!" And they all laughed again.

"Anyway…'sheep' or not, have they got all their gear?" Sir Richard asked, looking at Sir Hugh directly.

"And their shafts, Sir Hugh?" Matthew added, in all seriousness. "After d'Angély, I know just how many they will need for a real fight. *Thousands!*"

"And who is their leader?" Richard queried swiftly, with sensible concern. "They must surely have one."

"And do I really want them?" Gui groaned, his head in his hands. "Three hundred and fifty of the wild buggers!" he went on then, looking up. "They are all mad in that country, Hugh. We'd never control them...let alone get them to be disciplined! Only the Irish are worse!"

"Slow down! Slow down!" Sir Hugh laughed. "Yes, they do have all their gear. No, I don't know about their shafts, but I suppose so...they must have brought some with them because you can't get clothyard shafts in Aquitaine for love nor money. But their leader is a problem, Gui, as he died of the fever two weeks back. A month or so after arriving here. A real shame as he was a fine man and a brilliant organiser, Sir William of Grosmont. Not a bad fellow, full of ideas, and a proven warrior with much experience of border fighting. Gathered all these men together on a wing-and-a-promise and persuaded them to go with him from Wales on the King's Crusade."

"They must all be mad! What made them do it? The Welsh have little love for the English at the best of times. And to journey Outremer? I am truly astonished!"

"He filled their heads with tales of booty and fighting, which they loved. Better than reiving English cattle and being hanged for it! They are Welsh after all, and the chance to use their weapons as they love to do is not easy at home now, too many restrictions. But against the Infidel? The chosen enemies of God?...meat and drink to a Welshman. They do love a good scrap, and the chance to make some money doing it seemed a great idea to them all."

"Hence joining the Crusade?"

"Hence joining the Crusade, indeed, and William believed in the longbow completely...which the King doesn't! As I said, our noble Lord and master likes the crossbow because he can use one...good with it. So William thought if he got some lads together from around Gwent, he could join Richard in the Holy Land, dish out the business to the bloody infidels, prove the longbow as an amazing battle weapon, do some good looting and come back with a reputation, a barrel full of golden bezants and red hot ideas on how best a castle should be built. Bringing those ideas which he would have seen Outremer, and planting them in the Welsh Marches. He would have been a real asset to you."

"Only he's dead!" Gui said dryly.

"Yes, as a proverbial door-nail unfortunately. As I said, a shame."

"Is that why the men have become a problem?" Father Matthew asked, giving Sir Hugh a raised eyebrow as he spoke. "Because their leader is dead? Do they not have any good sergeants?"

"Or competent under-officers?" Sir Richard chipped in lazily. "A Company that size must have at least seven or eight sergeants. One per fifty men and a full Master-at-Arms to rule them all, just as we do."

"Richard's right, Hugh. There must be good men amongst them to maintain order. Why have they fallen to pieces so badly? And who has taken command since Sir William died?"

"That's the real problem. No-one as yet, Gui. Though I do have a man in mind of whom you might approve. He's been on my staff for a while, and you know him, I think. From our time together up by The Wall. Welsh, and a bonny fighter. Helped save de Methley's hide that vile day when we were so viciously attacked…"

"Not Robert FitzMiles?" Gui queried with a wild whoop of surprise. "That wild lunatic out of Abergavenny…with a penchant for healthy girls with black hair, blue eyes and tits like melons. He's a rogue with twinkling eyes and a Welsh accent you could cut with a cleaver. But a bonny fighter, Hugh. A bonny fighter, as you say. Quick on his feet and brave as a lion…and nobody's fool either. Now he would be good to have on our side against de Brocas!"

"Also knighted now as you are, Gui… and lusting for a command of his own. He's out on a short mission for me just now, but will be back with us tonight. If you want him, he's yours and those bowmen too. They are a bit of a split unit just now, which is part of the problem, with some wanting to return home and others wanting to move on to join the King. There are good sergeants amongst them, but no Master-at-Arms. Sir William wouldn't appoint one. The man you need in that post is Gareth Morgan. He is one of the best sergeants I know and has striven mightily to keep his boys occupied and off the streets as much as possible. But with no clear leader to turn to…"

"…He's up a creek without a coracle!" Richard chipped in with his lazy smile and a swift chuckle. "Sounds like a good man, Sir Hugh. Gui and I, and John Fitzurse…and the good Sir Robert FitzMiles, will need to meet him soonest. But before any further decisions can be made, Gui and I need to meet with Sir Robert himself. A bonny fighter he may be, but unless he is willing to take orders from me, and fight under Gui's House banner, then it won't work. He may have a divided command to contend with, but we cannot afford that kind of nonsense, not where we are going. Yet those are the men we surely need alongside us, Sir Hugh, when we march out from here in three days' time. So let's hope he is truly amenable!"

"Richard is right, Hugh. Of course I would love to have Robert join my command. But he's a bit of wild man, our Robert, and Richard is my Guard Commander in whom I have complete trust. And no matter what I may feel about a former comrade-in-arms, Richard will have the final word. If he can't trust him to do as he's told, then that'll be a disaster just waiting to happen."

"He's Welsh...so of course he's mad!" Hugh replied to Sir Richard with a smile. "But he's not bad, and his heart's in the right place. You'll like him! And *of course* you want his men, Gui," he added with a wicked grin. "You just don't know it yet!" And at the sight of Gui's face, screwed up as if he'd been sucking lemons, they all laughed.

"Must be related to the last Earl of Hereford, Roger FitzMiles?" Father Matthew said, startling everybody. "Cousin of the Baron of Abergavenny, the one who got himself murdered in Castle Arnold twenty years ago."

"Yes," Sir Hugh agreed, equally surprised that a Spanish monk should know so much of English nobility. "His father married into the local Welsh gentry, as so many Normans have since the Conqueror set the Marcher Earldoms up a hundred years or so ago. But he is allied with the de Clares of Gloucester. Wears a golden dragon displayed, wings out like a bird and all claws, tongue and spiky tail, armed Sable on a field Gules... How did you know, Father?"

"I have met with de Clare," the tall Benedictine said in his Spanish lilt. "Long ago, when I was fighting with Sir Yvo for King Henry. I have not always been a Black monk. Must be the current one's father, I suppose. They are all red-headed and can be as mad as March hares when the fancy takes them; as fiery in temperament as the colour on their heads.

"Anyway, Hugh, why doesn't anyone want these lads?" Gui asked, genuinely puzzled. "I mean, I have seen what prime longbow archers can do to mounted troops in a matter of minutes, and it is truly stunning, almost horrifying in a way. De Courcy's men stood no chance; they were all simply wiped out!"

And he paused to drink, his mind suddenly miles away, looking blankly over the rim of his goblet:...*Sweet Wine of Christ! I saw what happened at Saint Jean with just twenty five of them. Just think what three hundred and fifty would do? Pretty awesome in skirmishing terms alone, obviously, but on a battlefield? If they were properly trained and disciplined? And well sited and protected? They could be just devastating*... and the breath rushed out of him with a hiss of excitement.

"Have you actually seen these boys in action, or practice?" Sir Richard asked.

"No, in honest truth, L'Eveque, I haven't," Sir Hugh replied swiftly. "Only by reputation and soldiers' gossip...but I am told they can *all* shoot a fine arrow! And then they ended up here by accident. The ship taking them to join the King's army at Marseilles got badly damaged in a sudden freak storm, and they only just got up the Garonne by good fortune. Now they need employment. Welsh knights are not wealthy anyway, and Sir William broke himself caring for his men. But apart from Robert FitzMiles no-one here speaks Welsh," Hugh added. "They don't seem to speak much Frankish, and longbows need to be handled differently if they are to be truly effective. So no-on here really knows what to do with them. Then Sir William died and the men got restive, especially as they have had no pay for several weeks. They're good lads, Gui, really. Just need sound organisation and good leadership…and a handful of silver coins in their pockets and they'll be the best troops in Christendom…will you take them?"

"God's Bones, Hugh!" Gui swore. "I don't know. Oh…Hell's teeth…Yes, why not? Just think what a stunning effect disciplined longbow archers could have on the battlefield…"

"…If you can control them," the broad-shouldered Seneschal of Aquitaine interrupted, looking the young Lord Baron of Malwood squarely in the face. "The Welsh are funny buggers, Gui. Remember they are almost all Celts; can be very superstitious, and lose heart quickly if things don't go their way in a battle. Oh, they are vicious enough, and can fight like the very Devil himself. But they can be proper sulky as well, and that makes them difficult to handle…and then morale can be questionable on the field of battle. If things go hard for them they may not stand. So be warned. But if they like you, and trust you…then they can be devastating. It's very much your call."

"Richard?"

"Well, I hear all that Sir Hugh has to say. And I agree with him in many ways. The Welsh can be real funny buggers. But I have also seen them in action, and if we can win them over, and put good officers in charge of them; and if Sir Robert is willing to make a proper 'go' of them all, and will do as he is told when necessary...then I say 'yes!'"

"Very well then Hugh, very probably I will…God knows I need them! But first I'll need to speak with Sir Robert. And second I want my Master Bowman, Dickon Fletcher and Allan-i-the-Wood, the Under Sheriff to the Earl of Southampton, the Chief Verderer of The King's New Forest, to see them in action. They are two of the very best of the best I know with a shaft, and if these boys you so want to get rid of are any good, or even half-way good, with true potential, then, God help me! Yes, I'll take them all, Hugh, *and* pay them their wages. Oh, *Christos*," he added, covering his mouth with hands. "I bet the wretched bastards can't ride!"

"No! They are all mounted, Gui," Sir Hugh replied with a laugh. "No problems there. Welsh mountain ponies and beautifully cared for…The Welsh are good with their beasts. But they are all rather shaggy. Need clipping, especially in all this heat."

"So…mounted are they indeed?" And he whistled through his teeth. "Now, by God's Throat, Hugh, that *is* a real bonus!" Gui replied with a grin, throwing up his hands in mock surrender. "Well, you smooth talking Chancellor-of-all-Aquitaine," he said to Sir Hugh as he stood up. "You will owe me plenty! And the King, who will be getting really prime bowmen by the time my lads and I have finished with them, the like of which he will *not* have seen before, will owe me plenty, too!"

"Right! Then that's settled," Hugh said, rising too and giving Gui a bang on his shoulders. "You do me a great service in that, dear boy, and I will find you the twenty heavy foot you asked for earlier, maybe even a few more if you are lucky. But," and he smirked wickedly, "I expect..."

"*…They'll be half and halfers!*" Gui and Richard finished for him with a grimace.

"So, you've been there before?" Hugh laughed, unabashed.

"Yes, with Count William de Forz at Niort," Sir Richard answered with a wry smile. "But we managed. They're all good lads, and fought well at Saint Jean. I'm not complaining."

"Count William, eh? Good man. Loyal through and through. Excellent! One thing's for certain, this place will be a lot quieter after you've gone!" And he threw back his head and laughed again. "Oh, it *is* good to see you see, Gui!" he exclaimed, flinging his arm over his shoulder. "I have missed you, you mad bugger! Those were *good* days up in those wild hills of Northumberland, away up on the Scottish borders, eh?"

"Yes, Hugh, good days!" Gui replied with a warm smile, and moving to one side he raised his glass in a warm toast of comradeship: 'To good days and absent friends!" And all four of them drank long and deep together.

"Now, Gui," Hugh said briskly, putting down his goblet. "How about a hot bath and some proper food before you go to your rest? Sadly I have an execution to arrange, so I will join you later. And, no…Father," he added, seeing the tall Spanish Benedictine about to speak. "This has to be done, but I don't want you involved in it any more than you are already. You have done enough. Another priest can go to them both tonight. All the niceties will be observed I assure you.

"In the meantime, my castle steward will show you to your rooms and my officer commanding the castle guard will see to your men, and make sure they lack for nothing. We all eat in the Great Hall, and you can meet with Sir Robert then. He's actually a capital fellow, as you well know, Gui: mad about longbows and sheep breeding, seriously…oh, and building castles and brewing beer!"

"Yes, Hugh. He is a grand fellow, and it will be good to see him again and catch up on his wild love life. Whatever happened to Black Molly?"

"Don't ask, Gui! Don't ask!"

And while his guards held open the door to his chamber Sir Hugh Willoughby, Constable of Bordeaux and the King's High Seneschal of all Aquitaine swept out on a gale of laughter, leaving his guests to follow his Steward, stately as Sir James Bolderwood at home in Hampshire, with the same long ebony rod of office, to lead them to the rooms being prepared for them elsewhere in the great citadel of Bordeaux.

*

Later that evening, Gui walked on his own along the empty battlements of the enormous fortress that dominated the city, a blessèd relief after the bedlam of noise in the Great Hall which had been packed. The laughter and shouted conversations, the music, jongleurs and trumpets had all melded in amidst the general clatter from their dinner together, which had been both raucous and good humoured in every way, until he felt dazed with it all. The food had been varied and excellent after forced rations on the march, and the wine rich and free-flowing. But it had been wearing, and he had longed to escape and find a little solace for himself and his thoughts, right away from the rush and bustle going on around him. And despite all that had happened that day…it *had* been a jolly, rousing occasion, as Sir Hugh had wanted it to be.

The long top table, covered with beautiful napery, graced by Sir Hugh's slender lady, the Lady Anne, and her bevy of bower maidens…quick to cast out their lures for the two young English squires whom they swiftly reduced to blushing confusion with their giggles and sly glances...had been laden with good things, and the varlets had been well trained and attentive.

He sighed, and smiled.

The Lady Margaret would have approved: no goblet or beaker was left empty for long; clean bowls of warm rose-water and immaculate napkins had been brought to every diner on the top table with which to wash their fingers; the dishes had come and gone in smooth but bewildering profusion, and all as neatly carved and served as even Sir Yvo could have wished. Yes, his lovely mother, and his dear Papa, would have approved!

And as for Sir Robert FitzMiles?

To meet up with him again had been a real joy….*I had forgotten what a good table-companion he was!*...A tough, compact man, almost the same age as Gui with the blue-grey eyes of his Norman father with aquiline nose and hard square hands, and the dark hair of his Welsh mother with her shorter stature, long fingers and musical voice. Yet, small as he was in height, he was a proven fighter as Gui knew well, was as strong as an ox, rode a horse as if he and the beast were as one, and had a fund of wicked stories that kept them all laughing, especially his tale of Black Molly and the hobby-horse...*And I'm still not sure I believe him. He always was one for tall stories!*

But…oh how he had missed his beautiful Alicia.

She just loved parties like this and was always so funny afterwards with her mimicry and witty comments. She always made him laugh! That was half the fun of going anywhere like this together…the after party chatter. In their solar, or getting ready for bed…*especially in the winter when there is always a great fire to laze before, when the wolves howl in the forest and the wind rattles the shutters against their casements.*

So, when the meal was all over and he had done the 'pretty' with his hosts, arranged to meet with Robert the following morning; checked with Fitzurse and all his other Officers that their men were in good heart; visited Beau in his stable; and made sure Simon and Philip were safely housed amongst their fellow squires, he had slipped from his room below. And leaving Simon to sort out his things for the morning, and clean his armour until it shone, he had left to walk the ramparts and be alone with his thoughts…and a good goblet of the richest Bordeaux Sir Hugh had in his great castle cellars.

*

From the highest battlements the whole city lay spread out below him in a maze of twinkling lights and great flambeaux, especially down by the harbour where ships seemed always to be on the move or being made ready to do so. And the shouts of the stevedores and younkers, crewmen and wagoners came faintly up to him on the sea breezes as he leaned against a massive merlon, his silver goblet sitting comfortably on top of the wide crenel that lay between the huge 'tooth' of ashlar blocks he was stretched out against…and the next, in a seemingly never ending line of battlements and towers.

South-east from where he was lazing it was already dark, the countryside black except for tiny flickers of life where villages or distant towns still showed small signs of wakefulness. While away to the west, the after-glow of the long day that had brought them down to Bordeaux was still faintly golden, streaks of crimson and tangerine just showing above the far horizon, the vasty clouds of night, tinged purple and midnight blue, pressing them down into the sea while above him the stars were just beginning to fill the velvet sky with distant sparkles of silver light. All around him the air breathed softly, warm and full of scent from the city below him and from the sleeping countryside beyond; and from the huge river that wound its way along the city's edge and from its wharves and docksides.

And he longed for his Lady with all his heart!

Not just because he physically wanted her so badly that it hurt…he could live with that…but he missed simply being near her: to stand back and gaze at her; to put his arms around her and cuddle her when she least expected him to be there...*And it's always the little things that are so special: listening to her humming around the castle...and the cheery responses she always gets from the guards and castle varlets as she moves about the place. To hear her sudden giggle when someone says something funny; the small bunches of herbs and flowers she puts out for me to find; her scent in a room she has just left, the swish of her skirts amongst the scattered herbs in the hall, the busy trip-trap of her shoes along the stone passage ways...and always the ripple of her shining laughter somewhere in the castle...*For wherever his Alicia was there was always a sense of brightness and light, of warmth, as if she carried the summer with her, and her smile was like a huge sunburst that lit up her blue eyes and made them sparkle like sunlight on a lake of cornflower blue beneath an azure sky.

He breathed in slowly…and then sighed so deeply he felt almost bereft of the power to take another breath, reaching out into the night for her hands, so longing with every fibre of his being that he could just turn around…and somehow, like magic, she would really be there!...*With her arms open for me, her eyes alight with the love I need so badly, and that certain smile she always has for me when she wants me to hold her...*Just as he wanted to hold her now, wishing so much that he could just walk forward and gather her up into his arms and feel her softness melt into him as he folded her into his embrace for ever.

And he longed for her touch…*For her fingers on my arm, her hand against my cheek, or in the small of my back, the ruffle on my shoulder or on the back of my neck; for the sound of her voice and the love that is always in it; for the scent of her hair and the fresh smell of her body after she has bathed; for her laughter and the way she tosses her head and grins at me when she is feeling just wicked, and mischievous...*And he longed for the sheer joyousness of making love to her: of revelling in her breasts, so richly crowned; the silken smoothness of her skin; the luscious curve of her hips...*It's not just all that...It's how our bodies fit into each other so..so gently, yet with such a firm embrace...and she is always so willing to receive me. I only have to touch her and her body opens for me, soft and wet and ready; nuzzle her, and her breast is there for me to suckle, her arms holding me to her as if I am the baby she so wants to give us. Oh Alicia, you are so special for me. I love you so very much I feel my heart will break...*

Just to know she was there beside him was always wonderful.

Her breath soft in the darkness, gentle, slow; her long lashes closed against her face, her mouth just so kissable, her forehead so waiting to be caressed and stroked like the beautiful, adorable, great purring pussy cat she truly was!

And high on the deserted battlements of far Bordeaux his voice cried out softly to her from his heart and soul in the warm darkness of that summer's night...*My darling, don't give up hope. I am coming with flame and steel and thunder to rescue you. Wait for me! Wait for me!'*...And raising his glass to the north-east...where Narbonne and the distant Chateau Grise still lay undiscovered, and un-assaulted, he drank deeply.

Tomorrow he would talk with Matthew and Richard; sort out their wounded; garner fresh supplies; buy more horses; meet again with Robert, and with Gareth Morgan, and see to his new Welsh bowmen. *'Running in circles indeed!'* He laughed at their silliness. It had been a rare jest, and with a final chuckle and a lighter heart he went to his rest.

He knew without fail just where to find her...and would not leave one stone of the Château Grise unturned in his search for her

In three days' time they would leave. And in another week, God willing, he would have her out of that bloody place if he had to tear it apart with his bare hands! And the Baron and his *so* lovely daughter?...*By God's Throat! But I will have them too...flesh, blood and bones, everything: torn limb from limb if necessary!*...And he raised his goblet again to the north-east and draining it to the very last drop he hurled it with all his strength from the battlements...*a gift to the gods for good luck!*...then, grunting with satisfaction, twisting the massive gold ring with the huge Malwood Emerald set firmly within it on his right hand, he turned and strode away to his apartments.

Chapter 3...The Company of the White Rose view the 'Tiger's' lair.

Alicia, with her Household hedged in by the Baron's escort, caught her first sight of Gruissan, and the great castle that dominated it, as she crested the long hillside they had been following, and Lord Roger imperiously threw up his hand and called a halt, before drawing her off the road.

"Here, my Lady Alicia," he called out, beckoning her forward from amongst his men. "See," he said with obvious pride, "The Château Grise. This is my home, in Gruissan, as it will be yours also," he said, sidling his great stallion away from her to let her through..."after we are married!" he added with quiet definition as she came abreast of him, his dark, hooded eyes seeming to look into her very soul as he spoke.

Alicia paused then to give him a brief sardonic look...*over my dead body, you bastard!*...her eyebrow lifting quizzically for a moment as she brushed past him, Soraya and Agnes following, before giving a final shake of her head and ignoring him completely. Yet she was ever conscious of his presence, and of his eyes following her, and she was pleased to turn her back on him for once and look out across the wide vista that had opened out for her as she moved, her body swaying to her horse's gait, before halting where the land almost fell into the sea below, to give her this first view of the 'Tiger's' lair!

From where she was seated the dusty trackway beside her swooped away towards the distant town of Gruissan, following the coast right round a huge étang, like a vast bay, edged with sand, that stretched away in all directions, the far shoreline almost out of sight. Backwards to *La Robine*...the great canal dug by the legions to join with the River Aude, that had made Narbonne the great bustling port it was...and forwards to the wide Circle Sea itself, the beautiful Mediterranean, an impossibly, shimmering, glittering blue beneath the intense sunshine that seared everything it touched. And here, guarding the narrow entrance to the Circle Sea itself, stood the fortress that the Archbishop of Narbonne, Guillaume de Broa, had re-built thirty years before to protect Narbonne and its busy port from *Les Corsairs;* the ravening, Moroccan pirates that were such a terrifying scourge along those coasts.

The Château Grise, towering up into the flawless cerulean sky that arched above them, where the long dusty coast road finally curled to its destination, dominated the promontory on which it had been built, and Alicia was fascinated by it. Leaning forwards, resting her arms on the back of her tall saddle, she studied it with care…*Not bigger than Castle Malwood, but oh so very different. More like Castle Foix, in that it is built into a massive rock that lours over the whole town, the streets and houses with their scarlet pantile roofs huddled all about it…*But there the similarity differed strongly because, unlike Foix, the Château Grise was built on a circular promontory, all the streets running round and round it as they climbed, stopped only by the massive walls and towers of the castle itself which completely filled the very top of the hill like the highest tier of a giant wedding cake. And right in the centre of all, like a huge votive candle, its scarlet plastered walls melded with the pantiled roofs of the houses of the town below, was the *Tour Barberousse*, The Redbeard Tower, the very final citadel of the castle.

As she stared across the water at it, at the stark battlemented walls studded with great square towers; at the dry ditch that surrounded them, and at the tall gatehouse entrance above which floated two great emblazoned standards, so Alicia drew in her breath…*God help us! That is one powerful fortress…How will Gui ever get inside?…*And she looked again at the standards: one, the golden twelve pointed cross on its field Gules of the Lords of Toulouse; the other, the black boar's head on its field Vert of the Lords of Gruissan and Narbonne, while from the very highest point of the Redbeard Tower, covered with golden Fleur de Lys on their field Azure, flew the enormous standard of the Kings of France…*No wonder that bastard is so confident. The man has great allies. What can Gui do against the King of France?…*And she gritted her teeth.

Her eyes following every line of wall and tower, right down to the huge dry ditch that surrounded the whole fortress, the long drawbridge that crossed it, now open against its Lord's coming, and the enormous gatehouse entrance that guarded it…Alicia missed nothing.

As Gui had taught her, she let her eyes flow over everything seeking flaws…those little faults that jarred, the balance of walls to towers that faltered, the stone work that appeared uneven, walls that seemed recently repaired; stone ditches not cleaned out properly…*Sweet Lord. There are none that I can see! Like Malwood, this castle seems beautifully balanced, as well between sea and sky as between sea and land…*and Alicia's breath hissed over her teeth.

From top to toe it would be a real pig to assault!…*And if the ditch is revetted in stone, and all the ground around it scraped clean it will be even more so as there will then be a clear killing field between the nearest houses and the castle ditch…*Of course she could not see the other side of the castle, but there was likely to be a well-defended harbour there also, where supplies or reinforcements could be landed safely, well shielded from any land-based enemy if there was a siege...*The only thing this place does not have is a barbican defence before the main gateway!*...but then perhaps the Baron did not consider such a huge extra expense necessary. And Alicia could also see from the constant flicker of sunlight off polished armour that it was well defended, with many men on armed patrol constantly moving along its crenellated walls.

She drew in her breath sharply once more...*Yes...a real brute of a place! Only a wild, surprise assault could possibly work here...and that would be frighteningly chancy. A night-time escalade? Or a traitor behind the walls?* She shuddered at the prospects, her blood suddenly running cold through her veins...*And to batter a way through? Don't even think it! Impossible without full Royal support and a huge siege train!* She sat back and shook her head, and laughed with derision at the very idea of such a thing.

Dear Sweet Lord...however is Gui going to get in?

*

And as Alicia gauged the great Château's defences...so the Baron gauged hers, and smiled.

Now he had her he had no intention of letting her go, nor of letting her slip through his fingers as she had done in England. Especially not since he had tasted the soft sweetness of her lips!... *And it will do her no harm to sit her mare, study the castle and its powerful walls and towers, be aware of all those who man them and understand that this time there will be no escape. The Château Grise has been preparing itself for just this very moment for months. Nothing can stand in my way now!*...He knew she was King Richard's Ward, but Richard was journeying to Marseilles and then to Sicily...his whole mind set on his Crusade to wrest Jerusalem from Saladin. Surely he would not bother himself with one silly girl? Nor would he want a row with King Philip on the eve of setting out together on this ridiculous crusade. He would just want to get there...and then, God willing...*Insh'a Allah!*...he smiled to himself...*That big bastard never would return!*

And in the meantime?...*In the meantime I will conquer this delectable English citadel sitting her horse so securely. Batter her into surrender, breach her walls, overpower her defences and pierce her cool, withdrawn superiority to her very core!*...He would plunder her, ravage her, body and spirit until he broke her to his bridle...and he would ride her hard. God could have her soul, and Sir Gui de Malwood her heart for all he cared!...*But she, the Lady Alicia de Burley, she I will have. I am invincible!...*And he smiled ruthlessly to himself as he thought it. Her lands, her body, the fruits of his loins out of her womb...*everything will be mine!...*And through her the key to unlimited power from the Crystal, and he smiled again and shook his great shoulders....*Truly, life is good!*

And turning, his voice as warm as the sun on his back, he lazily hacked Charlemagne over to join her: "You like what you see, my Lady?" he asked curiously, his eyes black and still.

"Your home is very impressive, my Lord Baron," Alicia replied with condescension in her voice, privately thinking that it was a bloody military nightmare, and how in God's Name Gui would even get near it...let alone seize it, she did not know. "I hear you have a famous Roman Bath within your walls? Constantly fed with hot water?" she asked then, masking her thoughts.

"That is right, my Lady Alicia," he replied formally, smiling down at her. "I see Soraya Fermier has briefed you well. When my great grandfather re-built the castle he found natural water and a magnificent Roman hypocaust system dug deeply into the rock, part of a great palace built here a thousand years ago. He employed a team of clever engineers and water specialists, and an excellent master mason to refurbish it. So, now it all works beautifully, and there is plenty of easy labour with which to maintain the furnaces when needed in the winter time. It is fed from hot springs and is a real luxury. I am sure Soraya will show you everything when we get there. I hope you will like the apartments I have had prepared for you?"

"I am sure I will," she replied with a cool, enigmatic smile, looking at Rochine's tightly closed face as she spoke...*Now, what's going through her busy mind I wonder?...*"I can't wait to get there and see everything for myself. I hope you have suitable rooms for my people, too, my Lord Baron. As you know from his letter that I gave you yesterday; Prince Nazir was quite definite about them"

"Oh!" he exclaimed, his black eyes unreadable beneath his thick eyebrows. "I am sure you will be very satisfied...in every way, my Lady de Burley," he replied again very formally, with a slight bow...*God knows, I have gone to enough trouble!...*"They were my wife's private apartments. Constancia always loved them," adding with quiet satisfaction over his shoulder as he kicked Charlemagne on again: "It is where she died!" And he enjoyed Alicia's sudden gasp of astonished dismay almost as much as he enjoyed the sudden look of fear that crossed Rochine's face...and the furious, wicked sideways glance at Alicia that followed it.

*

Rochine, watching her father ride away with her cousin beside him, her small entourage close behind her, was wracked with jealousy and malice…and lust: lust for her father's time, for his affection, for his value of her…and for the explosive, rampant maleness that she had found only in his arms. All the more jealous since she had seen her father kiss Alicia on the lips. *How could he humiliate me so..so brutally? I hate her!*

Yes…she enjoyed the bodies of those women by whom she was tempted or, who like Soraya had been gifted to her by her father, and whom she'd had specially trained. But none of them could fulfil her the way he did! Her father. And even though the specially fashioned aids she'd had made in leather were good - made from patterns found on Grecian urns and Roman mosaics discovered beneath the castle in her great, great grandfather's time - they were not the same!...*I want him! I want him!...*was the sudden mantra that rushed through her. And the thought that he might make love to Alicia in the same way as he made love to her was just too much to bear…and her whole being writhed as if she were under the lash… *And what if through that conne anglaise…that piece of English cunt… he finds a way to make the crystal work without me? What then?...*

The very thought was simply unbearable…*Or if there should be a child?...*And she groaned in mental and physical torment, making her gelding suddenly jump and skitter. *Non!...Et non!...*And she gritted her teeth and snarled deep in her throat. A little while longer and the little witch would be gone, long before she lost all control over her father completely…and that simpering Agnes!...*And as for that putain! That salope! That 'Mistress Fermier!'...*She growled again, cocking her head from side to side in savage, silent mime…*She will be gone too! The price is fixed…it just needs my orders to put the whole plan into motion...*And she made her horse jump and skitter again as the hatred for them all rushed through her body.

But there was also fear as well.

Sudden gut-wrenching, palpitating fear that her father might, actually, know what had really happened to her mother, his lovely Constancia, whose bewitching beauty she had so wanted for herself…yet had never quite attained. She had her mother's lust, and her body…but she didn't shine and dazzle in her father's eyes as her mother had done. Oh, she could make him want her, and pant for her and ravage her…but that special look of melting love that she had seen so often on her father's face whenever he had looked at her mother…*That! I cannot achieve...No matter what I do he will not give just 'that' look to me!*…and she was still torn apart by jealousy because of it.

She wanted him all!...*ALL!*...And her whole body twitched and writhed beneath the lash of that all-consuming, desperate desire…*And this conne anglaise! This Lady Al-ic-ia!*... She mimed with a pert toss of her head…*The little bitch with the big, firm breasts and long nipples, narrow waist and rounded haunches; who could wield a sword like a man and ride like an angel; and who has suddenly so inserted herself into my father's heart and mind that he can think of nothing else? She must go! Must go! Go!*...And she almost shouted it out aloud in her anger and her bitterness.

In the meantime she would give herself to him like never before, her '*Lord Baron*'.

And she knew he wanted her.

She could always tell…by his eyes all over her, by his quickened breathing, by the way he clenched his hands when he saw her…especially after he had been without her for several weeks. But if nothing else he needed to know what was happening with that bloody bastard, that '*Chien de Malwood!*' that 'Malwood Dog!' she snarled, spitting out his name. And where he was now? And she smiled to herself again, her eyes glittering in the sunshine as she rode along…*For as long as he is still wearing the ring my father returned to him the night of the fire, the so famous 'Malwood Emerald'*… she sneered…*The very ring that had been given to my great aunt, Philippa de Brocas, when she married Alicia's grandfather*…he would know...*He would know!*...And then there would be an end to it once and for all! And she threw back her head and laughed….*Once and for all!*

*

Aquib and Aziz, with Najid close behind them, also looked out at the great castle opposite them across the bay, and then out to sea from where the *Morning Star* would soon be arriving to take them off at last. Knowing that while they had been struggling across the wilder parts of the French countryside, coping with the Lady Rochine and fighting off bandits and wild mountain bears, the *Star*, with all on-board, had been safely sailing round Spain, past the Pillars of Hercules, and into the Circle Sea. Aquib grunted in quiet frustration…*how I wish we were all safely on board, and not stuck out here like stray sheep waiting for a wolf!* Any day now might find her sails on the horizon and her oars beating the sea into foam…and any day might find them dead with The Lady's steel in their throats, or her poison in their bellies. And he grunted again...*Not if I can help it!*

In the meantime they still had their orders from El Nazir, which they were all sworn to do their best to carry out, not just because their Prince had so ordered them, but because they had come to value their charges for themselves, especially the Lady Alicia...*No Angel from the Koran could be braver or more lovely!*...But seeing the Baron again, and feeling the tensions between him and both the women he now had in his life, Aquib could see that this was not going to be easy, and looking at the great fortress with its multiple towers and massive walls he shook his head with concern.

"This is not good, my brother," he said to Aziz in his deep voice. "Our Lady is going to be in trouble. I can *feel* it! The Lady Rochine is in a very dangerous mood."

"True, my friend. But what can we do? I know we have our orders from the Prince, and that our Lady has given his letter to the Baron. But if he does not honour it, what then? I know we are the best...but, *By the Beard of the Prophet,* Aquib, we cannot fight the entire castle guard!"

"No...my Aziz, but we must do our very best to stay nearby her...and to Mistress Agnes and Soraya too."

"Our Lord Prince has told us we must do so. Sadly the Baron is not a man to be trusted, Aquib. I think he plans harm to our Lady Alicia?"

"I hope not, old friend," he sighed, watching Rochine following her father. "I would hate to draw steel against our Lord Prince's only infidel friend!" Then, turning towards Aziz, "I wonder whether the Baron knows he has two tigers by the tail now...not one?"

"The Baron's daughter...and our Lady?" Najid interrupted.

"Yes, Najid. The Lady Rochine. She is the one you really have to watch out for most. Everything you cook...and you are still doing that, remember...*must* be safe, little brother. It was the Prince's most insistent order for you. If you think The Lady has been near something you are preparing, then give it to a questing bird, they are always screaming for scraps, and start again with something different."

"Our Lady also still has the box that de Vere gave you, Najid," Aziz said to him quietly. "You must ask her for a spoonful of that powder in a vial, sealed with wax, and we will try it on a stray cur from the town. Then we shall really know what we are dealing with!"

"That is good advice," Aquib said, looking down at the little cook with a smile. "If anyone falls ill they will all think poison...and will kill you first!"

"I always have my khanjar," the little man said tersely, opening his coat a shade to show its ivory hilt.

"Good, my brother. *By Allah!* Keep it sharp. Truly you are '*usama*' Najid," and there was a short burst of laughter. "Now, kick-on! We must not get left behind."

Chapter 5...How the Lord Baron wooed the White Rose of Malwood.

A short while later the Baron moved them all forward again, down the long slope of the hill and then around the edge of the huge étang that led to Grise at last. Or 'Gruissan' as Alicia was learning to think of it now, as she walked her horse down the sloping road, the sun hot on her back, the blue sea sparkling as far as the eye could see...*It is all as beautiful as I have been told. That sea is amazing, and the sky? Incredible! It is all so bright my eyes hurt!*...Distant ships sailed like painted toys on a huge ruffled blue carpet, their sails shining white against the far horizon, almost dusky purple where the sky's blue edges met the sea.

And she was tired!

They all were, especially after the scares of the day before yesterday when in fleeing Rochine they had run right in to the Baron's arms...whom she had found herself greeting with unexpected warmth as her immediate saviour, arms closed around him, his deep voice in her ear telling her all was well...and his lips pressed to hers in a sudden unexpected kiss. A kiss that had shaken her to the core; both for its sudden warmth and because it had shown him as a man of passion, and not just the ravaging pirate that she knew him in very truth to be!

It had been a shocking moment.

Not because he had kissed her, that was bad enough...but because her whole body had responded to his touch in a manner beyond both her desire and her understanding. *How could I after Gui? How could my body so betray me?*...She loved Gui with all her heart and soul, of that she was certain. But de Brocas's nearness, and his strong maleness, and the sudden safety that his arms had offered her from all the terrors she had suffered on her journey had left her suddenly vulnerable...and in that moment he had kissed her.

She must take care that he did not do so again!

After which meeting they had then returned to a nearby inn, the 'Fox and Goose' which, by chance he told them all, he had apparently been visiting when word had reached him that there were bandits threatening the road beyond Limoux...an infamous band of desperate renegades and lawless men. Wild killers all, so he had heard from Monsieur Perdrix the *aubergiste.* Murderous wolfheads who had been terrorising that area of the countryside for some while, especially up in the mountains. And he had ridden '*vent à terre*' with his men to lend his support to the local authorities…and had found her instead! Such a surprise! Who had apparently been running in terror from his daughter, thinking her men to have been these same robbers! While actually it had been his own Guard Commander in control all the time…she remembered Gaston de Vere? Came with him to England? Yes? Of course she did!...And there was he racing with his men to rescue her from these same robbers and fiercesome outlaws! *Quelle horreur!*

And he had thrown up his arms in mock dismay to much mutual laughter!...'*Ho! Ho! Ho!*'…and all of it completely hollow as she knew, with absolute certainty, with what wicked spite and fury Rochine had actually been pursuing her! All of which had made her laugh hugely inside at the whole mammoth hypocrisy of it all!...'*As if I am some stupid 'numpty'*…as Gui would have said, '*Wi' nowt bi straw in't 'ead instead o' brains!*'…And she snorted with derision.

Nevertheless, rescue her the Baron surely had, for when Rochine's men had then come rushing up with drawn swords and armed crossbows ready to fire, her troops had been just as appalled to see the Baron out on the road…and just as surprised, as she had been herself!

So now, to Alicia's own personal chagrin, she had been forced to dine with him in the inn, then entirely taken over by the Baron and his entourage, alongside his daughter, who had sublimely managed to put aside her jealousy and hatred as if they were not there, both of them proving to be excellent company.

As Soraya had said on board the barge, sitting with a sardonic smile on her lovely face, The Lady could behave as if you were indeed her very best friend ever, only to turn and rend you limb from limb the very next moment…and you *never* knew which she was going to be until she started!

And, of course, over dinner, to everyone's astonishment and praise, out had come the tale of the outlaws and the bears! How she and Soraya had stood their ground in all the fury of the *mêlée* that had followed the attack upon themselves by Fermier's men, and how her little Arab household, themselves an astonishing gift from El Nazir, had rescued them with the help of one very angry She-Bear and her two cubs.

But of Paul Fermier's role in that whole saga none had clearly spoken, nor even of what they had all really been doing there in the first place…in desolate forest lands so far from the main Toulouse road out of Foix! Both facts which had sent Rochine's brows flying up and then settled in a grim line of dour speculation…*Now, what is that conne anglaise hiding? Why has she not told Papa it was from me she was fleeing? That bitch is more cunning than a barrel full of monkeys!*…Confident that she knew the truth about the outlaw leader, from listening through a copper bowl held against the wall of their bedroom…Rochine was yet unwilling to draw still further reproaches from her father than would be helpful at that very moment. So she had kept her mouth shut and her thoughts to herself.

Then that very morning the Baron had led them back on the road again for Narbonne, all three of them still in a bright mood, if somewhat brittle, Alicia conscious of the armed men around her and the massive presence of the Baron himself. Never far from her side, his dark hooded eyes flickered over her body as it swayed to the movement of her rouncey as they rode along….*You can look all you like, Baron, but this is one 'cat' you won't touch. Let alone skin!*

Now properly clad in a long scarlet kirtle of finest Egyptian cotton, with white silk chemise under a short sleeved gold embroidered corset of azure satin, that hugged her body and showed off the firm shape of her breasts to perfection, Alicia was woman enough to relish the clothes she wore enormously. Even though she deplored their giver, she loved the effect his gift had achieved, and with Soraya and Agnes similarly dressed but in different colours, they shone out amidst their armoured escort like brilliant kingfishers amongst a whole parliament of rooks.

*

At lunch time they reached Carcassonne.

A huge fortress city with its multiple walls still in construction, one line of massive curtain walls designed to overlook another; and a hundred narrow twisted streets crammed within it: shops, houses, stables, inns, churches, store houses, blacksmiths, breweries, baking ovens and the citadel itself. The city was the greatest in that whole region and flew the flags of France and of Count Raymond of Toulouse from every tower. You name it and it was surely to be found there: goods and trinkets from all across southern France and beyond; spices, peppercorns and rose tinted sugar; precious cloth of damask, velvet and finest silk from far Cathay; gold, silver and glittering jewels from India along with all the yells, bells and smells you could possibly imagine. No wonder the Baron preferred to stay outside the city rather than within it, Alicia thought, unless it was the very Citadel itself…and even that, she had been given to understand, was crowded at times beyond bearing! So, with his eye on Alicia and her welfare…not to mention that of his daughter as well...he had insisted on moving on and they had stayed in the nearby village of Trebes instead.

This was rather a pretty place, with a good *auberge, Le Canard Volant*...The Flying Duck...which the Baron had promptly taken over, his men throwing out all those who were staying there, in one case quite literally! And the whole village was forced to cater for his men. But despite Alicia's inner fury at what that 'Man-of-Blood' had done to her, and her despair over Gui...*How will I ever know what has happened to my dearest of men?*...The Lord Baron had proven to be both an excellent host...and a good companion, which she had not been expecting.

And glacial as she was towards him, sufficient to make anyone else shiver, he was merely amused by it and laughed, to her complete chagrin, making her feel both foolish and horribly *ingénue*. Which of course was what he had intended, and only served to make her crosser still! So it was a very uneven dining party that had finally met together that night in the *auberge's* large main room, with warmth and heartiness at one end and frozen, winter tundra at the other. Which Rochine enjoyed hugely, making every effort to woo her father's interest, while casting mocking glances at Alicia and her companions.

"This is insupportable!" Alicia growled at Soraya. "Look at her making cow's eyes at her father, while mocking me...us! It makes me want to tear her eyes out. What a *slut* she is, Soraya! Even he deserves better than that. How can he let her?"

Soraya looked at her then, and sighed.

Now that Alicia was finally here, almost at the château, and in the Baron's power...from which she believed there to be little chance of escape, despite all their hopes and longings...*it is time she is told some truths about the Baron and his daughter*...and leaning over towards her she said quietly: "Alicia, sweetheart, it is because of the Crystal!"

"The Crystal?" She replied, bemused.

"Yes! my love. The Crystal! A huge glass ball of amazing clarity and power. A Seer Stone, some call it. It is the very seat of the power that *Monsieur le Baron* has over everyone. It was gifted to him years ago by a great Emir...like El Nazir? Only more powerful...The Emir of Samarkand, a great Infidel Prince. Greater than El Nazir, or even Saladin, and one for whom the Baron had done a service *très grand*...very big. But, to his fury, the Crystal, it would not work for him!"

"Until?" Agnes asked unwisely loud, her eyes wide and glittering in the candle light.

"Until what, Mistress Fitzwalter?" The Baron interrupted her sharply, with a smile that lit his eyes with intrigue, while reducing his mouth to a narrow slit.

"Until..Until.." Agnes fumbled desperately, her hands fluttering wildly: "Until we get to your Château, *Monsieur le Baron*," she almost gasped out at last, her heart pounding. "I can't wait until we get to G..Gruissan…and..and the castle! I have heard such wonderful things about it. And is the sea as blue as they say?" she pattered on desperately. "And…and do mermaids sing and dance in it, as sailors I have spoken with tell me they do?" She went on, developing her theme. "Luring them to their deaths with their beautiful bodies and music that can steal the soul?"

For just a heartbeat the Baron stared at Agnes in such a way that she felt her bones turn to water and her heart race, until she was almost panting. Then his eyes closed and he threw back his head and laughed.

"No, Mistress Agnes. There are no mermaids in the Circle Sea that I have ever seen. Sailors tell all sorts of weird tales to fearful people; it is good for a full stoup of ale…or a kiss from a pretty girl," he added looking her up and down, his teeth showing as he smiled. "You should not listen to such wild tales. But the sea *is* as blue as a cornflower to match the sky, and as warm as milk. And my castle..my Château, is all that you have been told and more, as you will see tomorrow.

"It is as strong as the great rock on which it has been built my dear, and filled with a thousand armed men to protect you, he exaggerated with a sly smile in his dark eyes…*so don't you forget that my pretties!*…Have no fear Mistress Agnes Fitzwalter," he said, switching his gaze to look keenly at Alicia as he spoke. "No army can pass its gates unless I grant it passage to do so….and no bandits or stray villains, such as your mistress and her men slew yesterday," he said, his eyebrow lifting as he gave Alicia a sardonic smile, "will ever reach you except across a field of my spears and swordsmen!"…*so don't go thinking that some armed gang out of nowhere is ever going to break in and seize you, my Lady!*...And lifting his own personal goblet he drank silently to Alicia, with a smile as warm as any shark's, his eyes black holes, iron gimlets that bored into Alicia's deep blue ones as if into soft wood, before turning away to address his Guard Commander about arrangements for the night.

It had been but a brief engagement, but it had left them all trembling.

And trembling as much from the force of Lord Roger's personality as from the fear engendered in each one of them from what he might have overheard them talking of…or might know anyway, for even his very presence could be baleful…*and that last bit certainly told me what he thinks is in my mind!*...And Alicia vowed that before the night was out she would know what Soraya had been hiding from her all this time...but in the meantime she would now sheathe her steel and seek to draw the Baron out, if only to show Rochine that King Richard's Ward, the betrothed Lady of one of his most favoured knights, and a woman who could slay with a naked blade as well as many men...was no *ingénue*, but a Lady to be reckoned with indeed.

And so she did, being every bit as vivacious as previously she had been like stone, and what had started as a very difficult evening ended with both parties apparently reconciled to one another; and not just reconciled but in rare good humour with each other.

As Alicia had said to Soraya later: 'If you can't beat them, join them! But always on your own terms.' And her terms did not include surrender...*far more an armed truce to make that French bastard strive for what he wants. That way he will surely value me all the more*...and in his efforts to win her, he might make such a simple mistake of over-confidence as to enable them all to escape. And a melting lady, with stars in her eyes, was far more likely to achieve that than an ice maiden with frost in her breath and a body hard as steel!

And the Baron had responded in like manner.

Dropping his hauteur he had made every effort to draw her out...and to shield her from any possible malice or rancour from Rochine; offering her the choicest morsels from the many platters that he had ordered placed before them, including the dishes that Najid had also provided, at the Baron's insistence, from the inn's kitchens...and, earlier, making sure her room was as lovely as any the great château could provide.

And, despite herself, Alicia had been impressed.

All through that day he had not tried to make love to her, nor flatter or cajole her. Not even to kiss her hand. *Mais au contraire!* He had been courteous, formal...almost distant in some ways, and scrupulously polite...and gently humorous, even self-deprecating, which had made everyone smile.

She was also intensely aware of him!

Not that he hovered around her, he did not; but after that meal, whenever she had entered the main room of the inn in which they had stayed, or had walked out into the herb garden attached to it, or to the stables to check her mare...and he had been anywhere near...her eyes automatically seemed to 'find' him...*Why is that when I despise him so?*...And though she missed Gui enormously, and loved him deeply, the Baron aroused her feminine curiosity. His black, hooded eyes seemed to compel her to look at him, and when she did so, she felt almost aroused by his interest. And...yes! She was flattered by the fact that this powerful, dark visaged man, with his undoubted royal connections and enormous wealth should have gone to such extraordinary lengths to bring her, an English maid from the rural simplicity of Hampshire, to his sophisticated home in France.

And, beautiful though she knew herself to be, she was under no illusions with regard to the Lord Baron, Sir Roger de Brocas. He could have the pick of almost any women he might choose as a bride, yet he had chosen her, and taken extreme measures to achieve the success he so desired. So, what was this extraordinary man really all about?...*After all there is nothing truly special about me. I am just a maid from The Forest!...*And what was this 'game' she was now playing? Did she really wish to snag him in her woman's wiles? Make him love her…only to discard him again later when he realised he could never have her?

She didn't really know herself…only that she felt hugely flattered…and not a little aroused!

But until such time as she could discover where Gui was, and how to reach him, she now realised that she must dissemble as artfully as she knew how and woo the Baron as he would hope to be wooed…as he clearly intended to woo her, with every semblance of agreeability and friendliness without allowing him to have any more of her body under his hand than she was willing for him to achieve. And she looked at him from the corners of her eyes, assessing him as only a woman can…and the sight made her purr like the great golden cat she truly was, for he would be a powerful lover, of that she was sure and she suddenly felt her breasts tighten with unexpected lust so that she quickly looked away, startled by her reaction, and turned to talk with Soraya instead, while her breathing settled and her body calmed down again.

*

Rochine, sitting opposite the Baron, had watched the swift by-play between Alicia and her father; had seen Alicia's face suddenly flush and her breathing flutter, and gritted her teeth, for she knew exactly what he had done! Scorned her, flattered her with his attentions and then subtly challenged her, giving her just that 'look' to let her feel she could control him, letting her believe she held all the aces!

And it was heady stuff, as Rochine knew only too well, and would end up in the Baron's great bed-chamber as it always did…no matter *how* artfully that *salope,* that bitch! thought she could control him…with the two of them making the 'beast-with-two-backs' and experiencing for herself just how thoroughly the Baron would ravage her. And jealousy roared through her so she had to clamp her hands between her thighs to prevent her from striking her cousin there and then.

Then she smiled, forcing herself to relax...*for I swear to every god I know, that that bitch will never have my father under her hand. Never!*...Knowing that the time would surely come when she could savour every moment of doing exactly what she wished with her!

Chapter 6...In which Alicia at last learns all about the Baron's Crystal

Later, in the safety of their own bed chamber, with Aziz comfortably standing the first watch outside their room...much to the fury of de Vere, who had wanted both giant Arabs out in the stables where his men could keep a close eye on them...Soraya finally told Alicia all about the Baron and his Crystal: how the Lord Roger had first been unable to make it work properly...and how he had learned to do so!

"*Non! C'était impossible!*...No! It was impossible. He could not make it work as he so wished; not until he was seduced by his daughter after his wife's death!"

"*No!*" Both Alicia and Agnes had gasped in horror.

"*Mais oui!*" Soraya had confirmed. "It is so. *Vraiment!*...In very truth! *C'est moi qui parles*! It is me who speaks and I would not a lie to you tell."

"But how? I mean...how do you know all this?" Alicia asked her, her mouth almost hanging open.

"Remember, sweetheart, I am – was, the personal body servant to The Lady. And servants know always everything! Far more than their masters would ever realise! So...I have learned all this since I was brought to the castle and to her given as a handmaid by *Monsieur Le Baron*. I told you of that when we were on the *Morning Star*, remember? I was about fourteen then, and she was about twenty. Her mother, The Lady Constancia, had died very suddenly when Rochine was younger, about the same age as me when *Monsieur Le Baron* took me from Papa...two years after my beautiful Mama died in the forest of the boar. She was already to her father very close even then...very protective and jealous of any one on whom he cast the eye. It is said she was even jealous of her mother, and she was used secretly to watch them make the love together...at first to her own mother and then later to the various other women *Monsieur Le Baron* took to his bed."

"Other women?" Agnes asked shocked.

"*Mais oui! Certainement*, Mistress Agnes ! *C'est un homme!* He is a man...and a man without his woman. So, of course, he needs..he needs.. *baiser*..to release his energy. His spirits of love? Yes?" she went on exasperated with Agnes. "Oh, Sweetheart," she added, rubbing her two forefingers briskly together. "*Baiser!* Oh...where is your head tonight, Agnes? He is a man who needs *to fuck!*" And as Agnes finally caught on, her hand to her mouth, both Alicia and Soraya fell on their bed laughing.

"Yes! But she wanted him wholly to herself," Soraya went on. "And on her eighteenth birthday she seduced him!"

"*No!*" Both girls exclaimed again, horrified, but fascinated at the same time.

"*Mais oui!* Oh, *nom-de-nom*! But you are both so…so…*ingénue!*" Soraya said then exasperated. "*Innocent!* The Lady, she was *très rusée*…very cunning…arranged for him, *un repas merveilleux*, a meal most wonderful, with all his favourite foods and wines, got him drunk, well almost, and happily relaxed…and then came to him later, bathed, shaved and perfumed in only a long silk chemise…"

"How do you now all of this, Soraya?" Alicia interrupted, amazed.

"She told me!"

"*She told you?*"

"Yes…everything! *Je t'dis…*" she exclaimed frustrated, flapping her hands, *de temps en temps*, French breaking out all over: "The words I cannot find! Ahh…I told you…she can be-be…*très donnante*…very giving. Very trusting…your best friend in all the world, and generous too. And then…*méchante!* Of the most wicked. So she told me how she had made love to her father…and how he had made love to her in return, again and again…*avec beaucoup d'énergie!*" she said, shrugging her shoulders with elegantly raised eyebrows and pumping her hand up and down fiercely, adding with a delicious knowing smile: "*C'est un homme comme un cheval!!*"

"*Soraya!*" Alicia almost shrieked, her face a picture of outraged excitement. "How do you know he is 'like a horse'?"

"Because I have been with him too," she said very matter-of-factly, with a slight shrug of her shoulders.

"*Both of you?*" Agnes stammered. "I mean you and The Lady? Together? With the Baron? All three of you?"

"*Mais oui, ma petite!* My little Agnes! Why are you shocked so? Is it not so in your country also? The Baron does not tire easily, and we are there to serve *Monsieur Le Baron*. Do not you serve Sir Gui, the same?" She asked Agnes, astonished.

"No…*she does not!*" Alicia answered crisply, her mouth suddenly clipped in. "Not that my disgraceful belovèd would not willingly do so if given half the chance," she added with a wicked smile. "But I do not intend to share my man in bed with anyone!"

"Well, maybe it is in France different then?" Soraya went on smoothly, her head on one side. "But Lord Roger is a man with energy of the greatest…and until he is spent the Crystal does not work. And it was on that day, the very first time, after she was lying in his bed, exhausted, flopped open like the ravaged oyster, that *Monsieur Le Baron* went to his great Crystal, took it out of its cedar wood box most beautiful, put his hands around it....and, and...*nom de nom!* For the first time it worked! Sweet Jesus, Alicia," she said taking her hand and squeezing it. "*But the thing really worked!* Full of clouds and shining light in many colours...so beautiful...so amazing! I have seen it too, sweetheart. *Tu comprends?*...You understand?

"Yes...Soraya." Alicia said quietly, squeezing the lovely girl's hand in return. "I *do* understand, honeyone...nor do I think foul scorn on you for anything," she added softly, before turning away, her mind in sudden turmoil...*Dear God! He fucked with his own daughter! I cannot believe it?*...And her whole body shivered with disgust and revulsion, as much as with a sudden frisson of prurient desire knowing Soraya's tale to be true, however demonic she felt it to be. And if she had despised Lord Roger before...she now loathed him not least because of the lascivious thoughts that had so suddenly coursed through her...*Yet somehow I must hide all that if I am ever to find out where Gui is, and escape this dreadful place. Mary, Mother of God aid me!*...And turning back to Soraya with a tight smile she urged her: "Now...*go on!*"

Soraya, who had felt Alicia's body tremble and watched her face, and the shock still written large all over it, sighed, and squeezed her hand again before taking a deep breath: "Alicia, it is the most strange thing ever, that Crystal. It takes from his body the mind. *C'est exceptionnel!* The Lord Roger never leaves the castle but it goes with him, everywhere! When he holds it between his hands you can see what he sees...night or day. It is as if you were a bird, flying across the countryside...or a mouse in a corner of the room. And sometimes you can hear as well as see. Whatever his mind turns to, the Crystal will take him there.

"Is it magic?" Agnes asked in a small, shaky voice.

"No, my love," Soraya said gently, putting her arm around the trembling girl. "Though many might think so. *No...somehow it is real!* I do not myself understand it. How could I? Nor does the Baron...only that it works after he has...he has, *'baisered'* The Lady. And then, much later, he discovered that if someone wore something he had given them...the Crystal gave him real power over them, so that he could almost see into their minds. That's when he can hear what they say, and can influence them into doing things for him that they might never choose to do for him themselves!

"And the more they '*baisered*' each other...the better it worked. But only with Rochine, not even with his belovèd Constancia! He did try with other women on their own, or in pairs, but only with Rochine...and only if she received his seed too did the great Seer Stone work! And he needs an heir, my love…which of course Rochine cannot give him."

"How come she has not fallen pregnant herself, Soraya? *Enceinte!* Is she barren? Or him maybe?"

"No, my love!" Soraya answered with a smile. "There is no problem for the Baron there. There are plenty of de Brocas faces scattered around the villages on his lands. The Lady?...I do not think so. She has her moon-times the same as I do…and *trés méchante* she can be at those times too. So…no I do not think it is that. But she uses a remedy for stopping her becoming so…becoming *enceinte*. Roman it is I understand, a sure protection against pregnancy, a cream, very thick, made of acacia oil and honey. She has been using that ever since she first lay with the Baron."

"Do you…?" Alicia asked tentatively, her head on one side.

"Help prepare her?"

"No, no, Soraya. That is not what I meant."

"Oh…you mean me?" She asked, blushing slightly. "Do I use it too? But of course. I do not want to carry any man's child until I am ready to do so. And the cream is cool and soft and takes any soreness away if he is too rough. I will show you, perhaps?"

"Perhaps," Alicia answered shyly, looking at her from the corner of her eyes. Then, with renewed resolution, and a little casually, she asked: "And-and do you…you prepare The Lady for these 'jousts'?"

Soraya laughed then and gave her a swift cuddle for her embarrassment. "*Mais oui, certainement!* Of course I do, silly. It is why he gave to her me in the first place, to be her handmaid and in every way make the care for her."

"Why he gave you to me to as well, I suppose?" Alicia interrupted her tersely. "Thanks, Soraya!"

"Well there's no point in getting about it the huff, my love," Soraya told her with a grin and an elegant shrug of her shoulders. "But it is why I am here, after all. To care for you…both of you," she added with a glance at Agnes. "It is what has brought us all together. And when we get to the Château, we really will need each other…and in ways that now only we can guess at! For the Château is huge, Alicia, many rooms and corridors and passages, many secret places. I know them all," she said, lowering her voice. "Maybe even some The Lady does not know about herself? And there are friends there who will help us if they can! If only we knew where Sir Gui was, my Lady? Then we could perhaps make for us a plan? Thank God for Aquib and his friends. El Nazir did us a greater favour than he could possibly have imagined when he put those men to guard us!"

"Hmmmm!" Alicia mused. "I am not so sure of that either, anymore. Gui uses a Yorkshire phrase for men like him: 'Long Headed!' And El Nazir is just such a man, of that I am certain. I could not for the life of me really understand why he decided to help us in the way he did. Now I think I begin to understand."

"But be sure of one thing, though," Soraya said firmly, looking at both of them. "He will of the Baron be his friend always…*toujours*…not ours. And certainly not The Lady's! He had much respect for Constancia de Brocas. Love even. Me? I know because I have heard *Monsieur le Baron* say so many times. He adored her, and he was shocked the very utmost when she died so suddenly. The very utmost! Many tears…Both him and the daughter."

"Tears, Soraya?" Alicia questioned, amazed. "From that monster of depravity?"

"*Mais oui, Alicia! Certainement…C'était un homme sans la vie! Sans sa grande amante!...*a man without life…without his great lover…He was no monster then as now he has become. The Lady Constancia would not have allowed it. Everyone says so. People say he has never really been the same since she died: darker, harder, more cruel…*plus méchant*…more wicked, and less caring of those around him…those who serve him.

"The Baron was away at the time when the Lady Constancia fell so ill. And Rochine cared for her mother devotedly. Everyone says so. Fed her the choicest foods of her own making, brought her the drinks she needed, washed her, tended to her needs…everything! And made sure her mother lacked for nothing. And that no-one else…physicked her…gave her her medicines…"

And suddenly her voice faltered, and she looked up horrified. "Special foods and drinks from her own hands?" She mumbled, appalled, the colour draining from her face. "And only she looked after her?...prepared her medicines…physicked her? *Non! Non! C'est impossible!*" And her voice suddenly trailed off into a desperate silence…and she sat for a moment stunned by her thoughts, while the same possible realisation trickled into Alicia's sharp mind, and a look of total devastation slowly stole over both of them.

"*No!*" Alicia said, turning towards Soraya, her voice hushed almost to a whisper. "She couldn't have? *NO!* Surely not? Not her own mother?"

"What are you saying, Alicia?" Agnes questioned her urgently, looking bemused..

"I don't know, honeyone. *I don't know!*" Alicia exclaimed, deeply shocked. Then turning back to Soraya, sitting beside her numb with the horror of what her thoughts might have revealed, she pulled the quailing girl to her and asked: "Is it possible? Sweetheart, talk to me. Could she have murdered her mother in order to possess her father?"

"*No!*" Agnes gasped then, her face white with the dreadful shock of what Alicia had just said. "*Murder?*" the word coming out on a husk of breath. "*Her own mother?* Sweet Jesus, Alicia what have we stumbled on?"

"*Yes!*...Yes..she could have, Alicia." Soraya whispered, her voice so soft as to be almost silent. "It is in her to do so, I think!" she exclaimed horrified, her hand up to her mouth. "Dear God Almighty! Is that the secret that El Nazir holds in his heart so closely? That Rochine has killed to protect; and of which her father has no suspicions. *Nom de nom!*" she exclaimed, putting her hand over her mouth, her eyes wide as a fawn's about to flee a tiger. "*Or maybe he does?*" She whispered, turning towards the others, sitting in shocked silence on their bed, holding hands like small children. "He is a very deep and secret man, *Monsieur le Baron*. Very dark, *très dangereux*. So..so..maybe he does know?...Or at least suspects? But needs her too much to confront her?"

"And she knows all his secrets!"

"And where all the bodies are! Both his and her own. Remember the two girls I told you about? And the pigs?"

"*She is a monster!*" Agnes hissed, appalled. "*A monster!*"

"I told you so too, remember? On the *Star*? And that, my love, brings us back...."

"...To the Crystal," Alicia interrupted her firmly through gritted teeth. "And to me and the Baron."

"But why you, Alicia?" Agnes asked her, still confused. "Why not just continue with Rochine...after all she has given him her all, literally. And if he needs an heir...why then, any girl of impeccable family would do for that!"

"Agnes is right, my love," Soraya replied earnestly. "So he could, and many would fall over themselves to be *La Chatelaine* of the Château Grise. So..so..why you?"

"For revenge, Soraya! Well, partly so, I think. It is something that Gui and his father were talking of before the fire. It is ancient family history...but clearly it has so infected his mind that he has become obsessed with it!"

"So?"

"So...Lord Roger's father, Thibault the Cruel, joined in King Louis' struggle against the Old King...Henry II, King Richard's father?...at the siege of Cahors, over the control of the whole County of Toulouse. Louis Sept...the seventh, the present King Phillip's father...it was years ago! 1158...'59? More than thirty years...a lifetime! And Father Matthew was there too, fighting with Sir Yvo and my father, Sir Henry de Burley.

"And when they broke through the walls, there was a terrible struggle in the breach. Frantic, awful! I have heard Sir Yvo talk of it many times. He and

Sir Thibault fought like furies. Hand to hand, with all the Hounds of Hell unleashed around them...and then Sir Yvo slipped, his sword flew out of his hand and he was at Sir Thibault's mercy...the Baron's father.

"But as Thibault lifted his sword above his head to kill Sir Yvo, my father slew him instead. Barged the Baron right out of the way then hacked him open with all his strength...and my father was a strong man! Hewed Sir Thibault upwards from his crotch to his navel, and then hacked off his head with his return blow for good measure! Sir Yvo always explained Thibault's death with relish, for he loved the way my father fought. The hack up and return blow was one of his favourites and Sir Yvo loved a good blow well delivered. But worse than that, my father slew the Baron before his son's eyes! Baron Roger was only fourteen at that time and it was his first real fight...but he was there when my father slew Sir Thibault and sent his head spinning into the fray splashing the boy with his father's own blood!"

"*Mon Dieu!*" Soraya breathed out, as the horror of that awful day came to life in her mind. "*Mon Dieu! Vin sucré de Christos*, Alicia!" She exclaimed again, putting her hand up to her mouth, appalled. "No wonder of all people the Baron should have so much hate. I had no idea!"

"Why should you, Honeyone? It is ancient history now...but in fact it is a feud that has been going on for years."

"Years?"

"*Mais oui, des siècles*...centuries! Truly. My family and Gui's came north to England in the days of the Old Conqueror...*Duc Guillaume de Normandie*...They held lands all around Rocamadour and Cahors at that time and had been at feud with the Baron's family for years even then. There was much bad blood between them. So my ancestors joined Duke William's army and fought at Hastings where they saved the Duke's life; for which they were heartily rewarded, being the very first of all his knights to be given lands in England. He personally enfeoffed them on the battlefield...gave them their lands and signed their parchments there and then amongst the dead, and for them it proved to be the beginning of great things. They never looked back."

"And the family of *Monsieur le Baron*?" Soraya asked

"*Pish!*" Alicia said dismissing the man and his family with a sharp snap of her fingers. "Evil is as evil does!" Alicia rasped. "The de Brocas family went from bad to worse. Sir Yvo always said there was bad blood there: quarrelling with everyone: fighting, brawling, treachery and lies...even drawing steel on the Church, and running off with an abbess! Then, after Cahors, they lost almost everything. Proclaimed traitor for breaking his word to King Henry over the defence of the city, all the de Brocas lands in Henry's

Empire went. King Henry seized the lot for making war against their Suzerain. They were lucky to retain their lives."

"But what about your grandmother?" Agnes asked. "The Lady Philippa? Wasn't she a de Brocas?"

"Your...your grandmother, Alicia?" Soraya stammered. "A de Brocas?" she queried, completely shocked.

"Yes...my amazing, extraordinary, astounding grandmother, the Lady Philippa de Brocas; grandfather Ralf's adored wife. She was the absolute love of my grandfather's life apparently: beautiful, vivacious, demanding and very French. *Exotique!*" She said laughing. "And my grandfather, Ralf de Burley, almost worshipped the ground she walked on...as did Sir Yvo himself who knew her well. She was the complete antithesis of her brother in every way possible. Loyal, honest and true, and she was a good, loving wife to my grandfather in all respects, and was particularly caring of the people on our lands; there were great crowds to mourn her when she died.

"And on their wedding day, his greatest friend, Sir Alun de Malwood...Gui's grandfather, gifted to her for her lifetime - the greatest treasure his family possessed, the Malwood Emerald. A massive emerald ring set in beautifully worked gold, very old, that had been found in the ground when the first Malwood castle was being built a hundred years ago. It was said to be Roman and was Gui's family's greatest heirloom...but when grandmother Philippa died, instead of returning to the Malwood family as it should have done...the great ring disappeared! Vanished as if it had never been. Then, on the very night that Gui and I were betrothed, the night of the fire that killed Gui's parents, and should have killed him, it turned up again."

"*How?*" Soraya asked astonished, her eyes on stalks.

"In the Baron's hands!"

"*What?*"

"Yes! It was his betrothal gift to Gui! He called him to his room after the banquet and just gave it to him, without any explanation. Tipped it out of a small blue velvet bag, and handed it over. Gui was simply stunned. He said afterwards that you could have knocked him over with a feather, he was so astonished. Same as this armlet that Rochine gave me," she said twisting the golden dragons that entwined her right arm.

"Yes," Soraya said, as Agnes admired it. "It is very beautiful...and very old I am told. It is one of a pair; her father has the other one. He wears it almost all the time."

"Well, Gui got his gift from the Baron just after Rochine and I had retired to my room for the night..."

"You 'slept' with The Lady…with Rochine?" Soraya asked, appalled. "I mean…" She ended in confusion

"Hmmm!" Alicia replied, her head on one side, a certain smile on her face. "I know what you mean, sweetheart. And it *is* what she had in mind when we undressed! And she certainly wanted me to…but I declined that honour!"

"You mean…you didn't?...She didn't?..."

"No, Soraya…we didn't! Oh, not because I wasn't tempted, she is very beautiful, and easily desirable; and she had 'fondled' me before the party. I am convinced now that she put something in my wine."

"Yes! That is possible," Soraya murmured softly. "It is of her a trick she has before used. Of poisons like that she knows too much!"

"So that was why I found you so flushed that night!" Agnes exclaimed with a squeak. "That night I came to trim you and dress you. No wonder your body was so on fire."

"*Mon Dieu!*" Soraya said, her green, almond-shaped eyes huge in her pretty face. "You resisted her *complètement?*"

"*Completely!* I told her such games were not for me. I would feel ashamed of myself in the morning."

"She must have been of the most furious!" Soraya exclaimed with a grin. Then, more reflectively, she added: "No…perhaps amused? Looking forward to the time when she would conquer you for sure…*certainement!* No-one, but *no-one* has been known to resist The Lady when she is determined on surrender! My love, no wonder the Baron wants you so badly. You are an original, but much, much more than that, sweetheart!" she went on urgently, grasping Alicia's hand as she looked into her face. "Without realising it you have revealed to me all, me who knows him so well. I now understand why he so wants you and you only for his wife, my love. Why he must have you! And it *is* all about the Crystal!"

"How do you mean?"

And taking a deep breath, still holding her hand, Soraya said: 'Of course you are right, Alicia, in that for *Monsieur le Baron*, 'revenge' does have its part to play in all of this..but..but I think it is of the soul much deeper, and of far more danger than that. So bear with me, please, Alicia, and I will try to explain." And she paused then a moment while she collected her thoughts. "Alright, we know the Crystal works after lying with Rochine…*après le baiser…oui?*…because she is his daughter, yes?

"Yes!"

"*Bon!*...And it works in no other way that we know? Of this I am certain. *Avec aucune autre personne?*"

"No! Only with Rochine."

"And she is of the blood, yes? *His* blood, yes?" She asked urgently.

"Yes!...Oh my God, Soraya I think I can see where you are going with this!"

"So...the Crystal works because Rochine is of his blood...*de son sang! Et de son sang seulement!*...and of his blood only!...And it will *only* work with her, because no-one else is of his blood, *not even with the Lady Constancia whom he truly adored!* He has proven that, many times. So it is not just the sex, the *baisering!*...Yes?

"Yes! No...not just the 'fucking'!" Alicia said then, with a shrug of her shoulders, like Soraya. "It is about the blood."

"And you, my darling Alicia..."

"...I am of the blood too!"

"*Enfin! Oui!* Sweetheart," Soraya exclaimed, pouncing on her words, her own almost falling over themselves to get out. "*Yes!* You are of the blood too, my Alicia. Because of your grandmother, the Lady Philippa, you are of the blood...and now you are the *only* one left! If he marries you, not only will he get all the lands he so desires, but he can stop plundering his own daughter... which she clings to. He can cease being an outcast from all the world and hold onto the power he so badly wants...*and* have a legitimate heir to follow him!"

"And if his wicked plans with Prince John and King Philip really work, and Richard never returns from the Holy Land, then through marriage with me, blessed by the church and by the King of France he will be legitimised in the eyes of all the world, and will be as great a power in England for John...as ever Thomas Becket was for King Henry! My God...it is fiendish!"

"*And that's why he wants you: to work the Crystal and fill your womb!...And why he cannot marry anyone else*!" Soraya added bitterly.

"Oh Soraya! Dear God...It has to be me! It *has* to be me! And unless we can escape, and soon, he will do exactly that!

"He will get his *so* good friend the Archbishop Berenguer of Narbonne to dissolve my betrothal, supported by the Count of Toulouse and King Philip of France...and then he will marry me out of hand, whether I will or not! He will force me to the altar...force motherhood upon me! And with Gui disappeared, and King Richard wholly occupied with his crusade, there will be no-one to help me! *No-one!* I cannot bear it! I cannot bear the pain of it! Oh, my Gui, my Gui!" She cried out in unbearable torment. "Where are you, my darling? *Where are you?*" and with that last pitiful cry she flung herself into Soraya's arms and burst into tears.

Chapter 7...The Company of the White Rose reach Narbonne and Gruissan.

The next morning they had left Trebes early, reaching Narbonne at midday. Their whole journey had been one long bustling parade, as with his huge house flag unfurled and rippling busily behind him from its standard, his current command under Xavier Le Brun now joined with that of his own Guard Commander, Gaston de Vere, and those men still with him...*and* Alicia and her small armoured household as well...it was a very powerful and impressive body of men that had gently cantered down the great Via Aquitania.

Overhead the sun had shone in brilliant splendour from a faultless blue sky, with a fine south-westerly breeze off the distant sea to blow their travel dust away from them, and on that early August morning, less than a week since the month had turned, the fields all around them were already filling with cheerful harvesters. With sacks over their shoulders, children, wives and men all together, they were a happy, colourful throng with sticks and sickles in their hands, barrels of wine and ale on a handful of broad tilt carts along with sticks and sticks of freshly baked bread and the cheeses for which the area was well known. Alicia and Agnes were delighted, and waved and cried out to them cheerfully as they passed, and the field workers shouted back at them with smiles and laughter too...so much like the first days of harvest at home that it had made them both feel piercingly homesick, and far away from all those whom they loved and cared for most.

And though the Baron glared at them and Rochine hoity-toited her head and sneered at their rural ways, both girls ignored them completely, much to Aquib and Aziz's quiet amusement, both pleased that their charges should show such happy oneness with the countryside and its people.

Then they were approaching Narbonne, the biggest city in that region and the only one with a great thriving port, based on *La Robine*, the broad canal dug out by the Romans over a thousand years before to link the sea with the mighty river Aude that flowed far inland. It was a truly mammoth work, and the legionaries of the Tenth Equestrix, Caesar's favourite legion to whom he had given land to create Narbonne, had also built a magnificent bridge that crossed their canal to carry the Via Aquitania across it and into the city. This was a lovely bridge of rich, red Roman brick, a bridge with six great arches over the water, a bridge to link the Via Aquitania coming in from far Bordeaux in the west, to the Via Domitia coming up from Rome itself in the east. Up over the towering Alps where Hannibal had once marched his elephants and then, with Narbonne as its mighty lynch pin, it swung away towards Spain, Rome's greatest province before Gaul was created.

Below the bridge was the port itself, full of ships of every sort: small cogs in from northern Europe, and small galleys from the Circle Sea, along with countless boats and barges, especially barges laden with goods from the great cogs and busses that had to offload their hogsheads and bales below where *La Robine* started because they were too deep to get up the canal itself. And all were plying for trade, the wharves and docksides packed with merchandise of every sort imaginable...and if Bayonne had been frantic, Narbonne was a real maelstrom of activity: people, beasts, carts, wagons and pack trains everywhere. The noise was almost overwhelming.

And for a moment or two Lord Roger halted his command as it crossed the bridge to look down upon it all...for there, anchored away from the rest, like a great shark amidst a shoal of sardines, there was a huge fighting dromond; very like the *Morning Star*, only broader and longer. Twin-masted the same, the fore mast higher than the one behind it, but with a great central rudder, like the *Mary*, and two enormous ballistas bow and stern, instead of just the one that the *Star* carried; while out from the bows below her forward artillery was a great iron siphon for spouting Greek Fire upon her enemies, and below that, jutting out nine feet beyond her stem, the brutal fangs of her ram, a great wrought iron ring of forged and hammered teeth sufficient to burst through the sides of any ship she might choose to attack.

Unlike the *Morning Star*, the *Ajax* carried sixty oars aside in two great banks of thirty each, not the twenty five aside that El Nazir commanded, and on her decks were her marines, fifty men armoured-up and armed to the teeth and twenty archers with Syrian bows, all under strict command and carrying out a string of exercises and orders that had them all scurrying about under the fierce heat of the noonday sun. Nor were her officers sparing themselves either as they strode amongst their men, their voices harsh and loud, as they bellowed at their troops and sailors.

Alicia sat back in her saddle and watched amazed.

"What ship is that?" she asked, pointing. "Surely she is even bigger than the *Morning Star*? More rowers, and wider. And there are no steer boards. She has a great central rudder, like the *Mary*. And her ballistas are bigger too!"

"You are very observant, my lady," Aquib said in his deep voice from just behind her. "That is the *Ajax*! The biggest armed dromond in the whole Circle Sea, and the fastest. She is Valerian Dodoni's ship...see, there!" he pointed urgently to a tall dark haired man in black leather chausses with a white shirt open to the waist, hanging out over the ship's wide deck from the ratlines that ran up beside her foremast. "That is Valerian Dodoni, from one of the oldest, most respected families in Venice…they say there is nothing he will not trade with given a good price…except freeborn Christian women!"

"Dodoni! He is just another pirate!" Alicia snorted in disgust. "All Venetians are pirates!" She sneered. "I have heard Tommy Blackwood say so many times," and she screwed her face up with distaste. "And not trade in Christian women? Bah! They'd sell their grandmothers if offered enough bezants! I am told if you do a handshake deal with a Venetian…count your fingers!" and she laughed. "How do you know of him, Aquib?"

"Everyone who sails these waters knows Valerian and his *Ajax!*" he snarled, his voice rising in anger. "He has the only ship the Prince would rather not tangle with, the *Ajax!* Twenty pounder ballistas on turntables. Twisted animal sinews as tall as a man…and huge timbers to take the recoil. *Allah* knows where the infidel got such technology. My prince has not been able to replicate it!" And he banged his huge fists against the bridge parapet. "But one of these days we will have to fight her…if only to prove who is best!" And with a shrug of his massive shoulders, her usually very placid escort leader turned away. With a final look across to where the tall Venetian ship captain was drilling his men, Alicia kicked her rouncey on again too, over the long bridge, past the cathedral, through the city walls and away again at last.

*

And now here they were, luxuriating in the warm afternoon sunshine outside the 'Tiger's' lair. That very same 'Tiger' whom Father Matthew and Sir Yvo, with the King's help, had tried to trap at Malwood; from whom she had escaped the night of the fire, and beside whom she was now riding in seeming friendship, if not love…*dear God, there is a power in him that any maid might be seduced by!*…and alongside all those whom she held most dear, save Gui himself and his closest commanders. *Holy Mother, help me not to lose my way in all this,* she thought, looking at the Baron from the corner of her eyes…*There is such danger here for us all if I cannot hold it all together*…A chilling thought that caused a sudden shudder of pure terror to rush through her, lifting her skin and her hair, making her whole body tremble as she and the Baron's party entered the narrow streets of the little town, and began to wind their way upwards to where the vast bulk of the Château Grise loomed darkly over them.

With the late afternoon shadows lengthening, and the heat gently fading from the day as the sun began to sink towards its rest, the small tiled shops and houses that made up the little town leaned closely to one another, like bent old ladies whispering together of their jaded past. That each house was closely shuttered, its face closed tight against the world as if blinded by the fierce heat of the southern sun, was strange enough...but save for the rustling breeze that fluttered gently round them, the bright singing of the birds and the mewling gulls that soared and gabbled everywhere there was no other sound within its streets. Save for the steady clopping of their horses' hoofs upon the iron hard road, now giving way to neat cobbles as they entered the town itself...the whole place seemed deserted, empty, dead, with no-one stirring.

Alicia suddenly shivered again, as much from the shadows she found herself riding through as from the unnatural atmosphere that had been so apparent the moment their horses' feet had struck the roadway...*something is terribly wrong here*...and she looked instinctively round for Aquib and Aziz .

Surely the place should have been thronged after a busy day? The little shops still open, the people, bright as starlings, and chattering as such amongst themselves, children and dogs underfoot; goats as well probably. And all the while the trumpets from the great Château high above them had been brazenly announcing their Lord's return for some time...even more reason for the Gruissan people to flock out and watch him riding by.

But there was no-one!

Clearly, even for Gruissan, this was not right and the Baron ordered his men to close up around the women, hedging them in with bright steel like jewelled peacocks in an iron cage. They would not be so isolated for long, for their Gruissan escort must already be on its way down from the great Château above them...that, after all, was what the trumpets signified. But even without them Lord Roger had enough seasoned troops to deal with a mere parcel of 'townies', even though they might clearly be in some danger, though from what as yet they did not know. But as they rode further up towards the centre of the town, sound did return to its streets as they became increasingly aware of a growing mutter and growl of many voices, of women howling and others crying out in anguish, of shouts of rage and the ringing sound of steel on steel as if there was a great fight taking place somewhere ahead of them.

Bunched tightly, with drawn swords and knees pressed in closely for instant action, Lord Roger moved his party towards the town square, constantly looking up, as well as around, for fear of being trapped amidst the narrow streets all about them...and then violently attacked from above. But what awaited them in the town square with its fountain and water troughs, made the whole situation instantly clear. Even Rochine went pale; and Alicia felt so sick that it was all she could do to prevent herself from being so. But poor Agnes was not so disciplined and could not contain the bile that rushed up from her belly and she was violently sick, hanging over the side of her horse, retching miserably till her throat was on fire.

*

Hanging from a rough timber gibbet at the edge of the square were the flayed bodies of two men, their faces blackened and swollen, tongues like pieces of charred leather protruding from their broken lips, and eyes picked clean by ravening birds who still clung to the gibbet from which their meal was swinging.

But it was not their ruined heads that caught the gaze so much as the raw, bloody meat that had once been their human forms. For their skin had been ripped off in broad strips, like torn cloth, and left to hang in obscene ribbons from their backs and chests, while their blood settled in dark pools on the ground. They had also been eviscerated, gralloched like deer killed in the chase, strung up for all to see, their bowels pulled out upon the hot earth and left to rot in stinking piles. Now they hung there like broken marionettes with the dull gleam of bone and twisted sinews glinting in the soft sunlight.

Alicia had never seen such a revolting sight in her life and drooped from her saddle in shocked horror, nauseous, appalled, the tears starting from her eyes. But there was no time for such niceties, for even as the Baron reached the centre of the little square, where two of his men with drawn swords confronted the mob of men and women already gathered there, more of the townsfolk flooded out from all the dark and hidden alleyways that ringed it. Jostling, striding, creeping, and in grim and bitter silence, they pressed forward 'til they formed a solid circle all round them.

Gripping whatever tools and weapons they had to hand, their hatred of this man they were all forced to call 'Lord' was a solid thing that pressed down on all who had gathered there that day, making the horses dance and strike their hoofs upon the ground in nervous anxiety. With a touch of the reins Lord Roger sent Charlemagne caracoling and snorting round the square, the big horse forcing everyone back and away from him as he had been taught to do, while with a whir of steel the Baron drew his sword and swung it in a wide arc above his head and shouted to the silent crowd.

"*You all know who I am,*" he roared at them. "Your Lord and master, the Lord Baron, Sir Roger de Brocas! Stay back from me, I warn you! Come no closer or my men will cut you down where you stand."

"You are no Lord to us!" A bitter voice cried out from amongst the murmuring press of people. "Those were our friends your executioner has butchered in your name; and all because they sought to question the taxes you impose on us."

"We seek redress, Lord Roger, for their wasted lives!" shouted another. "Your foul ways and heavy burdens crush us with their wickedness."

"You take our women and our lives," another voice cried out in anger.

"And still you expect us to produce the goods and labour for your luxuries," a woman shrilled out from within the press. "While we are left to rot in our hovels and feed our families on husks and berries"

"Justice and protection are the bargains that a good Lord makes with his people!" cried another. "We seek no more than that!"

"Aye, fair justice and protection," others began to cry out as they grew bolder, waving their makeshift weapons and stamping their feet on the ground. "Justice and protection! *Justice and protection!*" Their voices rose in cadence alongside the stamping of their feet, wooden clogs and hob-nailed leather building up a rhythm that might yet end in an instant of wild attack and violent blood-letting.

"*Get back, you dogs!*" de Brocas raged at them, whirling his sword around his head while forcing Charlemagne backwards against them, his charger's enormous hooves striking sparks off the cobbled square as Lord Roger pranced him round. "I'll not treat with such a rabble as you are; not now, *not ever!* Go back to your homes before my patience fails, and be grateful that I do not hang the lot of you and burn this miserable place to the ground and all of you with it!"

By now the people were beginning to press forward again, but warily, uncertain of what they meant to do; knowing only that before them was the man they held responsible for all their wrongs. But the Baron's words had delayed them long enough to allow the Castle guard to draw near; and the time to act had come at last. So with a roar of encouragement to his men, unarmoured though he was, the Baron led them straight towards the lines of waiting town and peasant folk.

The result was screaming pandemonium!

These were not fighting men but simple, rude, unlettered townsmen and serfs who had only sought to make their feelings known to their absent Lord. They had no real plan, nor hope of success, and their puny weapons were no match for the shining steel Lord Roger and his men put to their shrinking flesh and they fled screaming in fear from the maddened soldiers who leapt upon them, dropping their makeshift armaments in a desperate attempt to escape the killing ground they had created.

Left and right across their horses' withers Lord Roger and his command flensed at them with their swords…women, children and men, old and young alike; sometimes with the edge, but mostly with the flat of their blades. Nevertheless there was blood upon their steel and upon their horses' bardings before they were done. And many lay dead upon the ground. But by then their escort had arrived, and with that the fight, what little there had ever really been, went out of the people who had so suddenly hemmed them in. More than half a dozen lay lifeless on the cobbled stones, some gashed and hacked to death; others trampled by the horses or even by their fleeing friends. The old, the young and several women were amongst those killed.

But two of their leaders, the owners of some of the voices who had railed against him, had been snatched from the crowd by the Baron's men and were now brought before him, their arms twisted almost out of their sockets, their faces forced down in agony upon the stony square.

"*You pathetic fools!*" the Baron railed at them, swinging himself down to the ground, de Vere close beside him, their horses held by two of their men. "What did you hope to gain by all this nonsense? Did you imagine that by killing me you'd rid yourselves of all your problems?" And he kicked both of them in succession with his heavily booted feet, pivoting from one to the other as he did so. His blows making them cry out and twist in agony as his men continued to hold them down. "You are not fit to live if you hold such foolish ideas in your hearts! Slay me…and the King will just place another over you who will be *twice* as brutal as me. The more so following so foul and bloody a murder of your lawful Lord, appointed to rule over you by God and the King himself! And I promise you your end will not be half so easy as the one those hanging there were given," he added pointing at the flayed cadavers hanging from the gibbet.

"Kill us if you wish." The older of the two men replied fiercely, struggling to raise his face as he spoke. "Yes maim us, torture us as well. But just hear this, my Lord Baron; for every one of us you murder there will be two shall take his place. We will not rest until we've rid this place of you, and every sign that ever a de Brocas lived here. You are a greater scourge than ever we could hope to find again, and your destruction will be the very high point of our lives, I promise you."

"There will be no high point to your lives beyond the gallows, I assure you," de Brocas menaced him darkly as he sheathed his sword. "Unless I have my men cast you alive off the highest of my battlements upon the very roofs your people live beneath. And you will *beg* for death before my men have finished with you!"

"What are our deaths compared to those of you and your family?" The older of the two shouted at him. "You and that *bitch* you rut with? Yes, My Lord Baron. All men know what you and that witch you call your daughter get up to when the moon is high!" And he gave a high pitched cry as the soldiers holding him twisted his arm still further up his back and forced his face into the hard cobbles.

"*You dog!*" the Baron hissed venomously. "Stand him up!" he shouted to the men holding him, then with the speed of a striking viper he whipped his gauntleted hand across his face and back again, while the men pinning the man's arms struggled to hold him upright.

"You black-souled son of a cobbler's harlot! I know you now," Roger de Brocas said, gripping the man's broken face in his gloved hand before violently twisting it away and shaking the blood from his fingers. "I thought I did! You are Guillaume, the cobbler's son, his heir; and that grovelling idiot over there must be Ralph, your younger brother. Well I hanged your father for his loud voiced complaints last year. I might just as well hang the both of you as well, and be shot of the whole scaff and raff of you. But not until my executioner has introduced you to his iron maiden. That will be a sharp experience from which no man has recovered!" And he laughed uproariously, along with his command.

Then, just as suddenly the Lord Baron stopped, and with his piercing black eyes he looked around the crowd, mostly now muttering and shuffling their feet, many with eyes averted, others looking steadily at the ground not wanting to be recognised; and all wishing they had never started this upheaval.

"That reminds me," he said softly with a smile, turning back to look into the older man's tortured face, one eye now closed with blood and purple flesh. "There is a girl, too, somewhere isn't there? You have a pretty sister!"

"*No, you bloody swine!*" The younger man cried out in horror, kicking himself to his feet, the Baron's two men struggling to control him. "Leave Isabelle out of it! She has no part in this!"

"*By God's Blood!* But you people make me sick!" Lord Roger bellowed. "'*Has no part in this?*' 'Has no part in this,' you stupid moron?" he roared, turning to hitting the man in the belly…*one - two!*…with explosive force, his clenched fists driving the air out of the man to leave him gasping and retching for air in the fierce grip of two of de Vere's burly troopers. "She's your bloody sister. Of course she has a part in this!" Then turning swiftly away he spoke quietly with de Vere who turned and shouted: "Come, Le Brun! I want the town searched for the girl. And when you find her, take her to The Lady's chambers...The Lady Rochine. I'm sure she can find something good for her to do at the Château!"

Then, while Le Brun's men rushed to organise themselves for their search, Lord Roger turned back to de Vere: "Bring these *canailles* along with us, Gaston. Tie them to a horse's tail apiece and then run them up to the Château. The exercise will do them both some good...and if they cannot stay on their feet then they shall be dragged through the town as they deserve. Take them away!" Then gesturing with his arm at the people standing there, he continued: "And as for this rabble, they can go back to their hovels, and their husks and berries, and thank God I only take these two, and do not raze this whole stinking midden to the ground!" And pointing fiercely at the disgusting remains still swinging off the gibbet, he added: "Let that be a warning to you all of what can happen to those who defy me!" Then, with a curt nod of his head, he swung himself back onto Charlemagne's broad back.

Gaston de Vere, having re-mounted his own horse, was just about to turn and move off when Alicia spurred her rouncey forward, Aquib and Aziz following too swiftly to be stopped, and drew up across his path, the two enormous Arabs in close escort behind her, their hands on their great curved scimitars in readiness for any order she might give.

Turning in her saddle, she addressed Lord Roger, who had not yet kicked-on, before all the people who had now been penned in by the timely arrival of the castle escort.

"Lord Roger, do not harm these men, I beg you. There has surely been enough blood spilled here today already, and spare the girl. You wish to marry me, the chosen ward of a great King? You wish for my betrothal? Yet you strew my pathway to your castle with blood, not rose petals; I am greeted with riot and the stench of death...not garlands and dancing. This was supposed to be a day of great rejoicing...yet you have shown me a charnel house! And you have given me no present yet, my Lord Baron. So what could be a better gift than the lives and limbs of these three young Grisians?"

"No my Lady, you ask too much!" Lord Roger replied, thunderstruck. "Those two have been behind much insurrection on my lands these past few years, and they know too many names of those who support these incursions for me to let them free. The girl also. I want her where I can be sure of her."

"Hear me, my Lord, this once." Alicia persisted, backing her horse to prevent de Vere from moving. "Please, walk your horse beside mine and let us talk a little. Please, Lord Roger, it is such a little thing I ask."

"Little?" He rasped, kicking forward to join her. "You call this..this outrage *little*!" he snarled, waving his arms around him, his eyes like burning coals. "These men defy me, their rightful Lord, *and* dare to smirch my daughter's name before me. No Lord in the land would deny me the right to deal with this…this parcel of town and village *rats!*" he spat the word out, "as I see fit! No, and no Lord in your precious England would stop me either!" he added, turning away to stare furiously around him.

"No-one denies your rights, my Lord." Alicia answered him firmly. "But if you treated them all a good deal better than it seems to me you do," she added scathingly, "then outbreaks of violence like this," she gestured fiercely with her hands, "would never happen! Such things are unknown on my manors, whatever you may say, and those of Sir Yvo's also. The borel folk loved their Lord for his justice which was always fair, and for his kindness in difficult times. For his humanity. This-this disgusting *mess* that I have witnessed here does not give me any cause to love you, my Lord, nor learn to love you either. Only to despise and hate you for the bloody tyrant you appear to be!"

He looked down at her then, from the broad back of his great charger, her face flushed with anger, blue eyes sparkling…and grunted with frustration, his mouth a stiff line of resistance, his black eyes still, hooded…*God's Blood, but the wench has courage to face me down on my own lands!*

"How dare you speak so to me, Madam!" he snarled at her then. "And on my own lands too! We do things differently here in France as you will be swift to find out. Now, out of my way, I pray you. What's done is done, and I cannot change it! We have lingered here long enough; and I will not make a raree-show of myself, and you, before these redeless peasants!"

"Then listen well to this, my Lord Baron," she said calmly to him, her heart racing so fast she could barely breathe…*God give me strength!...* "You continue in this manner towards me, and I assure you that you will *never* lay a hand on me. Letters to King Richard about my plight have long been sent from England…and I have written also, from Foix…*Sweet Mary help me, I surely meant to, but he does not know that in the end I did not do so!...*My King loves me like his own. He is now in Marseilles, awaiting his transport to Sicily. How far by boat to here, my Lord Baron? A day? Two at the most? And there are no tides to wait for in the Circle Sea. I know my geography, my Lord Roger. I *know* that Marseilles is just across the bay from Gruissan. Richard's men are probably a little bored just now. Yes? Do you want the Lionheart on your very doorstep to rescue me? Do you think he would not come if I begged him to? Are your walls so secure? Are your men so trustworthy that I could not get a message out? My Lord…I am no milksop maiden! Nor am I made of marble either. Woo me with this request and you shall see how kindly I can be towards you. What would you have on your arm, my Lord? An implacable enemy, or a melting heart? The choice is yours." And leaning over she looked up at him with a brilliant smile and put her hand on his arm...*And pray God his need of me is greater than his need for vengeance for this riot against him today!...*

The Lord Roger de Brocas, Baron of Narbonne and Gruissan, lord of all he surveyed, looked into Alicia's enormous blue eyes and was amazed.

The only person ever to address him in so a bold manner had been his adored Constancia...*Now here is this chit of a girl giving me an ultimatum that in all honesty I cannot ignore. How like my Constancia she is!...*King Richard, who was about to embark on this mad crusade of his...*from which he is not expected to return, true...*was still in Marseilles, his troops held up by his fleet not arriving, and bored troops would leap at the chance of action. Especially King Richard's Englishmen! They were renowned for it.

And bold as Sir Roger was, the thought of the Lionheart actually at his very doorstep in a mere matter of days, was enough to make any sane man quail. And then there was that promise of loving warmth and the hint of Alicia's agreement to marry him. He sat back in his tall saddle and looked down at her smiling face...and at the dark, hawk-like faces of the two enormous men behind her...*two of Nazir's best. I know them both and they will do what this girl commands, no matter what...They will cut me down as soon as look at me if she should so order them!...*And with a rather fixed smile he inclined his head towards her and nodded.

"So be it then, my Lady Alicia de Burley," he said, his arms crossed and his mouth a grim line in his doubtful face. "So be it! You choose to challenge me over a parcel of swine? I give them into your hands this day, life and limb. Do with them as you will. And you may have the girl, Isabelle with you too. But come to the Château she must. That I must insist upon. That is our bargain for the time being and I will call off Le Brun.

"But be assured, my Lady, if that girl is *not* with you by sundown...then I will order my Officer of the Castle Guard, and his men, to tear this stinking town to pieces in search of her. And be advised my lovely 'White Rose'," he added quietly, his black eyes enjoying her sudden shock at the use of her pet name, plunging down into her blue ones like fire hardened spears. "You lie in my debt, twice now, my Lady fair...Once, at Limoux and again here. I hope, my dear Lady Al-ic-ia," he said, sounding each syllable with great directness, "that you are as good at paying your debts as you are at incurring them! I will leave you with those men who are holding those...those *vermin*," he snarled, turning Charlemagne away as he spoke. "They can show you the way up to the castle later; you and all your Household."

And with another smile and a bow of his head towards El Nazir's men, he waved his hand in a broad circle around his head and kicked forward, his whole command following, clattering up the cobbled roadway in a sudden shower of sparks and fresh droppings, towards the great castle that awaited its Lord's return.

Chapter 8...Alicia seals her pact with Guillaume Soulier.

Finding herself suddenly and virtually alone amongst a mobbing crowd still anxious and unsure of what was happening, and still inherently angry, while just beginning to take stock of what they had done, Alicia felt surprisingly calm.

Jumping lightly from her saddle, followed immediately by Aquib and Aziz whose massive bodies simply overawed everyone, she ordered the immediate release of the two young men whom she had rescued. Dragging them towards her, the men holding them threw them down at her feet and stepped back, hands on their swords in case of further trouble.

But as soon as they were freed both men came up and knelt down before her: "Lady, who are you?" the elder of the two asked, his face mauled and bloodied by the Baron's fists, amazed by her grace and courage. "We both expected to die here. Yet, out of nowhere you have saved us, and I thank you for our lives! Surely you are not French, nor do you come from anywhere near here or you would know how evilly regarded is the man whom you seem so nearly to be pledged to."

"Come, stand up like the men you are," Alicia replied quietly, reaching her hand down to both of them. "And you are right, I do not come from here. I am not French, but English. I am the Lady Alicia de Burley, and that man whom you all despise and hate so strongly, is not my friend by any means...nor am I here of my own desire, or will either. I have no wish to remain here one moment longer than I have to...so we may yet become allies in your struggles. Only time can tell. Yet for all that the Baron is my only sure protector at this time...and for reasons I cannot tell you I must do all I can to maintain that support.

"I do not know what goes on here, but I can guess. And be advised, nothing is as it seems. Do not believe all you hear and see. I am pledged in marriage...but not to the Lord Baron, Sir Roger de Brocas!" She exclaimed to the people around her, who were listening almost open mouthed to every word. "However...as I said, I must do all I can to serve the Baron for the time being, and in doing so it may yet be that I can help you all as well, but 'til that time comes I beg you not to do one thing more to anger him."

"My lady, you are both brave and beautiful," the older man said, walking with her towards the fountain where he did his best to cleanse his face where Lord Roger had so cruelly struck him; while all around them the town slowly came back to life again. The dead were removed from the cobbles...a little priest in a brown habit with his cowl over his shoulders fussed kindly amongst their shattered families; the shutters opened all round the square...and the women and children came out to draw water from the well that stood a small distance from the fountain, both fed from springs deep within the rock. And all looked constantly at the strangers who had come so suddenly amidst them, the three women in jewelled clothes and the three Arabs in outlandish mail and sun-darkened faces, fearful as to what such things could mean.

"And I, Guillaume Soulier, will always be in your debt," the man said, dabbing his broken face and swollen eye with a rough pad of linen soaked in the cold water from the fountain. "My brother, Ralph also," he added, indicating the younger man who was being helped by some of the women. "If you should ever be in need of a friend, my Lady, then go to the house with the blue door opposite the fountain. That one over there," he pointed with his free hand. "And ask for us, the brothers Soulier. As to the rest, I can make no promises. You've seen how we are treated here and must live out our lives taking each day as it comes. But soon there will be a bloody reckoning, I promise you. Then, if you are wise you will stay in your rooms that day, for everything else will be destroyed, there will be no holding them."

"How will you do this?" Alicia asked, astonished. "The Château is one of the most powerful castles I have seen, and I have seen many, and there are a host of proven warriors within it. You and your people are not fighters; you would be slaughtered and the whole town destroyed."

"I don't know how, my Lady," Guillaume Soulier replied, with what Alicia was coming to know as a Gallic shrug. "And you could hardly expect me to tell you, either. For I know nothing of you. But something *will* happen, I know it! Someone *will* come...it is our most ardent prayer, and surely the Good Lord will not refuse us for ever. And when our saviour comes we will be ready for him. One trumpet call, and the whole countryside will rise up beside him!"

Alicia looked deeply at this young man whom she had just rescued, with his strong, dark good looks, albeit marred with blood and seeping wounds, and loose limbed stance...and smiled at the almost religious fervour with which he sustained his hopes. She shook her head, and looked at all the people around her...*Impossible! Unarmed, untrained peasants against mercenaries with steel on their backs and in their hands? It would take a miracle...or a man with a scarlet lion-rampant on his back!...*And then turned her face towards his younger brother, Ralph, standing tall, thin, and glowering, beside him. And she was deeply tempted to tell him about Gui, and the real truth of her situation in Gruissan.

But while Guillaume might be straightforward, a man to be trusted…she was by no means sure of his younger brother…*an imprudent hothead, if ever I saw one…and..not trustworthy either, I think!…*So prudence kept her mouth closed for the time being.

"Very well my friend, so be it. But I pray you do me one further office." Alicia asked, turning to stare appalled at the gibbet and the ghastly human remnants that dangled there. "Cut down those foul remains and see they have a decent burial for I cannot bear the sight of them hanging there and swaying in the wind a moment longer. No, Ralph," she said sharply, holding up her hand to stall the younger man who was clearly about to speak. "I don't have time to hear their tale! Please just have them taken down, and ask that tall Arab behind me, the bigger of the two," she added smiling at his confusion, "for some money from my purse that I may pay for their burial and for something to help their families, and those of any others who were slain this day, and let me know at some later date if there is anything more that I can do. It is my Christian duty to do what I can here, however little that might be. Now," she went on, turning back to look into their eyes. "I am afraid there is a price to pay for your release."

"What price?" Ralph spat at her. "What foul bargain did you make with that fucking bastard?"

"Is your brother always so foul mouthed?" she asked Guillaume scathingly. "Especially towards those who are trying to help him?"

"Help us?" Ralph snarled back before his brother could reply. "*Help us?* You are nothing but that foul bastard's whore! What are we to the likes of you? You are a filthy…"

But before he could say another word Aquib struck him with his fist between the shoulder blades with such force that he was flung bodily to the ground as swiftly and as forcefully as if a whole mountain had fallen on him from the sky, and as he lay there completely dazed and breathless he heard a soft swish of steel and saw before him the biggest, widest, most terrifying blade of shimmering steel he had ever seen in his life…and a voice filled with stones grated in rough Frankish in his ear: "You say one more thing against our Lady…*one more!* And, *Insh'a Allah*, you will join your ancestors without your head! Not from my blade, *mon petit homme*…I would not soil it with the blood of such an ignorant, foulmouthed *cochon*, as you are. *Non, mon ami!* I will just shake it from your shoulders!…*Agitez de tes épaules…avec toute mon énergie! Toute mon énergie ! Idiot!!*"

Alicia who had seen and heard it all smiled quietly to herself, knowing that it would take a great deal more than that for Aquib to lop off Ralph's head.

Aziz...maybe not, he could be a cold killer if she ever needed it...but not Aquib!

"Guillaume," she replied, calmly, coldly turning her back on his younger brother's prostrate form. "The true price of your release is that you *must* send your sister, Isabelle, to me at the Château. I know. I know!" she said, putting her hands to his shoulders as she saw his immediate distress. "But you heard the Baron, he was most insistent...and I am pledged to care for her myself. She will be safe with me, I promise you. You see these men around me...not just the two big ones, but also the smaller man too? They are my personal bodyguard. And Mistress Soraya Fermier, whom you may know?" she added, pointing to where Soraya sat her horse with a smile on her lovely face. "And my English friend, Mistress Agnes Fitzwalter? They will also help me to care for your sister, your Isabelle, who is so dear to you both. But, you must comply with this request, Guillaume, or the Baron will send Xavier Le Brun back down to search the town. And he will not be gentle, I think. It was either that or he would have killed you both for certain, and half the town as well, for all I know. You must do as I ask, or everyone will suffer because of your refusal."

"*Isabelle?*" Ralph cried out, struggling now to get out from under Aquib's massive foot that he had placed firmly in the small of his back. "No...No!...you cannot, she is only a child," he shouted out writhing beneath Aquib's weight. "You bloody bitch! *You fucking whore!* You are no better than he is, that son of Satan, and his bloody bitch of a daughter! You are *une conne...*"

But that was the very last thing Ralph Soulier said for a very long time, because Aquib simply swept him up in his massive hands and shook him, and shook him, until his head almost really did fly off his shoulders of its own accord and after violently throwing up over everyone nearby, he passed out without so much as a whimper. "My Lady," the giant Arab growled at her in his deep voice. "I did tell him! I did warn him...but he would not be told!" And tucking Ralph's collapsed body beneath his arm as if it were a baby he stalked away with it to a nearby water trough and dumped him in it, arms and head flopping over its sides, while the whole crowd was stunned into total silence at this simple display of such casual, devastating power.

"No wonder those bears had no chance!" Soraya said quietly with a soft chuckle, her eyes no less startled than others around them. "He is completely...?

"Amazing?" Agnes gasped, her eyes like stars.

"*Non, impressionnant!...awesome!*" Soraya said with a smile, putting her arm around Agnes while doing her best at the fountain's edge to wash off the vomit that had soiled her dress. "Whatever was in El Nazir's mind when he assigned those three men to our protection I do not know...but, Agnes dear, I thank God for them every day!"

"Well done, my Aquib," Alicia said, touching the huge man's arm lightly with her fingers, then was startled beyond measure when he silently took them gently in his huge hand and kissed them, then touched them to his forehead in a manner that made her whole body shiver, and Aziz's eyes almost pop out of his head.

"My Aquib, I..I do not deserve such an honour," she stammered. "I am an infidel, a *Nazraani* woman. You are of the Koran. Will you not be in frightful trouble?"

"I am a freeman, my Lady. And I give honour where I find it. And in you," he said simply, in his deep, rich voice: "I find it! And it is my pleasure."

"Thank you, all of you," she almost whispered, awed by the huge man's gentle and utterly unexpected obeisance...and eyes full of sudden tears she put her hands together and bowed her head briefly to all her Arab household...*Holy Mary, Mother of God, these men are beyond my understanding!*

Then turning she said, her voice slightly shaking: "And I will have no more bloodshed today." And walking to her horse she spoke briskly to de Vere's troopers, who were even then moving towards Ralph's completely collapsed body: "No! Leave that man alone. His brother will see to him now!"

A moment later, with Aziz's help, she was back up on her rouncey, and moving to where the older of the two Soulier brothers stood waiting for her.

"Guillaume Soulier," she said with quiet firmness when she had walked her horse over to where he was standing, still somewhat bemused by all that had happened. "Your sister, Isabelle, please, as you value her life, and those of your people. To my apartments as soon as maybe! She is your surety, yes? And control that foolish hot-head," she added pointing to where Ralph still lay in a sodden stupor. "He could ruin *everything!* And keep a watch out for any messages I may need to send you. Yes?"

"Yes...my Lady Al-ic-ia," he said, stumbling over her name.

"Good!" she said giving him her hand to kiss, and a long steady look. "Good! Now, I must go, for the Baron awaits me at the Château, and I have no wish to anger him any further either. And remember, I took a frightful risk this day as well. I don't suppose anyone has dared to speak to that man like that since his mother!" And she laughed, the brightness of it bubbling round the little square like a fresh mountain stream. "God keep you both, farewell."

And with a final bow Guillaume left her, to drag his brother's soaking body by the scruff of the neck to join their friends who swiftly clustered round them; while Alicia and her Company of the White Rose, and the soldiers who had waited behind for her, equally stunned by what they had seen in the square that afternoon, turned to walk their horses slowly upwards through the startled town, and towards the castle entrance at last.

Chapter 9...The White Rose of Malwood enters the Tiger's Lair.

The road leading up to the castle, though steep, was not impossibly so. Even heavy wagons could manage it, though more than a pair of horses would have been needed as the last pull up the hill before the town ended was steeper than the rest. From there, as Alicia had seen earlier from across the huge étang, there was a completely cleared space of nearly eighty paces between the last houses of the town and the walls and towers of the great fortress itself.

This was a clear killing field, as she had earlier surmised, not only because the whole area had been cleared of all obstacles, but also because any dips or curls in the ground that might shield an attacker had been filled in, and it was under intense scrutiny from every angle of the walls above. And not just from the massive round Donjon, the *Tour Barberousse*, that towered over everything, but also from the Gatehouse, which itself was a huge obstacle as its twin towers were taller than any of those studded around the walls.

Alicia's heart quailed in her breast at the sight of such frightening defences...*Truly this would be a dreadful place to attack! Not even an army could assail this fortress with any hope of quick success!*...Castles like this could only be taken by trickery, sudden unexpected assault or a high placed traitor within the walls. And she shivered again, as she had done when first she had seen the castle from the other side of the étang, her whole body suddenly so shaken she almost dropped her reins...*Dear God in Heaven...how would he even get near the place? Or how would I get out to find him? Save him from throwing his life away to rescue me? For as eggs are broken to fry in a pan...so this great fortress will surely break and fry him too!*...And her heart cried out to him... *Oh Gui! Where are you? Where are you?*..., while her eyes took in every detail of the Château Grise and its formidable towers and battlements.

Close-to, the Château actually showed the signs of much rebuilding, and changes not visible from the other side of the bay were now quite obvious, for where new towers had been built, or old ones altered, the new masonry and mortar was a paler colour than that of its surrounding stones, and some had yet to be plastered. And as they moved onto the bridge that spanned part of the great ditch that surrounded the castle, Alicia could clearly see where it had been both deepened and widened; alterations impossible to see from across the water. And both sides had indeed been revetted with stone to give added strength, making the job of digging a sap even more difficult.

She was only surprised the Baron had not actually flooded it from the springs she knew fed the fortress and filled its well, turning it from ditch to moat, making the castle even more unassailable. And the bridge itself was not trestled timber like the one at Malwood, but of vaulted stone that could not burn, and jutted well out into the great dry ditch that surrounded the Château. Fifteen feet deep at least on the landward side, and thirty feet across at the bottom, with the main walls soaring out of it, rising fifty feet of smoothly plastered ashlar stonework into the azure blue of the sky above.

And coming to meet the stone bridgehead was the drawbridge itself, over sixty feet of enormous timbers supporting a corduroy of log-work across which a roadway of smooth oak planking had then been laid. Pivoted on a massive iron roller, the whole huge structure was counter-weighted with immense blocks of granite at either end, themselves held in place with iron straps the strength and thickness of which Alicia had never seen before, the whole thing swinging down into a beautifully crafted, curved and stone-lined drawbridge pit. Thirty feet deep behind the main entrance, the same depth as half the drawbridge was long, it created a frightening obstacle for any armed force attempting to break in by smashing through it.

Then, just as they were about to cross over and enter the castle itself, Alicia saw a tiny doorway set very low down to the left of the pit, nearly at the base of the left hand tower. Clearly it was a sally port, some twelve feet from the foot of the ditch, but there seemed no way of reaching it…and no obvious way of climbing up the other side either. Maybe there was a hidden path to the top that could only be seen from the wall head? She would bear it in mind; such tiny scraps of information could save one's life in times of desperate need. Yet she must be careful not to question anyone about it, but with Soraya's help would secretly do her own investigations. Indeed Soraya might know the way down to it anyway.

Passing between the huge double entrance gates…nearly twelve inches of cross-laminated oak planks studded with iron plates, and hung on a number of massive iron pintles…they rode on beneath the first of three portcullises drawn right up to the ceiling above them. And as they did so, high on the Gatehouse overhead, trumpets peeled out a fierce brazen challenge, making her rouncey jump and skitter, and immediately the chains on either side of the entrance tightened with a fierce rattle. Almost the same instant four men ran to pull out the locking bars that ran through great hoops of wrought iron that, with the chains above, held the bridge open. And with a terrifying groan the whole great drawbridge slowly began to pivot upwards off its bed and downwards into its curved pit until with a vast, sullen *bang!* that shook and reverberated all around them it crashed into place leaving a huge thirty foot gap, thirty feet deep, between the leading edge of the first portcullis and where they were all standing.

The drawbridge pit itself.

At the same time the first portcullis that hung immediately behind the doors themselves was lowered to the ground, its huge bulk graunching and rumbling down its stone cut channel until it, too, banged into place, its great iron-tipped teeth grinning evilly in the evening light that filtered through from the far end of the entrance passage. Finally five of the Baron's men ran out from the nearest guard chamber with tall oak stanchions, joined by a number of light chains, that they slotted into place all across the entrance passage so that no-one could easily fall into the enormous pit beyond them. It was all hugely impressive and frightening, because not only had they entered the 'Tiger's' Lair at last...but they were now trapped within it also!

Soothing her startled mare, Alicia looked up at the ribbed vaulting that ran across the ceiling above her head and took in the five meurtrières that lurked there between each set of portcullises, the scarlet painted wood that covered them, like sightless eyes, just waiting to gush forth scalding water, or boiling oil...or even super-heated sand that would destroy all on whom it fell. And between each portcullis, set into the walls on either side of the entrance passage, were pairs of arrow slits showing where hidden passages ran within the thickness of the walls themselves, with doorways and hidden guard chambers on either side leading into the gatehouse and then onwards and upwards through its levels to its very topmost battlements. And away at the far end of the passage was a third portcullis that could be closed off by a final pair of double leafed doors...*Holy Mary, Mother of God!...*She thought looking at it all...*But there would be very little hope for anyone who got caught in such a terrible trap, for there is no way out of it that I can see. That cunning bastard has built well...Really well!*

Not even the King's castle at Dover had such elaborate checks against an enemy. She would do well to remember all this, for the time might come when her knowledge could be vital, and her heart trembled for Gui and his men who would have to try and assault this monster!

*

As Alicia and her small Household rode out of the shadows and into the warm evening sunshine again they found themselves in a wide bailey, not nearly as large as the one at Malwood, but impressive enough for all that, and to her astonishment the whole area was covered with beautiful slabs of pale, gold limestone paving rather than grass and cobbles, which reflected back the sunshine making the whole castle feel lighter and less oppressive. She and Agnes looked at each other and smiled, shaking their heads at the extravagance, while shrugging their shoulders and lifting up their arms in cheerful acceptance of this simple display of Lord Roger's great wealth and station. And no sooner had they appeared at the open end of the Château's entrance, than a large company of soldiers came running out to line the paved way that led up to the massive round Donjon that reared above their heads.

This was the *Tour Barberousse*...the very heart of the Château's defences, and it dwarfed the whole castle with its vast, scarlet bulk. Towering up into the evening sky, now brushed with gold and pink, it seemed to lean over everyone, its stone battlements standing stark against the orange glow of the retreating sun like black dominoes; and from behind them came the flash and gleam of polished steel as the castle guard patrolled its distant walkways, stairs and parapets.

Around the outer walls were numerous stone buildings for the troops, their women and their families; the castle forge and stables; barns, granaries, storehouses, armouries, rope and leather works...and all the other trades that such a great building required to keep itself in front-line readiness, and all roofed over with red pantiles or dark grey slate. There was little here that would burn easily.

Alicia shivered again.

This impressive stone pile was a far cry from the warmth of her own home at Castle Malwood. Here was no Hall of homely grace and beauty but a fighting castle of great power and strength that could defy a besieging army for months, years even if supplies held out! And there was indeed a good harbour on the seaward side of the fortress, just as she had surmised and Soraya had confirmed for her earlier. And she thought again of Gui as the Lord Baron himself came down the wide steps...*Carrera marble no less according to Soraya*...to greet her and welcome her formally into his home.

God aid me...she prayed in her heart as she moved forward to greet him formally...*My, but he is a handsome man. And richly dressed for me, no doubt. But give me my Gui and his stained leathers and open cambric shirt any day!*...And her lips quirked as she watched the Baron now striding down the great forework that led into the Donjon above her, magnificently dressed in black and gold, a long cape of true cloth of gold flowing behind him that made her companions gasp at its opulence and shimmering beauty.

At both ends of every white marble step, shimmering with silver mica, a polished trooper stood. Two gleaming armoured men on every step right to the wide marble plateau at the very top that led to the gated entrance of the great Donjon, itself protected by its own drawbridge and portcullis. Here a huge house flag of green satin with the Boar's Head erased Sable, scarlet tongued and tushed, boldly emblazoned in its centre, flew to greet her. And besides that, to her intense surprise, and unexpected pleasure, flew her own personal blazon: the Stag's Head erased Gules, attired Or on a field Ermine that she had not actually seen flown since her father had died, and the sight of that noble scarlet stag's head with golden antlers on its ermine background brought the tears to her eyes for she had loved him so very much.

Now, with Aquib massively by her side, Agnes and Soraya two steps behind and Najid and Aziz two steps behind them, Alicia led them all forward to meet with the Lord Baron formally as the Lord and Master of Gruissan and of the great castle that was its heart.

"Welcome to the Château Grise, my Lady," he said to a flourish of trumpets, bowing over her hand as he kissed it. "And may you find much peace and happiness herein...though much more of *that* out there, my bird, and I shall not be pleased," he growled softly as he took her hand.

"I thank you for your kindness my Lord Baron," she said loudly for all to hear. "And I look to enjoy in full the peace of mind and heart you speak of... And don't you *dare* berate me before such a mawkish crowd of gaping onlookers!" She hissed back at him as she curtsied. "And don't you dare to presume too much either, my Lord Roger. That was the Devil's work down there this afternoon. I do not want to see it repeated...please!"

With a bright, fixed, smile he took her arm firmly and led her up between the ranks of soldiers and servants that stood to greet her, and finally to Rochine who waited on the wide marble plateau at the very Forework top before the entrance, surrounded by her own personal entourage of servants and hand-maidens. Clearly she had chosen them well for they were all striking in their way; but none were as comely as Agnes...and none more beautiful than Soraya...and no guardsmen in the *whole castle* were as striking or as massive as her two giant Arabs, and Alicia felt neither small nor eclipsed by Rochine's fine Household, as doubtless The Lady had wanted her to be, and looking round she smiled serenely as if she had not a care in the world.

Turning she held out her hand for Rochine to kiss and curtsey over...as she had kissed and curtsied over hers in England...as the dictates of their society demanded, and if Rochine's fingers trembled with rage and her face was flushed with it, Alicia ignored it and smiled down at her cousin as she curtsied to her, and purred as Rochine rose. Her eyes like green chips of ice as she looked into Alicia's violet blue ones, she then turned with a swish of her long skirts and a toss of her head, to lead the way into the great building as its chatelaine she still was.

And so Alicia followed her cousin on the Baron's arm...Aquib's massive presence at her back giving her great comfort...right into the very heart of the 'Tiger's' Lair; Agnes and Soraya following, Aziz and Najid close behind.

Once they were inside Lord Roger turned to Alicia and released her arm, allowing her to step away from his side. "Come, my Love, don't quarrel with me. I gave you what you wanted today against my better judgement. Our ways are different here from those in England. Here I rule absolutely on my own lands. My word is law throughout my household and I hold the power of life and death over everyone who serves me...even over my own family if I so choose."

"That is not what I am used to, my Lord Baron," she said tersely...*and don't think to cut my head off too easily either!...*"Sir Yvo taught me that gentleness and understanding go further with people than the rod and the stake. Our serfs and villeins always give us the best service they can because they know their Lord is just, and will see them fairly done by. Such happenings as I have witnessed today are wholly foreign to me! Nor would Sir Yvo ever have been allowed to treat his people in such a foul manner. The Church would have stopped him...and so would the King!"

"So, you seek to draw swords against me my Lady," De Brocas answered her, taking a step forward as he spoke. "You will find it a perilous enterprise my Alicia, I assure you, but intriguing," he said earnestly. "But how I run my estates is my own affair. You may not like the way I do things, but look around you," he gestured with his broad hands. "These are the benefits it brings. The luxuries you enjoy are the fruits of the labours of my peasants, and I will drive them any way I feel. You would not take kindly, I am sure, to anyone who tried to tell you how to run your estates? So, please do not try to tell me how to run mine!"

"My Lord Baron," Alicia replied icily. "You forget that I am not here as your honoured guest...but as your prisoner!...*So let's get that straight, right from the start you bastard!...*I am not here because I wish to be...but because you stole me from those whom I love and from the man to whom, in the sight of both God and man, I am legally and religiously bound by oath and agreement of the King of England!"...*So think on that before you get any grand ideas!...*

"How dare you speak to me like this!" He thundered at her then, his voice sending his servants scurrying for cover, knowing their master of old.

"*And how dare you speak so to me*!" She shouted back at him then, her face suddenly flushed and eyes flashing with rage. "With the aid of Corsair pirates, you seized me on the high seas in the first place, as if I were a common piece of merchandise to be haggled over and bargained for, yes? I am your prisoner, my Lord Baron," she sneered up, at him, her heart hammering in her breast as she moved closer to Aquib. "And, God help me," she snarled. "Yes! I may yet marry you…*if death be the only other option!*...But until then show me some compassion and some understanding for my situation…*and* show some to those poor wretches below us in the town, and in the countryside, who sweat and swink in your fields and in your vineyards, and in your olive groves no better than the beasts amongst which they toil," she continued, her words panting at him as she spoke.

"Woo me with compassion, my Lord Roger de Brocas. Show me you are more than a brutal pirate and a heartless, ignorant Tenant-in-Chief to your Lord the King of France…and who knows what may yet happen between us?" And with a sudden, brilliant smile, she curtsied and held out her hand for him to take…*Now chew on all that, you smug bastard. You will not take me without a fight!*

Baron Roger, looking down at her with blank eyes, was astonished, and stepping towards her two enormous Arab guards, their hands hovering over the hilts of their great scimitars…*whatever had El Nazir been thinking of to saddle me with two such massive problems?*...he took her hand and lifted her up, kissing her fingers as she rose…and was suddenly enormously proud of her!

He must be well over twenty years older than she, and a man of great power already, with more just waiting for him to seize hold of…yet here she was, surrounded by enemies, defying him in his own halls! *Truly she is amazing. I could love her for it!*

And he suddenly laughed, a great booming guffaw of noise that startled his servants and his soldiers, and made Rochine grit her teeth with rage….*What is Papa doing? That putain has just defied him and now he is kissing her hands and laughing! No! No! No!*...And she spun on her heel, and looked back towards the entrance gates unable to watch the two of them together one moment longer.

"Come now, enough of this fratching, Alicia! When we are married and our inheritance is joined, I will give you a say in what goes on here. And, yes, we will see if you are right, and can get more out of the idle hounds who laze in my fields and barns, than my reeves and bailiffs. But until then, leave well alone! Don't anger me, I beg you, for it will spoil all the pleasures that I have in store for your enjoyment."

Alicia, no less astonished by the Baron's reaction than his servants, looked at Soraya who was actually standing nearby with her mouth open and her eyes on stalks with surprise, shrugged her shoulders and smiled again, so that it seemed as if Apollo himself had entered the great building alongside her:

"It seems, my Lord, I must be content, but promise me this one thing Lord Roger. Please don't hang any more of your filthy work where the world may call you to account for it, or I. And if you care at all about me, leave your people in peace and see what benefits it may bring to all of us." And she held out her hand and curtsied to him again in all gentle humility, her huge blue eyes twinkling up at him through her long black lashes.

"Alicia, I will do what I can," he said quietly, almost as astonished by his own reaction to her as his servants and his daughter had been... *What is happening to me?*...and raising her up he kissed her fingertips. "I shall promise you no more than that.

"Now go with Rochine, she will show you and your people to their rooms and will appoint you a maid to help you with your clothes and make you comfortable. We will meet again before the evening meal. We shall eat together in the Lesser Hall as we have done these past few days. My Seneschal, Sir Raymond Marceau, an old family friend and a man of great honour, shall call for you later. And I will take Najid with me now to prepare your food. I have read all that Sheik El Nazir has said in his letter and would not dishonour him by refusing any of his requests. Oh...and I have chosen the clothes for you to wear, I hope you will approve."

"Chosen them my Lord?" she asked surprised. "How come? I have only been in your company a short while; and we've only just arrived here. Surely no seamstress could run up a gown in so short a time as must exist between now and our next meeting?"

But the Baron only smiled, bowed to them all, and strode away leaving her looking quizzically after him as he turned a corner and disappeared. So, full of unanswered questions, she turned and went to join Rochine who was waiting for her at the foot of the great polished marble staircase that wound upwards to the family apartments, high up on the third floor of the great building.

Chapter 10...How the Lord Baron, Sir Roger de Brocas honoured Alicia.

At the top of the long staircase, Rochine turned and forced herself to smile...*though it kills me, I will 'do' the pretty by my cousin as Papa has asked of me. But, by God's Blood...it will not be for long!...*and resting her finger ends on her cousin's arm as she came up to join her she said:

"You know cousin, it is not wise to press my father too hard. He is a stark lord at times I assure you, and will not brook a rein upon his actions."

"I know that, Rochine. But I couldn't stand by and say nothing after what happened in the square. I don't want my dreams marred by any further horrors like those I witnessed today." ...*As if you cared!*

"Oh, as to that, the death of a few of those miserable wretches merely helps to keep the rest in line. No worse than my father's game wardens, what you call 'Verderers'? Hanging vermin up by the heels to warn off the rest?...*I cannot see why she is making such a fuss over a parcel of swine?*...Come, don't give it another thought. *Les canailles*...the common rabble...are not your problem, Alicia. Keeping my father happy is everything, and I will honour you for that," she said, coming to a halt opposite a beautifully polished door of oak and beech wood together. "Neither of us may like what my father has planned......*me least of all you English bitch!*...but you are here now, and I cannot stop him. I may not like you, cousin...not yet anyway. But I do admire you, and hope to come to respect you. Maybe even love you?...*By all the gods...how can I say all this?*...But I have cared for my father for a very long time..and..and have given my all to him, so I will find it hard to hand over to another that which I have done for him and with him myself for many years now since my mother," she hesitated, looking momentarily haunted, "died. So...so unexpectedly...*Dear God, how is my soul not burdened by her murder?*...So...please, try and respect my feelings too."

And before Alicia could say a word in response to Rochine's extraordinary and wholly unexpected out-burst of feeling, her cousin lifted the iron latch and flung the door open...*for if I have to say anything more about my mother to this putain I shall be sick!*...standing to one side as she did so to let Alicia and her ladies through, while Aquib and Aziz remained outside

"This is your room, Alicia," she said a moment later, coming in behind her cousin...*and it should have been mine! Mine!*... "And when you are settled and ready Soraya will take you all down to the Roman pool for you to bathe in and enjoy. She knows all our ways here at the Château, some of which may be strange to you…and some of which may be quite beyond your experience," she said with a bob of her head and a hard stare into Alicia's blue eyes. "But they are essentials here. My father will brook no alternatives. We live in a very hot part of *la belle France*, and cleanliness will prevent both sickness and disease, I assure you…*Why am I telling this to you? Die! Die!*...My Father has proved that many times over. If you need any further help Soraya knows from whom to seek it…*Truly I will kill that salope yet for her treachery!*...Your men, also, will be equally cared for. They are desert Arabs and also know the importance of being clean.

"Rooms have been prepared for them close to this apartment; Najid will bring you your food as he did while you were on the *Morning Star*, and when you are settled you may go where you wish, unheralded and without need of invitation, except into my father's apartments…*Papa must be mad to let them have such freedom. I would have them both in chains!*...Not even I go there except at his request. Only my mother was allowed total access to him at any time. Those have always been his orders."…*And you had better learn to follow them, you witch, or your life will not be a happy one!*...And she smiled.

Alicia, stepping forward into the room, was momentarily dazzled because it was so lit up by the setting sun with a wonderful flush of gold and pink that it almost took her breath away, but it was not just the light that was so stunning as the actual beauty of the room itself: of its fittings and furniture, its tapestries, carpets and polished oak floors.

"Oh…Rochine," she exclaimed breathlessly. "It is beautiful!"

"Yes, lovely isn't it?" the dark haired woman said, looking all around her with a sad smile. "As my father said, this was my mother's room…*How could he have honoured you in this way?*...It is where she died, and has never been used since. Even when the Château has been packed out, this room has still never been used. It is kept as if she would walk into it again at any moment. Freshly aired and with fresh linen and flowers almost every day. My father honours you greatly, Cousin…*and how I hate you for it!*...'Constancia' was my mother's name. She was half French and half Italian and Papa adored her. People say I am very like her to look at."

Looking all around her Alicia was amazed, and Soraya too awed with The Lady standing so close to her to touch anything. Agnes just stood in a corner and looked stunned.

"How do you feel about me having your mother's room, Rochine?" Alicia asked her, softly, reaching out to touch her arm in sudden compassion…*for this cannot be easy for her, and she is clearly hurting.* "Your father must have loved your mother greatly. It is truly beautiful. I have never been in so lovely an apartment."

"Don't worry, my sweet." Rochine replied, silkily, sliding her arm round Alicia's waist in a sudden display of cousinly friendship and affection...*If only you knew how I really feel, you fucking bitch!* "I would far rather it was lived in and loved by someone my father really cared for...than by just anyone. Anyway, you are to marry Papa! He has said so, so it must be so. It is ten years ago this month that my mother died. I was fourteen, on the verge of womanhood, when a girl needs her mother most, so losing her was very hard...*Harder than anyone will ever know...especially my dear Papa. But it was so necessary for her to die. I wept for days!*...But I am now a woman grown in every way and have become used to the life I lead...and I love every moment of it, so do not pine for me!...*And isn't that the real truth, God help me? For I just love all that I do, and the power it gives me*...Now, I must leave you, for there are many things I must do between now and then.

"I understand we are eating in the Lesser Hall tonight. My father's Seneschal...Sir Raymond Marceau? Good, my father clearly told you downstairs. He will call for you an hour before the meal. I will see you then...and pausing only to give Alicia a swift, soft kiss on each cheek and one on her lips, she closed the door...*One moment more and I would have strangled her! Dear God, I feel quite sick. How could Papa do this to me? I do not know whom I hate more tonight...my wretched English cousin...or my foolish French father?* And with those thoughts running through her she swiftly strode away.

*

To say that the room was sumptuous was surely an understatement. The hard stone walls were almost covered with glowing tapestries and the polished oak floor with magnificent eastern carpets of the most intricate and beautiful designs. Here the main body of the room faced south, but because of the curved wall of the Donjon it was also lit east and west as well so in the morning, and the evening as now, the room was awash with coloured light. There were long embroidered padded cushions upon the carved wooden seats that lay beneath all the windows, and elegant little settees and armed chairs for people to relax in. Handsome chests of cedar and cherry wood stood against the walls, and there was a beautiful refectory table and chairs beneath the farthest window, with tall Venetian goblets in beautiful coloured glass with a tall silver gilt flagon of ruby wine already on it, all resting on delicate mats of painted cork. And the great fireplace, with its beautiful marble surround, was full of flowers and scented greenery.

But it was the bed that drew Alicia's attention most, for it almost filled one whole corner of that great room, with magnificently carved corner posts that rose up almost to the ceiling beams and were hung with rich damask coverings and fine silk curtains of the palest blue. She had never seen such a magnificent creation in her life and an involuntary gasp of amazement slipped out before she was even aware of having moved her lips.

The mattress was of thick canvas stuffed with horsehair with a white quilted cotton over-cover, itself enveloped with the finest Egyptian cotton sheeting, almost like silk, and deliciously cool to the touch. At the bed head was a long cotton bolster with a host of cushions and pillows, and overall a beautiful bed-shawl of palest ivory cotton, stuffed with the softest down and embroidered with singing birds in scarlet, green and blue that flew and perched amidst a forest of swirling leaves embroidered with the purest gold and silver thread.

Suspended on broader leather strappings than Alicia was used to, and battened tight against the wooden frame, so they would not give too much... especially when being energetically used, she thought with a wicked grin!...the mattress was much firmer, and springier to rest on, and was large enough to take all three girls and still leave room for more.

Alicia, Soraya and Agnes took one long look all around them, and then, with a great shout of joy at being safe at last…they flung themselves onto it as much for the sheer enjoyment of not having to awake at dawn again in time for yet another 'Roman breakfast', and yet another long punishing day in the saddle, as for the simple joy of the thing itself, and they all burst out laughing.

There might well be fearful troubles ahead...but with Aquib and Aziz outside their door, and Rochine and the Baron somewhere else completely in this huge building, this was as close to heaven as they were going to get for a while and they had every intention of enjoying themselves!

Chapter 11...The true evil of the Lady Rochine de Brocas is revealed.

Rochine heard the burst of joyous noise and almost strode back and shouted at them!

Only the massive presence of the two enormous men who stood either side of the door, their hands resting lightly on the great pommels of their scimitars, naked steel points down on the marble floor, stopped her…so she continued to walk away…*How dare my father give that wretched girl my mother's room after all I have done to serve him... both with my body and my mind! And those other salopes too! Yet I, who have given so much, am denied it!...*And by all rights it should have been hers.

It had been wholly renovated to suit her mother's needs and her desires. And her mother had been so beautiful. So warm and loving to her small daughter…and so fierce too sometimes, when her hand-maidens had trembled in her presence and her father had roared like a lion she had once seen on a trip they had made to Morocco. Her mother…her room! Surely? Only her father had refused, turning it instead into some sort of shrine that he had not wanted her to share.

Ah well, she reflected, it would not be her cousin's for long! De Rombeau, her personal enforcer, was on his way, and Valerian Dodoni with his *Ajax* was at Narbonne awaiting her orders. And the agreed money, in leather bags of a hundred coins each, in two iron-bound oaken chests, was all safely on board. Six thousand golden bezants…equal to a hundred and forty four thousand silver coins in any nation's coinage! A huge amount of money for two Christian girls…but what girls?…*One fully trained, and stunning to look at; the other yet more beautiful and oozing appeal from every pore….my fucking Cousin, the Lady Al-ic-ia de Burley! That bitch!...*And she laughed. Wazzim would not be disappointed, even though he was buying sight unseen, relying on Valerian to prove the merchandise before sailing, as he always did.

In fact Wazzim was going to do even better with his deal because she would throw in the other English girl…*That pathetic little conne anglaise...that Agnes...*for nothing! *She's pretty enough, with pert breasts and good rounded buttocks and a brave smile when she chooses to show it. When properly stripped down and prepared she will do well on the blocks. All bashful tears and simpering...*She laughed again…*The slave dealers will love her!...*Not nearly as beautiful as Soraya of course, and nothing like her mistress…but good enough to let Wazzim think he was getting a bargain…*Just pray Valerian does not discover the true provenance of what he will be carrying!*

She smiled.

Who would have thought a Venetian trader would have such scruples?... *No free-born Christian girls?...Bah! What arrant nonsense…*He was being paid handsomely indeed for this little contract…more than any other trader on the whole Circle Sea! But he was the best. She snorted and tossed her head, realising she would simply have to offer more if there was a problem. After that it would be between him and Wazzim to sort it out.

She would deliver the merchandise, as agreed, and when stated…well almost. Just let the wedding be soon, with enough time to secure all the land contracts…*After that who cares what happens to the stupid little bitch with the huge blue eyes, big tits and softly rounded arse. Papa will have had a few nights of bouncing pleasure out of her and that will be that. Pouf! Gone for ever...and all those glittering bezants will be mine!...*And she grunted with satisfaction.

Yet she had come so close to killing them both.

Had so wanted to. Even planned it…until they had all fled at Foix. Even now jealousy raged through her body…and when that happened she could still lose all control over herself. Now that she was back with her father, things would be better, and with her deal with Wazzim, de Rombeau and Valerian Dodoni already set up and agreed...all she had to do now was wait, and it would all come right…*wouldn't it?*

Then she and her own adored Lord and Master, the Lord Baron, Sir Roger de Brocas…could both get back to being together again!…and she literally purred at the thought. He was such a splendid lover, and the very wickedness of what they were doing only served to make it better. *Delicious!..Would Mama have been shocked?...*The beautiful, sensuous Constancia?

She didn't think so. *Hadn't her father taken her into his bed before they were married?...And hadn't she already slept with both her own father, and her uncle, before she had married Papa? Incest! Taboo! Yet it happened all the time. Fathers with daughters. Mothers with sons. Even Popes were not averse to sex with their family. History was full of it! So why not me?...*And she chuckled at those thoughts as she walked the marble corridor towards her father's apartments

So the beautiful Constancia was hardly a shrinking violet when she had been slipped into her father's bed on their marriage night. Like mother…like daughter, and she smiled wickedly to herself, knowing that before the day was out she would be back in her father's bed…back where he wanted her, and where she so wished to be...where she had sacrificed everything to achieve...*everything!* Stripped and open for his touch; watching as he removed his clothes and his great manhood sprang free, leaping out of his loins like a great tree from amongst a wild froth of ferns and thornless brambles…and she pressed her hands to her breasts, feeling her heart quicken and her breath pant to her thoughts and rushing emotions…*Dear God, make it soon! Make it soon!*

Then, turning a corner, she came to a large seaward looking window with a long padded armed couch beneath it in green and silver, with the Boar's Head erased Sable in the middle of the back…the whole thing lovingly appliquéd, especially its scarlet tongue and great scarlet tushes. It was a favourite place of hers, with some of her mother's finest work, and she loved to come here and kneel up on it, lean against the wide stone windowsill, and gaze out across the vastness of the Circle Sea, the beautiful Mediterranean, especially on a gorgeous, sunset evening like this one.

She sighed as she settled her chin on her arms…*Her darling mother! The beautiful, sensuous Constancia...whom her Papa had so adored and who had, in turn, so adored her lovely daughter...Me!*

And kneeling up on the long bench, as she had as a child, resting her arms along the windowsill, her chin nestled on her arms, she gazed out with sightless eyes as far as she could see, the busy hum of the castle stilled in her ears as she did so, the swifts and swallows suddenly flying on silent wings, the crooning pigeons from their tower loft no longer softening the evening with their song.

Such a radiant lady, the so beautiful Lady Constancia de Brocas; with a sunburst smile and a melting look, but who stood between her father and what she had come to see as her rightful place beside him…and who always held something back when making love to him. And she looked out across the vast étang to the sparkling sea beyond, now golden red, like the juice from some vast blood orange, as Apollo drove his chariot towards the far horizon, the sails of distant ships silhouetted black against the intense orange of the sun as it slowly sank into the west.

Such distant thoughts!

So deep…so far away…*My lovely mother...so exotic, yet so denying my dear Papa at the same time!...*Of course she had watched them, often, from behind secret passages and lofty eye-holes that they had no idea even existed, and that she had been shown by Old William, the castle's most respected Watch-Guard, an aged retainer whom her father had known when he was young. Old William and he had gone everywhere in those far distant days when both were young, and the old man had shown her all that once he had shared with her father, and with her grandfather, the Lord Thibault - whom

Alicia's Papa had killed long ago at Cahors. And once she knew everything he had to show her...she had killed him!

She settled her head more firmly on her arms and sighed again...*Strange that it had been so easy really*...she thought, watching the swifts tear through the air on their scimitar wings, and so unplanned...so spontaneous...But then *perhaps that was how things should always be?...Spontaneous!*

In those far off days she had loved to watch the great drawbridge swing up and down into its huge pit: the graunching, rattling, groaning timbers...and the huge, echoing *bang*! when it crashed home. It always made her scream and clap her hands. Old William liked to take her to watch...enjoyed her excitement, and then, one day, he just fell down the pit!

Such a shame he had to go really. And she sighed...smiling at the memory...*Of course I pushed him, the silly old fool*...but still she had screamed and cried out... *'Oh...my poor William! Oh...my poor William!'* And she snorted at her cleverness. *Only ten and she had fooled them all!* They had always seemed such friends together, her and Old William, and she shushed the air out across her teeth...*It was expected she should cry and wail!*...And she smiled and wriggled her body as she gazed out across the shadowy garth below her, counting the dancing fishing boats, with their lanterns and patched sails as they began to sally out for their night's fishing.

Yes...Old William had been my first. The thought spinning the pictures of it over in her mind like a kaleidoscope, and she giggled at the remembrance of the shock on his wrinkled old face when she had pushed him over...*such puckered surprise, and his mouth a perfect 'O'!*...She laughed.

So funny! It had been after his fall that the guard-rail the men had rushed to put up today was created.

But how could she possibly let him live after he had shown her all the castle's secrets?...*He might show them to another, or tell others what he had shown me. Old men like to boast about their doings. So the daft old bugger just had to go. One swift push when no-one else was looking and over he'd gone*...And then the lovely *C..rrr.uuunch* when he hit the bottom...and she made the noise again...*C..rrr..uuunch!*...and she chuckled.

He had been so surprised!

Because of the old man's secret knowledge she had been able to watch her mother and father as lovers...*from all the little peeping holes that great grandpa had known of, and Old William had shown me*...And the whores who came to her father's bed as well, and the strong things they did together which her mother would not do! Though sometimes she did come and watch them, even join with them, a great dildo of black leather strapped to her loins. And she smiled again and wriggled her body...*The same one I use myself now... 'Big*

*Charlie'...beautifully crafted from Italy, with tiny seed pearls stitched along its shaft, such quality, and from Rome itself. Just like the pictures on the Greek and Roman vases found when the Château was first built by great, great grandfather. Amazing how nothing has changed in all those years?...*But Constancia did not relish pain herself, and though she would thrash the whores her father used when she was ordered to do so by her husband, she would not let him use the lash on her. They had rowed about it often. And *that* was when she had decided she must take her mother's place...*Because I, Rochine de Brocas, can serve my adored father better. I like pain!*

And she loved giving pain to others... *the smack of leather on flesh; the red lines leaping out, the writhing body, the cries... such power in my hands!...*And as her body had developed and she had experienced all the fierce sexual urges that were normal in anyone growing up, she had decided she must find out for herself what she really liked...and so she had done a deal with her father's favourite whore...*The luscious Janine Croest...the one who came most often to Papa's bed, who had the richest figure, and who was joined sometimes by my mother in slaking Papa's constant needs. And they are constant!...*she thought with a quiet smile, as the sun sank further towards the purple sea of evening, pressing her hands against her breasts, feeling her nipples tighten...*Constant!..*

They had waited until both her parents had been away in Cyprus...and then Janine had shown her how to make love. How to suck and how to caress; how to twist flesh and take the lash and how to give it too! Not so as to tear the skin, but to criss-cross it with red lines of fire; breasts and nipples, buttocks, flanks and thighs...and even between the legs...*And always the finest twisted silks, clouds of them on a long black leather-covered handle, so that the pain washes over you, almost soothing you until your whole body is glistening with sweat and your loins are watering...and you just want it to go on and on and on!*

And she loved it!

Having my own nipples bound with silken bands until they are almost purple with the pressure is delicious...Love it!...Love feeling the blood rushing back through my body when the bindings are removed...exquisite! To take the leather hard across my buttocks, and all down my back, so..so exciting! The very thought of it made the breath *shhhwish!* through her lips, and her whole body quiver like a hound's at quest.

And she wriggled in anticipation, couldn't help herself, feeling her breasts swell and tighten as she did so, and the soft lips of her vagina open wetly...for her father loved to bind her nipples with scarlet silk, as much as she loved to offer them for binding, until they stood out like fat sticks of crimson dogwood in winter…and she could barely wait to feel his hands upon her again.

Janine had always made her blood race. She was exciting and knowledgeable, knowing as much about a woman's body as a man's, and she had been as good and willing a teacher as Rochine had been a student…but, of course it had to end.

Supposing the girl was to tell others of what they did? Or threatened to? So Janine Croest, butcher's daughter from Narbonne, had been found washed up, drowned upon the beach after a lively boating party, when having had just too much to drink she had fallen in and been swept away by the currents.

How sad! What a dreadful accident! And she giggled at that too. Drunk?

The girl had been completely sozzled…she had seen to that! Drugged her with a sweet tasting posset from Stanisopoulos' cunning wife, Eugenia…*Slipped into Janine's goblet as they sailed, and then time and an unstable little boat had done the rest...*Laughing and singing with all the others, she, Rochine, had rocked the boat hard just as Janine had stood up swaying…*And over she had gone...splash! Water everywhere, and such shrieks and cries. And when the gasping girl had struggled to the surface, I was the first to push the boathook out for her to grasp onto. But while everyone was rushing to save her, to shout and cry out and give advice, amongst all the shrieks and cries...including mine of course!..I was cunningly slaying her. Screaming and flailing the hook at her as if in a panic to save her, but really drowning her...pushing her under instead, bobbing her up and down in the sea, and hitting her head...by accident of course...at the same time until she finally sank down and disappeared without trace.*

She laughed.

So easy, really, yet so sad also, and she sighed with rapture at the ease of it. *No-one had ever suspected. And poor Janine. She had known of course... tried to cry out, looking desperate...but I just pushed her under!...*And she laughed again at the memory. *Poor little Janine Croest…But so necessary!*

The girl was a disgusting little tart with no breeding. *Une conne française!* A juicy, willing and experienced teacher, but how could she possibly have left her alive? Especially after she had finally taken her mother's place in her father's bed! *No, Janine just had to go…*and that just left her mother...*My beautiful, generous, loving mother...whose single glance could melt Papa's heart to butter. Such a shame she had to die too. Quelle dommage, ma belle maman!...*She thought as she looked out across the darkening bay, the soft, warm summer air caressing her body…*My beautiful mother…*

And she groaned deep in her throat, and wept a little.

It wasn't that she hadn't loved her mother, of course. She adored her mother, and had wept bitterly after her death for days. But it was all her mother's fault of course. *If only she had been a better wife, I never would have had to kill her!* And she growled then in her throat at what her mother had forced her to do. Remembering how she had refused all comfort after her death until her father had returned, and swept her up into his arms…as she had so planned he would do...and they had wept and comforted each other. And so it had been from that day to this, and that all-consuming love for him is what had made it so easy for her to take her mother's life.

It was *why* her mother had had to die!

She smiled then and breathed in deeply; her thoughts drifting, spiralling, surging backwards: the years speeding past, a myriad swirling thoughts and images.

*My poor, beautiful Mama. So lovely, so unsuspecting of me...her own devoted daughter...*and she giggled.

Her father had been away…*in Cyprus? Morocco?...No!...Morocco. I remember now, he often went there to visit the Barbary Sheiks…*

He liked Arabs.

Found them intellectually stimulating, 'clever men with wisdom, and artistry, and culture,' he was used to say. So different from most Franks who only wanted to kill and butcher infidels wherever they could find them! 'Madmen dressed in steel, with swords on the brain!' he called them, and she smiled….so her father found them infidels to kill!

It was all so easy.

He visited the Sheiks…they indicated which of their fellow Arabs were causing problems; he arranged for the Crusaders to attack and kill them…and everyone made huge profits out of it all!

Had done so for years. How else did this castle look so magnificent?

So, with him away, her mother had fallen ill. Not a big illness at first; just a bothersome cough…she smiled, and giggled again, an inane sound that echoed through her head.

Eugenia had been *so* clever with her powders and her tinctures that no-one had ever suspected. Scented waters with which to bathe her face and body; sweet oils dissolved in boiling water and then breathed into her mother's lungs under a beautiful cotton shawl to clear her chest…*Everything lovely, everything clean and fresh...and everything poisoned!* So…the cough got worse, her throat filled with mucus, her nose ran with it, her eyes became red and swollen and she soiled herself. And all the time she had cared for her mother devotedly: would allow no-one else near her for fear someone else might catch what she had...*And I fed her with my own hands the dainties she most liked, brought her every drink she needed and physicked her, and cleansed her...and all of it was poisoned!* Such pathos, so many tears, so much praise for her devotion.

She chuckled.

*Everyone thought I was being a wonderful daughter to my adored mother, right until the end. Right until my beautiful mother finally realised what was happening to her...what was really being done to her by her adoring daughter, by which time she could no longer speak!...*Only look...haunting, choking, desperate looks of fear and beseeching...looks that still fleered at her in her dreams...*Looks which even I could bear no longer and finally stopped with the softest pillow I could find...pressing it down upon her poor tortured face and desperate breathing until it stopped. Until her gasping, rattling chest stopped its noise, her desperate hands stopped grappling my fingers and her body stopped heaving up at me, and heaving up at me again, and again and was...finally...still!*

And her whole body shuddered at the memory so that she cried out, burying her face in her arms to stifle her cries. But at the time she had howled her loss and her misery to the whole world...and everyone had come running to comfort her! So simple really, and she sighed deeply, her eyes staring glassily out across the wine-dark sea as the sun sank slowly towards it in a final blaze of glory.

So straightforward...and so easy to get rid of Eugenia Stanisopoulos as well after that, and so necessary!

To have her mother's poisoner still alive to tell tales? Unthinkable!

And she smiled at her cleverness in getting rid of the dark-eyed little Greek wife who had taught her all she could, who had occasional palpitations and small pains in her heart that made her breathless and pant and wheeze: 'You're overdoing it, my dove,' her husband, Dmitri would say as he pored over his roots and herbology. 'You must rest more, my angel,' he would say, easing her into a chair. 'Drink this, sweetness. It will ease your chest.'

She laughed out loud then, and clapped her hands together at the memory: 'Need to rest more!'...well, and now she was, too!...*Resting with the blessèd angels, filled with the digitalis I gave her in her favourite drink before church, and that carried her off between the Host being up-raised before the people and the last 'Hail Mary, Full of Grace'!...*And she laughed again at her cleverness. Not even Dmitri himself had ever suspected her.

And now this!

This English *putain* who had so suddenly come between herself and her father...and his great Crystal. Well, let her enjoy her mother's room while she could, because she would allow nothing to stand in her way between her father's needs and her own. Let him marry her...*Yes I think I can stomach that*...Get all the papers signed and properly sealed to secure the lands...then, *pouf! Gone!*

He was due to journey to Jaffa alone three days after his proposed marriage taking her precious Arab guard with him on the *Morning Star,* leaving Alicia wholly unprotected. And when he returned she and her whole entourage would be gone...she, the girl Agnes and that treacherous bitch Soraya...all gone! Vanished on one of her trips to the mountains she had spoken of to her father. Vanished like a puff of wood smoke on a windy day!

Fallen down a ravine; eaten by bears; drowned in the sea; taken by pirates off the sea shore...who knew? They'd gone off on one of their excursions, refused an escort, and never come back! They had searched everywhere but nothing had been found...only some blood-stained, torn-up clothes...she would sort out the details later. But her precious cousin and her ladies would be gone, never to be seen again. And she laughed at her cleverness.

Then let him take a different wife...an 'ordinary' wife for whom the Crystal can never work...and then, like Abraham's Sara...with that great Patriarch's concubines...she would take the birthing child into her own hands as her own. Feed the child from her own beautiful breasts...she knew how to stimulate milk in a woman's breasts who had not borne the child herself. Another of Eugenia's cunning tricks! And then that child would be hers to give to her father...as if it were her own!

The wife? No problem. She would go the same way as all the rest! In the Souks of Damascus; drowned in the sea; fallen off her horse; shot while hunting? The choices were everywhere...and there were always the castle swine anyway!

And she giggled to herself, remembering the screams of those two young whores whom she had slain and how their hot blood had come spurting out over her naked body..."*Grunt! Grunt!*"...she rooted with a wicked smile. "*Grunt! Grunt!*"...Pigs would eat anything! Or maybe a wild boar on a hunting day? A giant black sanglier from the depths of the forest on the Pech Redon? Look at what had happened to Soraya's mother that awful afternoon! The same could happen to another just as easily.....

Rochine stayed watching and looking from the window for some time, as the sun sank through the far horizon at last, a giant, shimmering ball of scarlet-orange fire that washed the whole western sky with crimson and gold like a flowing river, the clouds above tinged midnight blue and purple with the velvet blackness of the night still yet to settle down upon them from above.

And with a deep sigh…regret, sadness, expectation?…running through her she straightened her dress, and pulling the material tight around her breasts as she knew her father liked, so that her nipples pushed out at him, still sharply aroused, she swept towards the broad staircase that would take her to his apartments where she knew he would be waiting for her. As urgent to take her, to be one with her and to feel her gripping him with her loins as only she knew how…as she was for him to do so. Her body already weeping at the very thought of him plundering her…*delicious!*

And then afterwards the Crystal would flame and sparkle into coruscating beams of rainbow light, the clouds within the great palantir would clear, and from within them the images would appear in perfect clarity. Then they would know at last just where that English *bastard* was, that *chien*, Sir Gui de Malwood, so they could plan his total and complete destruction!...*Let my cousin...the so fair Al-ic-ia, with the blue eyes...enjoy these next few days as best she can, for Insha'Allah...they will be the last good, happy days she will enjoy for years and years to come!...*And with a beatific smile on her lovely face, giving her taut breasts a final squeeze and a sharp twist to their firm crests to make them thrust out ever harder, she mounted the first of the green carpeted marble stairs that would lead her up to her father's great room above…and to her own pathway to the stars.

Chapter 12...Soraya takes Alicia and Agnes to the Roman Pool

For some time after Rochine had left they all just lay without speaking, or moving, spread out on the enormous bed like giant lilies, basking in the gold and vermilion light of the sun as it slowly sank beneath the horizon.

Just lying there with her friends all around her, and her Arab Guardians on the door, Alicia relished being still, warm and in comfort for the first time in days...*No Roman 'breakfast' for me tomorrow thank God!...*And no-one was willing to move and no-one wished to speak either...all loving the silence, punctuated as it was by all the usual sounds of castle life: the distant clash of arms as some soldiers practised their weapon skills; the clatter of hooves on the stone paved garth below; the shouts of men and the laughter of women; the patter of feet in the marble corridors, the creels of the castle children whose parents lived and worked in the huge building, and for whom the place was home. It only needed the lowing of cattle, and the shouts of the drovers taking them back after milking for Alicia to be at home in the Forest...and not an honourable prisoner here in southern France!

"Ladies, this will not do!" she said at last, sitting up. "The Baron promised us a bathe in his famous Roman bath that Soraya has been telling us all about these past few days at least, or more," she said giving the French girl a mighty push in the ribs, making her squeal. "So let us be about it, and enjoy the ministrations of this well-practised and adorable masseuse!"

"*Right!*" Soraya exclaimed brightly. "And I will be delighted to do so, not least because you all stink like pigs in the midden, as I do too I am sure, and I hate not being clean all over. But I have to warn you ladies, that bathing is always accompanied by cleansing in the Château! I told you all, remember, on the *Star*? About being shaven smooth, all over your bodies? The Lady said the same thing just before she left. The Lord Baron insists that every visiting Lady, and every woman who works in the Château amongst the guests must be properly smooth at all times, for cleanliness, freshness and no disease!"

"*No!*" Agnes squealed. "No! Trimmed...I understand trimmed, and have been trimming my Lady here since her fur first grew. But shaven? *NO!* My lady, I could not! She added becoming ever more expressive. "Alicia do not make me! Please? I could not. I have never been seen naked by anyone except my mother, let alone been touched on my-my 'parts'!"

"John Shipley?...Agnes, dear?" Alicia teased her, her eyebrows sky high. "He was all over you like a rash for weeks?"

"Not all over me, my love. Only all over *bits* of me! And they weren't the 'lower' bits either!" she said blushing. "And so I told him, the varmint. I told him those were very special, those-those 'lower' bits, and I was keeping..."

"...them for the 'King of France'!" Alicia chimed in to finish off one of Agnes's pet sayings. "Yes, honeyone, that may well be so. But your 'King of France' is somewhere north of here, God willing, with the king of my heart and all his men, and we are here in the Baron's power not our own. So, my lovely Agnes, we will follow one of Father Matthew's favourite sayings in conditions like these: 'When in Rome...do as the Romans do!' He told me that Saint Ambrose once wrote that to Saint Augustine...the original one, not the one who was sent to Kent by Pope Gregory...when he found himself in the Holy City and did not want to offend his hosts by fasting when they did not! And if that was good enough for Ambrose, one of the Church's greatest saints, then I am willing to be so groomed by Soraya as to be silken smooth *all* over to please our hosts here....And if *I* can endure that, my sweet bird, *then so can you!* So no more nonsense out of you, my girl!" she added sternly, and giving her a swift cuddle to re-assure her, she turned briskly back to Soraya with a smile: "Now, my love. What do we need? We are all yours!"

And despite Agnes trying to hang back from a fate she clearly regarded as being just short of death itself, it was still a very giggly trio of ladies who made their way down into the depths of the Château, below the foundations of the great castle and into the very rock on which it had been built. The steps, of pink marble laced with golden quartz, were wide and comfortable to take, much more so than Alicia and Agnes had been expecting. The walls were plastered and painted with scenes of Roman bathing life, and there was a lovely thick, deep crimson, silky rope to hang onto as they went down; with huge crimson and silver tassels hanging from each iron stanchion, and bronze oil lamps in carved niches to light their way.

"This was once the site of a wonderful Roman Palace," Soraya told them. "And when the foundations for the great Donjon were being laid in Lord Turold's day, the Baron's great grandfather...Lord Thibault's grandfather..." she chattered brightly. "The pool was found. Filled in of course and in a desperate state, but Lord Turold refused to have it destroyed; found water specialists to help him with the plumbing, expert masons for its restoration, and fresco artists from Italy who could put paint into wet plaster...and got it all to work, better probably than before, because the water now flows out as swiftly as it comes in...which even the Romans could not do...and is always crystal clear and always warm. The pool is deep enough to swim in, neck high at its deepest, and has the most beautiful mosaic floor you can imagine, and all round the edges are more wonderful shapes and patterns. You will be amazed! See, we are here now," she said indicating a wide door of polished oak and beech wood. "If Aquib and Aziz will stand guard outside we can go in. There will be no-one there but us so we can have a really good splash about before I need to cleanse you!" She giggled again. "You both look as if I am going to cut you in ribbons 'down there'!" she exclaimed with her ringing laugh. "But you will be safe, I promise you...and afterwards you will wonder why you did not do so years ago! Not just your loins of course, but your legs also, and under.

"What's the 'under'? Agnes asked, nervously.

"Under your arms, Silly," Alicia answered with a chuckle. "Or anywhere else that's 'under', like your round bum!" she laughed, giving Agnes a hearty *smack!* on her rump as she said it. "Stop fretting, sweetheart, and follow Soraya," who, without another word, had opened the polished beechwood door, that had stood closed before them a moment earlier, stepping through to usher Agnes and Alicia past her.

Inside was a large open landing of red and white marble squares set like diamonds, with polished cedar wood tables around the sides, great fluffy towels on them for those who needed them...all leading to a short flight of marble steps down to the most stunningly beautiful mosaic floor of Roman gods and goddesses in all their glory.

Alicia and Agnes had never seen anything so wonderful, so intricate in their lives. Red, green, blue, purple, orange, yellow and white tesserae, some of them tiny, had been immaculately laid, with deep black ones to set off the patterns wherever necessary. There was also a fantastically complex border of richly coloured twisted shapes and fantastic animals, some real, some mythical; and right in the middle, a deep sunken oval pool with dolphins leaping and twisting all round the edge and Neptune with his trident in the very centre. Surrounded by dancing Nereids, those naked sea nymphs who always accompanied the sea god, and looked after storm-wracked sailor-men, he looked magnificent. The effect was simply stunning, and for several moments all Alicia and Agnes could do was stare in silent amazement. The pool, filled with perfumed water constantly on the move, steamed gently all the time, the misty vapour flowing out across the floor in cloudy waves, and was reached by a broad flight of wide steps that disappeared right down into it on which you could sit or stand as the fancy took you.

Overhead, suspended on chains from the rocky ceiling, hung four great clusters of burnished silver oil lamps that could be raised and lowered with pulleys and which bathed the whole area in warm, golden light. While at the foot of the stairs, and just to their right, was another low marble topped table with a tall silver gilt jug and three beautiful glass goblets brimming with the dark red wine of the district.

Close by were a number of long padded couches as well, with small marble tables beside them on which were vials of rich oils, pots of scented creams, powder in beautiful enamelled jars with huge puffs to go with them and the finest steel scrapers that Alicia had ever seen. Almost as fine as those that Father Matthew had used to cut into Gui's shoulder that dreadful night after the fire. And she shuddered. But here the air was soft and balmy, and smelled of lavender and camomile, not blood, sweat and fear, and as she ran lightly down the stairs, Alicia felt she had never seen such a gloriously inviting sight.

While Soraya turned to close the door behind them, secure in the knowledge that their massive Arab guardians were comfortably seated with cold fruited water beside them in big horn beakers, Agnes also tripped down the stairs. Pausing only to kick off her travel worn shoes and pick up one of the tall drinking vessels, she went and joined Alicia in dipping her feet delicately into the pool's steamy depths...only to find that the water was marvellously warm, the very scent and essence of summer rising from its fragrant surface. And it was constantly circulating; as fast as it flowed in from one thick outlet pipe, it disappeared through another, the two pipes balancing each other so that the pool never actually flooded and was always clear.

Turning back from the top of the steps that led down into the water, Alicia called to Soraya to help her from her dress and was surprised to see the girl was herself already naked, her firm pointed breasts and smooth loins glowing softly in the lamp light.

"Sweet heavens," Alicia gasped, eyes wide with sudden amazement. "You really *are* shaven! I know about your arms of course, and your lovely smooth legs, I always have done...but your loins? I had really thought perhaps you were joking! And I have never seen you completely naked before. Oh, Soraya...truly you are very beautiful! Look at you? You are gorgeous. May I-er-may I?"

"Touch me, sweetheart? Of course you may touch me, but fair's fair, my Lady Al-ic-ia de Burley," she said annunciating each syllable with relish, "off with your clothes first!...And you Agnes," she laughed, watching the girl trying to hide herself behind the large towel she had picked off one of the tables on the marble landing.

"I told you. All the women who work as personal servants of the Lord Roger and Lady Rochine are shaven. The Lady herself is so cleansed, as you know. It is cleaner in the hot climate in which we live, Alicia. Fresher, and much more comfortable, I assure you. It is one of the many things that separate us from the town and country folk that live beyond these walls."

Alicia giggled as she thought what a screech Judith and Annie would set up if she should ever suggest such a thing at home in Malwood! A screech that Agnes was trying hard not to give, cowering behind her towel like a frightened rabbit faced with a hunting weasel. But even as the thought raced through Alicia's head she laughed, the ringing dancing-water laugh that Gui knew so well. "Oh, how glorious that will be, Soraya. I *love* being clean! So, honeyone, me first. Then I can hold Agnes down while you skin her alive!" she shouted, making a dart for the terrified girl as she spoke, who had shrieked and dashed away to hide in a different corner.

"Right, my love. You first," Soraya said laughing. "The Baron expects it and I have been given the most explicit instructions by his daughter as well to use all my skills to ensure your comfort and well-being at all times. Alicia, it will feel strange at first," she said running her hands over her own smooth mons veneris and her labia, but it is a most lovely feeling to be so soft and smooth down there. Very lubricious," she added, running her fingers lightly between her cleft of Venus, while giving Alicia a most wicked smile as she did so.

"Now?"

"Yes. Now! This is the custom Alicia, for I must bathe your body for you first while you then bathe mine, and then we two will bathe Agnes. That way we all keep fresh and well. I know it may seem strange to you, but it is one of Lord Roger's most definite commands, and in very truth, as I have said before, there is less sickness and ill health here at the Château than anywhere I know. Come on. It will be fun I promise you! And once we have this dress off you, my love, then we'll both grab Agnes and throw her in."

"Clothes and all?"

"Clothes and all, then we can strip and scrub her all over! I have been dying to do so for ages, because, my dearest Al-ic-ia…she stinks worse than you do!"

"You ready?"

"Yes!" And with practised ease Soraya unlaced Alicia's dress and eased it gently off her shoulders so that it fell in a soft pile to the ground, then not bothering to lift her dirt stained shift, she simply took it in both hands and tore it off Alicia's back, throwing it in a soiled heap against the wall. Alicia, still sipping her wine, stepped out of her discarded robe and turned to face her, her breasts swaying gently as she moved, her white skin a sharp contrast to the golden tan of her companion.

"Where is she?" she whispered with a wicked grin.

"Behind you, trying to be a fluffy white 'rock', where no rock belongs."

"Right. You go left, I'll go right and we'll have her soaked and naked in no time!"

And with that they turned and dashed to where Agnes was cowering, who screamed and fled like a hare, dropping her towel as she ran...but she was no match for Soraya and Alicia who swiftly caught her, one on each arm and with a great shout flung all three of themselves into the water. With no clothes of their own to worry them, and with shrieks of laughter, and a lot of screams, they soon had poor Agnes stripped naked in the warm waters of the Roman pool.

And once they were all there together, all frolicking happily like water-babies, and had become used to brushing their bodies against each other as they played...and then washed each other with the scented soaps and unguents that Soraya had brought with them, even Agnes lost her shyness, as pleased to have her breasts admired, soaped and her whole body lovingly fondled as either of the other two. For, in truth she was a comely girl, and if her body showed greater strength in thigh and calf than Alicia or Soraya's, her waist was trim and her buttocks firm, and her breasts were swelled beautifully to balance her hips, and richly crowned. Her arms, muscled from carrying tubs and buckets for her mistress at Castle Malwood, were well toned and just as white as Alicia's, and her wrists and ankles were prettily formed.

Still it was Alicia whom Soraya groomed first: laying her down on one of the long couches near the marble stairs, expertly shaving her under arms, which were quickly done; then her legs, until they were as smooth as silk...and finally her loins.

First trimming her fur as Agnes had done in England before the banquet, using exquisite hand shears delicate enough to cut silk, with gold and silver chasing on the handles and the blades, Soraya than washed the fur away into a large marble bowl with the softest cotton cloths Alicia had ever felt. Next, with a cheerful grin, and a swift kiss, she poured beautifully scented oil all over Alicia's loins and lower belly, wickedly rubbing it in with her fingers and cupped hands, especially deep between her thighs until her Venus' mount, and every hidden petal below it glistened, as did the soft cleft in her buttocks and her dusky rose, the massage leaving Alicia softly panting as it was designed to do.

Then, taking up the finest of metal blades in a beautifully constructed holder, Soraya firmly brushed her skin with its edge, gently razoring away every last bit of her softened fur till the skin over her mons of Venus and the pouting lips that sheltered beneath its plump curve were as silken smooth as her own, and as she ran a practised hand over Alicia's quivering body, so she felt

Alicia touch her also, as she had said she could, running her fingers ends over every one of Soraya's shaven curves and upwards, between her open petals, into her slickly wet loins making her gasp, and Alicia's eyes twinkle in response.

"Mmmmm, my love," she murmured with a grin. "As you said, verrry luuubricious!"

With a giggle, Soraya smacked her hand away and then washed every part she had shaved with warm scented water and the loveliest creamy soap which she removed with a great sponge, collected from the Greek islands and used especially for that purpose. And having patted her loins dry with a soft towelled cloth she first poured the most wonderful thick aromatic oil all over her body, which she gently massaged into her freshly bathed and scoured skin until she glowed with vitality and felt unbelievably relaxed and at ease with herself. Finally Soraya picked up her largest puff and with it she whisked the softest, scented powder over every part of Alicia that she had cleansed, like any mother would pamper her adored child after its bath.

And bending over her she gave Alicia a kiss on her mouth, lightly flicking her lips with her tongue, her breasts just touching Alicia's as she did so.

"You, my girl, are a naughty tease," she said with a smile, standing up, her big puff in her hand. "And are your breasts fuller than I remember on the *Star*, my love?" she asked, her head on one side as she studied her. "And your nipples darker?" she asked, brushing them upright with her giant powder puff. "Or is it my imagination?"

"It's what you have been doing to me, you wretch!" Alicia said with a smile into Soraya's emerald green eyes. "Much more of that and you might really have me spinning. It is all so…so sensuous. So soothing and lovely," she went on, holding her breasts and lifting them in her hands. "You have made me feel wonderful, Soraya…*Oh God! How I wish that Gui were here now...he would just love all this!...*So it's not surprising that they feel so full and tender. Now…let's seize that ridiculous girl and fix her too. Then we can go back up and get ready for this dinner that *Monsieur le Baron,*" she said mimicking Soraya with a laugh, "is preparing for us. Can't wait; I am starving! And I know that Najid has something special in mind for us tonight too. So, where is *la petite*, now?"

"Behind the table over your shoulder...shall we?"

"Yes! Left, right?"

"Mmmmm…" Alicia nodded, with a big grin. "*NOW!*"

Chapter 13...The Lord Baron and The Lady make the Crystal work.

Upstairs, in Lord Roger's great apartments, on the wide bed between its beautifully carved mahogany bedposts, Rochine lay as spread-eagled across its rumpled silk sheets and coverings as any of the three girls below her in her mother's bed chamber.

Only she was naked.

Her body sheened in sweat and with a criss-cross pattern of fine scarlet lines across her breasts and buttocks, she was as sated as he was. Both of them driven to an excess of passion and pleasure they had not shared together since their woodland rutting the afternoon of the banquet at Castle Malwood.

Again and again he had taken her, thrusting into her so deeply she was sure he had touched the very edges of her heart...and she had ridden him as he so loved to be: with her feet on either side of him, almost up on her toes as a jockey rides a stallion, weight slightly forward so her breasts were near his mouth, and the great stiff pole springing from his loins impaled her to the very hilt as she rode him to oblivion.

Meeting every powerful thrust of his hips with a fierce downward drive of her own, she built a fantastic, galloping rhythm that always broke him. With vigour and sharp cries of joy she rode him until he clamped his big hands on her hips and forced her loins down on him again and again as she bucked fiercely onto him with every stroke, thrust meeting thrust until her mind and body were beyond control. And all the while he roared and shouted-out like the very bull he was; until he powered them both into the stars, and with a scream her body finally collapsed on top of him, both glistening with sweat, both panting for breath, both with chests heaving and thighs quivering as if they had just raced an eight furlong classic.

Looking down at his daughter, Lord Roger smiled and kissed her fingers and the palms of her hands, murmuring sweetnesses and honeywords as he did so; caressing her breasts and gently milking her thickened teats through his fingers, making her moan and toss her head...*She is, truly, so very lovely...and so exciting! So wanton..so lustful, so exotic..so unlike her mother...*Loving to stand, upon her very tiptoes ,with her hands tied to the golden ring on its simple pulley that he had fixed high up in one corner of his room, her arms stretched high, her body taut as a bowstring, while he flicked her with her own silken lash. Each twisted thread leaving a fine scarlet line across her body, until her breasts, her belly and her haunches were all marked, her nipples swollen beyond their normal size and her juices running out of her…and she had climaxed at least once as he had done so, her whole body jerking and leaping as she cried out in ecstasy…*Constancia would never have done that! Never have let me take her, and take her and take her until she passed out…but Rochine will! And then come back for more.*

But with Rochine it was truly about power. With his Constancia, it had always been about love. She loved to be held and fondled and cuddled…without the sex. Rochine wanted to be possessed and taken…without the courtship. *The need for power through sex is what drives her…drives me too!…*And he grunted…and then sighed…*Yet what I really want is the feel of a loving pair of arms, soft lips and a melting heart. That's what made Constancia so special, for she was lust and love blended into one, with a warm and caring heart that Rochine, no matter how hard she tries, just does not have!…*But which he was certain would come from Alicia, his newly captured English White Rose…but never his own daughter with whom he so loved to be joined as he just had been, and whose lusts were as fierce and rampant as were his own.

He was certain about it…the Lady Alicia de Burley… *'de Brocas' as she soon will be*…and he smiled at the thought…*But not Rochine. Sadly that would have to stop. But not yet!* And he sighed, and stroked his daughter's forehead before bending over her to caress her eyelids and her mouth with soft kisses that made her stir…*She was going to be a real problem. So lovely, so exciting…and so hard to resist!…*And leaving her still prostrate, he padded naked through to another room, to his Crystal Room, beyond his enormous greeting chamber with its tables, chairs and armed settees, through to his most private inner chamber where, in its carved and polished rosewood box, on its shaped cedar wood stand, covered with black velvet weighted with emeralds and pearls, lay the very heart of all his power.

For this was his great Crystal, his Seer-Stone, his Palantir, gifted to him by the Emir of Samarkand who had himself received it from the hands of *Sheik Raschid-ed-din Sinan* himself, the 'Old-Man-of-the-Mountains', the most feared leader of The Assassins and the one man throughout the Holy Land who was more feared by both crusaders and infidels than anyone else. And sitting down before it in his armed chair, whose padded back rose to his naked shoulders, he unlocked its beautifully carved cover and lifted it off to reveal, in all its purest beauty, a perfect ball of matchless crystal ten inches in diameter, with no flaw within it and no bubbles around its side.

White, glistening and clear as a mountain stream.

Lifting off the black velvet cover that hid its matchless face, he put his hands around it and looked into its unfathomable depths. Staring into it until his mind was like a falling leaf off a giant tree in autumn; like a small, rounded pebble tossed into an abyssal pool of silent water…and he breathed deeply, concentrating his mind, closing out all other sounds, channelling his deepest feelings until he was at one with the great Crystal Seer-Stone he held before him. And with all due reverence he bowed his head to the cool glass, gleaming in the sun's last rays, resting his forehead on its ice-cool, polished surface, and as his breathing slowed a deep silence seemed to gather in all the corners of the room, spreading towards him like smoky shadows.

And for a moment all was still.

Then, slowly, great clouds and swirling vapours appeared within the Crystal: deep purple, midnight blue and black shot through with jagged streaks of scarlet and gold lightning that made his whole body quiver. And as they spun and whirled so they changed from black to grey to a shining, blinding white…and suddenly the immense ball was filled with beams of coruscating light, every colour of the rainbow that flickered and shimmered in the dusk of his room as if it were filled with a myriad flying lights from a shattered star…until they too cleared completely, leaving an amazing map of the whole countryside beyond the castle's walls. Every field and hill and rushing stream was clearly to be seen as if you were flying above it like a bird, like a kite, swooping over slow, sunlit rivers and shadowed valleys; over towns and villages; meadows, forests, and distant moors.

And as his mind quested, seeking to complete the link between the twisted dragons on his arm with the great emerald ring on Gui's finger, so did the Crystal carry him on the wings of that hot summer's evening.

Northwards he flew in his mind's eye to Narbonne and beyond: to Carcassonne and far Toulouse, over great rivers and deep forests; mountains, hills and valleys, past tracks and roadways to a small *auberge* off the great Via Aquitania...*Le Pigeon Bleu*...the Blue Pigeon at Marmande. *Marmande? I know Marmande, just forty or so miles south of the great city of Bordeaux, the centre of English power in Aquitaine, and on the ancient Via Aquitania the Romans built to link Bordeaux with Narbonne.*

And he was amazed!

Sitting back in his chair, still holding the Crystal between his hands, he was stunned yet again by the power the Crystal gave his mind, and through that the power to direct men's lives. For now those English bastards were upon that ancient road, the Via Aquitania, that would carry them all the way to Gruissan…there was no other way a body of men and carts could travel so quickly nor so easily.

The Blue Pigeon. He smiled then. *I have those fucking bastards now! And with that knowledge I have the means to crush them too. And how apt... 'The Blue Pigeon'*...like one of his own trained birds outside, crooning everywhere, circling, swooping and swirling out of their tower loft. Despised by so many as no more than food for peasants...yet those humble birds were how he had always managed to keep one step ahead of the rest, and he smiled again. *Who would have thought that such delicate feathered creatures should yet be the very harbingers of Death himself?...So, that's where they are? Marmande!*

And he grinned.

A small village some forty miles from Bordeaux. By the saints, but the 'boy' had done well to get there in a day...*The 'Boy'*...he growled, remembering their fight at Castle Malwood the night of the fire...*The Devil seize him, he should be long dead*!...And the next moment, the Crystal had swept him within the shabby building itself. It was if he was right there amongst them: Gui de Malwood; Richard L'Eveque, his Guard Commander, lounging back in his lazy, drawling manner.

And the bloody Black priest!

That Spanish Benedictine wanderer, Father Matthew...the one man amongst very few who could close him down should he so desire. He knew that now, after the disaster at Malwood. It was he, through the Lady Alicia, who had wrenched Gui from his control the night of the banquet. And it was he, again, who had rescued Alicia from his grip in her chamber after he had set the castle alight. He knew that now...*just as it must be his presence that is stopping me from listening to their conversation*...for though he tried he could not, this time, hear them speak. He snarled his frustration and then shrugged his shoulders...*I do not need to. It is enough I know where they are, today. Even as I am sitting in my great Château in Gruissan planning their destruction!*...And he chuckled deeply to himself as he watched the young English knight play with the great emerald ring he had returned to him the night of the fire.

The so famous 'Malwood Emerald' that his aunt had worn until she died. The ring he had arranged to disappear with the little nuns all those years ago...*The ring that indelibly links its wearer to me through the golden armlet I always wear. It will yet be his doom, and that idiot thought I was being generous!*...And he threw back his head then and laughed, for his arm bracelet was the pair to the one that Rochine had given to Alicia, and that enabled him to know exactly where each wearer was at all times he chose to seek them out!... *Dear God, but I am good!* "*Allah Akhbar!*" he said softly. lightly kissing the cool surface of the great Crystal he still held between his hands: "*Allah Akhbar!*"...'God is Great'!

And as he spoke he felt Rochine join him, standing naked beside him too as she so liked to do at these times, her heavy perfume mingling with the sweat of her excitement, drenching them both with the scent of her lust. Her body still quivering, her skin warm and silky to the touch, her loins soft and smooth and wet…he felt the pressure of her hand on his shoulder, the softness of her left breast against his cheek, which he turned and suckled immediately, as she held it for him, her teat thick in his mouth, her lips on his forehead, his left arm already going around her haunches.

"Mmmmm," she moaned softly. "I love you suckling me after making love so furiously. It always makes me want you even more," she sighed, pulling away from him, her nipple puckering as the cool evening air flowed around the heated flesh of her areola, chilling it swiftly, and moving behind him she cradled his head against her breasts, her arms going around his shoulders and down over his naked chest, her cheek resting on the top of his head.

"Have you found them?" she murmured softly, kissing him.

"Yes, sweetheart," he said, moving the Crystal so she too could see into its amazing coloured depths. "See for yourself. They are stopped some forty miles south of Bordeaux at an *auberge* called the '*Blue Pigeon*'.

"Do you know it, *chéri*?

"No…but I know where it is, at Marmande. If they keep going like this they will be at Narbonne by the middle of next week, maybe even sooner. Far too close for comfort. We must take them out before that."

"How many are they?"

"Still only a handful I reckon…I have not scryed them for that. Their numbers are not my concern for they cannot have received any re-inforcements. There is no-one in all France to help them until they reach King Richard at Marseilles and by then it will all be too late." And he turned then for her to kiss his cheek, his big hands running up the back of her thighs as she did so.

Then he grunted.

"*God's Blood*, Rochine!" He swore fiercely. "This will be the third time we have tried to get him killed and his command sufficiently destroyed to make their efforts worthless and drive the remainder home!"

"You worry too much, my Lord," she soothed him with her deep, husky voice. "You and the Crystal have never failed…not with me to help you," she purred at him, rubbing her breasts against the back of his head. "Come now, my Lord and Master," she breathed into his neck, kissing his nape all across as she did so, a frisson of desire running through him as she did so. "How will you do this?"

"Mmmm. Send a pigeon to Jules de Saint Sauveur in Carcassonne. They should be at Castelserrasin in three days, two if he pushes hard and Toulouse one night after that."

"What about Neel Chambertin at Toulouse? He has a powerful following there, and the Count is an ally. They and Saint Sauveur would make mince-meat of them!"

"*Non, ma mie!* I cannot drag the Count into this. Philip would be appalled, and anyway look what happened when I divided our forces the last time? So...no pigeon to Neel, my love," he said kissing her deeply for a moment. "This has to be done by 'our' men and 'our' men only. And this time we *must* succeed. I will lose face badly if that bastard gets away from me a third time! And if I know anything about that young Englishman he will be pushing his command forward briskly. He will not want to miss a single hour's travel time if he can possibly help it. He is driven by love and honour, and they are sharp spurs in anyone's side."

"So...his men will be tired and their horses drained," Rochine murmured softly, rubbing her breasts against her lover's neck. "And getting closer to their quarry may make them careless. You plan so well, my Lord," she added kissing his neck again. "You see everything."

"Of course, ma mie," he snarled, grasping her buttocks more hotly. "It is why I do not lose! Jules will have to muster his men from all those who follow me in that area and take Malwood and that 'mob' of soldiery he calls a command the other side of Castelnaudary. The Fresquel runs right past the town, and it's deep and fast flowing, so he can't cross it...but he will have to water-up his horses. And he won't do that this side of the town. I know that stretch of river well; it is treacherous above the town, even in summer. If Jules gets it right, he should trap de Malwood between their spears and the river. He can't run..."

"...So he must fight," The Lady interrupted him, languorously rubbing his chest with her long fingers, feeling his big hands running over her thighs and buttocks as she caressed him, her breasts stiffening as he did so. "And our men will overwhelm him. He cannot have many left now. Not after the *Morning Star* so raked him, and the battle at Saint Jean d'Angély. Did you ever find out what happened there, my Lord?"

"No!" he growled softly. "Not really...though I did get a pigeon from our agent in La Rochelle that it had been a bloody slaughter on both sides. Those two idiot Vernaille brothers were taken trying to flee, and later executed for treason by that English bastard at Bordeaux, Sir Hugh Willoughby, and their whole command scattered!" And he grumbled deep in his throat, digging his hands into her buttocks as he did so, making the breath swoosh through her teeth as the sudden pain shot through her, making her loins weep.

"What happened to de Courcy I do not know! He was a real fighter...*and* his man, Victor Jonelle! They alone should have prevailed. There was some rubbish about 'arrow storms' at the end of the report! Don't see how? The English only had a few bowmen, and de Courcy's men were all experienced lancers. It is as if the ground just swallowed them up."

She hissed again then as he casually plundered her wet loins with his hands and she closed her eyes, the air seething through her lips, opening them to breath in sharply a moment later as he entered her with stiffened fingers.

"Look at them all, jostled together in that inn, my Lord, drinking and swapping tales," she gasped, her body twisting as she spoke, feeling his thick fingers moving inside her. And while her whole being was suddenly swept by excitement, her green eyes stared at the bright images in the Crystal, watching Gui sit back, laughing at something the dark clad priest had said, the great emerald ring of his family glittering in the light coming from the large oil lamp in the middle of the table.

"If I was a lip reader, my beauty," he said to Rochine, turning his face up for her to kiss him. "We would know what they were saying. Just think how horrified they would be if they knew we could see them as they truly are, right now! Worse...that it is *his* family's ring that links him to us, my *so* succulent mistress!" He went on, sliding his fingers more firmly amongst her wet petals as he spoke, stroking the very soft insides of her loins, making her whole body quiver and twist again. "As Alicia's arm ring links her to you!" he added huskily, swift lustful passion coursing through him...and he kissed her deeply, reaching for the black velvet square as he did so.

"Come ma mie, I have seen enough! We have better things to do now, I think? Yes?" And covering the great glass ball with the gem-fringed square of black he had just gathered up, cutting out the light so that it slowly died away completely, he swung round and picked her up in his arms and crushed her to him, nuzzling her neck and her scented hair as he did so.

"Mmmm. You smell so delicious, my beauty. And see," he said looking down at his manhood now filled with hot blood and boldly standing up for her to hold. "You have made me hungry for you again. The sun has yet to sink completely and we have time to spare for further jousting. I see you have my favour in your hand already, ma mie, and your body weeps for me to pierce you," he grinned wickedly, and he tilted her in his arms to put her down onto her knees on the thick carpeted floor, her head on her arms, her rounded haunches raised invitingly before him in a posture she knew would enflame him further.

“It would be such a shame to waste it, my lovely Tournament Lady,” he grunted, as he spread her buttocks firmly with his hands; and feeling her hand stroking him and guiding him as she opened her loins for him, now wet with lust, he thrust into her with one great surge of power that shook her breasts and left her gasping out for more.

Chapter 14...How Alicia met Bertrand du Guesclin and received a great shock!

Later that night, in the Lesser Hall, they all sat round a long table at the head of the room, placed on a raised dais of polished oak beneath the flags of their houses...Capet, Toulouse, de Brocas, and de Burley... Alicia's scarlet stag with golden antlers on its ermine background, that had greeted her when first she had arrived at the Château that very afternoon, was now up there proudly with all the rest.

They were the only diners that night, as Lord Roger had presaged, with the exception of Sir Raymond Marceau, Gaston de Vere, and one, Bertrand du Guesclin, the youthful son of a local baron staying at the Château for his education, as so many young squires did, and whom Soraya seemed to know quite well...and whom the Lord Baron kept looking at with his black, hooded eyes as if he was intent on listening to everything the boy said.

So it was a rather sedate meal to say the least.

Najid served Alicia and her ladies with rice and diced chicken cooked in a light creamy sauce with wild garlic and local herbs, some of his precious eastern spices and a handful of almonds and sultanas, having already fed Aquib and Aziz earlier so they were able to stand guard behind them, their shadows enormous across the white plastered walls of the hall they were seated in.

The talk was small and light, and somewhat forced at times as Rochine looked flushed and disinterested, and Lord Roger preoccupied and far away from all of them, so it was left to Soraya and Alicia to keep chatting, if only to relieve the almost unbearable tension that seemed to rack the young squire, Bertrand du Guesclin. He was as nervous as a kitten and ate silently and fast, as if he were just desperate to get the meal over and himself away to his own narrow pallet in one of the less exalted corners of the great Donjon, his eyes constantly flicking to the Baron and away again.

But, little by little they drew him out, even more so when he realised the Baron was no longer watching him like a hawk as he had been earlier, but busily talking with Raymond Marceau on one side and De Vere on his other, Rochine similarly occupied. So, with the flattering attentions of two of the loveliest women he had ever seen, he soon began to blossom, to slow down his eating, and lose the dreadful haunted look he had been wearing since they had met at the start of the evening. Such that by the time they all came to rise for the grace from the castle chaplain, a small, wizened scrap of humanity whom the Baron barely tolerated, Bernard felt sufficiently brave enough to ask if he could show them around the castle next morning, or maybe make an excursion to the seaside itself…if the Baron would allow?

"Dear Bertrand," Alicia cooed over him gently, her huge. deep violet blue eyes mesmerising him like a fawn being set down by its mother. "We should so love you to show us around. Soraya knows all the girly places to visit," she said with dipped eyes. "But you know the things that only a man could know. And we have no man to look after us," she fluttered at him wistfully, dropping a soft kiss on his cheek as she spoke. "We would be so proud to rely on you to care for us," she oozed over him shamelessly, until he was visibly expanding, if not actually floating on thin air. "Do you think he would dare to, Soraya?" she asked, her eyes huge pools of blue water that any man would die to drown in. "Do you think he will be the brave young knight we so need to help us find our feet in this great castle…Mistress Agnes and I being so far from home?"

"Oh, my Lady Alicia," Soraya replied meltingly, her eyebrows almost beyond her hairline. "I am sure no true knight would ever turn down two damsels in such distress…would he? He would be cast out by the Queen of Courtly Love itself!" she exclaimed, turning to kiss the boy on his lips, his whole mouth an open 'O' of breathless simplicity, pressing her breasts against his chest as she did so.

Agnes, sitting close-by, just goggled at the pair of them, her face such a mass of stifled giggles, that she had to whisk herself away to join Sir Raymond a few yards away. He, like Sir James Bolderwood at home, always had a kindness for a pretty face and gentle manners, of which Agnes had both in abundance. So she missed the way that the stunned look that their wicked attentions had wrought on the boy slowly changed to one of great determination and pride…and a ready willingness to jump off the castle's tallest tower if they should ask him to. Or slay dragons with his bare hands; or fight anyone who dared threaten the two queens of his heart, *to the death*, even if only armed with a toasting fork and a pudding spoon!

As Soraya said later as they were just at the door of their room: "I swear that boy was as close to passing out as any young man could be who had been so shamelessly courted by two such Jezebels as you and me. Did you see his face when you kissed him, Alicia? Poor child could barely breathe!"

"And what about you? You hussy!" Agnes squeaked, her face creased with laughter. "When you pressed your breasts against him and kissed his lips I was sure he would just keel over. I was amazed he could even walk in a straight line! Talk about melting butter? He was just a puddle of grease by the time you two had finished with him. I had to get up and leave for fear I would burst!"

"Cowardly custard!" Alicia teased her. "We have turned one frightened rabbit into a guardian fit for a queen. There is nothing he would not do for us now, of that I am certain. He is far more afraid of letting *us* down, than he would be of dodging the Baron's orders, no matter what they might be! Trust me...he will be our Champion, I am sure of it. Now, please open this door someone, I am exhausted!"

"Allow me, my Lady," Aquib rumbled at her from behind, his massive hand reaching forward to lift the iron latch that held it closed. "Aziz and I will be close by all night. No-one will disturb you, I assure you."

"Oh, Aquib! Forgive me?" she said, touching his arm gently, as the others skipped into their room. "In all the fuss of getting here, I have not assured myself of your comfort, forgive me. What must you think of me? Are you and Aziz, and little Najid, well placed? Comfortable?"

"We are *fine,* my Lady Alicia. All is well with us I promise you; all in accordance with the orders my Prince left for the Baron. He has not let the Prince down, despite my concerns to Aziz earlier. So...sleep well. You have much to prepare for in every way!" And he smiled down at her, his face as enigmatic as ever, his eyes just as twinkly as she had first seen them on board the *Morning Star*...and just as puzzling!

*

Inside their room, however, there was a surprise waiting for them, for standing in the middle of it, her few clothes and belongings clutched to her thin breast in a small blue canvas bag, was a young girl, her hazel eyes flecked with gold huge in her white face, itself streaked with tears, too frightened to do more than breathe...and that not very easily either!

"*Sweet Jesus*, Soraya! I had quite forgotten," Alicia exclaimed, as soon as she saw the child. "This must be Isabelle Soulier, William and Ralph's little sister, whom I promised the Baron I would take charge of. She was the price they had to pay to stay free! Poor child, she looks petrified. You or me?" she asked then, quirking her head as she often did when she had a problem to solve.

"Me, I think, my love," Soraya said softly. "She won't know you from Eve. But me? I have seen this little one before. She comes sometimes to play in the Château with one of the castle children...Naomi I think?" And so saying she knelt down and held out her arms to the shaking child, the loveliest smile on her face as she did so: *"Oh, ma chère petite. Tu es Isabelle Soulier, oui? Viens ici, chérie"* she exclaimed. " *Nous ne te mangerons pas! Nous ne sommes pas des ourses!*" 'We will not eat you! We are not bears!' She laughed. "*Non! Je suis une tigresse!*" and with her hands held out like bunches of claws and a fierce roar she leapt at her!

Isabelle took one look at Soraya leaping towards her like a wild beast, and with a fierce scream fit to lift the hair clean off the scalp, she dropped the bag she was holding and rushed towards her, hands also like claws and feet going like pistons as Soraya caught, lifted the child up in her arms and with a great shout flung herself onto the bed, both of them growling and snarling like furies, while Alicia looked on in horror not sure which part of whom to grab first, and Agnes screamed blue murder.

Moments later, into the middle of this appalling cat fight, strode Aquib who plunged his huge hand in amongst them both and plucking out Isabelle, like a cork from a bottle, he held her up by her bunched clothes while she kicked, struggled, screamed and *pffizzzssted* with impotent rage like a wild cat. Agnes stopped screaming, and with much more plain forethought, used to such rages from Annie and Judith at home in the forest, simply reached for a bucket of water put down nearby for their bedtime washing and flung it all over the child; while Alicia rushed to Soraya's rescue, convinced she must have been scratched and bitten all over…if not ripped in pieces!

But to Alicia's open mouthed amazement, Soraya rolled over and sat up laughing her head off, rocking with glee, her clothes in shreds…but her face and arms as flawless as ever…shouting "*Tigres!*" *Tigres!*" while Isabelle hung from Aquib's enormous grip like a drowned rat, her clothes also pretty well torn apart, shocked into temporary silence, while the water ran down the huge Arab's face and body in warm streams.

"*You wretch!*" Alicia shouted out at last, once she had got her breath back. "You absolute beast!" she added pummelling Soraya mercilessly. "You were funning! The pair of you! That was no ghastly fight…that was a game! Look at you both? And poor Aquib? He's soaked too, poor man. And as for Isabelle…it would serve her right if she spent the night in the Baron's dungeons! Well done Agnes…just what they both badly needed!

"Reminded me of Annie and Judith at home!"

"Very true, sweetheart!" she replied with a laugh. "That really was some cat-fight! But this isn't the Lower Courtyard at home. This is The Baron's belovèd wife's rooms…so we'd better get them cleaned up, before we are all in dreadful trouble with everyone. Shame we can't give this one a proper soaking as well!" she added, giving Soraya a fierce look. "By God and the Pheasant! 'Tigers' indeed! What did you think you were doing?"

"Making a very frightened little girl feel at home, Alicia!" She replied sharply. "And not in the camp of the enemy who killed her father! Had you forgotten that?"

"Oh, Soraya!" She exclaimed, stricken, putting her hand to her mouth. "I had forgotten. This just does not seem to be my day today? I seem to be forgetting everything, as if my brain has turned to mush! Oh, come on, I'm not really cross, Just shocked! '*Tigers*' indeed! Look, you go and sort out that child, whom you know so well. And Agnes, the 'boys' and I will sort out this mess," she went on as Aziz and Najid also came in to see what was going on. "Then, perhaps we can all get to bed? Please? I am exhausted!"

"Are you alright, my love?" Agnes asked quietly. "You are not usually so easily wearied."

"No! I am fine, truly. Alicia replied, laughing. "Just tired I expect. So come on, help me get this lot put right and we can all get some rest."

*

The next morning, Alicia was sick!

Chapter 15...The girls become determined to escape the Château Grise.

Enceinte!" Soraya almost shouted. "*Pregnant!* Alicia, you...*you can't be?* I mean...it is *weeks* since you were last with Sir Gui! It must be something you've eaten?"

She laughed: "No, sweetheart! I thought that too at first. But I am late already. And I am never late! My moon times always run like clockwork...and, it fits in with everything else that is happening with my body, and my mind too! Ask Agnes. Isn't that true, honeyone? I am never late?"

"It's true, Soraya. Ever since her first time, when she thought she was going to bleed to death...remember the shock, my love? Her moon times have always been correct. A day or two late now and then, but very rarely. We always keep a calendar running in her room at home, so that if there is something special coming up, or Sir Gui was expected home, she would know what to do, what to prepare for. In all this excitement, and running away and fighting, I had forgotten."

"And my breasts being fuller and more tender?" Alicia said, holding them in her hands, "As you noticed yesterday, and my nipples are darker too. And I have started to forget things, which I never do, and now this, this beastly sickness thing this morning? *Urrrch!* It all adds up, children. I am pregnant!"

And she sat down on their bed and burst into tears.

Little Izzy, long forgiven for her 'fight' with Soraya the night before, was appalled at Alicia's distress and ran for a sponge to wash her face and a soft towel with which to dry it, while Soraya and Agnes plumped themselves down either side of their weeping charge, feeling utterly helpless in the face of such a disaster.

"Oh...Agnes!" Alicia cried, turning to her oldest friend. "This should be one of the happiest days of my life. I have *longed* to carry Gui's child ever since he and I first made love together and he made a woman of me, even more so as the time has passed. But now? After all that's happened, and Gui so far away? Not even knowing where he is? Or even if he is alive? And trapped here, with that *bastard* threatening...no, *promising*, to have my betrothal dissolved and then marry me by force. This...this baby," she said, putting her hands across her lower belly, is just the last thing I need! The very last thing, and yet I want it *so much!* Oh, Soraya...Agnes? What am I to do now?"

"When?" Soraya asked gently, sitting down beside her and pulling Alicia's head onto her shoulder. "I mean, how far are you along?"

"I don't know. After the fire, I think. That night I broke his fever. We loved so fiercely…so deeply. I felt then there was a certain 'flash' inside me. But just put it down to elation in knowing he was saved. And I cannot be more than a week late in my moon time, maybe two? So, about, six weeks?"

"Six weeks, honeyone," Agnes said, putting her hand on Alicia's lower belly. "That is not so bad, sweetheart. You will not start to show yet, though your belly is slightly more rounded perhaps," she went on running her hand across her. "But no-one who did not know you really well would have any idea."

"No!" Soraya said, covering Agnes's hand with her own. "No-one will notice for a while yet, but one thing is for sure, Alicia, we have to get you out of here as soon as possible. Our lives are in difficulties enough right now anyway. But if Rochine should discover this, then she will kill you for certain. And *Monsieur le Baron*? Once he discovers you are carrying another man's child…he will kill it! In your womb if he can, I have known it done. Or at birth, with a long nail into the brain of the emerging baby, so it does not even take its first breath…"

"*No!*" Alicia gasped, clasping her belly. "*No!* He would not, *could not* do so monstrous a thing! The Church…"

"*Yes!*" Soraya said, shaking her. "*YES!* I told you. I have seen it done. Rochine did it to one of her father's most favoured lovers: forced an abortion with a needle into the baby in its sac, when it was about three, maybe four months grown. The poor woman survived…just. But her child was slain. And at birth, with a..a long nail…I have known it done also. Have heard the Baron so order it. And the 'Church'? The 'Church' is in his pocket, Alicia! Remember? What happened with my father?" Soraya snarled her reply, sharply crooking her little fingers together. "Archbishop Berenguer will do whatever the Baron asks him to…and close his eyes to anything else that is required of him. How do you imagine he has got away with so much wickedness for so long? My father's lands are just the *tip* of what he has done these many years!

"Oh my God!" Alicia moaned, curving her body over her womb. "*Christos, aid me!* We must get out. *We must!* But how? And where to? And where is Gui? Where is my knight in shining armour now, with all his men? Escape we might manage, somehow. God alone knows how at this moment. But without immediate protection, and support, we would be re-captured in no time. In the blink of an eye. We must try and find out what has happened to our men? First plan an escape route that will work. Then..then try and find out where Gui is. For I tell you…*I promise you!*" She exclaimed vehemently: "He *is* alive! I know it. *Have always known it!* I just don't know where!"

There was a silence then, as they all sat and wondered what on earth they could do.

"I could speak with my brother," Isabelle said in a soft voice, full of the music of the Languedoc. "To Guillaume. He might help. He knows people who could shelter you. Here in Gruissan, and beyond, maybe. He has a friend called Armand Chulot who owns the 'Golden Cockerel', in Les Monges, a small village six or seven miles from here. It is a good *auberge*, well thought of, the very best I have heard it said. They are good friends, my brother and Armand, close. Do many things together. Armand might help. Guillaume says he has no love for the Baron...and I would trust my big brother in all things."

"And there's Bertrand du Guesclin, here in the castle whom we met last night." Soraya said. "He has no love for *Monsieur le Baron* either. Something to do with his father? He may help perhaps? And I know some of the secret ways about this place too. I have not been idle during my time here, I can assure you."

"*Right!*" Alicia said then in her usual forthright manner, sitting up while Isabelle refreshed her face. "Wash and dress first, then some breakfast, there must be food somewhere in this castle? And then we will talk with Bertrand, as we said we would last night. At least I remember something, anyway!" she exclaimed with a chuckle. "Then we will see. 'Let the dog see the rabbit,' Gui always says in situations like this. Then we can know which way to take up the chase.

"He always says that to make a plan 'puts you in control'. Gives you a purpose, stops you thrashing about feeling helpless. So, my children, we must all 'kick-on', and sharply too: dress, eat and make a plan! Find Aquib, Soraya, or Aziz; whichever one is out there," she added briskly with a smile. "And get them to give the castle varlets a swift kick on their fundaments, and let's get moving. Moping like a donkey in a nettle patch will get us nowhere!"

Chapter 16...The Company of the White Rose rides out, and more deep secrets are revealed.

And so they did...and over the next week they bustled about with some purpose, always sticking together, always asking the right permission, always with smiles on their faces as if there was nothing going on in their minds but the pursuit of simple pleasures.

Meanwhile, despite her deep aversion to the whole project, Alicia allowed the Baron to believe her change of heart towards him to be both real and permanent; as everywhere they went together her hand was on his arm and her face was filled with smiles just for him...while Rochine watched them with growing fury.

And though Alicia continued to refuse him any physical favours, beyond that of kissing him on his cheek, and he hers, she allowed him to wrap his arms around her and believe that it was only a matter of time before she would allow him to savour her body to the full as he so clearly wished to. And by those means she kept him from immediately forcing her into his bed...as otherwise he might well have done, as it was quite clear from all he said to her, and the small gifts with which he showered her almost daily, that he truly was deeply smitten.

So while she dissembled and played the flirty coquette, the Baron's preparations for their marriage began to gather speed around her, with visits from dressmakers, seamstresses and jewellers...for measurements and the choosing of fabrics and magnificent stones of every kind that Lord Roger thought might please her...all of which gave her great concern, and made her agonise over her situation...*God knows how long I can keep him safely at arm's length...for he is persistent to say the very least. We must find a way out of this place, and soon! We must! Before it becomes impossible to do so!*

But every day she and her small Household spent together, with Bertrand and Isabelle now added to her entourage, so they learned more about their surroundings, and were able to discuss and to explore every avenue of escape they could devise. And everywhere they went, Aquib and Aziz went with them as their escort, with little Najid riding ahead as he had done so many times before when they had fled from Foix.

From the Baron Alicia sought no further escort than those she'd had with her the day she had met him on the road to Limoux...and he was happy to allow her that freedom; content that de Vere should keep his weather-eye firmly upon her excursions, to prevent her from journeying any further than he thought it safe for her to do so. He had no intention of allowing her sufficient freedom to escape his hold completely.

Yet every day of such freedom as they had brought no obvious solution to their problem. There just was no way out that they could see!

And wherever they went, a shadow always went with them…though they were not supposed to know it. And everyone with whom they spoke were themselves spoken to later by one of de Vere's men. Check and counter check, subtle cat and mouse 'stuff' that made Alicia smile and grit her teeth.

Nevertheless, despite all that the Baron could do, there were many messages that were passed from hand to hand at that time that de Vere's watchers did not intercept, nor Rochine's people either, led by the Cousins whom de Vere had assigned to The Lady's escort, and who were equally vigilant in trying to discover what Alicia and her little Household were up to.

Into the town they went, to the fountain and through the twisting streets to the sea shore, to where the fishing boats were drawn up out of the water, the men and their wives clustered amongst them where the nets were hung up to dry or lay across their knees being mended; with dogs and children running noisily amongst them. Smallish men, burned dark brown by sun and sea, with dark curly hair and dark brown eyes, weathered faces and smiles bright with laughter and careless chatter…yet always alert to danger, uncertain whether to talk with these strangers, and their hawk-eyed Arab escort…or not. Yet with barely spoken word, by glance and nod and quirky smile, they let them know that help could be offered if ever it were really needed.

From the town they also rode up into the wild highlands above it, into the Pech Redon, the huge forested wilderness that stretched for miles, both along the coastline and far inland as well, as far as Les Monges where the 'Golden Cockerel' lay. Ostensibly they went to picnic and to enjoy the woods and glades…but in reality it was the well-known *auberge* and its mighty *aubergiste* that they so wanted to get to.

But every time they tried, even amongst the most desolate of places, they were turned away by the Baron's troopers…clearly stationed for that very purpose…who made it quite clear they were not to be allowed to go there. And after the second such attempt had been foiled they did not try again, as much unwilling to draw attention to themselves, and what they were really doing…as they were to make Armand Chulot's position more perilous in the Baron's eyes than clearly it already was.

And if they were not out on excursions around the town and its messuages, then they were in and about the Château, exploring its passages and its battlements, even into the great gatehouse, with its portcullises, winding chambers and massive drawbridge. They visited the pigeon tower and met again the Baron's Pigeon Master, *Raheel al Moukhtara*, admired the beauty of his birds, the care he took with them, the pride he had in his fastest flyers, and were reminded how the messages were sent out and shown which birds flew to which lofts. Each special set of birds was held in separate large, caged areas of the tower, given the best feed, and the best care before being released back to their own home lofts.

It was time well spent in every way, as they were able to go almost everywhere, even as the Baron had said they could: into store houses and bakeries, the stables and the forge, across the enormous paved bailey that encircled the Donjon, even across the drawbridge and to the town itself. And every time they went out Alicia's eyes were drawn to the small doorway below the huge left-hand tower of the Gatehouse as you faced the castle, the right-hand one as you faced the town, that opened onto a small rock ledge some twelve feet above the bottom of the castle ditch. And though they did not try to get down to it, having been advised by Bertrand they would not be able to…not even he being allowed right down there…Isabelle could tell them all they needed to know. She and her friend Naomi had sneaked down there one dull afternoon, when Naomi's father had been on duty to surprise him; she was full of it.

"It is right at the base of a tiny winding stair," she explained the fourth day, as they were all seated not far from where the fishing boats were laid up, enjoying a simple picnic that Najid had put together for them, with fresh baked bread from the castle's ovens. "At the bottom of which there is quite a wide guard chamber…lit with two big oil lamps, and there are always two men on guard. Everything is natural rock down there, no paving stones, and right against the outer wall there is a door.

"Big door, sweetheart?" Soraya asked her. "And what is it made of?"

"No, Just tall enough for one medium sized man to get through, like Bertrand," she indicated, pointing to where Bertrand was skimming stones into the étang. "A tall man would have to stoop, I think. And the door is like the huge ones across the main castle entrance, very thick criss-crossed oak covered with iron, and held closed with two big oak drawbars that slot into the stonework on either side of it through an iron bracket.

"Is that all, honeyone?" Alicia asked her calmly, not wanting to shake her resolve.

"No…my Lady," Isabelle answered, looking right into Alicia's eyes as she spoke. "Right in front of that is another door. I have never seen its like before, as it is made wholly of thick bars of bent and twisted iron, all interwoven, and is set into the very rock on which the castle is built. It looks very heavy, and hangs to one side of the sally port itself. It closes across the whole doorway like a great latticed gate and locks deep into the rock with heavy drawbars of iron!"

Alicia sighed. "I know what that is, my love," she said warmly. "It's what is called a 'yett' at home. A very northern form of defence. Gui came across several along the northern borders and told me of them. It's really a Scottish form of defence. The Baron's father must have had a Scotsman amongst his builders when he had that put in place. But how do you get from the door to the castle ditch, Isabelle?

"By rope!"

"*By rope, young Izzy?*" Soraya asked her, amazed.

"Yes, Mistress Soraya," the young girl replied earnestly. "*Truly!* By rope. There is a great coil of it, right by the 'yett' thing Lady Alicia just mentioned. Thick as my wrist with big knots along it…"

"So…that's how it is done!" Alicia exclaimed, tersely. "I couldn't work out how you could get from the outer ledge to the floor of the castle ditch. A knotted rope. How simple, but how effective. But how do you get up the revetments the other side?"

"There are hidden sets of stepping stones up the other side of the ditch," Soraya said. "I just found out from Bernard today."

"That's right, my Lady," the young squire explained. "You cannot see them from above. But their undersides are painted white. So, once you are in the ditch you can see them. Mind you, you still need to know where they are!"

"Dear God…how do we get to the tower?" Alicia groaned, dropping her head into her hands. "And how do we get to that chamber? We have explored every possible avenue of escape and got nowhere…It is impossible!" And they all lapsed into a long gloomy silence into which Bertrand dropped his next words like sizzling firebombs.

"Actually…I think I may just know a way," he said quietly, looking round at them all with raised eyebrows. "But it is very risky, and truly horrid. I am not at all sure that ladies such as you are would like it. Or…"

"…Would even be willing to try it?" Alicia interrupted him with a snort. "Bertrand, we may seem like queens to you, elegant, demure, learned, beautiful…all of which we are, of course," she said with a grin at Soraya and Agnes. "And thoroughly 'lady-like' as well…so jolly precious as never to attempt such things!...But that is just not so, my Noble Knight," she said, turning back to Bertrand with a smile and a little mock bow, I can think of two famous queens who risked their lives for a noble cause. So, young Bertrand, do not hesitate to put your Queens in danger if by so doing you can help them escape their enemies!"

"Very well, my ladies," he said, blushing; and taking a deep breath he told them what he knew: "So be it! Then listen, because I can think of no other possible way of getting out without being caught. But…" He added, looking around at them with steady eyes…"It is surely not for the faint hearted!...At the right hand corner of the bailey, nearest the gatehouse, there is an old disused well …"

"…*Yes!*" Interrupted Soraya, excitedly. "I have often seen it, covered with an old iron grille."

"Well, when I first came here, I too was consumed by the desire to escape…as you are now, I suppose," he said. "Because I am just as much a prisoner of this…this *monster!* As you are." And to their dismay his voice suddenly trembled and his eyes filled with tears.

"Oh, Bertrand," Alicia cried out, opening her arms to the boy. "Come, my true and worthy knight, and tell your Queen what it is that this vile man…this 'Man-of-Blood', as my belovèd calls him, has done to you." And they all waited to hear his tale while he collected himself, and Alicia gave him her handkerchief to dab his eyes.

Then, looking up into Alicia's huge violet-blue eyes, he said quietly: "Like Soraya's Mama, mine was very beautiful too. She was called 'Elizabeth'. My father adored her…as did I of course," he added swiftly. "Everyone did. She was kind and loving and sweet-hearted and generous. The very best of mothers, and a true wife to my father in every way. But at some function they had to attend together, this Baron's lustful glance fell on her, and her guard being absent at that time for some reason with my father, he pressed his suit upon her. But she was loving and loyal to my father, whom she cared for deeply…as much as he cared for her. I know that their marriage was arranged, as many are…but theirs was a marriage sealed with true love none the less, and she would not bend to the Baron's wicked lusting, though he pressed her hard.

"So he waited until my father was away attending his estates elsewhere, and he came to our home one drowsy afternoon…no great lordly castle like this, but a moated manor house, with cherry orchards and olive groves, chickens in the yard and sheep amongst the trees. A homely place it was, my Lady; of plastered walls and great beams, red pantiles and embroidered cloths along the walls, bright with colours that my mother and her ladies had sewed together; bee skeps on wooden stands in her garden…always full of flowers and blossoms in their season. And happy people in the fields and the demesne. My father is a good husbandman to all those who work for him, my Lady…not like this Baron, this Lord Roger de Brocas, whose people live in fear and trembling all the time! This Lord Baron…this monster!...came while my noble father, my mother's protector and lover was away from his home, and I in the fields with my hawks on a cadge and my father's falconer…and he accosted my mother in her garden amongst her flowers and herbs, where she so loved to be, and sought to prevail with her. But she would not! So…so…"

And then he could go no further for he broke into bitter tears, and sobbed in Alicia's arms, his body shaken by his grief as she rocked him like a baby, finishing his sentence for him in a whisper: "So he forced her…and having raped her..he killed her! Slashed her throat open to the bone, blaming some other poor wretch for his wickedness and taking you as surety for your father's commitment to his web of lies and evil!"

"Yes, my Lady," the boy wept into her neck where she had cradled his head, rocking him in her arms. "How did you know?"

"I did not, dear Bertrand…but sadly it is an old story that has been done before by wicked men, and fits this Baron…this Man-of-Blood like a glove. So…he slew her!"

"Yes! I found her, my beautiful mother, her throat cut and drenched in blood, with my father far from home, and the Baron standing over her full of how he had just found her there with someone, unknown and never found, running away from her. I had to endure his evil lies and his wickedness in silence for my father's sake…whose life was surely threatened if I did not return with him that very day…and I have been trapped here ever since."

"No wonder *Monsieur le Baron* watches you like the hawk!" Soraya exclaimed with vigour. "Always he has the eye on you…and his ear to the ground also. Nor 'til this week has he treated you with any kindness. Oh, Bertrand. I am so sorry not to have realised sooner. But the Lady Rochine…

"Watches you as well," the young boy finished for her. "I have long wanted to talk with you…but I never had the chance. And was too shy to do so anyway. You are so very beautiful…and I just another scruffy youngster round the castle. I never thought you would listen."

"Oh, my Bertrand!" Alicia broke in then, giving him a brisk cuddle. "Truly this man deserves to die. But first we must escape his evil, and then do all we can to bring about his utter, swift destruction. Now," she said, putting the youngster on his feet before her. "There is nothing wrong with tears! No true woman will feel any the less for you, or of you, as a man, because you dare to show a softer side to your nature than you might wish others to know. Just don't drown in them! Now, come on, my perfect knight…we need your help. So, tell us all about this ancient well."

"Well!" And they all laughed, making Bertrand blush and bow his head in momentary confusion at his simple pun. "Anyway, I found a way down it. It has not been used for many years I think, and is bone dry. I understand that when Lord Thibault re-built the castle gatehouse they blocked off the watercourse that used to feed it. There are rusted iron steps down which you can climb, and at the bottom is a kind of very narrow bricked passage way along which the water must once have run. It is pitch dark down there...and scary. The passage presses down all around you...and there are rats!

"But I was determined so I took my knife and some fat candle-ends and went exploring. It is very tight in there, and you have to wriggle like an eel to get through, and crawl on your elbows, and right at the end the passage drops down to a different level, very wet and damp, and there is a solid brick wall that blocks off the end completely. You can hear water rushing by behind it and the wall is wet, which is a bit strange at first, but is quite safe.

"I think it must have been a part of the old Roman palace because I have found several old coins down there with Roman heads on them, and once a lovely gold and enamel brooch. Anyway...I was rooting around down there one afternoon when I dislodged a great chunk of brickwork out of the right hand side of the old water passage, and scrabbling my way forward I found myself in an ancient hypocaust system. Full of burned rubbish and blackened from long usage...and the air was thick and still dank with ancient soot.

"Nevertheless, I found my way through that at length, wriggling round the pillars on my hands and knees and marking my way as I went. First with chalk signs and scribbles, and finally with big clear arrows, until at length I came to another ancient fall of bricks above which are the actual foundations of the gatehouse itself."

"The foundations are on top of the hypocaust?" Alicia asked, amazed.

"Well part of them are, my Lady, right on top of the old palace. They seem to have cleared away as much as they needed and just got building. By design, maybe, rather than laziness, for a whole corner section of the main foundations have been firmly placed on top of the concrete floor and great flags of stone that lie locked together on top of the short brick pillars of the old hypocaust. They themselves are in turn firmly bedded into a Roman concrete raft which, despite the years that have passed by, has never lost its strength."

Alicia's face paled, and the others shuddered at the very thought of squirming their way beneath that massive weight of masonry like blind moles, not to mention the rats which she loathed the very thought of...so there was quite a pause before she asked Bertrand to go on.

"I thought that was the end of the matter, but by scrabbling around underneath them, as miners would at a siege, I found a small stone chamber..."

"Beneath the foundations?" Alicia asked, her voice awed by what she was hearing.

"No, my lady...a part of them."

"But why?"

"I've no idea. Perhaps the builders were lazy? Perhaps it was even planned that way? By design as I said, for there is a small flight of steps there that lead up to an ancient trap door..."

"*Right at the base of the tower?*" Alicia asked again, unbelieving.

"Yes, my Lady. Who knows what was in Lord Thibault's mind? Some kind of escape route in time of desperate need? Or maybe it was something to do with the build at the time? The thing is it's there, and though it took me several visits and much oil and grease on the rusted hinges, nevertheless..."

"*Go on! Go on!*" They all urged him, lost in his story.

"...in the end I managed to heave it open, and found myself in a lower storage room in the right hand tower of the gatehouse, as you look at it from inside the castle!"

"*No!*" Soraya and Alicia exclaimed together, completely astonished.

"Yes! And clearly not one in use any more as everything stored there was rotted with age and neglect."

"How do you know it was in that particular tower?

"Because the door was not locked, merely latched. So I was able to walk out of it as if I had every right in the world to be there. Which, in very truth, given my squiral rank...I did! And ...best of all, I was at the very bottom of a narrow spiral that leads up to the galleries that will take you down again to the sally port!"

"And have you been there since?" Soraya asked him anxiously.

"Yes. The next day. Doing the journey in reverse. Putting a goodly wedge at the bottom of the door from within the chamber, then leaving a small oil lamp in a corner, I lowered the trap behind me and went backwards through the whole system, leaving good candle-ends at every dangerous part of the route as I passed. And one night I also oiled and greased the small trap in the middle of the well cover, so that it would not squeak if ever I needed to use it for real!"

"*Bertrand!*" Alicia exclaimed with her lovely smile, giving the boy a massive hug. "Your Queen salutes you. My brave and perfect knight, for however dire, you have shown us the way to freedom," and she kissed him as he deserved to be kissed, as a woman would kiss a man she admired, as did both Soraya and Agnes, so it was one very unsteady youngster who tottered off a few minutes later to find himself a drink.

*

"So, this looks like it!" Alicia said a few moments later, as she watched Bernard getting a drink from Najid. "But Holy Mary, Mother of God, it sounds terrifying!"

"So much for brave queens then? Agnes said with a smile. "And rats! *I hate rats!*"

"Me too, honeyone! Remember the one that Gui killed in Lady Margaret's stables? As big as a small cat, complete with a long scaly tail Ughhh!"

"Who were the famous queens you mentioned?" Soraya asked her then, as they gathered their things together. "Those who risked all for a 'noble cause.'"

"Oh...Queen Eleanor of Aquitaine...our Lord King's dearest mother, when she was married to King Louis of France and went with him on the Second Crusade. She endured ghastly conditions, during which tens of thousands died. And the other was Queen Matilda, King Richard's frightening grand-mama, when she escaped from Oxford castle at the dead of night of a bitter winter during the Anarchy of Stephen. A terrible civil war that wracked our country sixty years ago! She was lowered down the walls in a basket, covered with a white cloak, and escaped across the frozen River Thames...the ice creaking at every step...terrifying! She was indomitable, and very scary! Anyway...enough of queens dead and alive, we had better get back to the Château before de Vere starts having kittens and sends Le Brun down to find us.

"Now that is one man I really don't like! Built like a barn door and with about as much feeling! I think he is almost worse than the Cousins...and they are truly vile! God knows what would happen if they ever had cause to lay their hands on us!"

Chapter 17...Alicia keeps her counsel and plays a dark game.

Rochine, watching all these comings and goings, gritted her teeth and fretted for her father's marriage arrangements to Alicia to be completed...*Sweet Wine of Christ, just let it be soon! Dodoni waits on my word, the money is all on board and the little witch is here...three nights after the wedding and Papa will leave for Jaffa, and this time he goes alone. That has already been arranged, for the Morning Star is due to take him and those three bastards with him! And when he returns...she will be gone forever. How can my father not see how wrong this bitch is for him?*

Knowing her father, she had allowed a week for all her precious cousin's frills and furbelows to be sized and sewn up, and for her to be forced into an acceptance of the inevitability of her situation, however much she might rail against it. Yet every night saw Alicia chatting to her father as if they were on the best of terms, even exchanging sweet kisses...*Dear God, how that makes me sick to my stomach!...*And using her searchlight smile to light up the lives of all those around her; even old Sir Raymond had been moved to complement her father on his choice of bride...*Why could the old buzzard not have kept his elegant mouth shut? His words have only served to make Papa even more determined to push through with this awful wedding business than before. Oh, God, how I hate her!...*

But with Wazzim having raised the money for the two flawless pieces of merchandise she had promised him, and two chests of gold burning a hole in Valerian's keel for want of securing them, she was becoming desperate to complete the deal and get the three girls out of the country as fast as possible, before she had Wazzim breathing down her neck.

That would not be a pleasing experience! The man was as rank as a bucket of pig shit on a hot day...*and as dangerous as a striking cobra!* But she relied on him for rare pieces captured by his slavers whom she could sell to the Emir's seraglios where he could not...*He trades the common herd that simply disappears into the Souks...the bottom end of the trade...where that mimsy-pimsy Agnes will end up*...and she grinned to herself. She only worked the cream, and was only using him for Alicia and Soraya because she dared not use a trade route of her own. That would be asking for trouble with her father!

So she chewed her finger ends ever more furiously and bided her time, while encouraging her father in every way she could to complete his arrangements and get the English *bitch*, that *conne anglaise* fixed to him hip and thigh…and the land contracts signed sealed and delivered as soon as possible.

*

The Lord Baron, Sir Roger De Brocas, too, was intrigued by his strange English love!

She gave every sense of being willing to be wooed, as she had said on that first day: by compassion, by kindness, by understanding, and he had complied as best he could. And his charm of manner and address was formidable. But though she would talk and laugh and smile with him…she would not let him touch her. The lightest of kisses only, when what he wanted was to plunder her, suck out her soul, make her blood boil with lust as only he knew how. He knew how best to treat a maid who seemed unwilling, yet was burning with desire beneath a cool exterior. But because she would not let him assail her defences too closely, he could not melt with hot kisses the ice that was still running through her veins.

He had expected reticence. Smouldering anger…even hatred!

But what he had seen was…friendly indifference. Oh, she was aware of him. He only had to enter a room where she was and soon her eyes would find him, and she would walk the battlements with him, her hand on his arm, or wander with him down to the sea shore beyond the castle harbour that he had shown to her, with its own defended entrance, towers, ramps and hidden docks. But always she was holding back from him that part of her heart and mind that he most wanted.

Occasionally the mask would slip, and she would greet him with the blinding smile that had softened even old Raymond Marceau's crusty heart. And in that very instant…that very moment of release...he knew she was the one woman in the world he really wanted. She had in her smile, in her eyes and in her very posture, the same power to melt him that Constancia had had, and which he had never thought to find again…and his whole spirit groaned, doubling him over as his heart felt the deepest pain.

With her in his life maybe, *just maybe* he could eschew the Crystal and all the power it gave him. Turn his back on all that the great Seer Stone allowed him to do, and just rely on his own skills and instincts to be successful! Put an end to his relationship with Rochine, which even he could see was poisoning her, and him too…and live a normal life.

So he allowed Alicia greater licence to wander, to talk, and to seek people out than he had ever allowed a woman under his 'protection' since Constancia's death. And in doing so he came to the staggering realisation that he was…*de facto et in semper veritas*…in love with this beautiful English girl whom he had gone to such extraordinary lengths to bring home to the Château Grise as his future bride.

And he growled deep in his throat, because, of course, she was not, truly, under his personal 'protection'.

She was under the protection of her own Household!

Those Arabs whom El Nazir…*God blast him!*...had placed to guard her, and feed her. Two giant men and one bloody cook! Nevertheless she was also his prisoner, stolen by him from beside the man she truly loved and brought here against her will...*But what was that in God's great plan for Life? What was one silly girl among so many? What do her wishes count for in what I have planned for us?*...He had her and in five days' time he had now decided, this very Saturday, willy-nilly, he would wed her here, in the chapel of his own Château, beneath the flags of Toulouse and the King of France…and it would be done!...*And no cock-crowing youngster with a rabble of soldiers and a liking for the dramatic is going to stop me...Nothing! Archbishop Berenguer has agreed the dissolution of the girl's betrothal...though she does not know that yet*...And he grinned to himself, delighted with his cunning. The contracts had been drawn up, and the bride clothes would be delivered any day now. The pigeons had been flown off to Carcassonne where by now Saint Sauveur would be readying his ambush, setting the stage for Gui de Malwood's final destruction at Castelnaudary.

With young Isabelle Soulier attached to Alicia's household in the castle, her brothers were quelled and soon he would send Xavier Le Brun to The Golden Cockerel to bring Armand Chulot's wife, Claudine, into the Château as well, as a surety against her large husband's behaviour…as he had been so thick with the Soulier brothers, Guillaume in particular.

As he had already done with Bertrand du Guesclin…*Stupid bloody woman! If she had just consented as I had asked, let alone demanded, there'd have been no trouble!*...Still…he had the father bottled up on account of his son, and he grinned again. 'Keep your enemies closer than your friends', was good Chinese advice, brought to him by his Arab friends who traded with the East…a certain General Sun Tzu apparently...and he was intent on following it…*But why won't the girl let me closer? Why won't she lie with me? Constancia did before we were married...why not Alicia?*...And he growled with frustration, banging his hands on the long table in his Great Chamber…*Let it be soon,* his heart and body urged desperately… *Let it be soon!*...while knowing that all was actually moving as swiftly as it could do. For him it just was not fast enough!

*

Aquib and Aziz were also concerned for the safety of their Lady. They could see what was happening all around the town of Gruissan and the Baron's wide estates, and deplored it. The constant maltreatment of the people, the wickedness of Rochine's behaviour and the duplicitous actions of the Baron himself, Sheik El Nazir's friend, in forcing marriage on Alicia when her heart and soul were set on Sir Gui, bothered them both greatly. Even though Gui was the man who had destroyed two of their galley consorts in the sea battle off Belle Île, one of them commanded by the Sheik Siraj, one of their Prince's many sons, they still honoured him for it. He had fought a fair fight under extreme conditions and, *Insha'Allah*, he had won. The Baron was devious and worse, he was also a deviant. All he did with his daughter was against the Koran...against all Christendom as well. And in their spirits they groaned for Alicia and her friends who, against all expectations, they had taken to their hearts.

And now their Lady was pregnant!

Both men could see the need for Alicia to escape the castle as quickly as possible, but could not see how to help her without compromising their position within the Château...and El Nazir's position as the Baron's great friend.

"What can we do to help our Lady and her people in this escape, my brother?" Aziz asked his giant friend later that same afternoon; after they had escorted Alicia safely back from the seashore picnic. "So far we have offered no counsel. Just guarded...both our mouths and their bodies. Surely there is something more that we can do?"

"It is a wise man who knows when to speak out and when to hold his counsel to himself, Aziz. I know our Prince to be an honourable man, as we have always supposed. See how he has put us here to safeguard our Lady until he himself can come to rescue us from our labours. I think he knows far more of what goes on here than we may imagine, and he will not expect us to desert our posts. *By the Beard of the Prophet*, Aziz, I think the crisis is very near. The Baron has sent a message to people in Carcassonne to prepare an ambush for Sir Gui so he cannot rescue our Alicia."

"How do you know this, Aquib?"

"Almahdi told me yesterday. That young man has survived against all the odds and is hot on our trail. He must have *Allah* and all his angels on his side, and is clearly pushing his command as hard as he can…men and horses both. But where exactly this attack on him will happen I do not know…but it must be soon, I am sure. The Baron will not want him to get too close to us here at Gruissan. All Almahdi knew was that a message about an ambush was sent to Carcassonne, not what all the message said for that was in Latin, which he cannot read. Nor any of us here either."

"And today?"

"Today he has sent out orders to Le Brun to seize Mistress Claudine, from *Le Coq d'Or* at Les Monges, the one place we did not manage to get to. She is the wife of the *aubergiste*, Armand Chulot…and the Baron takes her to make sure her husband does not make trouble at the time of the wedding which will now be in just three days!"

"*By Allah!* He has brought it all forward by a day. Saturday! Does our Lady know this, Aquib?"

"Not yet. And I do not wish to tell her until we know how best we can help her…and she has found out where Sir Gui is."

"But how can she do that? Only the Baron knows!"

"There is a way, my Aziz! But it is perilous in the extreme and would bring fearful troubles upon her, not least of which could be her death and that of the child she carries…and great dishonour as well. Were she to do this at home it would mean her death by stoning for certain. No Imam would demand less. But I can see no other way for her to find out what she needs. There may be some help there that we can provide…Najid has a plan…but until I am certain of it, my lips are sealed, and so, my brother, must yours be also!"

"But I know nothing of which to speak, Aquib!" Aziz almost wailed. "You talk in riddles that I cannot read. All I can do is follow. You always have been my master!"

"And long may it be so. Now, *hush!*" the big man ordered urgently. "Those two scorpions they call 'The Cousins' are close by. I can hear the foul mouthed one, that Lucas Fabrizan. Now there is one man whom I would love to slay!"

*

Later that evening, after their meal in the Lesser Hall had long finished, Alicia and her small household, including young Isabelle, were seated in their lamp-lit room with just the palest primrose orange of the afterglow still lighting the far western horizon, the midnight blue of the night sky now coming alive with stars.

It was Wednesday, the top of the week, and they had just four days before the Baron's decision to marry Alicia that coming Sunday, no matter what, would be forced upon her! All week she had smiled and bobbed her head at his suggestions. Walked and talked with him, her hand lightly on his arm, in gentle acceptance of a fate she could not fight any longer; determined to give every indication of capitulation…but on her terms not his. So, without fighting tooth and claw, she had mostly approved the contracts he had drawn up, only enforcing certain alterations concerning her own lands, and their administration…while leaving the question of the Malwood lands open. Though she had been determined to sign nothing that had been shown to her.

It was a role she had played to perfection.

But one that made her feel both sick at heart and to her stomach. How she had managed to refrain from vomiting up the black bile she knew was swirling in her belly, she did not know. And had it not been for the loving support and encouragement she received every day from those around her she would have collapsed long ago!

All through that week she had dissembled in every way possible, even allowing the Baron to kiss her, while filling her heart and mind with images of Gui. Yet every time he did so, her body shivered with anticipation of more. He had a most powerful effect on her, probably on all women, including his daughter who had watched them all the time with bitter fury in her green eyes…and 'green' in every sense of the word. Looks that Alicia had mocked with a toss of her head and a brilliant smile, while the Baron had patted her hand and brought her flowers, ignoring the turmoil that was tearing her cousin apart. That he loved Rochine was not in doubt…but that he now loved Alicia more was becoming every day more apparent, and just added to the dangers that she faced every day that she remained in the Château Grise. *God and the Pheasant help me if Rochine ever lays hands on me again!*

And now she was pregnant!

Carrying the most precious life it was possible for her to carry. Gui's child…*her* child, that she must protect from the monster whose death she longed for, yet must make every semblance of being willing to join with!

It was obscene! The whole thing was glaringly obscene!...*The very thing I vowed on the barge I would not do I am now doing the very best to perform that I can: dissembling, flirting, leading-on, lying, 'playing the game', being the simpering damsel on his arm*...she said to herself in English...*A real coquette*!

And now here they all were planning an impossible escape from a Château crawling with guards, and spies and informers...all the panoply of wickedness that this man and his daughter had gathered around themselves for their own aggrandisement...and for what? To join Richard's own hunt for glory in the Holy Land?...*When all I want to do now is to go home and grow my baby in the loving peace and beauty of Castle Malwood in the King's New Forest...in my belovèd England...and with Gui safely by my side*...She sighed, and sitting on one of Constancia's lovely settees, beneath the window opposite the dying sunset, she drank the fresh orange sherbet that Najid had specially prepared for her and called her Household to order.

"So...we think we now have a plan?" she queried looking round at them all. "Yes? A mighty risky plan, maybe. But still a plan, that with Bertrand's help, and a huge slice of luck we just might pull off. Getting out of this building should not be a problem. We can exit the Donjon from the very bottom level, where the laundries are, join with the drudges as they leave for their bothies against the north-west wall of the bailey and tail them around until we are right beneath the north buttress, across from the old well-head. And from then on we follow Bertrand's route to the right-hand tower of the gatehouse."

"What then, Alicia?" Soraya asked quietly.

"Then, my girl, we put our lives in our hands even more and make our way down that final spiral to the sally port...and then out of the castle and away!"

"What about the guards?" Agnes asked, her voice shaky. "There are always two of them, remember?"

"We will have to kill them!" she exclaimed, firmly. "Lure them, distract them and then, somehow, kill them."

"*Oh, My God!*" Agnes whispered, putting her hands over her face. "I could not, Alicia. Just could not..."

"No-one is asking you to, honeyone. Nor expecting it of you, either. Bertrand, Soraya and I will deal with the guards. God knows we had enough practice in the forest!"

"Bertrand's coming too?" Soraya said, raising her eyebrows questioningly.

"Yes, and little Izzy here. We cannot possibly leave them behind. They would be put down like dogs the instant we were found missing. There can be no argument about it. How could I face her brothers, seeking their help, knowing I had betrayed their sister to that brute-beast up there and his rapacious daughter."

"Aren't we all rather forgetting something in all this, my love?" Soraya softly asked Alicia.

"Mmmm?" Alicia replied, enigmatically, her blue eyes looking everywhere except into Soraya's green ones.

"The plan we have been discussing is only a part of what we need, sweetheart. The most needful part is to know where Gui is *now?*" She emphasised. "Where he and his men have got to? If we break out and have no armed support close by it will all have been for nothing! That bastard, or his daughter, will have us by the neck in moments."

"But there is the safe house that Guillaume told you about," Isabelle said softly.

"I know, Izzy," Soraya replied curtly. "But Guillaume's people cannot hold us there for long. The town will be the first place that will be searched. We need to get clear away in the swiftest time possible. I know Monsieur le Baron. He will scour the countryside for us for certain. He will leave no stone unturned to get us back. Him and The Lady, both. If we cannot find real armed support in the shortest time possible…it will all up with us!"

And there was a long pause then, as all in the room thought over what Soraya had said, knowing she was right…and knowing there was only one solution. Yet no-one was willing, or even daring enough, to raise it.

"Well, my darlings," Alicia said very heavily, looking at all of them, the tears swimming at the back of her eyes, making them huge in the golden lamp light. "I have a plan for that too, and I am the only one who can do this. No-one else can gather the information we need…as to where Gui is with his men. We..we all know that," she stammered. "And I pray to God that my Gui; my wonderful, loving, caring, l..loyal man will forgive me…" And she buried her face in her hands and wept.

"No Alicia! You cannot do this," Soraya cried out in anguish, guessing what she was going to say. "You are too precious to hazard yourself, my darling, girl," she pleaded, running to her and throwing her arms around her knees as she sat there on the settee in such distress. "And what about the baby?" she asked, kissing her.

"But this *is* all about the baby, sweetheart. And..and about you and Agnes and all the others, Bertrand, Izzy…and my darling, darling Gui," she added on a whisper, raising her head to look at them all, the tears welling out and falling unheeded from her eyes, as she sobbed in Soraya's arms. "I have no choice in this matter. I never did have. We..we cannot escape without knowing where our men are, and only I can do that. There is only one way.

Sweet Jesus...I have to try and make the Crystal work for me, as..as it works for Rochine. I am the only other one 'of the blood' in this castle who can...or anywhere else, as far as I know. And we know that it will only work with one 'of the blood'. So..so that m..means me!"

And looking into Soraya's stricken green eyes, themselves filling with tears as shc clasped Alicia to her, she said in a husky whisper: "*God and the Holy Mother aid me, Soraya!* I will have to sleep with that..that '*Man-of-Blood' after all!* I shall have to give my body to that..that *monster!*...And then pray the Crystal works for me too, or all will be lost!"

Chapter 18...Najid comes up trumps.

All the next day was spent in quiet preparations for their flight from the Château Grise.

These, though they were in no way elaborate, were most thorough: soft leather travelling clothes with cotton chemises under sleeveless leather jerkins and blue woollen cloaks with hoods, the same as the castle drudges wore when they were about their work outside; with black cotton wimples for their hair that tied behind their heads, and soft leather boots with stout soles. And for each of them a small leather bag of silver money and a few bezants each from Alicia's money belt, rescued from her armoured jacket after arriving at the Château, and now safely round her again beneath her chemise. All the loose coins had been carefully wrapped in soft cotton to stop them chinking...and there was a dagger for each of them as well, except Isabelle, who was outraged at not being allowed to carry a weapon.

Nothing else was to be taken, save for Alicia alone who was to take with her the golden locket that Gui had given her on their betrothal night. But before they could attempt to flee, they must first make sure of their reception beyond the castle...*and* discover where Gui was. Both of which would require careful preparation of their own, to say the least.

The first of those was solved by Isabella, sitting on a great tump of grass high up on the Pech Redon enjoying another of Najid's picnics: stuffed chicken breasts with crunchy lettuce and scallions, fresh bread rolls and delicate peach and apricot tarts, washed down with ale, wine and raspberry sherbet...who reminded Alicia of what Guillaume had said in the square: "'If you need help, go to the house with the blue door opposite the fountain.' That's what my brother, Guillaume, told to you my Lady. After you had forced the Baron to set him free that afternoon in the square."

"Who lives behind that door, Izzy?" Alicia asked her then, whose mouth was filled with peaches and apricots. "You must know. You know everyone in Grise."

"Mmmm...Gruissan, my lady!" Isabelle said with a laugh, struggling with the apricots. "And of course I do. Mmmm....Everyone knows that that is the home of Dmitri Stanisopoulos the Greek, the finest perfumier and herbalist along this coast. People come to him from all over for his herbs and infusions and his vials and special creams and potions. Everyone knows old Stanisopoulos."

"So…a good source of information for Guillaume and your brother, Ralph?" Alicia asked her.

"Oh, he is Ralph's man, not Guillaume's, my Lady. Guillaume doesn't like Greeks. But Ralph swears by him, and certainly he has passed on vital information on more than one occasion that has saved many lives. He is no lover of the Baron, nor his daughter!"

"You must get a message then to your Ralph, Izzy. Can you do that? Without being caught?"

"Yes, my lady. And to Guillaume as well, he also must be told. I have my ways, and Naomi will always help me. I would trust her with my life," she added, seeing Alicia's quirked eyebrow at mention of another's name.

"Very well, my love. Trust her. She is yours."

"And what about Aquib, Aziz and Najid, Alicia?" Soraya gestured to where Najid was tidying his things away. "We cannot just leave them in the lurch with no word about what we are doing."

"No…you cannot, my Lady Alicia," Aquib rumbled at her from behind, surprising her once again by how swiftly and silently he could move. "We all know what you have planned…and..and what you need to do," he said hesitatingly, giving her a hard stare. "And we understand what you are going through…the turmoil in your heart and in your soul." And he took her fingers in his huge hands and kissed them, before putting them to his own forehead, to her immense surprise and pleasure. "We know whom to honour, and how to show it, my Lady. But we cannot come with you, though we would all dearly love to, for we have grown close to you, Najid, Aziz and I. And to Mistress Soraya and your own Mistress Agnes, too. Closer than I ever would have thought possible. But we are bound by our Prince's orders, who himself is bound to the Baron. But we are not so tied. Najid has been busy on your behalf…your own *usama* now…and has something rare and special to give you that will help."

"My pretty Lady," Najid said, in very broken Frankish coming forward and bowing his head. "Aquib, Aziz and I talk long…hard, how best to help you, and now I for you offer the very best I can." And he patted his chest and bowed again. "There are roots and herbs I brought with me off the *Morning Star* that will help you!" And opening his hand he held out the roots and flowers of two plants, both very dried and discoloured.

"Val-er-ian….Skull-cap, My Lady Al-ic-ia," he said firmly, shaking them at her one by one. "Make the Bar-on sleep big!" He mimed with his head on his hand and snoring loudly, so that everyone laughed. "One, very good!" he said then, holding up the valerian. "Two, very *very* good!" and added holding up the skull-cap, and he lay back with his arms out, his head completely flopped on one side and his mouth open. "I boil, with sugar" he said, miming boiling. "And make good drink. Very strong. *Very strong!*" he said again slowly. "This drink I, in smooth oil, together have placed… flavoured with *cassis* that all Frenchmen like." And he shook an imaginary flask between his nimble fingers. "You," he said, blushing, "must pour on body! Your body!" he said then pointing to her. "Yes?" and he mimed that as well, expertly, while Soraya covered her mouth with her hand, her eyes dancing with stifled laughter. And when Najid then mimed the Baron using his tongue to lick the elixir off Alicia's breasts, even Aquib had to turn away, his whole body shaken with silent mirth.

"See, pretty Lady Al-ic-ia. Bar-on lick oil. Mmm-n-mmm," Najid mumbled with pleasure, rocking his head from side to side, a big sloppy smile on his face. "Then Bar-on sleep long, long time, and you run away!" And he mimed Alicia running on tip-toe from the Baron's chamber.

"We cannot help you with the Baron, my Lady," Aquib said at length in his gravelly voice, his eyes twitching with mirth. "That is beyond even our powers. Nor can we come with you through the tunnels, Aziz and I, we are too large for that," and they all laughed again. "But we will escort you for the last time to the lower staircase, and from there Najid will help you. He can go where an eel can! And his khanjar is sharp enough to cut the wind."

"Najid…will you do that for us? Really?" Alicia asked with her biggest smile. "That would be a huge comfort…to all of us. And I thank you for the herbs, most gratefully. And the oil," and she curtsied to him deeply to his enormous pleasure. If you can give it to me when it is ready, I will take it with me for certain. It will save all our lives. *Insh'a Allah.* Truly you are *usama,* Najid!" And she growled like a lion, with her hands like claws, before putting her arms around the little cook-warrior, and planting a soft kiss on his forehead before he could skip, blushing, out of the way.

"Aquib…will not this get you all into great trouble with Sheik El Nazir?" Soraya asked the giant Arab quietly.

"I do not think so, Mistress Soraya," he rumbled, his eyes twinkling. "Though he may well not be best pleased with us. But his orders were that we were to render you *every* assistance," he said with studied emphasis. "And to protect you, until he came to rescue us. This he has not yet done…and if we allow you to put yourselves in danger and do not lift a hand to help you, then, we believe, for we have all talked this over amongst ourselves, that we would not be carrying out the orders that our Prince gave to us when he put you in our care."

"Oh, Aquib, my *afdal sadeaky,* you are a *good* man," Alicia said. "Your Prince chose you well. What would we have done without you, and Aziz and

Najid? Truly we have been blessed!" And taking his enormous hand in hers she kissed the huge palm of it, and every finger end, and then curled it closed again. "From *all* of us!" And she turned and walked away, leaving the big man blinking back his own tears at her simple gift of thanks and love.

Chapter 19...Soraya prepares Alicia for the Baron's chamber.

So Thursday passed, and Friday opened, when Lord Roger then let it be known by letter that he had brought forward the wedding day to the very next morning...Saturday, not Sunday as he had previously stated. This, of course, was wholly unexpected, and shook Alicia to the heart, but, for apparent sudden...'*Reasons of State, the Archbishop is now unable to perform the ceremony as it had originally been intended*'...and so her wedding day had been brought forward!

He hoped that...'*my dearest Lady Alicia de Burley will understand and be accommodating, not least because I so wish to be hand-clasped to you in all reality as soon as possible. And would you consent to dine with me tonight in my own apartments? As my Constancia did before we were married many years ago*'...He also told her that had a special gift for her to wear upon their wedding day, and he would be delighted if she would join him, alone, for dinner. Soraya was to prepare her for the evening. Everything she was to wear would be waiting for her by the Roman Pool. And Soraya was to bring her to the foot of his apartments, from where she was to make her way to his rooms above, on the very topmost floor of the Donjon.

'His dearest Lady Alicia de Burley' was overwhelmed by it! So that her very soul shivered, and she held it out wordlessly for Soraya to read, turning away to the windows as she did so.

"There is no 'Affair of State' looming for which the Archbishop must change his plans!" Soraya sneered bitingly when she read what the Baron had written in his message. "That is a bare-faced lie to bring you to his chamber ahead of time! He never was going to wait until his marriage night before bedding you! He didn't years ago when he married his Constancia," she added bitterly, reading the words out aloud. "And before you ask, my Lady," she said, vehemently, turning to where Alicia was now seated beneath a tall window, "Rochine told me herself; was proud of it! That her mother had given the good Lord Roger so lively an account of herself in his bed that he could barely stand the next morning, while she was still as fresh as a dew touched peach!"

"Then I must do the same!" Alicia snarled in return. "At least he is clear in what he wants! Me in his bed at last," and her whole spirit quailed at the thought. "Dear God, Soraya. I now have just this night, and this night alone, in order to try and find out where Gui is, God bless him. So we must be prepared to flee tonight…and not tomorrow as we had planned! Thank God for Najid and his herby oil. Do you have it safe, honeyone? For without that, my sacrifice will be in vain, and all will be lost. The Baron will not let me out of his sight after tonight for certain until his Devil's knot has been well and truly tied, and his ring is on my finger. I swear by St Michael and the Angel Gabriel himself that I will hurl myself from the battlements of the *Tour Barberousse* before I will actually marry that foul French bastard, that..that very breath of Beelzebub!" And she stamped her feet in rage at his wickedness and vile conniving.

"Well, my Lady," Agnes said in her quiet way. "That is not going to happen. If you were to do that then you would be condemning all the rest of us to certain death, for without you alive and kicking, there is no need for Soraya and me to be kept alive one moment longer. And what about Aquib and the others whom El Nazir has placed here to guard you?

"I know you of old, my dearling," she went on, taking Alicia into her arms. "You are hot with rage just now, but in a moment your head will be in charge of your heart again, and all will seem better, I promise you. Of course the oil that Najid has prepared will work, and you will be back with us in moments to lead us from this awful place. You to Sir Gui, and me to Alan-i-the-wood," she ended on a rush with a brilliant smile. "For in truth, sweetheart, my heart does beat more strongly for him every day!" And to much merriment she blushed.

"Well," Alicia said then, standing up and holding out her arms to Soraya. "Perhaps I was a bit dramatic! But that man is enough to drive anyone insane! And to change everything now is just…just *maddening!* And so like him to do it. Perhaps he knows something we don't? Archbishop Berenguer is far too much in Lord Roger's pocket to make him change everything for some 'Affair of State' about which not even you know anything…"

"Maybe King Richard is nearby?" Agnes queried.

"Maybe El Nazir's ship has been sighted closing Gruissan, and the Baron wishes him to be present at your bedding?" Soraya chipped in.

"And maybe the moon is made of blue cheese?" Alicia added, pulling herself away from all of them and moving back towards one of the tall windows that overlooked the bailey.

"And, just maybe, he has had news of Sir Gui?" Agnes said quietly, adding softly: "Maybe he knows that Sir Gui is alive and closer to Gruissan than anyone could believe possible?…"

"…And has brought his marriage to you forward for that very reason?" Soraya ended on a rush.

"Sweet Jesus!" Alicia exclaimed suddenly, turning sharply away from the window. "Do you think so? Could that really be the reason? That he and that hell-bitch have used the Crystal and discovered that Gui is not only alive and well but almost breathing down their necks!

"Dear God, were that so, I would sleep with the old bastard willingly. Before God and the Pheasant, my body were a small thing to give were that to be true, and that by so doing I could find out where Gui is and thus how to find him. Oh, Soraya, do your very best with me tonight," she said then, swiftly turning towards the lovely young woman, gripping her by her upper arms and shaking her firmly. "For this night I will woo the 'good' Lord Baron, the old bastard, as he has never been wooed before. I will offer him my body as if on a golden plate to do with as he pleases until he has sucked me dry of every drop of Najid's oil! And then, *Insha'Allah*," she added with a withering glance and a toss of her head in the direction of the Baron's private chambers, "when he is slumbering and sated with his ardour…I will find the way to my belovèd Gui and then, together, we will all flee this dreadful place and so be free again at last!"

*

And so Alicia spent the bulk of that final day in her apartments, much of it curled up on her bed, while her Household spun around her in changing moods of pure terror…and then bold confidence that they would carry all off as successfully as they had planned to do. While Rochine, from secret spy-holes, watched them apparently fall apart with glee…*I must make sure the Cousins are on duty by the sally port tonight. Oh how I wish I could hear what they are saying...and see their faces when they are caught!*...so her father prepared himself to receive his bride-to-be with some trepidation. Not at all sure, himself, quite what he was expecting? A raging virago who would push him to the limit of his patience…or a melting Lady, accepting his *force majeure* with smiles and even grace?

*

Mid-morning,…and Najid came and gave her a single glass vial, about as long as her middle finger, and about as wide, filled with a rich golden coloured oil, very finely scented with musk and flavoured with blackcurrant, with which she was to anoint her body in such places as the Baron was bound to explore with his mouth. He did this full of blushes and stammers, and downcast eyes.

But he had produced the necessary unguent, as he had promised he would…and Alicia was hugely gratefully to him for his courage and his friendship. And holding it in her hand she turned it from side to side, watching the thick oil slide around inside, and she smiled, knowing just how she would paint herself with it in Lord Roger's full sight especially to enflame him…and exactly where she would pour it! Where his mouth would be most voracious, her body the very wettest and his tongue the greediest. And once ingested and worked into his system by the energy he would express in making love to her…then, even as Najid had mimed so perfectly, it would surely engender great drowsiness and a deep, deep slumber…*Dear God, but this had better work!*…"How deep will he sleep, Najid?"

"I do not know, My Lady. But it laid out El Nazir's favourite bull from his herd for a whole day!" he said with a grin and an expressive shrug of his shoulders. "This man? Who knows? And do you care?"

"No, Najid. I do not care, so long as he is out long enough for us to escape this castle, and for me to find my own man again at last. Pray God…*Allah!*…that Gui will forgive me for what I am about to do. At least this child is his, she said, pressing her hand across her lower belly. "Of that much he can be completely certain."…*and right now that is the only thing I truly know!*

*

Evening came at last after what had seemed an endless day.

And when Soraya came to collect her, having spent much of the afternoon with her own preparations on the Baron's orders, Alicia was calm and composed, and they left together with their arms around each other, tawny and rich chestnut heads pressed close, whispering sweet words of comfort and exchanging soft kisses as they went, Aquib padding dutifully behind them, and before long they had reached the pool door. Here Alicia took leave of Aquib, relieved beyond measure that he and Aziz would still be on guard outside her room when she returned. And defying all protocol she pressed a kiss on the big man's cheek, before dashing the tears away from her eyes and slipping through the door into the pool room.

A moment later Soraya joined her.

"He was just as moved by your leaving him," she said, slipping out of her dress. "I have left that enormous mountain of a man quietly weeping into his sherbet. He feels he is deserting us by not coming too. But I have told him that he has done all he can for us, and that after he has finished his beaker, he is to go and wait for me beside the second staircase that leads up to the Baron's rooms, and I will meet with him there when I have safely delivered you into Lord Roger's keeping. Now, come on, sweetheart. At least I can care for *just* you for a change, and not everyone else as well!" And bending down to pick up a cake of scented soap from a nearby table, she followed Alicia towards the water.

Slipping off her dress, the Lady Alicia de Burley walked with delicate footsteps to where the wide marble steps led gently down into the pool, and with Soraya close behind she walked slowly down into the steaming waters. To be clean all over at the same time was the most luxurious feeling and she readily submitted to Soraya's expert ministrations. The girl's hands were so deft and gentle as they caressed and soaped her body, teasing her nipples with her finger ends and rubbing her own firm breasts against Alicia's until they were both in a state of some excitement.

"You are very lovely, Sweetheart," Soraya said as she washed the creamy suds off her with a huge sponge. "Your breasts are just perfect. Pregnancy will only enhance you more," and she lifted Alicia's breasts and kissed each one lovingly, with languorous gentleness. "These are beautiful enough to make any strong man weep…or girl either. My figure is ripe, I know," she said, twirling in the deliciously warm water. "But yours, my darling Alicia, is just gorgeous! No wonder Rochine is spitting blood and splinters over you."

"Oh, I don't know, honeyone," Alicia said then putting her arms around Soraya from behind and floating off with her. "You are sensuously beautiful as well. Your teats are longer than mine too," she said milking them from the base of her areola, pulling her breasts into sharp cones as she did so. "And just as peaky too! Now where's that soap gone? For it's my turn to wash you all over, you wicked tease."

*

And all the time Alicia was aware of a heightening of her own desires. Whether from Soraya's attentions, her own suppressed feelings or even the very air she breathed she did not know; but what was certain was that her body had never felt so alive, so tinglingly aware of its own suppleness and beauty.

Eventually Soraya led her out of the water, and laughing ridiculously to hide her nerves, Alicia lay down on one of the long flat padded couches, while Soraya knelt beside her and neatly and efficiently began to razor away the wiry down that had grown again so innocently across the very point of her desire. Alicia knew her loins were wetting already, but there was nothing she could do about it, and yet she must keep absolutely still while Soraya groomed her perfectly. It was the most exquisite torture for she longed to hold her breasts, caress her loins, anything to ease the pain and ache of the unfulfilled wanting that now seemed so suddenly to be consuming her.

And her situation was made worse by the tingling sensation of the hard steel blade Soraya was so expertly using on her, and the gentle rubbing of her soapy, oily hands against that softest most vulnerable part of her body until she was panting, each touch of Soraya's hands making her gasp and almost cry out, until finally the job was done.

"Sweetheart," Soraya said at last, looking down at her. "Truly you are the most lovely creature! But before you dress, there is one more thing that I must do."

And getting up she crossed the steam filled room to a low chest that stood against the wall, returning shortly with a large glass phial filled with a heavy amber fluid, and leaning over Alicia she first drew the thick cork from it and then slowly poured the contents across the prostrate girl's naked body. And Alicia drew in her breath, for this was no ordinary fluid but musk oil of the very finest quality that filled the air with its heady perfume; and ran across her breasts in deliciously thick golden rivulets.

Gathering it in her hands Soraya slowly, lovingly, rubbed it over Alicia's breasts and between her thighs, across her belly and around her arms and shoulders, and over her shaven mons and the soft pouting lips of her vulva until Alicia felt she could stand no more...until she felt Soraya's caressing fingers slip inside her at last, mingling the musky oil on her hands with the salty tears from Alicia's own petals now more open than ever before.

Then turning her gently over Soraya continued the massage, over and between her buttocks, over, around and even into the dusky rose that nestled there, making Alicia gasp and whole body leap and squirm, and then over the soft top of her thighs, until Alicia's body glowed in the soft lamplight that filled the room, and when she was done Soraya briefly kissed her.

Running her hands lightly across her neck and then firmly around her breasts, she pulled Alicia's dark areolas upwards with her finger ends, milking them until they pouted up at her, thrusting her swollen teats into even harder prominence, before deftly painting both nipples and areolas with gold, as Soraya's had been when she had first met her, that first day on the *Morning Star*. And she smiled up into Soraya's face, knowing exactly why she had done that to her, taking her hands and kissing the palms of each one in turn, before pulling the lovely girl down for a final deep kiss of gratitude and love.

"Now, my Lady, truly you are ready for that bastard upstairs. Any man would desire you, Alicia, or any woman. You are so beautiful that it almost takes my breath away! Come quickly now, before I take you in my arms and kiss you all over myself. He will be enchanted, I am sure. Do you have the vial from Najid safely?"

"Yes. I have it close, and know exactly where I shall paint myself with it...and how lasciviously I shall do it too. I am no maiden in this butcher's arms tonight Soraya; but a woman grown, and a woman with some knowledge too. *God aid me*, Soraya, that it stands me in good stead tonight. I am risking all on a single throw of the dice. If I cannot find the Crystal...or it does not work for me, then I am lost...*we are lost!*"

"You fret too much, sweetheart. His great Seer Stone will be in its rosewood box in his inner, most private room...where it always is. No-one else, on pain of death, is allowed to touch it, let alone move it. Not even Rochine herself would dare to do so; and *Monsieur le Baron* never leaves the castle for any length of time without it. And as we discussed the other day my darling girl, *you are 'of the Blood'!* And the Crystal only works for those who are *'of the Blood'*. And your so great love for Gui...your own true heart...will lead your spirit to him as sure as eggs are eggs! Only be courageous, my love, and determined and you will succeed...I know it! Tonight you only need your wits and your natural beauty, my darling, to entrap that man's interest...and his black heart. Clothed you are beautiful...disrobed you are magnificent." And she bent and kissed Alicia again.

"Oh, Soraya! What would I do without you? Agnes is very dear to me and has been since I was a little girl. But you? You have proven to be the very truest friend and I would be lost without you!" And she kissed her most tenderly. "Now, my love, you'll have to help me a little for you have left me in such a state that I can hardly stand, let alone walk. What was in the water and in that oil you have glossed me with? For my body is so alive, so hot and tingling that I feel on the verge of the greatest climax of my life. I cannot begin to describe it adequately, but unless something happens soon I shall go gypsy wild and fling myself at you!"

"Whereas I think that would be rather wonderful," Soraya chuckled merrily, kissing her on the mouth, letting her tongue brush Alicia's fleetingly, pressing her breasts against her as she did so. "Now is neither the time nor the place. One wood-wild nymph would be bad enough…but two? Impossible!" and they both laughed.

"As to the balms and oils," she went on, slipping her arm around Alicia's waist. "They are a secret that I may one day pass on to you, I promise you. But I can tell you that the balms I have used on you are very old, they go back to the time of the Egyptian Pharaohs, so I understand. They will not harm you, only heighten your desires, so enjoy the release they give you Alicia and just let yourself go. You are here for a purpose, my darling, I know, but there is no reason why you should not enjoy it. Duty does not have to be a penance…it can also be a joy!"

Then rising again, she moved to another chest before returning with the most beautiful dress Alicia had ever seen. Made of the finest white silken gossamer, with curling fronds of gold and silver thread, and strewn with tiny seed pearls that seemed to cup her breasts, it shimmered in the light like silver stars…and when she stood up in it, it floated round her naked body like a cloud, revealing all her charms yet shrouding them in mystery at the same time.

"Come now, we must cover ourselves for our return. It would never do for the castle guards to see either of us like this…they would all pass out!" And picking up a long, beautifully embroidered robe of blue silk for herself and another in palest cream for Alicia, with light cork heeled sandals for their feet of the softest blue and delicate cream leather, and soles of scarlet, they left the pool chamber, closing the heavy door behind them as they went.

Despite the light-headedness she felt and the glowing sensations across her breasts and loins, Alicia soon began to feel in better control of herself, and after an initial helping hand, was able to walk quite steadily back up the way they had come. With Aquib following, his armour softly chiming, his great scimitar across his arms, they retraced their steps and avoiding all the other guards on duty that night they were soon back in the family wing of the great keep. And without pausing to return to their own room, Soraya led Alicia along the marble corridor and then to a broad spiral staircase that wound by stages up to the fourth floor of the massive building where Lord Roger had his own private set of rooms, quite separate from the rest of the old family apartments.

Here, at the foot of a short flight of marble steps, themselves lushly carpeted in forest green, at the top of which were a pair of great double doors bound over with delicately fretted ironwork, she finally stopped: "Alicia, this is as far as I am allowed to go, and where I must leave you; for the female house-servants are never allowed up those stairs without special orders to do so, and those have not been given to me tonight. Go on. Enjoy yourself, my love, and leave all your troubles behind you for a while.

"What is it that Jesus said to his friends, sweetheart?...'About tomorrow do not worry, for tomorrow will bring its own worries. Today's troubles are enough for today.'...Just ride this storm, Alicia. The Lord Roger may be an evil bastard...but he is good at what he does! *C'est moi qui parle!* And I should know, believe me...and I have not suffered because of it. So, my girl, give as good you get, and then walk away. You need your freedom, sweetheart, as we do. Don't agonise over it, Alicia. Just get in there and get it over with...*and smile!*"

"Soraya!" Alicia whispered huskily. "I am suddenly very afraid. What if he doesn't like me, or my stubborn nature angers him? "

"*Are you mad?* Alicia! He has engineered this whole dreadful 'thing' just to get you in his arms and into his bed. And not just his bed, sweetheart...*but his marriage bed!* You are stunningly beautiful...those lovely breasts of yours are enough to turn any man's head, and you have a bottom like a peach. Just let your own feelings flow through you and let your natural instincts do all the rest. Go on now, he doesn't like to be kept waiting, even by you!" she said, passing Alicia a small clutch bag with handkerchief, perfume and Najid's precious vial carefully tucked inside it. "And remember, sweetheart, we will all be waiting and praying for you, Najid as well I expect!" And with a final kiss Soraya turned away and trip-trapped back down the stairs.

Drawing a deep breath, Alicia walked up the last few carpeted steps and pushed open the doors that stood before her at the top, and was amazed at the ease and quietness with which they instantly swung apart. Then pushing them closed behind her, she moved through the narrow ante-chamber that lay beyond, and turning through a heavily carved stone archway, she entered the Baron's private suite of rooms for the first time.

Chapter 20...The White Rose lays down her honour in the dust.

Inside there were two main chambers, both huge, and sumptuously furnished with the finest embroidered silken hangings on pure white plastered walls, and thick eastern carpets in glowing colours on the polished oakwood floors, such that Alicia stalled at the very entrance, almost open-mouthed...*This place is just stunning! How can someone so foul, create something so wonderful? I am amazed!*

Everywhere she looked there was beauty: from the finest Venetian glassware and Byzantine icons in shimmering gold and glowing colours on fine beechwood chests inlaid with rosewood and ivory, to shining ornaments of gold and silver, many encrusted with jewels...for emeralds, rubies and sapphires glowed with colour in the dying light of the setting sun. But unlike her own apartment, there was also a great table of some beautiful dark wood, polished to the most gleaming finish, that stood in the middle of one room with a number of ornately carved armed chairs of a similar dark wood placed around it, each one padded in the finest green leather with the de Brocas Boar's Head with scarlet tongue and blooded tushes immaculately stitched on every back.

One whole wall was lined with magnificently bound and gilded books. Great thick tomes all hand written and no doubt lovingly embellished, but all locked tight with cunningly wrought golden fastenings. And there were lights everywhere, sweetly scented candles as well as silver oil lamps inlaid with gold, so that the room glowed in the soft early evening darkness that lay outside the tall arched windows. Off that were two other rooms, one seemingly much larger than the other. And there were several padded settees, and broad window seats, intricately embroidered with the same birds and foliage as on her bed cover, and with great blue and scarlet silk cushions in each corner on which to lean back against the painted plaster work.

And seated alone on one of them, bathed in the warm after-glow, was the Lord Baron, Sir Roger de Brocas of Narbonne and Gruissan. Dressed quite simply in a pure white satin jacket with short sleeves, his left shoulder emblazoned with his own great livery of the Boar's Head erased, and soft hose of forest green wool, with green suede half boots on his feet, he looked both quietly composed and formidable. His arms were bare, corded with muscle, and each bound round above the elbow by great ornamented arm-rings of heavy chased and twisted gold. The one on his right arm the mirror of the one she still wore herself, only larger and heavier…twined lovers on one side and fighting dragons on the other.

Seeing her enter, he paused first to watch her face, pleased by the look of awed surprise that ran across it, before rising and coming forward to greet his lovely guest…*like some great cat stalking its prey*…she thought, and taking her hand he brought her forward into the light.

"So, you are really here at last!" he exclaimed, lifting the silken robe from her shoulders…*dear God she looks magnificent. No wonder my blood runs so hotly through my veins!*

"Did you honestly think I wouldn't come, after all the trouble you have been to, to make me feel at home?" She answered him coolly. "I am not so churlish my Lord. I was taught better manners than that!"

"No, it wasn't that, but I thought you might have been too tired after everything that has happened to want to enjoy my company tonight. Especially with tomorrow being such a special day?"

"It will be indeed…*Not if I can help it, you bastard!*…But you mistake me, my Lord Baron, for though I must confess myself to be a little nervous, I am not such a miserable maw-worm as to draw back at the first sign of outright desire from my future husband. Many a maiden in my place would be shrinking with fear and uncertainty, I know. But I am no maiden, and am made of sterner stuff, I assure you."…*just what I said to Father Matthew, you dog, before he cut my Gui open to remove your bloody arrow!*…And she fought to maintain her composure.

"Are you well?" he asked suddenly, seeing the pain that had just swept across her face.

"Yes! Of course"…*Sweet Jesus, but I must be more careful!*…"Just that I stubbed my toe coming up the stairs. Marble is surprisingly hard, even cloaked with green," and she laughed. "Truly it is nothing, I assure you. Nor have I been bothered by the heat, as I thought I might be," she chattered lightly to further distract his gaze which was still bent upon her. "Your home is beautiful indeed, my Lord Baron," she deftly added, looking round the room. "More beautiful than anywhere I have been before…even King Richard's palace in London."

That amused him. "Not that I am like to enjoy your King's hospitality!" he exclaimed dryly. "Not after making off with one of his Royal Wards in so," he paused a moment, "in so masterly a fashion." And he smiled again, and studied her carefully for her response….*Now what do you think of that, my lady fair?*

She smiled at him in return, complete with a slight dip of her head in acknowledgement of his sally…*You bastard! How dare you flaunt your wickedness at me! Dear God, but I hate him!...*"Well, my Lord. That is between my Lord King and yourself. My decision has been made concerning you and me. As I said.....I am made of sterner stuff."

"So, I see." he said with a smile, conducting her towards a large padded settee covered with sumptuous blue woollen cloth, gold and scarlet silk cushions scattered across it. "I was not mistaken in you, my love, and may I say that you are looking absolutely ravishing...*Dear God, she is good enough to eat!...*Come sit by me and let me give you this trifle that I am hoping will grace your neck tomorrow when we are married." And so saying he passed her a square box of polished rose wood for her to open...*Now! Let's see what she makes of this gesture of my love.*

And on doing so she gasped with surprise and wonder, as indeed he had expected, for inside, on a bed of white silk, lay the most magnificent necklace of interwoven gold links and great, liquid blue sapphires, sprinkled all around with enormous square-cut diamonds, the very sight of which brought tears to her eyes.

"Oh, my Lord Baron, this is a mag..magnificent gift!" She stammered, completely thrown. "Far too grand for me. I..I cannot take it!"...*Dear God! These are as like my mother's sapphires as any I have ever seen, only with diamonds instead of pearls. What a swine this man truly is, to tempt me with something so like that which he stole from me in the first place! Bastard!*

"Yes you can, my Lady," the Baron insisted, lifting them up to show her. These are not family jewels. They are *your* jewels. I had them specially made just for you, and I will feel deeply dishonoured if you will not accept them from my hands." And leaning forward he placed them round her neck, almost with reverence. "Now give me your lips for I have not yet tasted their sweetness," he said huskily. "You have kept me at almost arm's length all week, and I can wait no longer to hold you in them...and please, no formality here between us. You must call me 'Roger' and I shall call you 'Alicia'...as my adored wife Constancia was please to call me, and I her."

Alicia was stunned by the sheer bare-faced magnificence of his gift, and by his intimate comment...*Sweet Heavens, he mistakes me for his former wife! Perhaps he does, now, truly love me? Poor bastard! God's Blood...but he makes me sick! How can I go on with this?...*And taking a pace forward she reached up her hands and gently kissed his face: "Oh..Roger.. they are just beautiful. Lovely beyond words. Come, my Lord," she said holding out her arms. "I told you ages ago that I was not made of china. Just hold me tightly and say nice things to me, for I am feeling lonely tonight," she added, writhing inside at her words.

"Alicia, no man could hold you in his arms and not want you near him always; and I am no exception. You are made for love, my beauty. In truth I don't know how I have managed to keep my hands and body under control for so long. Come with me now, the meal can wait 'til later, but I cannot!"

Alicia chuckled as he said this, but holding out her hand she allowed him to draw her towards a studded door in the wall of his first chamber that clearly led to another room beyond... *Well! Dear God...here we go!...*And she gritted her teeth as he led her forward...even as she smiled at him.

"So soon my Lord? I thought a goblet of fine Bordeaux at least, and more honeyed words before attempting me. I might fight and struggle, you know, or scream for help!"

Roger smiled at her wolfishly and caught her to him, holding her close against his chest so tightly that she could hardly breathe: "It would do you no good my pretty one," he growled, his voice thickened with desire. "My servants have been banished, there are no guards, and no-one will come near here anyway, for I have given the strictest orders that I am not to be disturbed for anything. And no-one, my Alicia, ever disobeys my orders, except on peril of their life. Tonight you are mine to do with as I please, and you will not be disappointed, that I promise you."

Alicia, despite her deepest feelings against this man who had done such scathe to her and all those whom she loved the most, could feel herself beginning to respond....*Sweet Mary, but the man has more power in him than I had realised. I am excited by him already! How can that be with a man I hate so much?...*And though she felt a little afraid of the heated passion she was deliberately intending to raise in him, yet the woman in her purred delightedly.

She was also deeply conscious of the weight of gold and precious stones he had just placed round her neck! No girl likes a weakling for a mate, and Alicia particularly had always warmed to strength and masterful attention in a man.

Then before she could reply she was whisked off her feet, and holding her gently in his arms, Lord Roger kicked open the door and carried his melting lady into his great bedroom, and placed her down carefully upon his bed. This was not unlike the one that lay in her own bower below and had probably been crafted by the same hand, but before she could follow up that line of reasoning a step further, the Baron knelt down beside her and taking her in his arms he kissed her... *Gui! My Gui! Forgive me for this. I do this for our baby and for you. Oh...Dear God...I am lost!...*And with that last cry in her heart, all Alicia's other thoughts flew out of the window as she surrendered to the Baron's overwhelming passion, for with that first kiss it was as if she was suddenly filled with fire, for his tongue was a dancing flame, and the hot male essence of him sent the blood surging through her body.

That first burning kiss re-awakened all the feelings that Soraya had aroused in her earlier, and left her panting with the heat of her own fierce, unexpected desires…it filled the awful void left in her senses since she had been so brutally torn from Gui's side…and drove her to seek more. Moaning softly she reached up her hands and caressed the back of his head, pulling him closer to her as she did so and kissing him back fiercely, driving her tongue over his again and again, sucking it into her mouth and savouring every drop of him she could.

Dear God forgive me…but I want this man!

And her whole body suddenly ached to feel his hands on her: on her breasts and loins, on her taut buttocks, across her back and shoulders…and to feel the hard maleness of him come alive beneath her touch, and then to ride herself to exhaustion upon its thick strength.

Breathlessly letting go of her, Roger sat down on the edge of his bed and watched her briefly, before running his firm hands over her body with murmured words of pleasure and surprise at her beauty, that still lay shadowed and inviting beneath the filmy gauze of the dress that he had chosen for her… and reaching for the neck of the garment, impatient of its value, he simply tore it from her body. In one swift, powerful movement he ripped it away so that he could enjoy the sight of her nakedness: her firm breasts and swollen nipples jutting from their silken haloes, dark areolas and thickened teats all painted gold…her smooth haunches and the soft naked fruit of her mound of Venus thrust out so deliciously, so plumply towards him.

Pausing only to remove his white satin jacket, the Baron lay down beside her and slowly began to make love to her, gently at first with butterfly kisses and finger tips, then harder as he caressed her vibrant body more firmly. Fondling and kneading the smooth flesh, he ran his hands and fingers across her back, and between her thighs and over the firm globes of her buttocks. Parting them and closing them again as he did so, he worked his strong fingers nearer and nearer to the burning seat of passion that was now truly lubricious from the flood of desire beginning to flow so fiercely through her veins.

Then, when she felt she could stand no more of his passionate teasing, he slowly slid his fingers into her, first one, then two, then three and played her with them, thrusting them into her 'til they were wet with the tears of love that flowed from the soaking lips of her vagina.

And Alicia moaned with pleasure…"*Go on! Go on!*"

Her body swiftly running out of control, she kissed him fiercely, eyes closed in bliss, driving her tongue over and around his, while she covered his busy hand with one of her own, pushing him deeply into her again and again until she was gasping, drawing his hand to her breasts so that he could wet her nipples with her lust, and then dipping him into her again and again, until lifting her lips from his, she put his hand to her mouth so she could suck his fingers, taste her own saltiness on every one, before thrusting them back inside her again, only to draw them out and savour them all over again, and again…loving the sweet and sour taste of her loins on her own tongue.

And never had she been so wet!

The juices simply flooded out of her over the smooth, shaven softness of her vulva until it was deliciously slippery, letting him wet her sphincter and her buttocks with them so he could pierce her soft dusky rose with his thumb to excite her demon passage while his fingers busied themselves fiendishly in her vagina. Every thrust of his hand made her cry out with pleasure, as he plundered every part of her body, going where even she and Gui had never trespassed…and loving it, so that her body leaped and bucked to his hand's demands until she felt she could take no more.

Alicia was ecstatic, her only thoughts…*Oh fuck me! Fuck me!*

Lost in the glory of her passion as she lay beside and over him, she quivered to his touch like a silver birch bending before some great tempestuous wind. All she wanted now was for him to enter her, to take her there on the floor if need be, bent forward on her hands and knees or straddling him like a rider does a horse…*as I do with Gui!*

She didn't care.

She just wanted his hardness buried in the very depths of her; and kneeling over him, fingers fumbling in her excitement, she unlaced his hose and pulled it down, so that his phallus, thick and swollen with desire, bounced free at last into her waiting hand.

Like an iron pole encased in flesh, hot to touch, silky, it rose before her, the head glistening in the warm lamplight, the very essence of his manhood, strong and powerful, and with the lightest touch of her lips, she savoured it, ran her tongue all around it…and then as gently she released it. And putting his own hands round himself with a smile, she turned and rose to seek the little clutch bag that Soraya had given her, while the Baron tore at his remaining clothes, struggling to free himself from them as swiftly as he could. Then, lying back he gently caressed himself, relishing the strength of his erection, as he watched her move languidly around his great chamber, gracious in her nakedness, enhanced by the barbaric splendour of the great golden collar of sapphires and diamonds she still wore round her neck and nestled on the white slopes of her breasts, her nipples startlingly erect and gleaming golden in the candlelight.

In moments she found the bag where she had left it on the edge of the table in his outer room, and opening it, she took out the perfume it contained, and the vial of golden liquid that Najid had given her, and with them in her hands she returned to where the Baron lay, naked on his great bed, gently caressing his phallus with the oil and juices from her body…and smiling at him she took her small perfume bottle and tipped it on either side of her neck and between her breasts.

Without a word being spoken she unclasped the jewelled collar he had given her and laid it with great care back in its box, turning and bending over before him as she did so, her haunches and buttocks deliberately displayed, then standing again she turned back towards him, and looking into his dark, black eyes, she lifted her breasts in her hands and sucked and twisted each teat until every vestige of gold paint was gone, then while he hungrily watched her she slipped the small cork from the slender vial Nijad had given her and poured a gout of the rich oil onto each breast until both swollen tips and their dark haloes were thick with its golden sheen.

"This is oil from the gods, My Lord," she whispered. "Given to Soraya by the Lady Rochine for your special pleasure with me tonight. From the top of Mount Olympus, from the herbs of Aphrodite herself it comes, and of Diana, the Goddess of the Moon. It enlarges *everything*, my Master, she said softly moving towards him, now watching her almost open-mouthed.

"I am going to put the rest of this Oil of Olympus where you will love it the most, where your questing tongue and hungry mouth can drink from my chalice, that which the gods themselves so loved." And taking the tiny vial in her hand she tipped every last drop onto her cleft of Venus, letting it run down over her labia, over her petals, chasing the golden liquid with the fingers of one hand while with the other she teased her nipples so that each one stood out thickly from her body, glistening with the golden liquid that Najid had given her.

And giving him that special smile he had so longed for all week, she came slowly back to where he was lying and holding her breasts out for him she drew his head onto her so that he could suckle from each breast in turn, as a baby would, standing for him as he reached out for her soft flesh with his hands to feed from her. And as a drought-stricken man would suck the last precious drop from a skin of fresh water…so the Lord Baron, Roger de Brocas sucked every last golden drop of scented oil from Alicia's breasts, while, like the good mother she was so longing to be, she encouraged him in his greed with small sounds of love and praise, while holding his flaring manhood in her free hand.

And with her breasts cleansed of oil, she knelt down beside him on the floor, and holding his phallus in both hands she first kissed it then ran her tongue around it, before with a smile to him of infinite pleasure, she finally drew its swollen head deeply into the velvet smoothness of her mouth to savour it completely.

His hand pushing on the back of her head as she did so, she thrust her face down onto his rampant penis, suckling on it, slathering it with her mouth, and then drawing back again; rubbing her teats with it; pressing its glorious hardness between her juiced and oiled breasts and swallowing its strength until he could take no more as bobbing her head faster and faster she drove him towards his first climax, loving her power over him, as he threw his head back and groaned his pleasure to the distant stars, thrusting into her mouth and throat as he cried out, flooding her with his semen which she gorged on as greedily and without restraint as she always did on Gui's.

But that climax was just the first of what the Baron intended for them, and drawing her head away from him, he picked her bodily up from the carpet on which she had been kneeling and flopping her on her back on his great bed he went down before her, and with her legs draped over each shoulder, he bent his head and drove his tongue into her, sucking the golden oil off her and out of her, lashing the hard little nubbin he knew was standing there so pertly to attention and sucking her labia with his mouth, sharply nipping her swollen bud with his teeth as he did so.

And her whole body bucked like a wild mare, like a leaping salmon or a mighty pike upon an iron gaff, as his tongue pierced and savaged her loins and her clitoris. Again and again he thrust his tongue into her, bringing his hands up to play with her as well, his fingers thrusting deeply amongst her petals and buried beyond the knuckles in her dusky rose as well as he worked her hard, while she crushed her breasts in her hands and pulled her swollen teats with her fingers until she was in a complete frenzy of overwhelming lust.

And Alicia screamed..."*My God! My God! What are you doing to me?*"

Then kneeling up to her, pushing her legs over his shoulders as he did so, he put the dark, swollen head of his phallus to the soaking lips of her vagina, and with one long, powerful thrust he drove into her at last, pulling her hard against his loins as he did so, until Alicia cried out again, reaching her legs round him as he pulled slowly back...only for him to thrust into her again, and again, her head and body jerking to each great drive. And each time she pulled him into her with her thighs, gripping him with them as she would ride a bucking horse, her hands seizing onto his shoulders as well, her whole body shaking as he rammed his stiff manhood into her with rampant vigour. Next, before she could cry out, he turned onto his back, carrying her with him as he rolled so that she was suddenly above him, her breasts hanging down over his mouth for him to suck on, her knees now clamped firmly on either side of his body, his hands pressing her hips onto him as he moved.

Never had she been so completely filled…so extended and gorged with human flesh before.

She felt as if he would touch her heart so thoroughly was he thrust within her. She was speared, staked, impaled upon him yet unable to prevent herself from moving her body up and down on him. Gently at first then harder as the rising tide of desire swamped her ever more strongly, she rode the solid stake upon which she was so gloriously thrust until she felt completely dizzy, all cogent thoughts of Gui, Soraya, her friends, her home, completely lost in the driving, pounding primeval urge to find release.

For every movement that she made, her tormentor matched her, thrusting his loins up to meet her as she hurled her body down onto him, squeezing her oiled breasts hard between his hands as he did so. Then falling back, he pulled them both further onto the great bed while she bent over him, pressing he breasts into his mouth so he could suckle her, pulling at each pouting swollen teat with his lips and tongue and teeth, moulding with his hands the rich fruits that she so willingly held out for him.

Then he made her sit up on him, her feet either side of his flanks as any rider would on short stirrups, and thus firmly mounted, his thick shaft deep inside her loins, she rode him hard, her back straight and her shoulders back so that her breasts thrust out at him in their pride…and as they bounced he struck them sharply with his big hands, making them spring and leap from side to side as he did so, and each time she gasped and cried out as the pain lanced through her loins, making her body buck wildly on his manhood. And each time she bucked…so he thrust into her again, and again until she reached a peak of absolute, overarching desire, and throwing back her head she ground her hips down on him, gripping his thick phallus with the strong muscles in her vagina, screwing her hips down onto him as she did so, making him cry out at the added pressure she now put him under.

And smiling at his torment, she lifted her breasts in her hands and squeezing them together, she bent her mouth to ease the burning in her nipples from his heavy hand, lashing each throbbing crest with her tongue, drawing them into to her mouth, and sucking on them until they were soaked with the wetness of her own loving, gleaming and golden in the lamp and flaring candlelight.

Yet when she was almost on the brink of falling into the greatest, deepest whirlpool of her life, he suddenly withdrew from her, and flipping her over onto her knees he knelt behind her; and lifting her drove his tongue deeply into her instead. Alicia gasped, for his tongue was a thing of quicksilver in her saturated loins and plundered rose, first stabbing at the raised bud that nestled there among her juicy folds, running between the rounded globes of flesh that usually protected it…then right through the centre of her rose, while he worked her *conne anglaise* into a fresh maelstrom of almost unbearable delight.

But she was desperate for him to enter her, begging and crying out for him to do so again: "*Oh…fuck me! Fuck me!*"

And lowering her to her knees on the very edge of his great bed, so that her breasts brushed the bedclothes, and her swelling, rounded buttocks pushed back towards him, he filled her as Gui never had before! Standing behind her he parted her buttocks with his big hands, splaying her open, nuzzling her soft dusky rose with his hot, swollen phallus, now soaked with her juices and filled with warm oils where his busy fingers and thumb had already plundered her. And as she opened for him so he slowly eased his great manhood into her demon passage to the very hilt…and pausing a moment to savour the wet softness pressing so tightly all around him, he withdrew almost to the full…before thrusting deeply into her again.

At that first touch Alicia's eyes flew open and she gasped…"*Oh, God! What are you doing to me?*" her breath hissing over her teeth and then she groaned deep in her throat as he thrust right into the very centre of her fundament, her whole body trembling with a depth of feeling that wracked her to her very soul. And as he slowly withdrew and then thrust into her again more strongly, she cried out and tossed her head, her body shuddering with the sudden force of it, and lifting herself onto her hands she pushed back onto him with equal force. Gripping him with her sphincter so he could not easily release himself from her, he cried out again and again as he now plundered her without mercy: "*Ride me! Ride Me!*" And so she pumped his great phallus through her rounded buttocks, now sleeked with sweat, while he smacked them both resoundingly as he did so, each sharp blow serving to drive Alicia into an ever increasing frenzy of lust and wild abandon.

Never had she experienced anything like it!

Never had her whole body been so on fire, her breasts so swollen nor her loins so wet. Now she had no cogent thought save to find release, save to fly up into the stars and experience that wild, rushing blast of energy that would surge through her like a fierce torrent.

And she screamed out loudly as she rode him: "*Oh, God, you bastard! Make me cum! Fuck me! Fuck me hard!*"

And pulling out of her demon passage with a wet rush, the Lord Roger picked Alicia up and pushed her towards the head of his bed where the long padded rail ran from one side to the other, and together they made the 'beast with two backs'. Thrusting into her vagina to the very hilt, he now plundered her loins as she had desired; his body furiously pumping…her arms rigid against the bed head to support her, hands gripping the padded top as he powered into her. Again and again he stabbed deeply into her body, making her moan and cry out, before withdrawing almost to the very gates of paradise before lunging forward once more into her wildly jerking and tempestuous body, harder and harder and faster and faster as the rising tide of lust gripped them both ever more strongly.

Loving the torment he was giving Alicia, Lord Roger shouted out each time he thrust into her, but now he too was reaching that state of nirvana that precedes oblivion, and firmly grasping her buttocks he sank deeply into Alicia once again, drawing his loins back to power into her; and reaching for her breasts as he did so he squeezed and twisted their rigid stalks between his strong fingers until, at last, with his hands over her hip bones driving her onto him again and again…he hurled them both over the edge in one final surge of power, slamming himself into her with every drive, until she was beyond all possible control, her breasts shaking and jerking at every thrust, her arms pushing her loins back into him each time he powered into her, hands clenched over the bed rail, thrashing her head from side to side and moaning incoherently every time her sleek buttocks met his rigid thighs.

Not even with Gui had their loving been filled with so much wild passion and naked lust…and with a final great cry she was there at last: falling, spinning, drowning, her body and her mind suspended somewhere in the vasty distances of space among the myriad stars that swung and sparkled there. And as she climaxed so he followed her, groaning and roaring like the great bull he was, like a lion, pumping his seed into the very deepest parts of her body, to seethe there briefly until time and distance brought all to an end. Releasing her gently, he turned her onto her back and kissed her fevered body, brushing his mouth over her swollen breasts and nipples, her eyes, her neck and her softly parted mouth. Then turning on his side he drew her against him and held her tightly in his arms.

Yet long after he had withdrawn from her, her body continued to jerk and quiver every time he touched her, and she mewed softly in her throat, warm murmuring purrs of pleasures given and received. But after such a heady joust words, like reality, lose their meaning and so with deep kisses and soft fondlings they settled for the night. Pressed close together like spoons, nestled snugly into one another, with Lord Roger's arms around her and his big hands cradling her naked breasts, Alicia was too exhausted to do anything but lie there as slowly her breathing settled and her heart stopped pounding.

And as she lay in the candlelit darkness of the Baron's bedchamber, remembering once more the whole reason for her being there, she was deeply wracked with guilt…*How could I do this when I love Gui so much? I am ashamed! May God forgive me*...Furious with her body for betraying her, her heart and soul cried out for forgiveness.

But, exhausted from her violent joust with the Lord Baron of Narbonne and Gruissan, now lying asleep with his arms around her, and while waiting to be certain that he was deeply and truly slumbering before attempting to move and seek his Crystal…and without ever meaning to…she softly fell asleep!

Chapter 21...Sir Gui meets with the Bowmen of Gwent.

Three days after meeting with Sir Hugh Willoughby, Gui's command left Bordeaux.

Well rested and mounted, and all with a good meal in their bellies to see them on their way, they left early; the hot August sun just beginning to warm their backs, a cool breeze across their faces, and ready for anything the world might throw at them.

Gui, seated with his knights around him, now all on their handsome destriers but with sturdy rounceys at the trail to save their precious chargers on the long journey south, felt enormously proud of his command as they rode past him in review on that superb August morning. Now starting on the last long leg of their drive to take the Baron down, every man rode upright in his saddle, arms and armour burnished and shining in the brilliant sunshine that lanced down upon them from yet another cloudless day.

Five hundred men had come forward when their sergeants had called the muster at daybreak: heavy foot, gisarmiers, crossbows, longbows and lancers. Three belted knights, supported by their Squires, led them; their own chaplain and surgeon and eight big wheeled tilt carts with two horses for each were also in their train. And running at the rear on long leading reins were still the girls' mares, Sunburst and Gillygate, along with the Vernaille brothers' own great destriers, far too valuable to be left in Bordeaux, their late owners' armour carefully sacked-up and placed on board one of the big carts.

"Well, young Gui," Sir Hugh said as he sat his own charger to watch them pass out in review, Sir Richard on his other side, Sir Robert on his big grey, Monmouth. "That is the finest bunch of men I have seen trot-march out of this fair city for some time. The Count's men, those from de Vernaille and your own from Malwood I can understand, they are used to taking orders, to drill and training. So are the heavy foot I have given you to play soldiers with, poor buggers. But that Welsh rabble I forced on you, Gui? I mean just look at them today! Helmets and mail jackets polished and shining, bow cases neatly across their shoulders, riding upright, faces to the front...well most of them," he added with a smile, as he saw several tanned faces turn with shouts and grins to friends, family and the dazzling flock of pretty girls who had all come to see them off. "I am amazed! God knows what you did to them, Gui? I just wish I had the trick of it myself!"

Gui looked at the swagger his new men were putting on for the crowd who had gathered around the northern gate of the city to shout and cheer and wish them well as they rode out on their sturdy Welsh ponies, and then at his former mentor almost scratching his head with astonishment…and smiled….*By God and the Pheasant, Hugh is right! They do look bloody good this morning. But, Christos, it has not been easy!*

*

That day after their arrival in Bordeaux - the very morning after he had walked the battlements and raised his glass to the north-east - had been one of the hardest of his memory.

Leaving his men in the charge of their own under officers, and giving them four pieces of silver each with which to have some fun in the good city of Bordeaux…*God help Hugh's city marshals for my lads are a lively bunch at times like this!*...Gui and Sir Richard L'Eveque, with Father Matthew close beside them on his big skewbald, had sallied forth in their bright Court clothes to meet again with Sir Robert FitzMiles and his wild Welshmen of Gwent, all of whom had by then been committed to Gui's command by order of the High Constable and Seneschal of all Aquitaine, and ultimately of the King himself, as the great parchment Gui had collected from Sir Hugh's Office first thing before breakfast had clearly stated.

With them went all his other senior commanders, properly armoured-up and with long swords at the sides: John Fitzurse, de Beaune, Bergerac, Allan-i-the-Wood…a Master Bowman in his own right; Dickon Fletcher, his own Master Bowman from Malwood, and John of Hordle, his Master Swordsman, with a great coil of hemp over his massive shoulders…together with the Bashley twins, Wat and Ned, a great chest of silver coins carried on stout poles between them. Almost all the biggest men in his Command.

Having met and fought with Robert FitzMiles in Northumbria Gui knew him to be a cogent, sentient being if somewhat wild at times, but a good man at heart as Sir Hugh had said: one of the new breed of Marcher Lords who took more to his Welsh dam's side in size and speech, than his tall Norman forebears. Dark haired and lean, he was committed to the welfare of his men…which had well-nigh emptied his slender coffer! He was enthusiastic and had good weapon skills, did not suffer fools gladly and was not easily daunted; so Gui was intrigued by what he might find. He was also amused by Richard's enthusiasm for their new brother knight, being especially pleased to have found another man who preferred the point of his weapon to its broad sharpened blade!

As he had said last night after dinner, in his inimitable drawl: "Any man who can discourse about the importance of 'machicolations' over 'hourdings'; understands the difference between a 'batter' and a 'glacis'...and fights with the point rather than the blade, unlike the Herculean barbarian I am talking with...cannot be all bad! Mad...undoubtedly because he is Welsh and they are all completely mad anyway! But not bad! And infinitely better than the Irish who are all quite beyond the Pale!" And they had both laughed hugely at the wit of his comment!

"Give the man his chance, Gui. At least he has kept his boys together and that, when dealing with Welsh soldiery, is no mean feat, I can tell you!" And with his customary lazy smile he had lounged away, twirling his wine goblet in his hand as he went, a snatch of song on his lips as if he had not a care in the world.

And now here they were, at the Welsh encampment, and Gui was not impressed for it was one mass of tents and scattered equipment, chickens, sheep...*My God! They really do have sheep!*...goats, big tilt carts and shaggy ponies tethered all over the place as if no-one gave a damn about anything! And yet...as Gui's sharp eyes noted it was not all bad: latrines properly dug away from food and water; horse dung removed to a single great midden right on the far side of their encampment, away from everybody; their weapons and armour sheened with oil...no rust anywhere. And their bows were in their cases, their arrows in their quivers...and every man was busy doing something. *So someone is doing the right thing, poor bastard. Get him placed in proper control of this lot under Robert's command, and we might yet really make something of them!*...But with their own leader dead and no-one yet formally appointed to take his place, and no designated Master-at-Arms to take overall control of the men themselves and their training, everything had slipped. But clearly not to the point of complete disintegration, so there was lots of good here still; just their personal hygiene and the general state of their camp left much to be desired...and they appeared to have a complete disdain for authority.

All of which he was quite expecting, having done his own homework beforehand, spoken at length with Sir Robert about his problems and about some of the families he had amongst his command...and had made some keen preparations of his own accordingly.

Nevertheless he still looked extremely grim when nobody stood as he and his officers approached on horseback...especially as the camp had known they were coming! And nobody moved when Sir Robert called them to order either. They just stood, or lounged where they were...and glowered.

"Dear God!" Sir Richard exclaimed as he looked around, swinging off Merlin's broad back: "Did you ever see such a filthy mess? And look at them! They are just about the scummiest, scruffiest, stinkiest set of rapscallions I have ever seen! How on earth do we make soldiers out of this lot?" and he sat down on an upturned bucket and almost put his head in his hands.

Gui, now off Beau, patted him consolingly on his back and laughed. "The same way we made excellent fighting soldiers of the rubbish I found up north when Robert and I went there before our knighthoods."

"And how was that, dear boy?" Richard groaned at him. "With prayers and magic?"

"No! Idiot!" Gui chuckled, banging the man on his elegant shoulder. "By example! By raising expectations, paying properly when promised, and in good coin; by unwavering determination, fair but strong discipline and by kicking arse…very hard!"

"Well, this I must see," his tall Guard Commander replied slowly with a smile, standing as he did so, Merlin's long reins still in his hands. "Who am I to deny the knowledge of experts? Go to, O my Master, your humble disciple awaits his revelation!"

And giving him a gentle cuff, Gui laughed and under the interested gaze of those men lounging nearby he beckoned the two Bashleys towards him, and having first placed the large chest they had brought with them on a ladder they'd found nearby, resting it across two convenient tree stumps, Gui ordered them to open it. And signalling to Fitzurse, William Bergerac and Hordle John to stand by him, and with Sir Robert, Richard L'Eveque and Father Matthew now also dismounted behind him, Gui gave the order for the camp to come to attention and to assemble on the wide area before him immediately with a ringing…" Come to order in the camp! *Stand and take muster!*"

At first nothing happened.

Then, with a grunt one man stood, almost grizzled in appearance, but lean in body with long legs and the powerful shoulders and strong knotted arms of a true longbow archer. Gaunt was his face, weathered and seamed like old leather, but he had bright, dark brown eyes, almost black, under bushy eyebrows…and dressed in dark green leather, with long sword and dagger either side he looked what he was, a tough, experienced soldier. And as he stood…so too did half a dozen more men, similarly clad in dark green and similarly armed, and with them the remainder of the camp gradually came to order, though with much glowering and grumping as they did so.

Gui, several parchments in hand and looking around at his unrelenting new command, laughed at their half-hearted reluctance, searching out the first man to stand to his order, nodding at him in stern gratitude. And dragging up a large upturned chest with a broken lid, he jumped lightly up and read out what was in his hand. Namely that, by order of the King…and he flourished Richard's Great Seal at them as he spoke, to their amazement and dismay…they were now under his complete command, and would remain so until he, Sir Gui de Malwood, released them from his service. There was no appeal to the orders, and refusal to accept any instruction, or order from his officers, or from those appointed amongst them as officers, would result in an immediate punishment ranging from a fine, docking of wages, restriction to camp and extra duties…to mutilation, by the removal of the two middle fingers of their drawing hand, followed by dismissal, or even outright execution by hanging. They were in effect under orders directly from the King himself, and any major infringement of his, the Lord Baron, Sir Gui de Malwood's orders could be taken as treason…with all that such a charge would imply.

And he stepped down to a sudden wave of unrest and immediate outcry, the men before him, and in their crude bothies around him, shouting, swearing and waving their fists.

"Well," Father Matthew said with a bark of sharp humour. "At least we know they understand English!"

"Now what?" Sir Richard asked.

"Mmmm. Richard, get down there with Ned and Wat Bashley and bring me that man who first stood, and I bet that will be Gareth Morgan. Yes? The man whom Sir Hugh singled out as Best of the Best? Robert, take John of Hordle, Allan-i-the-Wood and Dickon Fletcher and get hold of those others in dark green leathers and long swords. They all seem to be dressed as leaders…and let's see what goes on here. I will tell the rest to sit down."

And standing back up on the broken chest, while his men moved to carry out his orders, Gui ordered all the remainder to sit down which very reluctantly they did, wondering as they sat what would happen to their leaders in the meantime, not least because of the hangman's noose that the giant sergeant was making with the rope he was carrying over his shoulder. And there was a concerted gasp when having finished his work the man threw the rope over the arm of a great tree standing a few yards away, so that the noose hung in sharp, horrifying silhouette against the clear blue of the sky overhead.

*

Moments later, Sir Richard led the man Gui had singled out before him, with the hulking figures of Ned and Wat Bashley on either side of him. And while Richard L'Eveque remained there, the twins stepped back half-a-dozen paces and drew their swords.

"Gareth Morgan?" Gui asked grimly, his eyes hard as steel.

"Yes…my Lord." the man said hesitantly, clearly uneasy, and with two massive men behind him with drawn steel, a hangman's noose swaying in the breeze not fifty paces away, and a ring of very grim armoured men now immediately before him, he might well be too! "Sergeant Gareth Morgan of Skenfrith."

"Well Gareth Morgan of Skenfrith, I am the Lord Baron Sir Gui de Malwood, as I said over there, and Lord of the King's New Forest. I am appointed by Sir Hugh Willoughby, and through him by our Lord King himself, to take command of you and all your people until the task I have been given by the King, here in France, has been fulfilled. And from now on you will answer first to Sir Robert FitzMiles of Abergavenny, who is now your immediate commanding officer and then up the chain of command to me. Do you understand?"

"Yes, my Lord." He replied firmly, looking into Gui's face as he spoke.

"Good! Now, Sergeant, what is the meaning of this appalling lack of respect for the King's officers…and this..this midden in which you are living?" he snarled at the man, gesturing furiously around him. "You are an experienced soldier, Sergeant Morgan. A professional, so I am informed, and I am ashamed of you! As Sir William of Grosmont who brought you here would be too, were he still alive to witness to what levels his chosen men have sunk. Right now you are a disgrace to the army, and I demand an explanation from you before I strip you of what rank you hold and throw you out onto the streets!"

"My Lord, I and my fellow sergeants have done what we can," the big Welshman replied fervently, leaning forward as he spoke. "Sir William of Grosmont was a good man, and kindly, and good with his weapons; and I respected him greatly as did all of us in our own ways. But he was no disciplinarian, Sir Gui. And without his complete support it was very difficult to deal with the men anyway, and since his death even more so, not least because none of us have been paid since he died so food and supplies have been very hard to find. And until today, no-one has been assigned to take command either. At least I and my other sergeants have done our best to keep the men healthy and their weapons cleaned and ready…"

"Yes, Sergeant," Gui interrupted tersely, his eyes still hard as they bored into the man standing rigidly to attention. "That is the one thing that is likely to save your life this day. That, and the fact you did stand up when called upon to do so, even if it was unwillingly…and in doing that you gave the men the leadership they needed to follow suit. Well done."

"Th..thank you, my Lord!" the gangling Welsh archer replied, with a startled look and the hint of a smile. "These are mostly good men, Sir Gui. Always some bad apples in any barrel, and some going soft," he said in his sing-song Welsh voice. "But the bad ones we can weed out and the soft ones we can still knock into shape. All the lads need is firm leadership, m'Lord, and a clear understanding that discipline will be upheld. You've shocked them all this morning. And I for one was never more pleased to hear you say what you did," he added. "Just show us what you want…give us a sense of purpose, and we will follow!"

And there was a pause then as Gui looked first at Sir Richard and then at Father Matthew standing nearby, who both with the slightest of inclinations showed their agreement with his coming actions, knowing beforehand what was in his mind.

"So…Master Gareth Morgan of Skenfrith. Will you serve me? Faithfully, truly and to the very best your ability until I give you leave to be discharged with honour?"

"Yes! My Lord Baron, Sir Gui de Malwood, I will do so!" The man exclaimed immediately, astonished at the turn that events were taking. "And so will the men, I assure you!"

"Very well, Gareth Morgan of Skenfrith, I believe you! And I hereby appoint you Master-at-Arms of the Gwent Company of Longbows, and take you into my small army, under your new Commander, Sir Robert FitzMiles of Abergavenny. You will also be answerable to my Master-at-Arms, John Fitzurse; to my Guard Commander, Sir Richard L'Eveque whom you see before you and, ultimately, to me, the Lord Baron, Sir Gui de Malwood, myself under direct orders from King Richard of England. Do you accept this charge?" he asked finally, his face as hard as before, eyes chips of blue ice.

"Yes, my Lord Baron." The man replied, saluting him with his right fist to his forehead, both astonished and delighted by so unexpected a promotion with all the authority and wages that such a rise would give him, and he beamed, his craggy face breaking up into wide wrinkles of pleasure that spread everywhere.

"Good man!" Gui replied, holding out his hand, a broad smile on his own face, his eyes warming instantly. "Sir Hugh Willoughby recommended you to me, Gareth. He was not wrong! Now, let's see what we can do about the rest of these lads of yours, yes? And then I would like to see you all shoot! Come on then," he added, clapping his tall new Welsh Master-at-Arms on the back. "Time and tide wait for no man, Gareth Morgan…so this might yet call for a demonstration. So, Master-at-Arms," Gui said stopping in mid-stride, to swing himself face-to-face with his new officer, his voice hard and sharp: "Whatever else you do, or whatever else you may hear from me this morning, you must trust me absolutely to know what I am about. No matter how shocked you may feel, or how 'mad' you may think my actions, you must trust me completely, and neither *do* anything, nor *say* anything, about what will happen next! Do you understand me?" he said then, looking into the man's anxious brown eyes, his voice level, his eyes hard as blue granite: "*You do and say nothing!* And remember, in this case today, *nothing* will be as it seems!"

"Very well, my Lord Baron," the man replied puzzled. "I will do as you say, you have my word!"

"Good! Let's to it then!"

And patting the tall bowman on his broad leather shoulders, Gui turned and walked back towards the upturned chest, and with Gareth Morgan beside him, and his own officers now returned to their positions behind him, the remaining Welsh Sergeants clearly under their command, Gui grunted, and signalling to Hordle John and to his two Master Bowmen…who immediately strung their great bows and thrust a score of arrows each into the ground before them, to the obvious consternation of the camp…he dusted down the blue woollen bliaut he was wearing and stepped forward again, fists on his hips above his side arms, his face as bleak and angry as any of his own men had seen in a long time.

"*Right!*" Gui roared at the men now seated before him, jumping up again onto the upturned chest as he did so, his own men standing behind him, the Welsh sergeants with them in a small disarmed group close by, all looking very fearful, as all his officers drew their swords, their sharp steel blades flickering in the bright morning sunlight.

"I warned you all what would be the penalty if you should refuse a direct order from one of your officers placed in authority over you. You are *filwyr wael. Ac ddrwg iawn!*" He snarled at them in their own language, "You are bad soldiers. Very bad indeed! In fact right now you are '*Nithings!*' He swore at them in Saxon: "Men of no honour! No pride!" And he blistered them with his scorn, making many of them drop their heads and shuffle their feet in shame. "Look at you! Look at the filth and squalor you have allowed yourselves to live in! And you dare to call yourselves soldiers…*milwyr?*" No! I tell you that you are *filwyr wael*! Bad soldiers! *Ac ddrwg iawn!…very bad indeed…*and deserve all that you are going to get!

"*So!*"…he bellowed at them in a voice of brass…"By the power invested in me by the King, through his High Constable, Sir Hugh Willoughby, and having discussed this issue with your new Master-at-Arms, Gareth Morgan, who has assured me of his *complete* trust," he added looking around at the tall bowman standing next to him, his eyes like black stones, his face rigid. "And so that you will all understand the nature of discipline in my command, I have been informed by Sir Hugh of the theft of a number of valuable items from within Bordeaux that have been traced back to this camp.

"I have assured Sir Hugh that I will deal with this matter in a summary and immediate manner. As I know that there is no chance of securing the true culprit of these offences, *I will now hang one of you by his neck until he is dead!* John of Hordle, William of Bergerac, seize any man you like and bring him to me. Jean de Beaune, Wat and Nat Bashley, draw your swords. You will slay *any* man who intervenes. Master Fletcher, Allan Wood, draw your bows. Shoot any man who moves! And any man who moves after that!"

And with that came true shock and dismay: dark threats and vile curses, as Gui's men, armoured-up and armed with sword and mace in hand, forced their way amongst the crowd and pounced without mercy on their chosen victim…and a cry of horror and dismay rose up from the ranks as they did so. For the one man that William Bergerac and Gui's Master Swordsman seized upon with their iron grasp was the youngest amongst them all, and the most favoured.

A youngster with a fresh open face and a handsome smile, bright-eyed and merry…a mere boy of less than fourteen years, now quivering and petrified…his father grovelling on his knees for his son's life before Father Matthew, in the pathetic hopes that the Church might save his son, where the military powers clearly would not do so.

Master-at-Arms, Gareth Morgan still stood where Gui had left him, his face truly horrified by what he had witnessed was yet clinging to what his new Lord, Sir Gui de Malwood, had said to him just minutes before: 'in this case, *nothing* will be as it seems!' And desperately hoping his trust had not been cruelly misplaced, he stood there like a pillar of stone, his eyes hard, his hands clenched by his sides.

Now, whereas before, the camp had been sullen and wholly unwilling, most of the men not caring about their appearance nor their profession as soldiers…now the whole place was fizzing with emotion, fear and anger, as they watched the huge figure of John Fitzurse make ready the great hangman's noose he had made earlier and that would shortly kill the boy who had been seized, while Hordle John drew up a pony beneath it on which to put their chosen victim, held fast in William of Bergerac's great meaty hands.

The next moment there was a sudden surge as the great crowd of men now gathered before them tried to attempt a rescue, and immediately the air was filled with arrows as Dickon Fletcher and Allan-i-the-Wood fired into the crowd, the *twang* of strings, the swishing flicker of arrows and the sharp flacking *thunk* as they hit their targets resonating all around the camp. For those arrows were not fired indiscriminately into the shouting, milling crowd of angry men and fearful followers, but with matchless aim and speed. Striking shoe heels, leather scrips and wooden bow cases; quivers, knives in hands, mugs on tables, crocks of food, wine and water skins…anything that in itself was not human, but of human origin or creation…and they stopped the whole encampment dead in its tracks. Every single archer there that day knew they were witnessing a superb display of rapid, precision shooting such as they had never seen before, and would remember all their days after.

And as Gui saw them all stagger to a halt, he immediately raised his hand and the frightening deluge of arrows immediately ceased. And as they ceased so all looked to see where the boy was now standing, with the great hangman's noose behind his head, upon the back of a sturdy Welsh pony, the rope above him stretched taut as Hordle John and the two Bashley brothers held the shaggy beast firm and steady, ready to do whatever their Lord should order them, Gui's giant Master-at-Arms close beside them.

And now Gui addressed the crowd again.

"You have seen my men shoot, and they are but two of many…and I am a man who keeps his word! I will have order in my Command, and firm discipline and you, and Sir Robert FitzMiles, are all now *in* my Command and under my orders. As are your sergeants!" He called out to them waving his credentials in his hand again, showing them the High Constable's seal as well as their Lord King's. "*And I will hang Willy Davies if you make me!*" he roared, the boy's name bringing absolute stillness to the crowd of men, and their women who had now come forward from amongst the many tents and bothies to join the scene.

"Yes!" he spoke to them all crisply, his words dropping amongst them like great pebbles in a mill-pool. "I know who he is, and who his da is today…and who his ma was. Your new Master-at-Arms has told me…your new leader, Sir Robert FitzMiles of Abergavenny, has also told me. I even know where the boy lives, between Grosmont and Pontrilas, on the estates of Sir William's family in Gwent. And I know he has done no wrong…*nothing!* Except to fall among thieves and ignorant vagabonds, pretending to be '*milwyr*'…'soldiers'…who have led him astray," he shouted at them, pointing as he spoke.

"There are those amongst you who have taught him that honour and duty and loyalty mean nothing to a Welshman…only lies and deceit and greed! But someone must pay for those thefts, and he is the chosen one. The poor scapegoat for all your manifold sins and wickednesses," he railed at them, his eyes ablaze. And a growl of anger and dismay rippled through the crowd, together with many rumbles of agreement at his words, shaken heads and much bitter talking.

"No! You don't like it, do you?" Gui continued, lowering his voice. "When someone points out to you the things you know to be true but do not want to admit, it makes you squirm! You who have lazed here like idle hounds off the leash, scratching for fleas and doing nothing but consume your leader's substance; rollicking in the town making your name, and that of all Welshmen, stink in the nostrils of good men! And, worst of all, you *filwyr wael*," he scorned them bitterly. "You have squandered your greatest skill by not practising your art! *You are a disgrace!* You are Willy Davies' killers today," he snarled, throwing his arms wide as he spoke, to embrace the whole sordid encampment. "But I can teach him another way!" He shouted down at them, raising his hand in the air to bring immediate silence to the whole crowd of men and women gathered there, as all waited to see if it would fall and poor Willy be hanged.

"And all of you as well, if you wish it?" He shouted at them. "I can show you how to be proud again of yourselves and of your skills. I can pay you a proper wage, *and in real silver*, as laid down for the mint by the Old King before he died last year. And pay it without fail and without you having to plead for it, or steal for it, or watch your family go hungry with famine in their bellies for want of your wages. *That is not my way!*" And gesturing to where the Bashleys had placed the money chest on the old ladder he shouted: "See! Here is my chest. Show them the coins, Masters–at-Arms."

And he paused then as John Fitzurse, accompanied by Gareth Morgan to whom Gui gave a subtle push, both moved forward, bent down and dipped their hands into the great box and then stood to let the mass of coins fall back down through their fingers. Like a clinking waterfall of shining silver, the coins flashed and flittered through their fingers in the brilliant light as they fell back down amongst the rest, the tinkling sounds seeming to go on and on for ever. And all those around them watched Gui's little display with open mouths.

"They are real, lads, I promise you!" Gareth Morgan shouted out loudly, allowing great fistfuls of coins to fall in glittering cascades from each hand. "Not tin blanks, nor adulterated coins full of lead. *These coins are real!*"

"Of course they are real, Master-at-Arms; and the men of my Command are out in Bordeaux this minute enjoying themselves with coins from another chest just like this one, because they have earned it…and because I dashed them extra for their unfailing and unstinting efforts on their way here. For their loyalty and courage under fire, and their discipline. Because they have proven their value to me with their bravery and with their blood…and I honour them for that.

"I can give you the same rights and privileges as all my men!

"And there is no distinction here. It matters not to me whether you are English, Norman, Burgundian, French…or Welsh! What matters is that you always give of your best. That you keep your word, as I will keep mine. That you obey your officers, keep yourselves, your camp and your weapons clean; practise at the butts whenever you can…and fight like all the fiends in hell when I ask you to. Don't steal from the town…you will hang for that I promise you! Don't get drunk unless you have my orders to do so…or I will flog the backs off you, and don't abuse by force any ladies you may come across…or I will have your balls on a silver plate, cooked fresh with cream and garlic, and make you eat them!" And a sudden gale of laughter ran through them all, and he smiled at them for the first time, broadly and with warmth.

"But this is no bed of roses to which I lead you, lads. Many of my best men have been killed already, and three more so injured that they may never fight again. But all have been cared for and their families will not lack for the loss of their men. That is *my* way, Men of Gwent," he called out to them, giving them a proper title for the first time.

"Come with me now, willingly, and your rewards will be great. There will be fighting a plenty that you will *all* enjoy, or so the High Constable tells me!" and they laughed at that. "There will be towns to visit and money to spend on your pleasures," and they laughed even more at that too. "And there is a mighty castle to seize and sack at will, the treasures of which will be free to *all* my men!" And they roared out to that without restraint.

"Now, you '*Dynion Gwent*'…you 'Men of Gwent'," he called to them, giving them their new name again, his arms outstretched. "Now is your chance! Now is your time to show wisdom and honour and true Welsh pride in your heritage and your skill with the bow. *Now is your time to save this boy's life!*" He called out to them, pointing to where Willy Davies still stood on the pony's broad back.

"Now, my '*Dynion Gwent*'…my 'Men of Gwent', of Grosmont, Skenfrith and the Black Mountains," he roared at them a second time. "Now…come to order in the camp! *Stand and take muster!*"

And with a great shout that made the seabirds lift and scream all around them in a wild panic of wings and feathers, all three hundred and fifty Welshmen, and their women and children too, rushed forward and stood tall before him, bows raised and shaken in their hands, as they cried out "*He! He! He!*" the great traditional cry of a successful longbow archer, and: "*He! He! He!*" again, at the top of their voices, as they all saw Willy Davies brought safely back to join his father, a single great golden bezant clutched safely in his grubby hands.

Chapter 22...Sir Gui sets out for the Blue Pigeon and Castelnaudary.

No...it had not been easy, but ever since that morning the difference amongst his new command had been extraordinary, no little aided by a gift of silver to every man who could wield a bow with skill, for every child whose family could prove the child theirs...and silver as well to those with lesser skills, so everyone had something to rattle in his or her pocket, and everyone could tell their new Lord Baron's word was true.

And now as he watched them stream out before him, past the three great emblazoned standards of the knights saddled-up around him...the scarlet lion-rampant of Malwood; the black lion rampant-guardant of L'Eveque and the golden dragon of FitzMiles...all held by their squires in shining mail and glowing surcoats, he was filled with pride. Not in himself so much, that was not a part of his way, of his upbringing...but pride in his men, in his Command; in what they were as soldiers and in what they could accomplish. He set them an example he expected them to follow, and never asked of his men what he did not ask of himself. Which was why they followed him so bravely, so completely, and Sir Richard watching him smiled...for that was why he followed him too!

"So, Gui," he said as he watched their men pass out of the city in review before them all. "Where to now?"

"To Marmande first, to the '*Blue Pigeon*' where Sir Hugh has arranged rooms for us against our arrival tonight, then straight on down the route of the old Via Aquitania all the way to Toulouse, then Carcassonne and finally Narbonne. A week's hard travel will see us there, Richard. And we will travel hard, I promise you!"

*

And so they had!

Enjoying their first night out of Bordeaux at the '*Blue Pigeon*', the only *auberge* in Marmande, where the *aubergiste*, Claude Bonfils and his team of servers, had made them most welcome. And after a hard forty miles of travel that had tested man and beast almost to the limit they were ready for his fare, tossing down the fine ale his wife, Mignette, had brewed, and which her girls were delighted to carry round amongst the men, and doing stout justice to the mutton stew he had prepared for them against their coming, with suet dumplings, fresh baked bread, good cheese and fresh peaches from the trees around the old *auberge*, with its twisted oaken frame and wide doorway…and the ever present olives in oil, smoked meats and balsamic vinegar.

With so many men now in Gui's Command, it had taken the whole village to accommodate them and their carts and horses, and after forty miles of hard travel they had kept the blacksmith busier than he had been for months, for many shoes needed tightening, and the carts great wheels checking for weaknesses of boss, axle and iron tyre. And so many men meant many silver coins to be spent as well, so it was a rollicking evening as the men relaxed and joked, laughed and squabbled amongst each other…and their huge Welsh contingent set up their butts and practised their art, while the whole village came out to be amazed at what three hundred and fifty prime longbow archers could achieve when their hearts were truly in it!

Later, sitting in the main snug of the inn, with Richard, Father Matthew and John Fitzurse around him, Robert choosing to be with his men at that time, Gui sat back and let out a huge sigh of relief.

"And would you truly have hanged that boy, Gui?" Richard asked quietly, looking across at him over the rim of his wine beaker. "You took a huge risk!"

"Well, Robert told me he was a kind of talisman for the whole Company: a youngster whom all men had a kindness for, as much on account of his mother, who was adored by all, as for himself with his wide smile and friendly nature. A really likeable lad, young Willy Davies…and his ma. Tamsin Bacon was her name. Brought up on Sir William's estates, went with her man to the wars and was mother hen to all the girls who followed in his train. She died of a fever, poor lass, only a few weeks ago. Her son is a favourite with them all."

"Still, Gui," Sir Richard persisted in his slow drawl. "A huge gamble none the less, dear boy. That new Master-at-Arms was stood there just goggle-eyed at what he thought you were going to do. He almost passed out when that lad was released. And as for that parcel of sergeants? They were simply horrified! What would you have done if someone had owned up to the theft?"

"Mmmm," he pondered, looking inscrutable. "But, you see, they couldn't have done," he replied with a wicked smile. "There hadn't been a theft. I invented it. Anyway, the boy thought it was worth it!"

"*What?*" Richard exploded with amazement. "That whole ghastly 'thing' was a set up? Sweet Jesus, you fiend!" And they all laughed, rocking with the black humour of it.

"Gui and I talked it over," Father Matthew said in his soft Spanish lilt. "We needed an 'edge'. Something to force those idiots to think...and think hard! Hence the chest of silver coins, the young lad and the hangman's noose!"

"Picking on the most vulnerable member of their whole company, the one most liked and most innocent, was the best way possible of cracking them open," Gui replied. "Anyway, don't blame me. It was all our Master-at-Arm's idea, wasn't it John?" He added, with a smile. "All I did was carry it through, with a great cast of willing helpers!"

"But would you have hanged him, Gui, truly? If your final call to arms had not worked?"

"Yes! Certainly!"

"By God, Gui," Sir Richard said appalled, his voice almost a whisper. "I would not have thought you to be so cold-blooded that you would have had it in you to do so?"

"Well...only because I knew Fitzurse here had fixed the lad with a special harness!" He said nonchalantly with a wicked grin, while everyone gasped. "Why else do you think it took so much time to get him on to the back of that bloody pony! And why Hordle John chose a tree so distant from us all. What do you take me for?" He asked then, innocently. "A murderer!"

"*You bloody bugger!*" Richard roared out. "*You fucking bastard!*" and he banged his fist on the table making it jump.

"Well," Gui said rocking with laughter at Richard's appalled face. "Serves you right for that rotten sheep joke! Claude, you idle hound," he bellowed as all around him burst into laughter. "More of your very best at this table, my man. There are a few here who need reviving!"

*

They left Marmande at first light, with the day still grey about them and masked with an early mist that floated around both man and rider in opaque patches, the ground heavy with dew and the men thick with sleep and the fumes of the wine they had enjoyed the night before.

As always with Gui, he insisted that they start with just cold spring water and fresh bread. Convinced that what was good for the Romans was just as good for his Command on any day...especially when that day was going to be long and hard beneath a boiling sun. And he ordered all his sergeants to check that the men's water bottles were not filled with whole wine, but watered wine only, half-and-half, and that all water skins were exactly that…water only! Finally that there were enough buckets to go round, especially for their large Welsh contingent whose shaggy cobs would need plenty of watering if they were to complete the journey safely and well.

Born and bred for their hardiness, and their carrying ability, the tough little Welsh cobs were the ideal animal to carry the bowmen and their equipment, and capable of great endurance. Bright eyed and fast at the trot, intelligent and friendly natured, they were easily trained, loyal to their masters and handsome to look at. But in the heat of the southern French countryside they would need plenty of water to keep going and, as Gui had discovered after leaving Nantes, buckets were essential! He also made a mental note to insist that every beast was properly clipped before they left their next stopping point on their journey south to even warmer climes.

"So, gentlemen," Gui said as his officers mustered with him outside the inn that soft, pearly morning, the air still cool and fresh. "Marmande to Agen today; Agen to Montauban tomorrow and Montauban to Castelnaudary the day after if we can manage it. All very hard going as we discussed last night, but all 'do-able'…of that I am certain, even in these hot conditions."

"I still think you are pushing too hard, my Lord," Jean de Beaune said gruffly. "That's a hundred and forty miles in three days. Roughly fifty miles a day, give or take a few wrong turns. As I said at Nantes, Sir Gui…this is not England!"

Gui sighed. "Look, we have had this discussion already! You could walk fifty miles in a day…and we are all mounted. Indeed well mounted compared to some sorry jades we have passed on our way here," adding in response to the sucked in breaths of all those around him, "and it's not even sun up yet, about 'Lauds' as Father Matthew would say…and we have the whole day ahead of us!"

"But, my Lord…" Robert FitzMiles started to say

"But me no buts, Robert!" Gui said sharply. "If we travelled at just five miles an hour…the speed of a fast walker, we could cover the whole distance in less than two days…and we are mounted. It is just fifty miles from here to Agen, our first stop…" At which point he was interrupted by a flurry of complaints and objections, so that he had to hold his hands up to quell them. "I know! I know!" he acknowledged with another sigh. "We have tilt carts with us, wounded, ill-trained men and unfit Welsh ponies…and no-one can keep going for ten hours non-stop. I know that! But we are not seeking any place within the town…we just need to get there before sunset, and we will have the river beside us all the way so there will be no shortage of water."

"What about Toulouse?" Sir Richard asked, as the hubbub swiftly subsided.

"I want to give Toulouse as wide a birth as possible," Gui answered him grimly. "Count Raymond is no friend of King Richard's and is a known ally of that black-hearted bastard we all know and love so well, the Lord Baron, Sir Roger of Narbonne and Gruissan! I have no wish for a fast pigeon to reach the Baron with a true tally of our strength. So after Agen we shall stop at Montauban for the night…that's only forty miles or so, and then make a really early start…Matins rather than Lauds and after Saint Sauveur cut across the back of Toulouse, going to Gragnague to drop down on Castelnaudary from the north, from Revel…"

"Excellent move," Father Matthew interrupted in his rich voice. "That will confuse any enemy who might be expecting us to come from Toulouse. Your father would have been proud of you!"

"I do try, Matthew. I do try." And he smiled, pleased with the gentle accolade from his father's best friend.

"Isn't that going to be longer, my Lord?" William of Bergerac asked him, from beneath a furrowed brow.

"Mmmm, maybe, William. But Father Matthew knows this part of France better than any of us, so if he thinks it's a good move it must be 'do-able'. I do not want to tangle with the Count of Toulouse's forces if I can possibly avoid it, nor anyone else's either if I can help it! We have lost quite enough good men already as it is. And a serious tussle with one of King Philip's major allies, on the very eve of the Crusade, will do nothing for our friendship with our own Lord King. Right?"

"Right, my Lord!"

"Good! Thank God and Saint Michael for that! Now let's kick-on and get this lot on the move, sharpish. We have wasted enough 'chat' on all this to last several lifetimes, and it would be good to get a few miles under our belts before the sun really gets going!"

And while his sergeants and other command officers cantered up the ranks with shouted orders, and the air rang with the crack of whips, sharp whistles and blaring trumpet calls, Gui, with Sir Richard and Father Matthew by his side, swung his long-legged rouncey onto the dusty road, and with their standards carried before them they began the long walk-march to Castelnaudary and Narbonne.

Chapter 23...Sir Gui's men prepare the ground.

Castelnaudary.

A pretty little town perched on a steep hillside above the banks of the Fresquel River, a tributary of the River Aude. Established by the Romans as a simple staging post on the Toulouse-Narbonne road, it was less than a hundred years old on that bright late sunny afternoon that Gui and his men approached it from the north.

Crowned with its church and tall spire, that could be seen for miles, and surrounded by shops and houses, the town was enjoying its busy Wednesday market, now just closing, for which half the countryside seemed to have turned out in force. Hosts of cheerful marketeers busily wending their way home in merry, chatting droves and all amazed by the long column of dour, dog-weary mounted soldiers that pushed them to one side as they approached the town three days later.

Exhausted, dust covered and saddle sore, they dropped down on the town from the north just as the sun was sinking, the whole sky changing from cornflower blue to aquamarine as it began to settle for the night, filling with long rollers of gold and crimson cloud from the west, shot through with orange and scarlet. And a cool breeze had sprung up heralding a change in the weather, bringing with it a long fringe of dark cloud from below the horizon, making the dust at their horses' feet swirl and twist as they plodded forward.

It had been a very tough three days journeying, few stops and camping rough by the trackside at night: assaulted by biting insects, sweat running off them and covered in the fine dust of hard travel. But never had the men seen such a wild array of colours, nor experienced such heat either on that long haul south. Strange fruits were in abundance: bright yellow and green melons, succulent peaches you could pick off the trees and fat purple figs that hung in great clusters. At night the cicadas chirruped ceaselessly and bright fireflies lit up the trees and bushes like dancing fairies By day green and brown lizards scuttled across the road and shivered over the walls as they passed by, or disappeared with a flick of their tails the moment you tried to touch them.

But now they had arrived and were hungry for decent rations as Gui had kept them moving forward all the time, and was now stood with his officers around him, their horses' reins in their hands, while Father Matthew checked the wounded, and their squires rattled round the closing market for fresh fruit and pies.

"Tough going, my Lord," William Bergerac said, tearing a small roll apart with his teeth, a chunk of meat pie in his other hand. "And can't say I'm not ready for a break just now. 'Specially after those bloody Welshmen rode right by my lads with their drawing fingers thrusting and wagging out at them and their bloody '*He! He! Heing!*'...and all because one of my lads had fallen off his fucking nag trying to adjust a stirrup!

"Yes! I saw that," Sir Richard laughed. "But did you see the poor fellow's face as he realised he was going over and couldn't stop himself? Mouth wide open and his eyes up to heaven!"

"Nothing like a little inter-unit rivalry to bring this lot together," Fitzurse commented, stretching his massive shoulders.

"Just so it doesn't get out of hand, yes?" Gui chipped in, biting into a fresh peach taken from a basket of fruit that Simon and Philip had brought them all from the town. "Jokey insults can soon become real..."

"...And then there'll be bloodshed," Sir Robert finished for him, with a grin. "And my boys love a bit of bloodshed! By God these peaches are good, bach," he said to Gui, sounding very Welsh, the juice running down his chin. "Those two boyos of yours have done a great job. Where's my Thomas?" he said, looking round hopefully. "That lad's never where I want him!"

"Well," Jean de Beaune said, with a wicked grin. "No need to worry about bloodshed today, that's for certain. This lot are too knackered to do more than stay on their horses, let alone indulge themselves in bloody horseplay!" And they all laughed. "As for your Thomas, Sir Robert. Last time I saw him he was off for a leak...behind one of those bushes!" And they all laughed again as Sir Richard banged the little Welshman across his shoulders, making him splutter all over his peach.

"Right, gentlemen," Gui said spitting out his stone. "We stay here tonight as planned. We'll water the horses on the 'down' side of the town. I hear that the river above it is more dangerous, swifter currents or something and the river runs higher there as it flows down towards the Aude and the Circle Sea beyond. But I don't want us camped-up close beside it! If anyone attacked us, with the river at our backs, we would find ourselves in serious trouble. The river's too deep to ride across and too swift to try and swim it.

"Are you expecting trouble tonight then, Gui?" Father Matthew asked him, sharply, coming to join them.

"Mmmm. Just a feeling, Father! We have had no problems for a while now...and it's three days since we left Bordeaux. Plenty of time for de Brocas to cook up a little mischief, don't you think? And we are getting closer to our 'Tiger's' lair all the time. He won't attack us close to his own base, of that I am certain. That would be far too dangerous for him, and though the good

Baron may be many things, gentlemen, he is not foolish! If he allowed us to reach within a few scant miles of Gruissan before assaulting us, who knows who might come out and join us against him? No! If he's going to *do* anything, then it has to be soon. Now! Before we reach Carcassonne tomorrow and definitely before Narbonne...so, yes, I think so, and if I were he it would be at first light, tomorrow. So we need to be really vigilant."

"Got a feeling in your water, dear boy?" L'Eveque drawled lazily, his eyes watching Gui sharply.

"Well, something like that, Richard. I've been getting a bit twitchy now for the past two days, ever since leaving Agen. Remember how we were nearly bounced at Saint Jean? If it hadn't been for Allan's verderers we would have sleep-walked right into that ambush and been cut to shreds! Well, I feel the same now. And though we have nearly four times the number of men, we have never drilled together, nor fought together, and I don't want to be caught with our bloody knickers down for want of a little forward planning!

"Hence all the stuff we've been gathering along the way, my Lord...and the oil?" Fitzurse asked.

"Yes, John; a little ruse that Matthew, Robert and I think might work."

"So, my Lord?" William of Bergerac asked.

"So..." Gui said firmly, his eyes looking around him as he spoke. "We'll camp-up against the western edge of the town, over there," he pointed, where the ground fell quite sharply away towards the swirling water. "And not in that lovely curve of the river that looks so inviting. The ground is sloping away from us here, and any enemy will have to attack uphill and be back-lit by the afterglow, as they were at Saint Jean. We'll picket all the Welsh ponies up behind us, along with our destriers...and all the rest, the sumpters, Jupiter and the mares we'll put where you would expect to see horses in a campsite like this one. To the side and away from our sleeping quarters. And all must be walked down to the river for watering...not ridden!"

"But that's nearly a quarter mile, Gui!" Robert FitzMiles objected. "And we alone have over three hundred and fifty beasts to water!"

"Robert, you idle hound!" he said sharply, stabbing at him with his fingers: "Two things here, I think: one...we don't want those bastards to get the idea there are many more camped here than they expected, so no torn up ground from riding. And, two: what would happen, if your horse picket lines were close to the river and we were attacked tonight?"

"Oh, well, bach," FitzMiles replied in his soft Welsh voice, throwing up his arms with a grin as he spoke. "There would be bloody chaos I suppose! If the lads couldn't calm them those cobs would snap their lines, get horribly tangled and many would probably rush straight into the river..."

"…Especially in the darkness, with everyone screaming and shouting all about them," de Beaune chipped in darkly.

"And with the river running high and fast, many would drown!" Sir Richard ended, clapping the little Welsh knight across his shoulders. "And no-one wants that, dear boy! No-one! So…"

"So, my lads will walk their mounts down to the river as instructed," the little Welshman said with a rueful grin. "Quite like old times, boyo!" he added to Gui, bouncing in his saddle.

"Mmmm. Not quite, Robert," he replied doubtfully. "So just keep calm and no heroics! And no dashing out on the enemy without my signal. Yes?"

"Wouldn't dream of it," he replied with a cheeky grin. "Wouldn't dream of it!"

"Mmmm," Gui murmured again, looking at the young Welshman with his head on one side, and a quizzical look in his steel blue eyes. "It's when you look just like 'that', young Robert…like butter wouldn't melt in your mouth, my lad, that I most worry!"

"You leave him alone, you big bully!" Sir Richard said with a swift grin of approval, giving the Welshman a bang on his arm. "He's a good man, our Robert!" He added turning towards him. "Knew you were a 'right one', the moment I met you. Any man who fights with the point has to be!" And he gave Gui a nod and his lazy laugh as he spoke.

"How do you want the picket lines, Sir Gui?" Fitzurse asked him then.

"Twenty five beasts on each line, and evenly spaced, John. Every horse to be watered and curried before the men do anything else. Those poor jades have had a gruelling time of it and need some comfort. And I want every Welsh cob to be clipped out properly," he said turning to their leader.

"Robert, I cannot let them go another day without it, 'else this heat will kill them, poor beasts! Have your lads got the necessary equipment with them? Good! Those poor animals are suffering and we still have a distance to go. But, if you need any help just give a shout. Get Gareth Morgan onto it, and those sergeants of his.

"Allan, take Dickon Fletcher with you and pick out a hundred of the best bowmen that Robert has. They'll know who they are, Sir Robert will too, and bring them, together with the twenty five we had at Saint Jean, to my tent as soon as you can, as we discussed last night."

"What about rations, Gui?" Father Matthew asked as he watched the weary column moving down towards the distant river. "Those lads of ours have come a long way," he said gesturing to where the men were now trudging along, dismounted, beside their weary mounts.

"And if you want them to fight well tonight," Sir Richard chipped in, pointing to the long dusty lines of nodding men and horses. "They will need to have a damned good feed. An army with no scoff is no bloody good to man nor beast!"

"I know, Richard," Gui said wearily. "I know. I learned that from Sir Yvo too, years ago. So...Matthew, take a dozen men and scour the town for what you can find. It will have to be cold rations tonight, but fresh bread and cheese with some of the smoked meat these people always seem to have plenty of will be better than nothing, and whatever fresh fruit you can find. And I'll send those three squires of ours with Fitzurse and a small detail to find an alehouse and bring back some ale or wine casks. French ale is good, but their wine is better. Get some of that into our lads and they'll all feel like lions and tigers, and fight like demons! And no latrine trench tonight, we don't have the time. Each man to dig his own pit amongst the trees and bury his dung beneath the turf...I don't want to be treading in any one's shit in the dark, thank you!

"Now, gentlemen, bustle about. We have a host of things to do in preparation for tonight, and don't forget I want a good fire lit as well, with enough fuel to keep it going and some good old logs to sit on around it. Food and drink for everyone, and no-one to leave this encampment without my orders. So no hobnobbing with the locals tonight! And Robert?"

"Yes, Sir Gui?"

"No archery practice! I don't want any long-eyed spy to see what our lads are capable of. Don't want our secret weapon unmasked before time!"

"Secret weapon, eh Gui?" The little Welshman asked, surprised.

"Yes, Robert! The French don't use the longbow, remember? Don't know what it is and have never seen it in action. They have no idea just what a devastating weapon it is. They use the crossbow, because it is easier and raw recruits can be taught to use it quickly. They are idle fellows at war, the French! That's why we keep beating 'em. So, let your lads keep their 'sticks' on their backs for a change. But make sure every quiver is filled, Robert, and that every man has two spare sheaves of arrows by his side! Yes?"

"Yes, Sir Gui. Bach." The little knight said with a firm nod of his dark head. "It will be so, and I will make sure all my good sergeants know it too. My lads will not let you down. I promise you!"

"I never thought they would."

*

Hours later, sitting under the wide canvas of Gui's command tent in the centre of their encampment, with Richard and Robert FitzMiles beside him, and de Beaune, Bergerac and Allan-i-the-Wood close by…smoked meat, new baked rolls with honey glazed apricot tarts and fresh peaches firmly on the menu, all washed down with beakers of rich Bordeaux…Father Matthew turned with a cocked eyebrow and asked: "So, my son, you think it will be tonight?"

"Tonight?" Gui murmured absently at first, as he chewed, his eyes miles away. "Mmmm, actually, Matthew, yes, I do! As I said earlier, if Sir Roger is to make an attempt against us before we get any closer to Gruissan…and I thought it might have been sooner…then it has to be here, and it has to be now! The next stop is Carcassonne…and not even he would dare to risk any form of engagement near that great city. The Count of Toulouse would never support it, he controls everything around there…and a short step from there is Narbonne and Gruissan itself. So…here and now! As I said. That's why we bought all that vegetable oil in Revel."

"Your thinking is impregnable, my son," the tall Benedictine replied with a smile. "When?"

"I think they'll come just before first light, between midnight and Lauds, when everyone should be at their lowest, sentries dozing and all the camp asleep. And I think they'll come in force, expecting us to be picketed out along the river as Robert would have liked, because they will be over-confident, and stupid, and think we are just lazy, ignorant, English clods who know nothing!"

"Sounds as if they have spied us out already, dear boy!" Sir Richard chuckled, as he drank wine from a beaker. "God knows we look scruffy enough. Let's hope they do, and get over-confident! After all, the whole town knows we are here. Not only are there an awful lot of us, but our boys have been through the place for food and ale like a dose of hollyhock and spiderwort! You know what they're like."

"Hence supper tonight." William of Bergerac commented, waving a large honey and apricot tart in his big hand.

"Hence indeed, boyo," Robert FitzMiles replied thickly, apricot-honey juice running down his chin. "By God, these are good!" And there was a ripple of laughter.

"So…er…what is your plan, my Lord?" Allan-i-the-Wood asked him tentatively, and with a sense of intrigue all his other officers crowded round him to listen to what he had to say. And with their officers so engaged, the men came together too, so very quickly he had everyone's close attention.

"Well, we've planted our tents and shelters low down this slope, and what I want next is that each tented shelter should have a goodly supply of flammable material in it, dummies as well to fool our redeless friends, as we discussed last night. The lads will love doing something so unusual as making scarecrow soldiers out of straw, sticks and melons. They'll throw their hearts into it...and they'll be inventive as well! Then make sure everything is well soused in oil...the ground as well...and long before first light, just around Matins, midnight will do, we will all move to the very top of our encampment and lie down, about eighty yards from where we are now. Easy bow-shot range. All the Welsh cobs and a goodly section of our horses have already been safely picketed there, right at the back, and I want whatever spare canvas we have left to be strung out like a screen to hide them all as much as possible...The rest to be picketed where you might expect them to be, at the extreme edges of our encampment, like the wings of a bird, angled out on either side. Bit like a funnel, with the camp in the centre."

"You don't think they know how many men we really have, do you my Lord?" William of Bergerac asked.

"No, William! I don't think they have a damned clue. We virtually wiped out their last lot! So they probably think we are now down to the very scrapings of our own barrel, not dreaming that we might have got any reinforcement along the way...which, to be fair, I didn't expect to find either. I bet they think that one more good push will see us off the map for good!"

"What about the town? If they have scouts out, and I've seen a few distant horsemen, won't they know our numbers?" de Beaune asked quietly.

"Townies are always hopelessly unreliable when it comes to numbers and soldiers. They may realise we are a goodly few, but we haven't allowed anyone near enough to make a count, so they won't know exactly how many we are...and they won't know what kind of troops we have either, especially as I have banned any archery practice tonight. It does not worry me."

"So...how do you plan to make this work in our favour, my Lord?" the young Under-Sheriff asked quietly.

"We trap the entrappers!" Father Matthew said, softly.

"That's right, Father!" Gui replied instantly, turning to the tall Spaniard with a grin. "I keep forgetting that you are as fine a strategist as my father was. Yes!" He exclaimed brightly. "They will see what they expect to see: tents, shelters, sleeping soldiers, dozy guards, long horse picket lines, a dying fire and a few big tilt carts...we'll hide the rest...and we will lure them up this slope by the very normality of what they can see. Let them spot some men moving about between the fire down there and these shelters. Not too many, John," he said, turning to his Master-at-Arms.

"Just enough for them to think we are still alive and kicking and not taking any care. And we'll let them come charging up amongst us, roaring and shouting, right up amongst the tents and amongst the dummies and the scarecrow guards leaning on their long spears. Then," he went on turning to Robert and Allan-i-the-Wood. "When they discover they have been fooled, and have stopped shouting and have started to mill about in confusion…then, on my order…*and on my order alone!*" he emphasised most strongly, looking each man in the face as he spoke. "No man to move until I say so! *Yes?*"

"Yes, my Lord," came the softly growled agreement from all those around him.

"Good! Then I want those bowmen we are choosing now to loose fire arrows into every tent and shelter and to set the whole slope aflame. All those men attacking will then be brilliantly backlit. At which, Robert," he added, turning to young FitzMiles sitting intently by his side, "on my trumpet call…a single long blast!...I want the remainder of your lads to leap up and give that whole screaming mob of mercenaries two massive twelve arrow volleys from both sides of this slope. Young William Bell will then blow the same call he did at Saint Jean, our flags will rush forward, we will all rise to the attack…and we will unleash hell upon them all. Your boys, Robert, are to drop their bows where they stand and just wade in with the rest of our men…and together we'll wipe those bastards out! *No survivors! No quarter!*" he said fiercely. "I want the whole miserable scaff-raff of them slain!"

"All of them, Gui?" Richard asked, slightly awed.

"Yes, Richard. *Every last one of the fucking bastards!* Then no burials, simply strip them raw of all their own gear. I want their armour and weapons, then dress them in some of our kit instead…and fling the whole poxy lot of them straight into the river, food for the bloody fishes, along with everything else they brought with them that the lads don't fancy."

"Spoils of war, Sir Gui?" De Beaune asked

"Absolutely, 'spoils of war', Jean. The lads have earned 'em! Except their horses. Those that are not slain, we will bring with us; the rest we'll burn, save a few for the butchers as free meat for the good people of Castelnaudary," he said, sitting back and brushing the palms of his hands vigorously together. "And that will bloody well be that!"

And for just a moment there was complete silence, as every man there thought of what Gui had just said: how his orders would affect each one of them….and how best they could carry them out.

"Phew! Good plan," Sir Richard said at last, the air whistling over his teeth. "Good plan! Short and bloody. They won't know what's hit them! And no quarter! That's brutal, Gui," and he shook his head, amazed at the young knight's utter determination, and his clarity of thought.

"So, young Gui?" Father Matthew questioned in his warm Spanish lilt, his eyes alight with approval. "When the bodies wash up down river, probably near Carcassonne, anyone whom the Baron will have instructed to keep an eye out for us, and finding them in our surcoats, will think they are 'us'…yes?"

"Yes, Father…exactly so," the young Lord Baron of Malwood replied eagerly. "And," he added, putting his hands together and bowing his head over them, his eyes sparkling. "You can say a swift prayer for their rotten souls as we tip them in."

The tall Benedictine bowed his head to his young leader and smiled. "Sir Yvo would have been very proud of you, dear boy. Very proud!" And he clapped his hands, the other commanders energetically following suit, to the sudden wild cheers of their men.

"Right, gentlemen," Gui said tersely, "That's it then. Pass the word around. And Robert…Allan, those bowmen to me as soon as you can. Yes? Good! Now let's to it, and let's do a proper job on these frog-eating bastards that the bloody Baron never will forget!

Chapter 24...Sir Jules de Saint Sauveur plots the Lion's downfall

Sir Jules de Saint Sauveur was a lean man of medium height, broad shouldered and strong of limb; dark haired with a hard face marked with a fine scar that ran down the right side of it, deep brown eyes and an engaging smile when he chose to use it, which was not then!

For two days he had been gathering his men together, drawing them in from all round Carcassonne to his home base at Bram, a small village just a few miles west of the great walled city, and not much further from Castelnaudary, so ideal for collecting together the troops he would need for the ambush that the Baron had engaged him to mount. And all without attracting the interest of the city's Governor, a lackey of King Philip's and Count Raymond of Toulouse, whose long nose was definitely not wanted anywhere near the Baron's scheme!

Over two hundred men had already come in to his quiet call to arms, with more to follow. Serious fighters every one: experienced, hardened killers as good with knife and garrotte as they were with sword or battleaxe. Well mounted and all wearing some kind of protective armour: boiled leather, shirts of mail, overlapping scales on leather with mail chausses, hauberks of chain and studded iron, all were mercenaries paid to do the job, and paid well. The Baron had proven to be a good paymaster to these men who had fought with Saint Sauveur before, and were always paid extra for a job well done...*But where the fuck are the enemy I've been recruited to sort out?*

Having gathered as many together as he could, he had then moved his whole Command to the little village of L'Espitalet, about four miles to the east of Castelnaudary, to the *auberge, 'Le Cheval Blanc'*...The White Horse...where the *aubergiste*, an old friend of medium stature, but great girth and wreathed in smiles, *Monsieur Le Rue*, and his petite wife, Annette, held cheerful sway. Taking his great money chest with him, his armour on a sumpter and mounted on his magnificent chestnut charger, 'Hercules', he had arrived in easy expectation of swift action...*mais rien!*...but nothing!

Not only could he not find the enemy, but his friend Neel Chambertin at Toulouse had seen neither hide nor hair of them either! Charged by the Baron to keep a sharp look out as their enemy passed by the city on the old Via Aquitania, and to keep him, Jules, equally well informed...he had seen nothing.

The whole company, all seventy or eighty of them, plus tilt carts according to the Baron's orders, seemed simply to have disappeared into thin air, which was infuriating enough as his men were keyed up and ready for a fight. But doubly so as he had already been paid a lump sum for the job…*and I am paying these lads by the day out of it!* So the longer the enemy could not be found, the less there would be for him when it was all over!...*So…where the fuck are they?*

He had sent scouts out all around Castelnaudary, but especially towards Toulouse from where he had been expecting news of his enemy's advance all day, and the next…but still nothing! *And until I have some idea of where those foreign bastards are, there isn't much I can do except wait - and I hate waiting!*...Something Sir Jules de Saint Sauveur did not do very well. But he did know the ground on which he would have to fight; had reconnoitred it, seen where the English picket lines should be beside the river; where he would hide his horsemen and where he would attack, and had placed men on watch to keep him informed.

He had his plan, which was simple but effective: assault before first light, straight up the middle, mostly on foot, but with the powerful back-up of sixty of his best men mounted on strong horses, easily sufficient to overpower the English knight's command by *force majeure* and drive them into the river...*Then mop up any who might have escaped into the town, or elsewhere…and no quarter!*...The Baron wasn't interested in prisoners, and neither was he…So, with the violent bit over they would divide up the spoils, knock off the wounded, toss the bodies in the river, as he had been instructed, and then back to the *auberge* to pay off Le Rue and the lads…A*nd back home for a late lunch in Bram and delicious dalliance with my adored Lady Thalia in our huge bed overlooking the gardens. All over by sunrise…Lovely!*...Love in the afternoon after a bloody skirmish…just what he needed…*A bloody fight always leaves me pumped-up and ready for a lively 'joust'!*

Always had done. There was nothing like sorting out Thalia's yearnings with a good bout of solid fucking! Lovely!...*I might even have time to play with the children…little Julia, with her golden hair and her mother's big blue eyes and his son, Bevis, dark haired like himself and ready for his first pony*….One of each, and much loved by both their parents.

But first this commission from Lord Roger.

And he sighed. Let this be the last one…he was a good soldier, a damned good soldier. But much more of this and he might yet end his days before time. And that didn't suit. Not at all. Ever since Thalia had entered his life, and the children had come, he had been seeking better employment…*It's just that the old bugger pays so bloody well!*

He sighed again.

Just get this one over, and he would definitely seek something better…*Meanwhile, where are the fucking bastards?*...And he was just about to go out and kick one of his Sergeants into urgent life, when at last a messenger came flying in on a lathered horse, swung himself out of his saddle and reported: "Found them, Sir Jules!" he rapped out, saluting with his fist, his armoured tunic dark with sweat. "Coming in from the north….

"…From the north, you say?" Saint Sauveur interrupted, sharply, his eyes glittering with interest.

"Yes, Sir Jules, from Revel. Bone weary and covered in dust…hundreds of the buggers!"

"Hundreds of them? From Revel? Can't be the lot we want, you idiot! The Lord Roger was quite clear: 'Expect about seventy or eighty, all mounted, with a couple of carts, coming from Toulouse!' André le Boeuf isn't it? God help me, beef by name and beef in the bloody head as well! Hundreds of them, indeed! You fucking moron! See to your nag and then go and get something to drink, while I think about this one!"

"Yes, Sir Jules," the man answered with a quiet smile, knowing his Lord's humour and saluting again as he did so before turning to leave.

"Wait, le Boeuf! Were you seen? Did any of those bastards you observed, observe you?"

"No, Sir Jules! Absolutely not! I didn't need to linger, and I was a goodly way off. But you could see their dust before you could see them. Didn't wait to see their scouts…it was enough I thought to report at once that the enemy had been sighted, and in great force."

"How many do you think there are, André?"

"Don't rightly know, Sir Jules. Hundreds of 'em. Column must stretch a mile, and they have many carts with them too. You can see their metal twinkling.

"That's a fucking useless report, you oaf!" he growled over his shoulder. "What can I gain from that? I am told to beware eighty men coming from Toulouse to the west! You give me 'hundreds of the buggers' coming from the north!" Go and feed your face, André, and send Sir Pierre Dumas to me. This is a puzzle!"

*

But as the day wore on, so more reports came in of a long column of mounted men, led by three knights, coming down from the north, with at least eight carts. One whole contingent of whom were smallish, dark haired men, mounted on ponies with sticks across their backs!

"Small men with sticks on their backs, and riding ponies?" Saint Sauveur sneered to his fellow commander, Sir Pierre Dumas, a tall, smiling Burgundian with pale blue eyes, a fine breadth of shoulder and white blond hair. "Is that the best this foolish English Lord can bring against us? Sticks and ponies? If these are our quarry, what on earth are they playing at?"

"Quarter staffs!"

"*Quarter staffs?*" Jules burst out with a shouted laugh. "Are you mad?"

"No, Jules! Not me, *mon brave*...the sacred blood fucking English! Those sticks will be quarterstaffs. They are noted for their skills with them, and of course they are mad! They are the bloody English! Who can understand them? What else can you expect from such barbarians?

"Sticks and ponies, indeed! *Mon Dieu, Pierre!* You might as well send children to fight as small men with sticks on ponies! *Bah!* We will eat them tonight."

"So…we attack no matter what?"

"Of course, my fine armoured friend. What did you think? These fellows *must* be the ones the Lord Roger means for us. Though from where they have found extra troops, God alone knows. They are the only forces on the move anywhere between us and Carcassonne, so it must be him, Sir Gui de Malwood, as the Baron advised us. Nothing else makes any sense!"

"But the ones we want are coming from Toulouse, Jules…from the west. These are from Revel, from the north. How can you be so sure?"

"Because Neel Chambertin has seen nothing of anything either! No soldiers, no horsemen, no carts…*nothing!*" he exclaimed raising his arms in exasperation. "I think this English knight has been very clever. He has bypassed Toulouse and come right round behind the city to avoid the Count. So…he comes to us from the north. But he knows nothing of us, Pierre! *Rien!*"

"…So," Pierre interrupted excitedly, "We take them just before dawn. Just as you have planned. You from both sides, and my horsemen straight up the middle after the camp has been overrun. Yes?"

"No, my big friend," Sir Jules said getting up with a smile, wine beaker in hand. "We hit them earlier. *Just after Matins and before Lauds!* As the darkness turns to grey, when all are at their lowest, before the first bird makes its song or the cock crows for the morning. When all those little dark haired men are fast asleep snuggled up to their bloody sticks! Then we shall see who can land the fiercest blows, young Pierre. Then we shall see!"

And putting his wine down he strode to the door and shouted: "Le Boeuf! Go now and bring me Sergeant Le Croix from your company, and all the other Company officers. Meeting in ten minutes in the bar. Council of war, Pierre," he said tersely to his tall friend, shaking his fist. "This fucking bastard has wriggled out from under two of Lord Roger's ambushes...he isn't wriggling out from under mine. Not this time...*not ever!*"

Chapter 25...Sir Gui plants his ambush.

Outside on the hillside above the river, below the edges of the town, as real darkness finally settled around them on that breezy August night, Gui and his men had made their preparations and now lay waiting.

Below them in the gloaming were the tents and shelters of their encampment now filled with dry kindling gathered from the woods around them; dummies made up of long bundles of straw gathered from the great harvest fields they had passed along their way, neatly tied in with cord used for binding sheaves of wheat, and all bought from Revel where they had found the oil they needed.

Some were placed lying down and covered with rough blankets, some sitting and some standing as guards with long bean poles for spears...and all soaked in the oil bought in Revel especially for the purpose. With heads made of melons, some with helmets on them, and arms and legs from sticks cut from the surrounding woodlands and all suitably dressed, from a distance, and in the semi-darkness of the early morning, they would looked truly realistic

The men had worked hard and with imagination...and much laughter.

Nothing professional, nothing special...but back lit by the fire his troops had built in the middle of the camp site, it would all look real enough to men sneaking up from the river and from the road half a mile away. On horseback, or on foot, they would see what they would expect to see: a peaceful camp, men seated, men leaning on their spears, men asleep and the whole sparsely guarded in such gentle countryside, with horses quietly cropping in their picket lines, or even lying down!

But, at the top of the slope, some eighty paces away, Gui had drawn up his command together, his hand-chosen bowmen, a hundred longbow archers from the Forest, from Castle Malwood and from the Black Mountains of Gwent in one group in the centre, a dozen broad head arrows apiece, each iron head with a bundle of cotton rags tied around it, dipped in oil, with a fire pot beside each man from which to light it and another soldier close by to hold it.

In front of them Gui had placed Bergerac's lancers, where their nine foot weapons would make a perfect fence of sharpened steel that no horse would dare leap upon, and where each man could shelter behind his great kite shield like an armoured rock upon which any enemy mounted horse would founder. And on either wing, above the picket lines, in two blocks of a hundred and twenty five man apiece, would stand the remainder of his Men of Gwent, bows in hand...their bow cases, the 'sticks' Saint Sauveur's scouts had sighted, behind them in the long grass that bordered the camp on every side. Each man with his chosen personal weapon by his side, and two dozen bodkins for each archer already thrust into the ground, waiting. This time every man had paced the distance, fired a few flighting arrows to check the pull of his bow, the angle of fire needed and the drift of his arrow in the breeze now blowing off the river…two flights of arrows they would fire, then down bows and at 'em with sword, dagger and the leaden maul each archer carried.

And in between his blocks of archers Gui had placed his heavy foot: his own Lions led by his giant Master-at-Arms and Hordle John, 'heater' shields on their left arms, and the Bashley twins closed by. All carried sword, mace or battleaxe and were joined by Bergerac's spearmen, with their lethal gisarmes, a wicked bill with a deep hook and a chopping axe on its back mounted on a thick six foot pike. And those men whom Sir Hugh had given to Gui, those 'half and halfers' they had laughed about in Bordeaux, were also stood stoutly ready beside them, similarly armed with mace, axe or sword, their big kite shields on their backs, or on their left arms, depending on what kind of weapon each man felt would suit him best.

And Gui, Sir Richard L'Eveque and Sir Robert FitzMiles were there too, of course, all clad in their full mail armour, glittering in the firelight, over quilted gambeson and leather. Thick chain mail to below the knees over chain mail leggings on supple leather chausses, the main coat of shimmering linked steel split to the waist for movement, the edges bound with tough leather. With reinforced mail on their back and chests, topped with shoulder and back plates of thick leather boiled in oil and hammered into shape, they were daunting figures indeed. All wore mail mittens on their hands with thick suede palms and finger covers, mailed sabatons on their feet, and by their sides their great helms of plated steel, well-padded with straw and fleece so they would not easily twist awry in battle, and held with a leather chinstrap. And over all the long cyclas, with each warrior's blazon glowingly stitched upon it: Lion Gules and Lion Sable, with the great golden dragon of Sir Robert FitzMiles between them.

Their squires, too, stood ready. Having dressed and armed their knights first, they then armed themselves with long sleeved mail coats over quilted gambesons, like their knights, but wore mailed chausses and long boots, leather gauntlets strengthened with small metal plates along their fingers, and conical helms with a strong nasal bar to split each open face, short surcoats bearing their knight's blazon over their armour…and all three stood by the furled colours of their knights that they would uncover and defend with their lives once the fighting started.

*

Earlier, all through the camp, Gui's men had readied themselves for the fight they knew they would soon have to face. Testing bow strings, flexing muscles, shaking arms to keep them supple, flensing the air with their weapons, cracking jokes and boasting of the deeds they would perform and the enemies they would slay…and queuing for their blades to be sharpened on the great stone wheel brought from England, the screeching noise and flashing sparks going on long after dusk had fallen. While Gui and his sergeants, with Richard L'Eveque and Sir Robert, moved quietly amongst them: a word here, a joke there, a bang on the shoulder, a punch on the arm. That 'little touch of Harry in the night!'

Unlike Saint Jean, here the men had had time to prepare, time to talk and jest and share a tale, to drink their wine and gnaw the rolls and chunks of smoked meat that had been put aside for them earlier…and relieve themselves amongst the trees and bushes of the camp; all waiting for Gui's order to take up their places and await their enemy's arrival on the battlefield, while Father Matthew moved amongst them with blessings and the promise of eternal life for all who might need that comfort before the fight.

Meanwhile word of their enemies had reached the tall Spanish Benedictine from the priest in Castelnaudary. A timid friar who had crept down to find him, alerted by others that there was a Black Monk amongst the soldiers who had swept through the town for food…to tell him that a large body of armed men were occupying the village of L'Espitalet, just four or five miles away, having suddenly arrived there two days before. No, he didn't know where they had come from. But they were led by two knights…one big, always smiling, lots of white blond hair, Burgundian by his speech; one smaller. Hard man, a big scar down his face. How many men? Oh lots of men, hundreds he had heard, and lots of horses. All grown men. No youngsters. Tough-looking and well-armed! No…no-one had seen men like them before…and he had then scuttled off, too scared of his own shadow to stay and eat with them.

"I think I might know that big Burgundian," De Beaune said later, when Father Matthew had reported what the little priest had said, all seated round the fire on great logs dragged there for the purpose, horn beakers of best Bordeaux in their hands.

"Chap called Pierre Dumas. Not bright, but a fierce fighter. Like me, he was knighted by the Duke of Burgundy himself for services to his family.

Superb horseman, never gives in and always smiling...a complete bastard, but as brave as a lion."

"You do mix with interesting company, dear boy," Sir Richard drawled at him with his lazy smile. "First those scoundrels at Nantes...now this big bugger from Burgundy. What about his chum, the chappie with the scar?"

"Well...actually, yes, Sir Richard," de Beaune said with a rueful grin. "If the big chap is Pierre Dumas, then the other one will be Sir Jules de Saint Sauveur for certain! You never find one without the other nearby...they are very much David and Jonathan when it comes to a fight like this is likely to be. Sir Jules will be the leader. Experienced but impulsive, and inflexible once he has made up his mind. Nothing will deter him from carrying out his orders, and he is quick on his feet with sword or battle axe. Ferocious swordsman. He's a good man, Sir Jules, married to a real gem and has two little ones he dotes on, so I have heard."

"You have heard a lot, young Jean," Sir Richard drawled lazily.

"In my trade, who you work for can depend on what you hear! He and I are both mercenaries. And I would far rather have Jules de Saint Sauveur on my side than against me. He fights like a demon, and draws good men to him like bees to a honey-pot. Shame he is working for so rotten an employer. The Baron has chosen his men well."

"But not well enough to beat us tonight, gentlemen," Gui said sharply, shuffling his big shoulders under their weight of metal. "If Robert's lads do their stuff, I doubt we will even get to draw steel!"

"Don't count your chickens 'til they are hatched, Gui," Father Matthew cautioned from the darkness. "And don't underestimate your enemy! I am off to check those fire pots for the lads you've chosen for that first flight of arrows, and then set up my dressing station. The weather is changing," he said, looking up at the darkening sky. "There is a fresh breeze and I sense rain. Now that could make life interesting, don't you think?" And with a chuckle he strode away into the darkness, his black robe flapping around his legs.

"That bloody priest," Gui groaned, ruffling his head where his helm had pressed down on it earlier when his squire had first armed him, while the others laughed. "Counting chickens, and then rain! I ask you? What more do I have to do to make this campaign work? Rain?...that's the last thing we need tonight. I need those tents to burn, and burn well...and the ground. A bloody great douche of heavenly water all over our heads is the last thing I need! *Fitzurse!*" he called out. "*To me!* and bring those two Bashleys with you. There's a job to do! And young William Bell, you too, you idle bugger, and bring that bloody horn of yours with you. You never know when you might need it!"...*Pray God the fucking rain goes elsewhere*...he thought, looking up with a frown into the clouded sky...*Or else we could find ourselves in real trouble. Shit...but that would be all we need to turn this bloody skirmish into a right bloody shambles!...*And he stalked away to find his squire and check his men yet again.

*

Four miles away in L'Espitalet Sir Jules and Pierre Dumas mustered their forces: three hundred and sixty men armoured-up and spoiling for a fight. All mounted on good rounceys, strong in work with well-muscled quarters, except the two knights who had real destriers between their legs, beautifully bred chargers: rich chestnut with white fetlocks, and dark bay with a white diamond blaze on his forehead, feet stamping and snorting with excitement.

Three hundred men to attack on foot with sword and mace and fighting spear, led by their sergeants and Sir Jules de Saint Sauveur; sixty mounted with lance and shield in support, led by Sir Pierre Dumas on his dark bay charger, now pawing the ground with his great iron shod feet. And with the moon now sliding down a cloud-pocked sky, they clattered out of the village and onto the long highroad beyond, the church of Castelnaudary on its hill a dark silhouette in the far distance as it thrust its tall spire into the sky. Above them Diana's silver light was masked by increasing wracks of cloud as a wind blew up and veered into the north-west, bending the trees and grasses that lined the road.

They were a long armoured column of well-mounted, excited men hell-bent on making serious mischief, weapons by their side, shields on their backs...and right at the back on a long-legged sumpter, strapped across the cruck that would normally hold big panniers, a small cage of fluttering pigeons.

"Are you clear with the plan, Pierre?" Sir Jules asked at the head of the column.

"Yes! I hold my lads back 'til I see your men going forward strongly and Raoul blows his horn. Three short blasts and we'll dig in our heels and come thundering through. Just make sure none of your fucking bastards are in the way, because they will just get mown down. Once we go, we go *à l'outrance!* To the death! No hesitation and no stopping, Jules. So just makes sure your lads know what they are doing. Do you know where they are?"

"The enemy? Yes! Word came in two hours ago that they are encamped below the town, close beside the river some distance off the Bordeaux road…right where we thought they would be! And there are quite a lot of them…"

"How many?" the big knight asked. "And what kind of men are we facing?"

"No idea! No-one could tell me more than they are 'soldiers'. Useless bloody townies. No-one knows how many there are down there, nor whether they have mounted armour, bows, spears or fucking sticks! Honest to God, Pierre, fucking useless! But certainly nothing we can't handle.

"Sticks and ponies! Jesus, Pierre, Who do they think we are?" And he spat onto the rough trackway with disgust. "Still, at least we know where they are camped and we have plenty of time…especially as I don't want to get there before the moon sets," he continued, looking up at where it rode the heavens the clouds fleeting across its face making it look as if it too was swiftly moving.

"We'll de-horse from the road beyond the town, picket the beasts, including my Hercules," he said reaching down to pat his destrier's enormous withers and gently pull his ears. "And then move forward on foot. De Nostre will lead the far company right round from the road to come up to them from amongst the trees nearest the river, with Danvier and Lécamp. Le Blanc, Varennes and myself will lead the other company nearest the road, and you and your lads can pad their nags up behind us, and then pull them right back amongst the trees where they can remain hidden for as long as possible. When we are near enough, we will advance together at the charge, roaring like tigers and fighting mad! We'll take the flanks, and push the poor bastards into the centre, where you'll come up and chop the whole fucking mass of them in pieces! As I said, 'job done and over by sunrise.'"

"And then?"

"Then we loot the buggers, and dish-up their wounded. No quarter remember? The Baron wants no-one left to tell a tale…so into the river with them afterwards, take their horses with us for sale as a bonus, send the Baron his bloody message, and then shog off home for lunch! What do you want, Pierre? A bloody victory parade?

"No you ass!" He laughed. "Just wanted to know what had you in mind afterwards…apart from the fair and beautiful Lady Thalia?"

"Seriously, Pierre, I'll send Lord Roger word of what we have done, immediately, you know what he's like!...*A real bloody bastard I wouldn't trust if I could help it...*Then we'll get rid of the bodies and sort the loot; then back to the 'White Horse', pay off the lads, and Le Rue, and then bugger off. What about you?"

"Off back to Burgundy for a spell," the big blond knight said, swinging his arms round to settle his armour more comfortably. "The Duke's made me an offer of employment I can't afford to pass over. He wants my sword for some local problem he's got, and it comes with good promotion and a manor on his estates. The old buzzard must have missed my cheerful face after all," and they both laughed. "Then again Rosa wants to settle down, Jules, and this lark is getting too bloody dangerous by far! I know the Baron pays well, but there's no proper bonus and no retainer. You really ought to find a better employer too. So, this will probably be our last skirmish together. I've been meaning to tell you for a while..."

"...But somehow, one never seems to find the right time to do so." Sir Jules finished for him, his big chestnut plodding steadily along the moonlit trackway. "Well, this lot should be a piece of apple pie!" he exclaimed brightly, with a warm smile. "All we have to do is what we have been paid for and we'll live to fight another day. You with the Lady Rosa, and me with my Thalia. So...when this is all over we'll sort out the bloody mess, and then off we go, as swiftly as a fox stealing chickens, and as quietly! I do not want to be around when Raymond of Toulouse finds out what we have done on his doorstep. Yes? Let de Brocas sort him out. He's his ally, not ours. We are in this strictly for the money and a good fight! And as long as our boys don't loot the fucking town as well, we should be alright. Not much chance of a good life in one of Raymond's bloody dungeons waiting for his headsman to do his stuff!" And they both laughed again, hands on their armoured hips as they swayed to their horses' long stride while their long column walk-marched towards Castelnaudary along the moon's bright silver highway.

Chapter 26...The Battle of Castelnaudary.

Meanwhile Gui and his men lay waiting in their chosen places on the sun-dried ground, weapons to hand, while darkness settled on the little town and on all the countryside around them, and the moon rose brilliantly into a star-spangled sky.

Diana, the Huntress, goddess of the moon, shining brightly down in all her silver glory, cast everything in sharp relief, in bars of black and white, her great beauty marred by cloud streamers across her face as the wind flared up, then down again, veering into the north-west, as she rode across the heavens in her silver chariot.

And as the wind tugged playfully at the tent ropes and canvas sheeting, and rustled through the trees and bushes all around them, so her bright light flickered across the camp site, making a host of shadows dance and flutter. But it also made the fire the men had built earlier roar up fiercely, sending great swirling columns of sparks spiralling up into the night sky like a million fireflies, twisting and spinning up into the moon-wracked darkness as the clouds raced by: the whole hillside awash with searing white light one moment, then just as swiftly plunged into inky blackness the next.

It was a true hunter's moon, full and brilliant...but no-one came!

And as the night slowly passed and the moon finally set, so the clouds grew heavier overhead, masking the stars and closing down the light. The wind soughed across the river, bending the tree tops, swaying the reeds and rushes, wafting the scent of passing summer over the faces of the men lying flat at the top of the slope.

Below them their tents and shelters were still lit by the flames of the great fire that had been kept fed all night, now dying down to a huge mound of embers that glowed and pulsed with sudden life as the wind blew through them. And as the last logs were thrown onto it, each one threw out a violent spurt of blue and crimson flame, a volcanic burst of sparks that danced and whirled and spiralled upwards until they vanished into the rushing darkness of the night.

And still they waited, with bated breath and hearts a-glow, ready for action...and still no-one came!

In each tent men could be seen seated, or lying down, while others stood at gaze on sentry duty, tall spears by their sides, while up by the horse picket-lines at either wing of the encampment others moved forward and back again, flickering shadows against the ruddy firelight that glinted across their armour and their faces as they turned, their bodies showing as brief silhouettes each time they moved…and there was the soft murmur of voices and the occasional shout of song or laughter.

And still no enemies eeled their way towards them through the distant trees beside the river, nor came on silent feet across the harsh pasture on which their campsite had been built...and still Gui's men waited at the top of the slope, dozed and woke again, fretted and eased their arms and shoulders, and flexed their toes as the long hours passed slowly by in uneventful, tense succession…and still no-one came.

Then, at the turn of the night, when all around was silent save for the wind's sigh amongst the leaves and grasses, the crake of a moorhen from the reeds along the river bank, the bark of a deer from a nearby wood, the distant howl of a lonely guard-dog away across the sleeping countryside…when all was still and all were sleeping, before the first bird awoke to make its song, or the first cock crowed for the new-born day…the enemy came at last.

Flitting like shifting shadows and wraiths of darkness through the trees that lined the river and the road side they came on silent feet, no chime of mail, no flash of light off their blackened armour. Running and pausing, running and pausing, through the coppice that lay beyond the camp's rough boundaries of bush and briar and tangled woods, weapons free, shields on their arms they came in a silent rush...and all their hearts and minds were fixed upon the slaughter of those they'd caught sleeping in their tents and shelters on the hillside just above.

Swiftly they gathered in great pools of darkness beyond the fire, now only a vast pile of glowing embers, a hundred and fifty men on each side, led by their sergeants and by a belted knight in full chain and leather plated armour, his great fighting helm on his head, a shield on his arm and a sword in his hand. And behind them, amongst the deepest shadows, hard against the trees that edged the whole encampment, a host of mounted men, on shuffling mounts with hides of bay and sable, had silently appeared with shocking suddenness and speed…and all now waited to attack with sword and lance and battle-axe, their faces masked with steel, their armour black and dented with hard use, and all had bloody violence in their hearts.

*

Lying above them in deep silence, Gui and his men had seen them come, a whisper of warning sighing round the ranks of hidden men, all lying flat as they had been ordered, all desperate to look and see, to know what was going forward as they heard the soft thud of hooves on the thick turfy ground, the rattle of a bridle, the snort of a horse, the urge to stand unbearable as each man stiffened his muscles or bunched his thighs in readiness to spring up from the ground and fight. But Gui would not release them, and their sergeants kept them down, as he and Sir Richard, with Gui's young trumpeter by his side, watched with blank, armoured faces as their enemies silently gathered below them.

*

Just beyond the close confines of the camp, Sir Jules de Saint Sauveur readied his men.

Straining his eyes in the fell darkness to see where de Nostre was with his Company, now running up from the river to bunch below the horse lines, he saw where several sentries stood at gaze, their heads drooped on their arms, while dozens of others lazed asleep in their shelters, and he laughed quietly with his men, flacking his right hand at the simplicity of the stupid, bloody English, who thought they could fight his veteran mercenaries with fucking sticks and ponies!

And looking across the wide hillside, he raised his sword high and then slowly waved it round his head. A second time he waved it, its blade just glinting in the firelight, and on the third time he gave a great roar of challenge that shattered the stillness of the night and with his sword he swept his men raging up the slope before them. All baying like hounds at the chase, they fell upon the camp and flensed it with every bit of furious energy they had. Snarling and howling like wild beasts as they came, their faces twisted with feral rage as they shouted out their war cries, and hurled themselves up the slope and into the attack.

*

And still Gui held his men in an iron grip, his dogs-of-war, his 'Lions', straining at the leash and growling, with lips curled back like ravening beasts, waiting until his enemies discovered that the camp was all a bitter sham. Waiting for them to realise they had been tricked, waiting for their fierce attack to stall, for them to stop in confusion, to stand at gaze and wonder where their enemies had gone, and for the wild fire of rage and fury to run out of them

And…so they did!

For as Sir Jules reached the first tents and his men swiftly overran them, thrusting with sword and spear at all the men they found there; roaring and shouting and smashing down in full battle-fury with axe and mace and gavelock, their howls of rage turned to shouts of surprise…and then of anger and deep disgust…*for all the men they had so furiously attacked were dummies!* Crude scarecrow figures of sticks and straw, not men of flesh and blood…and dummies rank with oil that ran down their fingers and across their angry faces. Too thwarted in their fury to realise the danger they were in, they milled about and argued; shouted, swore and bitterly exclaimed, and before Saint Sauveur could bring swift order back to his command…Gui struck!

"*UP! UP!*" he roared, leaping to his feet sword in hand. "William blow your horn! Raise the standards, lads! UP! UP!" And as he shouted, and William blew, so his men sprang to their feet with a mighty shout, and suddenly the whole crest of the slope above their startled foes was alive with armoured men, as if the ground itself had suddenly disgorged them.

"*Taraaa! Taraaa! Taraaaaa!*" Each blast of sound followed by the screaming rage of the men above the camp. And as the trumpet screamed its loud abuse so Sir Richard shouted, "*Loose!* You bastards! *Loose!*"

And with that the sky was suddenly filled with soaring flames as Gui's chosen archers opened fire, each arrow followed by the next, and the next and the next, a constant stream of flaming balls as if each man was tied to a writhing scarlet ribbon of fire that fell upon the tents, the shelters and like a fiery deluge from the very sky itself upon Saint Sauveur's men milling there in wild confusion.

Within a minute, fifteen hundred separate balls of fire rose up and fell upon them as if a volcano had erupted before their very eyes. And as the arrows landed, piercing men of flesh and straw alike, so the very ground burst into flame around them, as the oil and kindling caught alight, sending flames leaping and twisting into the clouded sky, veering and wavering in the wind, jumping over the heads of the living, and of the screaming dead and dying, as the storm of fire-arrows fell amongst them with devastating effect.

"Forwards! *Forwards!*" Sir Jules raged at his shattered command. "*Close the range!* Get close to the bastards. Follow me! *Follow me!*" And shield up and head bowed he drove himself and those who could still follow him up the slope and through the flames towards their enemies; the silence of the night split apart by the shouting fury of the fight, and the screams and cries of the wounded.

Below, where Sir Pierre Dumas sat his great bay charger at the head of his mounted reserve, it was clear that the attack was in danger of failing, and without waiting for Saint Sauveur's signal, he waved his axe around his head, stabbed in his spurs and with a great shout his whole Command took off up the slope ahead, leaping from standing start to full gallop in a dozen strides, the drumming of their hooves shaking the hard ground with thunder as they pounded towards the flaming camp; the air rent with their roars and shouts as they came, a raging tsunami of men and beasts and whirling steel.

Gui, hearing the distant shout and the thunder of galloping hooves, shouted to Sir Robert, standing beside his men on the right flank to be ready, and to William Bell beside him: "*Blow, William, blow!*"

And gathering his breath once more, young William Bell, Gui's trumpeter, blew the dawn apart. A different call this time, desperate, urgent, its tempo wild: "*Tan! Tantaraaa! Tan! Tantaraaa!*" Four wild, brazen blasts of sound, repeated and repeated as Sir Robert's Company of Gwent longbow archers opened fire at last.

No flaming broad head arrows these, their power blunted by wads of flaming cloth, but sharpened iron bodkin arrows designed to pierce armour, to burst through chain mail or leather as if they were parchment, to pin a man through his legs to his saddle. Arrows that would punch through four inches of English oak, or straight through a man's chest and body to come out the other side in a spray of blood and shattered bone. And so the little dark haired men with their 'sticks' now answered the trumpet's shrieking calls, and slipping their left feet forwards, drew their great longbows in one smooth drawing action, pulling their strings back to their ears with back and shoulders working as one...and loosed and loosed and loosed again...bending and firing, and bending and firing without pause until every arrow in their first strike had gone. Within a minute three thousand arrows fell upon Sir Pierre Dumas and his Command, on their proud horses and on his bold troopers until they looked more like stricken porcupines than men.

One moment they were thundering up the slope, immense in their power and might, fierce armoured men about to carry all before them with ease and majesty...the next they were a wall of heaped and struggling men, screaming and howling, the barely living and the dead: horses, men and equipment all scattered across the slope like broken toy soldiers cast there by a giant's careless hand. And a minute later came the second deadly flight, a terrifying sleet of death that wiped out all those who had defied the first, until there was not one man left alive of all those who had braved the slope that bitter August morning.

Up on the crest Gui heard the screams of dying men and horses, saw the wreckage his Men of Gwent had wrought on their mounted foes, the leaping flames, the terrified enemy staggering witless amidst the carnage, and calling William to him a last time he ordered him to blow the advance. And with the young trumpeter blowing his lungs out once again, as he had done at Saint Jean d'Angély, the thrilling *Tan-tan-tara-Tantaraaa! Tan-tan-tara-Tantaraaa!* of the charge blazed out over their whole encampment. Now with Gui and Sir Richard at the head of their men, a thick line of armoured warriors behind their standards, both defended by proven fighters with shield sword and shining axe, Gui's whole Command rushed forwards as he unleashed his men at last, his Lions of Malwood and of Niort, of Bordeaux, Gwent and the King's New Forest. And with both knights clad from head to toe in shimmering mail and toughened steel roaring out "*Chaaaaaaarge!*", swords furiously stabbing the way forward, the Lions of Malwood and all their allies gave one triumphant roar and fell upon the hapless survivors of their arrow strike like a steel avalanche…and slaughtered them.

Most were cut down where they stood in a welter of butchered arms and shattered heads and faces, others fought on fiercely in small, disparate groups while trying to get to where their own horse lines were half a mile away, but Gui's men were having none of it, and led by Sir Richard L'Eveque, Hordle John and Sir Robert FitzMiles they were quickly isolated and hacked down in a spray of smashed limbs and blood-boltered remains. No quarter begged for and none offered, till all were killed and the victor's swords and armour ran with the blood and brains of those they had slain.

Only around Sir Jules de Saint Sauveur was there any order left, as gathered around him were the best of those who had survived all three arrow strikes and were now fighting a fierce and bloody rear-guard action. With their horses still safely picketed where they had de-horsed earlier, this was a last ditch attempt to survive long enough to get there, and into this tempestuous *mêlée* of blood and flensing steel Gui strode with deadly purpose.

Immense in his armour, his cyclas still stained with the blood and brains of those he had hewn down on the *Mary* and at Saint Jean d'Angély he waded into that desperate fight as if he were inviolable. With one massive blow to the head of one of Saint Sauveur's men, that split his helmet and broke his brain pan open in a spray of bloody gruel, the Lord Baron, Sir Gui de Malwood smashed his way into the very heart of the fray going on around the enemy leader. And as he did so William of Bergerac's men, and those of de Beaune and Allan-i-the-Wood, closed in around him, their bill-hooked gisarmes doing dreadful service, wrenching men backwards by their arms or shoulders, while others hacked them down with the reverse axe blade, or smashed them down with mace and sword in a vile welter of crushed heads and eviscerated bodies, blood and shattered bone flying in bloody shards across their hands and faces. And with Gui's brutal assault the *mêlée* broke apart into its raging, screaming parts, each one of Saint Sauveur's remaining men facing half a dozen foes who rushed upon them without mercy and stabbed and hammered them to death upon the torn and bloodied ground, their shrieks and groans lost in the wild fervour of their deaths as their blood spouted from a dozen wounds.

So Gui came face to face with Saint Sauveur at last, Fitzurse behind his left shoulder, his helmet dented and his Rampant Malwood Lion torn and smirched with blood, Sir Richard on his right, his bright steel thick with the human debris of battle, his sword blade and his great helm running with the blood of those he had slain.

Light on his feet Sir Jules still was, as de Beaune had said, shield up and sword darting like a dragon's tongue as Gui, a giant in bloodied armour, his great sword over his right shoulder, now strode towards him. But Saint Sauveur knew how to fight, and leaping forward as if his mail were links of card not hammered iron, each link riveted through another, he halted Gui's advance. Thrusting at the English knight from every angle, now darting backwards, now forwards as he sought to pierce through his enemy's defence, he used the deadly point of his sword to keep Sir Gui at bay and his shield up to ward off any blow that he might make.

Stab! Stab Stab! His point flashing everywhere, so that Gui had to cover himself with both his shield and his blade, before striding forward once more to batter him with his sword: *crash!* on the man's shield rocking him on his feet, and *crash!* again as he followed up, with a reverse stroke across his front from right to left, pushing him further back. But it was as if Sir Jules were on steel springs, and moments later he danced back within range and delivered four quick stinging blows on Gui's shield arm and on his right shoulder, piercing his mail and his gambeson so he felt the prick of sharp steel and the warm trickle of blood down his left arm and across his shoulder.

"You fight well, Sir Jules!" Gui shouted at him, through the breath holes in his great helm, shaking his right arm. "But I will still pin you to the ground!"

"You may try, Malwood! You may try!"

"You know my name?"

"Yes! I recognise your blazon!" Sir Jules shouted back at him through his own helm, now dented across its right edge. Then darting in, he hammered at Gui with a wild flurry of swift blows that ended with a screeching block, both men's faces inches apart, both straining to break the others grip.

"You are the knight who put King Richard on his royal arse."

"Yes…and I will have your head for this, you bastard!" Gui snarled at him through his breath holes. "For this treachery, you will die!" And with a grunt of rage he flung the smaller man back and hewed at him furiously, his heavy blade sweeping past the man's defence to clatter his shield, carving out a great chunk of wood and leather from its rim and knocking Sir Jules sideways as he did so…only to have him spring back at him again, his sword a flicker of quicksilver in the flaring light from the burning hillside, that Gui parried in a shower of sudden sparks and shriek of steel.

Then leaping back out of range of Gui's lethal blade, Sir Jules mocked him: "See, you rabbit-eater, I am not finished yet!"

"But your Command is," Gui roared back circling as he spoke, whirling his sword about his head, his eyes flicking from Sir Jules' blade to his body stance as he did so. "Every man you brought with you is dead! You are the last man standing!"

"We thought we were fighting boys with sticks on ponies!" The Frenchman shouted rushing in, his sword point flickering all around Gui's guard, the blades snickering and sliding over each other in a screeching shower of sparks, bright in the glooming of the new day.

"Wrong, Sir Jules!" Gui shouted back, breaking off with a *clash!* of his shield as he forced Sir Jules' sword away from him. "You were fighting Welsh bowmen. The 'sticks' your scouts saw are their bows! They carry them across their backs. Big mistake, Sir Knight," he added, parrying two fierce blows as the man darted in again. "The 'ponies' your scouts told you of are Welsh cobs bred for war and carrying strong loads. They have covered miles of hard ground without strain."

And shooting his foot forward, he battered his opponent with a shower of hard blows that almost forced him to the ground: *crash! crash! CRASH!* Striding forward as he struck, overhead and from the waist; great strikes that would have slain a lesser man, sounding like a blacksmith striking red-hot metal on his anvil, sparks flying in all directions as he smote his enemy's sharpened steel with his raging blade.

Back Saint Sauveur came again with three more darting lunges at Gui's chest and shoulders, bursting through the leather chest pieces to the bright mail beneath, and with a final swingeing sweep he sheared off the rim of Gui's shield as if it were paper, scoring the side of his helm with a screech of tortured metal as he did so, rattling Gui's head and making him step swiftly back.

Shaking his head for several moments to clear his ears of the dreadful sound, and his eyes of the sudden stars that had burst across them, Gui circled warily, his whole body feeling red hot; sweat flowing in hot runnels all across his back and shoulders, and off his face and into his eyes so he had constantly to shake his head. But still he held his shield high…and, sword swinging, he stepped forward again to attack his enemy with renewed vigour, and raining a flurry of great blows upon his enemy he relentlessly pursued Sir Jules, who now only just managed to twist and parry them away with his sword and shield, losing a further great chunk from it that flew over his left shoulder, leaving himself dangerously open. And taking a giant stride forward Gui gave the top of his helm a terrific overhead *whack!* that left Sir Jules' head ringing, and almost drove him to his knees, his eyes full of bright stars and blood running from his nose. But though he staggered he did not fall; stumbling to his feet, his sword and shield still warding off the blows that Gui now rained upon him left and right.

For now the man was tiring fast.

His responses were not so quick, his breath rasped in his throat with the taste of blood in it, the sweat of battle poured off him, his body battered and bruised beyond further usage as Gui followed him mercilessly, picking his time and his blows until his opponent was clearly failing: *crash!*...to his shield, *thud!*...to his left shoulder, splitting his mail open, the blood spurting out and forcing him to drop his shield arm. *Lunge!*...to his chest, forcing him backwards…and in between swatting with ease the few desperate blows Saint Sauveur still managed to wield against him, till Sir Jules could only stand on wobbling legs, sword and shield arm sagging to the ground, helpless before Gui's vengeance.

It was time to make an end.

Up went Gui's sword, above his head, for his favourite overhead blow and down it came again, an avalanche of hardened, shimmering blue steel that, had it crashed upon Saint Sauveur's armoured head, would have split his great helm like a wooden box into shattered pieces and his head with it in a violent shower of bones and bloodied brains and tissue.

But it did not!

With a last moment twist of his body Gui pulled his blow, and swinging his blade up over his left shoulder he turned and brought it smashing back against Saint Sauveur's belly with the flat of his blade, knocking the man flying instead, and striding forward he placed his great armoured foot on Sir Jules' chest and shortened his sword arm to thrust him through his throat.

"*Yield, Sir Jules!*" he thundered through his breath holes. "You have fought valiantly, and with great skill. My men and I have shed enough blood. Yield and I will spare your life! De Beaune, take his sword and remove his helmet."

"To what end should I yield to you, Sir Gui?" Saint Sauveur gasped breathlessly a moment later, standing disarmed, his face red with effort, streaked with sweat and blood that flowed freely from his nose, and from his damaged shoulder upon the torn ground.

"Because it pleases me to do so," Gui replied, breathing deeply as he recovered from their fight. Then, handing his own helm to Simon his squire, as Sir Richard came over to join him with Sir Robert, wiping his own sweat stained face with a damp cloth which he next put into Gui's open hand, he added: "And so that you may reflect on today's events and on what it has cost you to be involved in the Lord of Narbonne and Gruissan's little schemes! Look around, you, Sir Jules," he continued, wiping his face, while he gestured to where the dead lay heaped and scattered everywhere. Dead horses and dead men all mangled up together, some poor beasts still wandering the stricken slope, pain driven, whinnying with terror in their eyes, arrows stuck in their quarters and their chests; while his men had already started to strip the dead, and collect the thousands of arrows that lay thrust up over everything like some foul feathered crop that had sprouted overnight.

"As I said…you are the last man standing! I can give you life, Sir Jules, or death! It is your choice. But I warn you. If you choose 'Life' from my hands, and I ever find that you have returned to your bloody reiving ways, or have involved yourself once more in any of de Brocas's foul schemes before I have put him down like the rabid beast he is, then I swear by the Archangel Michael, that I will return and destroy you and yours utterly, to the last stick of furniture you possess and the last member of your household and of your family!"

"That is my choice?"

"Yes, Sir Jules, that is your choice. Yield to me now, and I will spare your life. You may leave with honour, but without your arms or your charger, they are my right, and I will hold them. But I will mount you, clothe you and feed you, and have my surgeon bind your wounds. Where is your home?

"Bram! Some few miles from here."

"Then, on your knightly word, when I release you, that is where you must go, and I will give you money from my chest to see you safely there."

"Or else?"

"Death! Now, from my Master-at-Arms by the axe, before my men whom you sought to slay this morning…and your body stripped, as are your men's, and thrown to the fishes!"

Sir Jules de Saint Sauveur looked all around him: at the gritted faces and glowering looks of the men amidst whom he was now standing, at the shattered remnants of his Command and up at the sky, just flushing pink beneath a great pall of darkening clouds, sheets of cornflower blue behind them as the sun rose and the morning gathered pace… *I cannot leave my Thalia and my babes like* *this. They deserve better...*And then he looked back at the Lord Baron, Sir Gui de Malwood, standing before him, his officers at his back, his armour red with blood, his face like stone, and his great sword still in his hand...and he sighed... *This Englishman is said to be a man of honour. Perhaps in him I may find new life?...* "You give me little choice," he said with resignation in his voice and in his standing. "And life, and my family, are more precious to me than a pointless death." And dropping to one knee he bent his head and held out his sword in supplication. "I yield to you my Lord Baron, Sir Gui de Malwood, and give you my knightly vow that I will do as you have bidden me. I have a Lady who is very dear to me, and children whom I love, and I would not have them harmed in any way. I will pledge my sword to Truth and Honour from this day and I will forswear the Baron's schemes. I have no wish to stand upon a stricken field like this again!"

"So be it, Sir Jules! I accept your supplication," Gui said, taking the man's sword. "Now, give me your hand for I have never fought against a braver man nor so skilled a swordsman!"

"Nor I against so punishing an opponent!" Saint Sauveur said with a rueful smile, taking Gui's outstretched hand

And looking around him at the carnage that had been caused: the ripped and bloodied ground, the shattered human remains, the slaughtered horses, the bodies being dragged to the river's edge to be cast in one after another to float away downstream...he sighed again and shrugged his shoulders. "And to think we thought we would be fighting small, dark haired men with sticks!"

And, head bowed, he stumbled off with the Bashley twins as escort to find Father Matthew and his dressing station. '*All over by sunrise*,' he had said so short a time before. And so it had been...just not in the manner he had expected!

Chapter 28...The Lord Baron is fooled.

It was an hour or so later, while the clearing-up continued beneath a rapidly lightening sky, the coming dawn a tangerine blush squeezed beneath a rising blanket of grey and black ridged clouds, that Gui and his fellow commanders were startled by a distant shout and the sight of hurrying men.

And minutes later, two of Allan-i-the-Wood's verderers came awkwardly up from where Sir Jules's men had de-horsed before the battle, carrying a box carefully between them, another man beside them with a small bag in his hand. Gui and Sir Richard, standing around the growing pile of arms and equipment that their men were collecting, watched them with interest, while Sir Robert's Welshmen wandered all over the place plucking spent arrows out of the ground in their thousands.

About two feet square, the box was not large...nor was it heavy, but it was an awkward object with which to hurry if for no other reason than for what was in it. For as the two men drew closer, stumbling and cursing over the uneven ground, their companion following with a broad grin on his homely face, all those standing around were astonished to see that it had two birds in it. Both were fluttering desperately to keep their feet, their wings flapping and scattering feathers everywhere as they panted with beaks half open and eyes wide with fear...pigeons!

One black, slender, grey-blue sheeny feathers with white wing panels and tail barred with white, and one larger, with a deeper chest, slate blue with blue black wings tipped with white, and a black barred tail. Both had red feathered legs and both had brilliant eyes, bright and shining, red around the rim and deep orange in the centre.

"*God's Blood!*" Gui exclaimed, astonished, as soon as he saw what the men were carrying. "It's Peter of Minstead and Roger Fox isn't it? Two of the lads who scouted for us at Saint Jean? What have you found for us this time?"

"Pigeons, my Lord," Peter said, delighted to have been remembered by name. "We were tidying up like, Sir Gui, when we heard a commotion amongst some of they Welsh lads, who were rootling around same as we, and Foxy here said he thought they had found some pigeons."

"So we went over to them," Roger Fox said, taking up the tale. "And they were trying to take one of these out of its cage. Poor bloody bird was trying to escape, wings going wildly, feathers flying everywhere, and I was just about to ding him on his bonce, good and hard - bloody Welsh idiot - when the Under Sheriff came up and sorted them out...and sent us up here with these birds. These are no woodies, my Lord," the man said with interest. "These are different. Those bloody Welshmen wouldn't know a pigeon from a partridge…let alone a woody from a townie. Pigeons is different, you see Sir Gui. Sound different. Look different…and these are very different again. Sleeker, brighter eyed, prouder. So…so here they are, my Lord."

"You like pigeons, Roger?"

"Oh, yes, my Lord. Always have a few at home. They're clever, and pretty. And they'll come to your hand."

"Well, Roger…and Peter," Gui said, smiling down at them. "You have done a great deed today. Those are the Baron's pigeons! His famous messenger pigeons we have been so plagued with all along," and he smiled at their suddenly knowing faces. "I was never too sure whether I really believed what Father Matthew told us. But now I see it is true." And turning, he ordered the men to find a good flat spot on which to lay the birds down so they could get some rest, and not spend all their energy desperately flapping and fluttering as they tried to keep their balance.

"And what do you have in that neat bag?" he questioned the other man who had come up with his two friends. "Davy Coulter, isn't it? Joined at Malwood. You're the boy who found the Baron's message on the old *Mary*, after the fight with the corsairs!"

"Yes, m'Lord…and I still got that lovely box I found it in," the boy said proudly, looking now with confidence into his commander's face as he spoke. "Keeping it until I get home, I am. Hope to better myself with it, Sir Gui."

"Good man, young Davy! Good man! Now, show me what you have found this time."

And opening the neck of the small bag he was carrying, a neat pouch of softest yellow chamois leather tied with a cord of twisted green and black, the youngster tipped the contents out onto the broad palm of Gui's hand: two tiny brass cylinders with cork stoppers, a tiny roll of papyrus paper, a small cypher book, a quill pen cut very finely indeed, a small pot of black ink, a thick stick of green sealing wax and a small golden stamp, beautifully incised with the head of a wild boar…and Gui sighed with satisfaction if not with surprise. And he looked up at the man before him and smiled.

"You, Davy, and you Peter and Foxy too," he added with a terse nod of his head, each man delighted to have been known, "have all performed a more special service for me…indeed for this whole expedition...than any of you can easily have imagined. For, with luck, you may have handed me the very key to the Baron's castle…and the way to the Lady Alicia's freedom and that of her friend, Mistress Agnes. You have all done very well and I am more pleased with you than I can say. Now…away with you, lads," he said, slipping the handful of items back into their bag for safe-keeping. "But be sure to come and seek me out later for your reward, which will be substantial, I assure you!" And he threw back his head and laughed, while the three men scuttled swiftly off to join their friends, everyone amazed at their sudden good fortune.

Seeing the commotion going on, and the men milling about trying to see what the two verderers had brought across for the Lord of Malwood to examine, Father Matthew strode from his dressing station at the back of one of the tilt carts, Sir Jules trailing miserably after him, his wounded shoulder now stitched and strapped up, his face grey with pain and etched with the distress of capture and defeat, and the death of his friend.

"Right, you men," Gui rasped as he saw Matthew's approach, the chamois bag held firmly in his right hand. "You've all seen pigeons before…and mighty silly birds they are too! Nothing for you lot to gawp at when there is so much to do. If you've got the time to stand around and stare then I am sure Sir Richard can easily find more for you to do! Yes?" He questioned them smiling, with a fierce bellow. And with that they all melted away, chattering like a flock of magpies over what the young Lord Baron had said…leaving Gui and his officers looking down as the birds finally settled and began to bob their heads and croon.

"*Well!*" The tall Benedictine exclaimed as he arrived. "Told you that Man-of-Blood was using pigeons to carry messages…and you thought I was becoming one of God's own children? Well, there's the living proof…"

"…And bloody lucky we are to have it too," the Under Sheriff cut in, laughing, as he arrived to join them. "Those buggers of young Robert's were about to have them for breakfast, roasted on a stick!"

"So I gather. Two of Allan's men rescued them just as your lads were thinking of wringing their necks," he said with a raised eyebrow, turning to the Welsh knight bobbing around beside him, still pumped-up after the battle.

"Good eating is pigeon, bach," FitzMiles said with a grin. "And no need to raise an eyebrow at me, boyo!" he added, putting a hand on Gui's bloodied shoulder. "Mind you, the breast is all they're really good for; apart from that they're all wings and feathers. But the breasts are good. With a few leeks and peas and a bit of bacon in a rich gravy, and a hunk of bread to dip in with? Lovely!"

"Well, Robert," Father Matthew said in his Spanish lilt. "Pigeons are good eating, that is true…but these beauties are best left for flying. Certainly we can put them to better use than eating, I think," he added softly, squatting down to look at them as the slate blue bird with the black barred tail, stretched out his wing and nibbled between his beautiful blue-black feathers, preening each one back into perfect shape. "Certainly better than eating 'em!"

"And look what that other fellow found for us, Matthew," Gui chipped in. "That Davy Coulter…one of ours from Malwood."

"Yes, my Lord," Fitzurse chipped in. "The lad who found that gold and emerald box on board the *Mary*. A good man. Joined with us from Devon. What's he found this time?"

"Only these!" Gui exclaimed, with a huge grin, tipping the contents out again onto his hand. "The key to that bloody 'Tiger's' lair, I think. With these we might just be able to fool that bastard more thoroughly than even he could possibly imagine!"

"You mean send the good Baron a message, Gui?" Father Matthew asked sharply, picking the tiny golden signet of the Boar's Head Erased from amongst its fellows, and looking up at him. "It was in my mind to do so too."

"Mmmm. You and me both, Matthew. And why not? After all he is clearly expecting one," the young Lord of Malwood replied with a shrug of his armoured shoulders. "So why disappoint him and deny him his hour of triumph?" Adding after a pause, a sudden frown on his face, "Do you have the trick of it, Father?"

"Well, maybe…a little," he said, as Gui slid all the little pieces back again into their bag. "But we all know one who does," he said, looking into Gui's face with a grim smile. "Someone who will know for certain exactly what secret signs might be needed, or cipher, to ensure the good Baron knows it is the truth that he is being told and not a lie!" And with one accord they both looked over to where Sir Jules de Saint Sauveur was standing, just then looking bleakly across to the river where the naked bodies of his Command were still being thrown in, amongst them his friend, Pierre Dumas.

"Can't make him, Father," Gui said quietly, looking into the tall Benedictine's dark eyes. "Torture is not my 'thing'! But maybe I can shame him into doing it?" he suggested quizzically, his head on one side. "I think there is a good man in there trying to get out." And the Lord of the King's New Forest paused then while both men looked at the figure of Sir Jules, standing stark against the morning sky, as the sun rose behind him, its light a veiled disk, with streaks of apricot and blush pink beneath a growing blanket of clouds: his face still and his eyes blank and far away.

"Sir Jules," Gui called out to him then, carefully closing his hand over the small bagful of items they had all been looking at. "If you really intend to throw off your allegiance to Lord Roger…then there is a signal service you can do us," and he pointed to the cage that Allan's men had brought over. "Clearly the good Lord Baron of Narbonne and Gruissan will be awaiting a message from you to tell him of your expected success…"

"Yes. I have the paper in the saddle bags on Hercules' back; the cipher book, and the little brass carrying cylinders also."

"No...I have all those here," Gui answered him swiftly. "One of my men found all you need in this chamois leather bag." And he held it up for Sir Jules to see, at which the knight nodded and holding up his hands in acknowledgement, he drifted slowly towards them.

"Which bird?" Matthew asked him next, his dark eyes fixed on Sir Jules' face, his head on one side. "It will not be any old bird that will be expected, my friend, will it? It will be the best and fastest. And do not seek to trick me, Sir Jules," he added sternly, his eyes still fixed on Saint Sauveur's face. "I am not ignorant of the ways of pigeons, nor how they carry their messages either!"

And there was a brief pause while the South Frenchman looked into the tall Black Monk's intent gaze and then at Sir Gui, standing nearby, his hand on his sword; and then he turned away to gaze up at the changing sky while he thought of his wife and children...*Can I do this? Can I really turn my back on de Brocas and all the money he pays me? I have handed over my sword and surrendered my horse and my armour. If I do this that bastard will be my enemy for all time...is that what I want? If not, how will I hold my head up again, knowing how evil that man can be? Dear God! How do I wring honour out of this...and safety for my wife and family?...For my belovèd Thalia and for little Julia and Bevis?* And he sighed deeply...*No contest!...*

Gui watched his torment, and coming up behind his shoulder said softly...almost as if he had read the man's thoughts: "If you truly wish to wield your sword with honour, and to be as well regarded by others as once you were - then this is your chance to break free, once and for all. This Man-of-Blood; this 'Lord Baron'," Gui snarled with bitter disgust, "will be destroyed, and his power with it, of that I promise you. King Richard has demanded it. But to keep him in the dark a little longer will do our cause no harm, and may fill him with such glee as to make him careless. Let him believe that you have slain us all. That it is *our* bodies you have cast into the river, and *our* horses that have been burned. He will be ecstatic! Overjoyed...and bloated with his success he may let down his guard sufficiently for us to slip our steel beneath it and strike him to the centre of his foul, black, rotted heart...and send his soul to hell where Satan waits to welcome him with open arms! Again, Sir Jules...the choice is yours to make." And he looked at him with a face of stone.

"And if I decline?"

"Then you will still be free to go. I have already given you my word on that. But you will leave more stained even than you are already. For all men know how evil this Baron truly is and how corrupt his soul...and they will see you as just one more of his foul creatures. Worse, his active aider and abetter…and how will your wife and son view you then?”…*Come on man! Accept! Accept!*

“And if I accept?”

“Then men will praise you for your courage and your wisdom. And all Gruissians will laud you for your mercy in striking such a blow for their freedom that the tyrant who has blackened their lives for years can be destroyed at last.

“And if you seek true, honourable employment, and safety for your wife and little family, then go you to Sir Hugh Willoughby, the King’s Seneschal of all Aquitaine and Guard Commander of Bordeaux…the greatest city on the whole western seaboard of France…for I will recommend you to him, and he will welcome you and advance you for my sake, as much as for your own, of that, by God and Saint Michael, I surely promise you.”…*Pray God, you take this offer, you bastard. This might be the only chance I have of getting into that fucking castle!…*

Sir Jules de Saint Sauveur stood then and looked into Sir Gui de Malwood’s face…hot brown eyes into cold, steel blue…and then at the hundreds of men now busy all across the slope that had been the scene of such desperate fighting and bloody death so short a time before, and he smiled.

“Once more Sir Gui, you make me an offer I cannot refuse…To have such a chance put to me that will enable me to regain my honour, *and* give my Lady Thalia and our children the safety I know she craves for - and that will return us to the society into which we both were born - does not come to many men, and I know Sir Willoughby as a man respected for his good sword arm and his straight dealing.” And looking at Gui, he held out his hand. “My Lord Baron…I accept.”

And taking it in his own strong grip, Gui smiled then and shook it firmly: “Sir Jules de Saint Sauveur…Good! I have not been deceived in you!…*Thank God, for that. God’s Blood, I thought he would never get there!…* I thought there was a good man in there trying to get out,” he went on, tapping him on his shoulder. “I am delighted that I was not wrong. Now, let us get a pen and those papers and get this message on its way, and you too, Sir Jules: on your own charger, Hercules,” he added smiling at the huge shock of pleasure that rushed across the man’s face. “Take him as my gift to a brave man, as a sign of better fortune in the days to come. And take back your sword from me as well, and your armour, as a sign of my respect for a courageous fighter and a man of true honour after all!”*…And that’s how I do business, you lucky bastard. And don’t you forget it!*

"Now, Sir Jules," Father Matthew persisted quietly in his soft Spanish lilt, having watched the by-play of emotions across both men's faces, his eyes glittering in the sun's first shrouded rays. "Again, which bird?"

"Birds, Father," Sir Jules said with a grin. "We always send two birds when there is a distance to travel, in case one should fall victim to a stooping falcon. But…the first and finest is the one with the feathered legs and the brightest orange eyes. The slate blue one with the blue-black wings and the black barred tail, of course," he said, looking at the tall priest in his black habit with a smile. "He is called 'Gabriel', the fastest bird in all the loft, and the Baron's favourite. The other we will send is 'Chantelle', the bird with white wings panels and a white barred tail. She is not so fast but she is cunning and, like Gabriel, has never been known to fail. But you knew that, didn't you, Father?"

"Yes, my son, I did. I just hoped you did too!" And there was a sudden burst of laughter.

"But do you know about the Baron's mark?" he asked.

"No, no, Sir Jules. We did not," the tall Benedictine said, his face now wreathed in smiles. "Not until we found it a few minutes ago," and he opened his hand to show it off. "Nevertheless, I am impressed with your honesty in advising us of its need on any message sent to the good Baron. Our ruse would have failed without it!"

"Well, I don't know whether every message carries this particular mark, Father," Sir Jules said, picking the tiny stamp of a Boar's Head Erased from Matthew's hand. "But this one must," he said, looking intently at the neatly incised boar's head, then up at Sir Gui. "Perhaps, soon, it really will be erased…for good!"

And they all chuckled at his wit, as they clustered round the cage of pigeons to sort out the message they would now send off to Grise.

*

Half an hour later, with the sun up and the clouds streaked with gold and pale vermilion; a fresh breeze blowing and both messages ciphered and written on thinnest paper, Father Matthew reached into the cage and took hold of Gabriel. With his big hands behind his wings and round his strong feathered chest, he gently drew him carefully out so that Sir Jules could slowly extend his fine red leg, and with the greatest care tie on the tiny message cylinder with finest thread and a sliver of soft cotton cushioning, top and bottom round the grooves so carefully cut there. And then Chantelle, a slim, neat feathered beauty with delicate red legs and feet tipped with black claws was similarly burdened, each tiny capsule tight sealed with hot green wax, stamped with the Baron's signet, and tied to the longest part of each bird's leg.

Then walking away from all the bustle of the encampment now busily breaking up around them, both men carried their birds cradled in their two hands closer to the river, and in one swift upward movement released them with a flash of wings and feathers and at once they began to climb. Spiralling upwards on their great sickle shaped wings like a cast of falcons. they strove for height, and then, in an instant, they were gone, winging south-west away from the sun as it struggled to break through the rising clouds…towards the Château Grise.

Streaking at fifty miles an hour for the great tower loft that was their home, Gabriel and Chantelle flew like feathered arrows to where Lord Roger's Pigeon Master, Raheel al Moukhtara and his assistant, Almahdi aal Suriyyan, were as eagerly awaiting their return as was the Baron himself where he stood upon the great Donjon's battlements, watching for the swift black specks against the azure sky that would herald their arrival, and the fulfilment of all his plans.

Chapter 29...How Sir Gui took the road for Narbonne.

By mid-morning it was all done.

Every last body cast into the fast flowing Fresquel, and those poor beasts whom they thought they could save had been given into the care of Paul of Bartley and William Fisher, the two horse doctors chosen to go with them from Castle Malwood. All the rest too wounded for further life had been put down, dragged into a great pile where their fire had been, along with all the other slain beasts, and with the exception of half-a-dozen carcases left for the butchers of Castelnaudary, all had been set on fire; the smoke black and oily, the stench of burned flesh strong in the air all around them.

Already people from the town had finally plucked up the courage to make an appearance, and were flooding down to see what they could, and find out what had happened early that terrible morning, so Gui was pleased to order his men to mount up and move out before he had to face a barrage of questions from the town mayor or any of his fellow worthies. And with all the spare mounts left by the dead on long leading reins, Gui led his men back onto the road and forward to L'Espitalet from where Saint Sauveur had set out the previous evening.

There he rested his men and fed them properly, terrified the plump *aubergiste* into revealing where Sir Jules had left his chest, still almost stuffed to overflowing with the Baron's silver, and sat down with his officers to discuss what had happened that day and plan their next move.

"Is that right, Richard? Truly? That we haven't lost a man?" Gui asked amazed, after the aubergiste had brought them wine, fresh bread and olives.

"Not one! Oh there are plenty of cuts and bruises…and Matthew has stitched a few up, so we have plenty of walking wounded. But no dead! Those arrow storms really knocked the stuffing out of them completely."

"Are you surprised?" Father Matthew asked, leaning back with his wine beaker. "Those poor bastards expected to find a sleeping camp full of dozy soldiers. The place looked like that…it was meant to! Then, when they got up there and found they had been fooled, and before they could do anything, they were deluged with a rain of fiery death quite beyond their experience. Next thing their mounted support was wiped out before their very eyes, and moments later they had all the fiends of hell rushing down on them baying for their blood. If it had been me out there tonight, I'd have legged it straight away!"

"Well Robert," Gui said to their newest recruit, with a bang on his shoulder. "Your lads did brilliantly today. Brilliantly! I thought I'd seen something special at Saint Jean, when our lads had a good go. But what your boys did this morning was just terrifying! Proves it for me…the longbow is an amazing weapon. It will revolutionise warfare. Did you manage to salvage most of your arrows?

"Thank you, bach," the little Welshman said with a grin. "Quite like old times fighting the wild rievers of Northumberland and the Borders. And as for the arrows? Yes we did, though there are many that are past it. Lots of broken shafts, but we can get the heads off them and there is plenty of hazel about, so we can always make new ones."

"Good man, Robert! Well done, and thanks for waiting for my trumpets before charging out! I know you of old, you rascal," he added with a grin. "Everything forward and trust in the Lord," and he gave him a friendly buffet on his arm. "I hear from Richard L'Eveque and John Fitzurse, that you fought like a tiger…and with the point as well as the blade. Great stuff, Robert; proud to have you with us. I shall come presently and reward your men also, and mine, for a terrific job well done! And I haven't forgotten those lads of yours either, Allan," he added with a grin to the burly Under-Sheriff. "But don't forget those ponies, Robert, yes?" he said then, turning back to the little Welshman. "They must be clipped or you may lose some, and that won't do. Now, away with you, and find your lads. You've done really well, Robert." And as the Welsh knight pushed past them he was warmly patted on the back and shoulders by all those standing there with laughter and goodwill, until his good Welsh heart was bursting.

"So…where next, Sir Gui?" Fitzurse asked then, a fat sausage in his hands.

"Well…past Carcassonne today, I should hope. Matthew says there is a small village just beyond it called Trebes…"

"…Pretty place with a good inn, called the '*Flying Duck*,'' the tall Benedictine broke in with a smile. "Been there before. Good food and soft beds without bugs!" We should reach that easily before sunset."

"Sweet Jesus!" Sir Richard exclaimed, sitting back on his settle. "A real bed again? With sheets and a pillow? And proper food for a change instead of water, eternal smoked meat, runny cheese and bread rolls? My dear noble Lord and Master," he drawled in his usual laconic style. "You are positively spoiling us!" And they all laughed.

"Then, Friday morning we will be in easy reach of Narbonne," the tall Benedictine continued,

"And after that *'Le Coq d'Or'* at Les Monges!" Gui added. "'The Golden Cockerel', Tommy Blackwood swore by it. Armand Chulot and his wife Claudine are noted for their good food and comfort, Richard. So tonight may not be the last night in a good bed after all!"

"Heavens preserve us, the boy is going soft!" he drawled. "I'm not sure I am prepared for the world to come to an end just yet!" And a fresh gale of laughter swept the table.

*

Trebes...*Le Canard Volant*...'The Flying Duck', and it took Sir Richard and Father Matthew all they had to stop the young Lord of Malwood from rushing out into the night there and then!

All day they had travelled, with the weather changing around them as they journeyed. The clouds that had come up overnight and threatened the morning steadily filled the sky till by late afternoon the wind had turned chill, and the rain that Father Matthew had sensed the night before soon smirred the hills around them, the clouds coming right down till all was like a dreich day at home in November. And with their tents and spare canvas burned to cinders in the fight, they were even more determined to reach Trebes before darkness fell when they would be forced to shelter under the trees and hedgerows with only their capes to warm them.

So, it was with great relief that they reached the village just as the last light was dying, and the rain had finally caught up with them, a penetrating mizzle that soon covered them with fine droplets of cold water that quickly found their way into everything, making the horses flick their ears and toss their heads with irritation.

But no sooner had they arrived, and stamped their way inside than Gui was moved to rush out again into the gathering night and ride *vent à terre* to Narbonne and Gruissan immediately!

"God's Blood, she was here!" he shouted at Sir Richard and Father Matthew, dragging the *aubergiste* along with him almost by the scruff of his neck, his wife following, wringing her hands and crying out in fear. "This is Monsieur Agneau, and his wife Charlotte. That fucking bastard was here with his daughter, the precious Lady Rochine, Agnes, another girl I know nothing of called Soraya Fermier...*and Alicia!* Here! Damn and blast them...here in this very inn! Tell them, you bloody French moron," Gui raged at the little man, shaking him as if he were a terrier with a rat. "You cretin! Tell them!"

"*Gui!*" Father Matthew roared at him. "Put the poor man down, and pull yourself together! It is not his fault that Baron Roger chose his inn in which to stay the night. And it is our good fortune that he did so, for at least we can gain some knowledge as to how Alicia and Agnes are being treated…and who this other girl is."

"Leave him be, you great oaf!" Sir Richard joined in, prising Gui's hands off the *aubergiste's* scruff. "And let him go and get some supper cooking. I have not put up with you all this trip to have my good dinner spoiled by your tantrums...*Maintenant, mon bon Monsieur Agneau*," he said addressing the terrified *aubergiste*. "*Pardonnez-moi, mon ami. Il est complètement fou !*" he exclaimed, whirling his finger around his temple. "...completely mad! Il est *anglais?...Vous comprenez?*" He continued, waving his hands at the little man in his eagerness to be understood. "*Nous désirons le grand dîner! Immédiatement!*...dinner immediately! We are starving…*Nous avons très faim! Vite! Vite!*...Quickly!" And taking him by one arm and his wailing wife by the other, he ushered them swiftly out, smacking the French woman's round bottom firmly as he did so.

"Now, Gui," he said, turning round to his friend tersely. "Stop being such a bloody arse! Rushing around like a madman because Alicia was here a week ago, and frightening everybody half to death! That will achieve nothing except a burned supper and damp beds. For God's sake get a grip! Like this you're no damned good to man nor beast! I'm off to see to my men! Matthew," he said sharply to the tall black garbed monk. "You sort the stupid bastard out. I for one have had enough!" And he stalked out, more angry than anyone could easily remember.

*

But gradually calm descended.

Once again the village was turned upside down for their visitors, even more so this time as there were so many more men for whom to cater, and once more Gui and his commanders took over the inn. And after supper, which was an excellent roasted capon with crisp skin and bacon, fresh vegetables and a fruit compote to follow, Monsieur Agneau, and his wife, Charlotte, told all they could to their guests: of the sudden visit of the Lord Baron, Sir Roger de Brocas and the four ladies he had brought with him…and the three Arabs too; talking long into the night as they were plied with so many questions.

"Well," Gui said later, to Sir Richard from the door of the inn, relishing the scent of the freshly wet earth as the rain swept across Mistress Charlotte's sun-dried herb garden. "At least we know she is alive and well…and being cared for. She and Agnes…and that other girl, that Soraya Fermier. She sounds lovely from what the *aubergiste* had to say. But what about those bloody Arabs? Where in God's name have they come from? Seem to be some sort of bodyguard, as far as I could make out. And an Arab cook? I tell you, Richard. This is all turning out to be a very strange chase indeed!"

"At least you've calmed down," his tall friend said, joining him by the open door, breathing in deeply, the fresh scent of wet soil and grasses sweet to his senses as well. "I quite thought I was going to have to lay you out, you were in such a state."

"I'd like to see you try!" And they both laughed.

"I am sorry, Richard. And I have apologised to Monsieur Agneau and his wife. But I just got a bit overwrought, what with that bloody skirmish this morning…*was it only today?...seems like ages!...*And then discovering that Alicia had actually been here in this very inn! Well, it was just too much for a moment!" And he laid his arm across his friend's shoulders and rested his head there too…both lost in their own thoughts as the rain fell softly and a cool, wet wind blew across their faces.

"Come on, Gui," Richard said at last. "We have had an excellent meal and I for one have a real bed to go to…and so do you. The good Monsieur Agneau says that Narbonne is only half a day's ride or so from here, so no ghastly start in the morning, Gui - and no bloody 'Roman Breakfast' either! We can rise at a civilised hour, wash in hot water before we put our stinking armour on again, and have a decent meal. Fresh croissants, butter and honey, with peaches off their own trees…just lovely! And the good lady of the house, the fair Madame Charlotte, has taken our filthy cyclases for a wash and our underclouts." And he sighed with pleasure. "I haven't had clean clothes for a week, and neither has Philip, poor boy. Fine master I am proving to be!" And with a smile at his friend and a friendly arm to lean on, both men finally staggered to their rest.

*

Next day, though most roused at dawn having become so used to doing so, they did not leave the 'Flying Duck' until nearly midday, with fresh rations for their journey garnered from all in the village, and all well paid for from Gui's renewed money chest now completely refilled with Lord Roger's silver. And it gave him no qualms to pay their shot with Monsieur Agneau from the Baron's hoard, only intense satisfaction, and they laughed heartily as they rode away into a rain-washed morning. For overnight the weather had cleared leaving everything fresh and sparkling, the sun a shimmering blaze of light that poured its heat down on them from a sky of untouched cerulean that made every twig and leaf stand out in sharp relief.

Truly it was a glorious morning, and even their mounts seemed refreshed after the night's rain, tittuping along in fine style, heads tossing and shaking, ears pricked forward and fetlocks dancing as they clip-clopped onto the road and headed south once more, the sky above blue as a jaybird's wing, and the air filled with the scent of passing summer.

In the great fields all around them, with the stubble turning white, long rows of fat sheaves, their heads heavy with grain, lolled in the sunshine; while great flocks of small birds, and fat grey pigeons with white-barred wings, swooped amongst them for the gleanings left by the harvesters. And everywhere the vineyards were laden with grapes, hanging in great red and green clusters from every vine, and the olive groves were thick with green and black olives just waiting to be garnered.

Gui looked around him and sighed.

August almost over and summer was passing…and he was missing their own harvest at home, with the great wains going out to the fields, the shouts of the harvesters, the good will, the laughter and the songs in the evening. Before long it would be time for the Harvest Home supper…*the great hall in the Keep packed with the village come in for the revels, with new cider from their own apples, and new wine from Bordeaux, the fireplaces filled with roaring logs, the trestles groaning with food, and all the dancing, mumming and acrobats…*

Sir Richard looked at him and smiled.

"Thinking of home?"

"Mmmm. Yes, I was actually," Gui replied dreamily, turning towards his large friend. "Looking at these fields being harvested, and wondering how Sir James is getting on with our own at Malwood, especially with so many of the men away. And with the news of those who've been killed? It will be our Harvest Home soon – that's if there will be a harvest this year, after that dreadful storm. And poor Father Gerome gets so upset with the fires on the hillsides our people still like to leap through.

"That's Samhain, Gui; a bit later - October 31st. But I know what you mean; I was just thinking the same thing myself: the dancing, the singing, and the fun. I *love* Harvest Home…almost as much as I love Christmas! Surely the fields can't all have remained ruined?" And he sighed, resting his crossed arms on the high pommel of his saddle, letting his rouncey just plod its way forward, head bobbing happily while he looked out across the sun-filled countryside.

"Where do you want to rest up tonight?" he asked after a while, the gently clopping hooves and the sunshine making him feel drowsy.

"Oh…this side of the town, I think, Richard. We'll find a good glade just off this road, I expect. It won't rain tonight," he said looking up at the sky, blue and almost cloud free, just a frill of white high, high up. "Nothing up there to worry about, and the day after, according to Matthew, we'll be at the 'Golden Cockerel' at Les Monges."

"Yes that's right, Gui," the tall Benedictine replied, kicking-up to join them. "Lovely big inn just off the road between Narbonne and Gruissan. Armand and Claudine Chulot; the people whom Tommy Blackwood told you about. He has no love for the Baron, as Thomas said, and should prove a really useful ally."

"Bet he's not expecting three hundred and fifty Welsh bowmen, bach," Robert chipped in with a grin. "My lads have never been in such fine fettle since leaving Cardiff. They are 'up' for anything right now!"

"Well they made our day yesterday, Robert," Sir Richard said lazily. "They deserve to feel good. They've earned it. Just don't let it go to their wild Welsh heads or else there will be trouble. Let them keep their fighting for the bloody Baron and his minions…not my troopers!" And he laughed, remembering what Sir Hugh had said at Bordeaux about the Welshmen's fighting spirit.

"Oh, the lads'll be fine, Gui," Sir Robert replied, in his soft Welsh voice. "Just a bit of boasting and teasing…"

"And *He! He! Heing!*" Father Matthew, interrupted. "That is the strangest thing. I've never come across anything like it before."

"No…no more had those gentlemen yesterday come across so many clothyard shafts in so short a time either!" Sir Robert replied with a grin. "Sticks and ponies, indeed!" And they all laughed at Sir Jules' frightening error.

"I see you have got those beasts of yours clipped, Robert," Gui said to him quietly.

"Yes, Gui. All done and dusted. Should have done it straight away after I was appointed...just didn't think about it at the time. Too many other things in my head, I suppose. It has surely made a real difference, you can see it in the way those ponies lift their heads and trot on, hooves high and tails swishing."

"Right! Well, let's all kick-on. I want to be settled down properly long before sunset."

"And I want proper latrines dug for the night this time, Gui," Sir Richard said, looking around at him. "Last night was a bloody shambles, dear boy; shit everywhere despite your orders!" he moaned with his lazy grin. "But no shelters…we can all sleep out tonight under our capes and horse blankets…but the horses must be watered and curried, cooking lines set up and a hot meal for all. We bought the extra pans in Revel when we got the oil, so those villainous cooks we have amongst us can bloody well get going and show us their skills! Then I want helmets rubbed and polished and weapons properly cleaned and honed as well. You never know when we may have to fight again!"

"Well said, O my noble Guard Commander," Gui gently mocked him, with a bow. "And hot water to wash in for a change. It'll be so good to get out of this stinking armour for once and have the time to wander a bit in the Baron's own backyard without him knowing it, before moving on again tomorrow."

Chapter 30...*The Screech Owl with ill-boding voice portends strange things!...(Lady Mary Montagu 1689-1762)*

And so Narbonne at last!

A bustling, thriving port city, created by the Romans as the most important land link between the Imperial City and the Iberian Peninsula; with two great roads passing through it: the Via Aquitania to Carcassonne, Bordeaux and the Atlantic coast...and the Via Domitia up into Spain, Rome's greatest province before Gaul was conquered, and then down to Rome itself, the old Imperial city. Narbonne, as packed with wine and olive oil merchants now as ever it had been in the days of Ancient Rome, and all centred on *La Robine*, the great canal dug by the legions all those years ago, which linked the Circle Sea, the glittering Mediterranean, with the River Aude.

*

All day they had travelled through the heat and dust, men and horses both covered with the same fine grey powder off the road, bodies weary and throats dry; all hugely relieved when they found a great clearing just short of the town where there was a fine stand of heavy timber beneath which to shelter themselves and their horses. And all along the treeline a wide stream of crystal water, cold, untainted, rushed and bubbled between firm reeded banks where purple loosestrife and wild angelica rioted in a blaze of purple and white, mixed in with marsh cinquefoil, yellow water buttercups and fair-maids of France a plenty. Deep enough to swim in, and to let the horses stand and drink, it was not so deep that those who could not swim could still leap and splash and have some fun after so long and wearying a ride.

With no tents to bother with, nor shelters to build against the weather, which once more was set fair, with clear skies of celestial blue beneath a sun of blazing gold, it was not long before they were all properly sorted. The horses in long lines beneath the trees, the carts to one side and the folding trestles for holding the evening meal unpacked and set up close to where the cooks had built their field kitchens.

And all around were the men themselves, many sitting in groups, drinking, talking and cleaning their equipment; others on guard or collecting wood for a great fire on the edge of the clearing just down from their encampment; yet others, under the command of their sergeants, wandering off to sample the pleasures of Narbonne, safe behind its walls and towers.

And with them went Gui and his principal officers. Now out of their armour at last, and having visited the latrines and then flung themselves naked into the stream to wash off the dust and filth of travel, and thus refresh themselves, they were ready for some fun. Dressed in light chemises and linen chausses, with soft suede half-boots on roughened leather soles instead of their heavy work boots… all except Father Matthew who was in his usual black robe with studded sandals…they left their horses behind for a much needed rest, and so walked down towards the river and the town.

Crossed by a great Roman bridge of six arches, the wharves and warehouses along both sides of the River Aude were awash with people, merchandise and animals of every kind, and as Gui, Father Matthew, Sir Richard and Robert FitzMiles looked down on them from the bridge parapet they were amazed. Every kind of shipping was there to see, except for great cogs and busses like the *Mary* and the *Pride of Beaulieu* that were too deep laden for the canal. They had to moor up at *La Robine's* seaward end while their goods were brought up by barge, of which there seemed to be hundreds.

But amongst the many vessels plying their trade in the busy port, there was one great ship there the likes of which they had last seen making off with Alicia, having battered them and the *Mary* almost into oblivion. A fighting dromond, double banked oars and fully decked. One bank of rowers below deck, rowing blind, two to an oar and chained there as galley slaves; the upper bank working their oars from a long covered outrigger above the deck, one man to an oar, each long oar thrust through a rowlock held in with thongs, and each rower a freeman, as ready to fight their ship as any of the armoured mercenaries on board.

She had heavy ballista artillery fore and aft on oak turntables, a long siphon for Greek fire and a mighty ram with iron teeth right on the waterline beneath her finely shaped prow.

And they all stopped to stare at her, now making ready to leave, her marines busy on deck, while her sailors scampered up the ratlines in preparation to loosen sail, or gathered around her cat-heads where her twin anchors on great thick cables still held her moored to the bottom of the wide port basin fifty yards off the quayside.

"God's Bones…but that's like that bastard that raked us off Belle Île!" Gui exclaimed pointing. "Only much bigger! Look at her, she's enormous!"

"Biggest dromond on the Med,' she is," a passing merchant said, hearing the stranger's comments. "She's the *Ajax*. Captain Valerian Dodoni. He's a Venetian trader, and he owns every last foot of her. See," he added, pointing to where a tall dark haired man in an open shirt was directing his crew. "That's Valerian.

"She's been here more than a week, the *Ajax*, longer than usual; but she's leaving now. He's got good business, I hear, in Sicily. He's a fair man, is Valerian Dodoni, but better count your fingers if you ever shake hands to do business with him," he laughed. "He's the sharpest man on the Circle Sea!" And with a chuckle he patted Gui on his shoulder, turned and went on his way.

And standing back, with the sun sliding down the heavens behind them, the sky turning gold and crimson overhead like vast heated bars of iron from a giant furnace, they watched as the anchors came up and her oars lifted like wings to the great thump of drums deep within her, just as the dromond had that had so viciously attacked them three weeks ago. And with the next beat they struck the water, churning it to white foam as they dug in and drove her forward, her crew up in the masts ready to unfurl the sails once she was clear of the town.

Gui paused to watch the ship leave, her wake golden in the setting sun, each double set of marks beautiful whorls of shimmering gold and crimson as her oar blades dipped and rose in the still waters of the harbour. And with each beat and dip of her oars Gui's thoughts were filled with Alicia...*I am on my way, my darling. Like this ship rowing into the sunset, I am coming. Soon I will be with you again. Soon! God aid me, but I need a good plan! How will I get into that bloody man's castle, even though he may believe me dead? God and Saint Michael, show me the way!...*and with a deep sigh he turned and moved to join the others as they walked onwards into the town.

Today Narbonne, tomorrow the 'Golden Cockerel' and then the Château Grise!

*

Hours later, long after they had returned from the town to a meal of hot vegetable soup and the last of their thick bread and Cantal cheese, sentries were posted for the night at all points of the camp, and the men turned in for sleep, their minds fixed on the morrow when all knew that they would arrive at their final destination before the great castle itself, the Château Grise.

They'd cleaned and checked their weapons, honing their swords to a razor's edge on their portable grindstone and burnished their helmets 'til they shone. In battle a polished casque could mean all the difference between a blow glancing off…and being felled! Particularly when it came to arrows and small projectiles. And Gui, Richard and Sir Robert, and their officers, kept at the men 'til every dent had been lifted and the metal really gleamed.

But despite the lateness of the hour and the long day behind them Gui was unable to sleep, lying in his cape on a bed of woolfells bought from the town, propped up against his saddle, his mind full of dreams, and plans, and disembodied thoughts while he watched the great fire they had built slowly die, and the sentries Fitzurse and de Bergerac had posted as 'First Watch' move silently about the giant clearing.

Above him the thick stand of timber that sheltered them sighed and rustled, the warm evening airs shushing the leaves gently as they moved through them. All around him his men lay sleeping, even the horses were still, the only sound coming from the chuckling stream that ran brightly down the edge of the clearing they had chosen…just off the great road that led down into the town, where it flowed on its way to *La Robine*. Before him, the great fire the men had built earlier and sat round drinking and yarning, as soldiers do, had died down to a vast glowing pile of smouldering debris, that pulsed briefly like a beating heart each time the wind breathed gently over it, the heavy ash rising in little puffs each time it did so.

But it was the stars that moved Gui most of all, and getting up he slipped on his favourite rope slippers and moved out from under the trees and looked up at a star-dazzled sky.

Never had the myriad silver lights that hung there seemed so bright, so close, and even though the moon was still high, never had he seen so many of them. Spread across the black velvet heavens they winked and sparkled like diamonds, like the secret flash in the ring that sometimes felt so heavy on his hand. And as he moved nearer to the fire and lifted it to study the ring once more by the still flickering firelight, so the very heart of the great emerald that crowned it seeming suddenly to flare into startling emerald life.

And as it did so…she came to him.

One moment he was alone, his mind lost in the wonderment of the jewelled firmament that arched above his head, and of the ancient family ring on his finger as it suddenly pulsed with emerald fire…and the next moment she was there.

His Alicia…the one person in the whole world his soul was crying out for.

He thought afterwards he must have dozed off…dreamed it. But suddenly it truly seemed as if she was right beside him, her voice crying out his name, anguish in every cry: '*Gui! Gui!*' so clearly he actually looked for a moment to see if she really was there for he could *feel* her fear and desperation reaching out for him as he heard her cry out his name again: '*Gui! Gui!*' While all alone he stood by the fire on the edge of the clearing in the soft stillness of that warm summer night.

It was as if he could feel her touch, warm on his hand and her voice, the very sound of which could move his heart, calling to him. In fact so close did she seem that he called her belovèd name into the warm darkness: "*Alicia...Alicia!* Where are you? *Alicia*?" Then, thinking she had moved elsewhere, he called out, "I'm coming, my darling. I love you, *I love you!*"

And turning round in confusion, convinced of her nearness, he reached out to catch her to him, and as he did so a great white hunting owl, on wings so soft and silent that they scarcely seemed to move, swept past his head so closely its feathers lightly brushed his face in a swift caress that left him startled and breathless as it called out: '*Kee-wick! Kee-wick!*'...for that touch was warm, like the tender fingers of a woman's hand, and if he had not known otherwise he would have sworn that she had touched him.

For several minutes he was strangely disorientated, wandering the camp in a daze, softly calling her name. "*Alicia!...Alicia!*" while the great owl circled above him on silent wings. Indeed he gave one of the sentries the fright of his life, not expecting his Lord to come from behind him, just wrapped in his cape and not much else, calling his Lady's name amongst the trees and bushes.

But the only answer he had was from the owl calling as it flew: '*Kee-Wick! Kee-Wick!*' Twisting over the clearing in the bright moonlight, and back again over his head, '*Kee-Wick! Kee-Wick!*' And it was there that Richard found him minutes later, still bemused and wondering.

*

"What In God's name are you doing out here, Gui?" he asked him, amazed. "One of the sentries came and called me to say you were wandering about, calling out Alicia's name. He thought you were ill. You gave the poor boy a hell of a fright!"

"It's the owl!"

"What's 'the owl', you ass? God knows it's making enough screeching to wake the bloody dead!" he said, looking around for it....*has the lad had a touch of the sun?*

"I thought I heard Alicia's voice, Richard, calling me," Gui said then, breathlessly, clutching his friend's arm. "Truly I did. She sounded so frightened. I couldn't sleep and came out here to look at the stars, watch the fire, look at my ring…I don't know. And suddenly I heard Alicia's voice as close to me as you are now. God's Bones, Richard, I even thought she was actually here! That somehow she had escaped and found us. In fact I actually turned round to hold her…and suddenly that owl flew right by me. *Touched me!"* He exclaimed urgently, pointing to where the bird was still twisting and turning amongst the trees. "*Called to me!* Felt like Alicia's fingers on my cheek…" And he stopped in confusion.

"Gui, dear boy…it's just an owl," his friend said to him calmly…*Christos! A 'touch of the sun' indeed…Sweet Jesus, don't let him fall apart on us now!…*Look, there it goes," he said as the white bird sailed out of the trees and along a distant hedge row on great spread wings as if questing for voles, its sharp '*Kee-Wick! Kee-Wick!*' coming to them ever more faintly.

"You've done too much, my friend…*and isn't that the truth? He and Matthew carry us all…*You've just had too little rest and got a touch of the sun as well I expect, and God knows there's been enough of that! Come back with me now," he said, draping his long arm over Gui's great shoulders. "And we'll have a stoup of warm cider together with a few of Matthew's herbs in it…and you can get some proper rest. We are not starting out at the crack of dawn today for once, God aid us; and we need you on top form, dear boy…Top form!…*not mooning about chasing a bloody great owl because you think it's Alicia!…*and in the morning I'll get Matthew to have a look at you. Trouble is, you big lump…you think too much, and you know what 'Thought' did, don't you?

"No?"

"'Thought' got it wrong!" And he laughed in his lazy way. "So come on with me and share this cider. It's the last of the really good stuff we brought from Vertou. Narbonne today, Les Monges tomorrow, and if we are going to reach there in good time you are going to need it!"…*and if that doesn't knock him out nothing will!*

"The stuff with bee stings in it?"

"Yes, dear boy! Chouchen cider, guaranteed to put hairs on your chest!" he exclaimed with a huge grin. "Been keeping it for a special occasion…and seems to me this is it. Anyone who can turn his Lady into a bloody great owl bloody well needs it! That and a good night's rest will see you right as rain in the morning."…*Well, it better had, or we're all in deep trouble!…*And turning, with arms across each other's shoulders, they both laughed.

*

Suddenly, just as they turned, the owl soared out behind them into the moonlight and called to them again, '*Kee-Wick! Kee-Wick!*' The sound coming hauntingly on the breeze, the white shape, a ghostly shadow in the moonlit darkness rising and falling, rising and falling: '*Kee-Wick! Kee-Wick!*' Before suddenly diving down amongst the long grasses that covered the clearing, its cry still hanging in the soft air like a lost soul.

Chapter 31...Alicia awakens in the Baron's Chamber.

Lady Alicia de Burley's body twisted and trembled, her mind filled with broken dreams and tumbled thoughts as Gui strode through her wild imaginings...and always he was leaving her behind to the darkness of some dreadful storm that threatened to burst all over her.

No matter how fast she ran she could never catch up with him, her baby in her arms crying out as she held him up to the father who would not look at his child, a vast cloud of blackness rushing up to overwhelm them. And in her fear and desperation she called out his name: '*Gui! Gui!*' And in that halfway state between full wakefulness and slumber, she cried out to him again: '*Gui! Gui!*'...Her mind struggling to break free, to reach for the light, for someone seemed to be calling her name: softly, insistently, reaching back through the darkness pressing down on her, a voice of love and warmth and safety: "*Alicia...Alicia*!" over and over again.

And with the sound came recognition and awareness.

It was Gui!

She had no doubts about it. None at all! Somehow it was Gui who was calling her, tapping her mind, reaching out to rescue her, and with that her eyes flew open, her body bathed in sweat, her heart racing.

Dear God! She'd fallen asleep!

And suddenly she came instantly awake...dreams and nightmares splitting apart like shards of splintered glass, for today was the morning of their escape, and panic gripped her: how long had she slept? What was the hour? Had Najid's potion worked? Was Lord Roger really sleeping as she needed?...*Sweet Lord, how is Gui calling me?...And where is the Crystal?* she thought in a sudden wild panic. The one thing for which she had risked everything! Heart fluttering, breath panting, she forced herself to calm down, to slow her breathing and her thinking, and take stock before she did anything else.

Desperate not to alert the man she had slept with, she sat up slowly, slipping gently out of his embrace to leave his arms empty, then she turned to look down at him with slitted eyes: the Baron, Lord Roger de Brocas, now lying prostrate beside her in the bed, head turned to one side and breathing deeply. His powerful body and great shoulders were quite relaxed in sleep, his heavy, spatulate fingers uncurled and still, himself as naked as she was.

Very gently she got up, terrified in case she woke him...the urge to flee coursing through her, and swinging her feet onto the floor she looked out across the wide room that lay in deep, dancing shadows around her. The candles that earlier had burned so brightly were now low, guttering heaps of wax from which their flames just flickered and wavered palely in the darkness, and the oil lamps, too, had burned down to thin glimmers of orange flame.

And all around her there was a stillness that was somehow unreal, a heavy quietness broken only by the gentle soughing of the warm breeze through the room from the wide-open windows that pierced the far wall. Around the bed the fine gauzy curtains that the Baron had let down danced and whispered quietly in silken dalliance, wafting the heavy incense of late summer around Alicia's naked body. And she strained her eyes into the glimmering blackness of the room, seeking movement or some human presence, but the pools of dark shadows that cloaked the corners and flickered round the walls masked her sight, and she could see nothing.

"*Alicia...Alicia!*"

The soft sibilants called again, breathing round the chamber, making the wall hangings flutter softly, and her spine prickled with sudden fear, the hair rising off her arms and the back of her neck as her flesh sharply pimpled. But feeling her feet pressing onto the soft, rug-covered floor, Alicia forced down her alarms, and very gently, very quietly, she stood up, her body a pale shimmer in the bright moonlight that poured through the open windows in cold beams of silvery light.

Quickly she looked behind her, but the Baron had not stirred. He still lay as she'd left him, deeply asleep, drugged she hoped with the golden oil she had so liberally poured over her body for him to drink from in every way she could devise, and so he had, and now his great muscled frame was spread out across the coverlet, with his head turned towards her, facing the far side of the room. Pausing only to gather up her torn dress, she slipped on the cream over gown she had worn earlier and crept away from the bed towards the door that led through to the other room, following the voice that she could still hear calling to her.

"*Gui?*" she called wonderingly, softly. "Where are you, my love? Don't go! I'm coming, I'm *coming*!"

"*Alicia...Alicia!*"

The deep breathed voice drew her on tiptoe over the thick Persian carpets that lay strewn across the polished oak floor and hesitating only briefly, she passed through the door and entered the great room that lay beyond. There the candles and lanterns had all gone out and the harsh moon-beams that flooded through the great windows were the only light there was to see by. Everything caught in them threw up huge, stark shadows against the walls and stiff hangings, strange shapes that made her gasp and put her hand up to her mouth in silent fear, while the rest of the Baron's apartment was plunged into shadows so solid they were almost palpable.

By now Alicia was trembling from head to foot with quiet terror as she poised on the threshold like a frightened deer, ready to start away at the first sound or sense of danger. But drawn inevitably forward by the heady breathing of her name she continued, step by hesitant step, to move towards another room from whence the voice appeared to come, and pushing open the door she found herself in a much smaller chamber, lined with ancient books and rolled manuscripts, facing a table with a large dish of fruit in its centre, and a short backed chair with padded arms facing her...and suddenly she stopped, her heart beating so fast she could barely breathe.

For there on the table before the chair, beyond the glass dish with its cornucopia of fruit…in the darkest corner of the room was the black, formless shape of something that seemed to pulse with hidden light. All the colours of the rainbow seemed to be contained within it, yet the light was not clear, but shrouded, and seemed to glow from beneath a dark hood, a thick cowl that hid its brightness as a dense cloud hides the sun. It was from beneath this, and through this, that the radiance was bursting out, and it was towards this that Alicia, shaking with a greater terror than she had ever felt before, was being steadily called, having lost any power she might have had to resist.

Then, without being aware of having moved at all, she was there, with her arms stretched out before her to grasp the great shimmering object that lay hidden from her sight beneath a pall of rich, black velvet, cunningly embroidered with threads of gold and edged with pearls and gemstones. Taking one deep breath she pulled the covering away…and instantly the voice stopped, and she stared in shocked awe at the object that now lay before her.

It was the Baron's great Crystal…the very thing for which she had sacrificed so much to find.

Placed on its heavily carved cedar wood stand when the Baron had returned to the castle, it now lay in its deep wooden cup filled with coruscating light, the vaporous clouds within it spiralling round and round in endless confusion.

Unable to prevent herself, Alicia sat down in the great armed chair in front of it and put her hands round its smooth surface and leaned forward to peer into its swirling, mysterious depths, and as she touched the glowing orb she felt her entire body shudder and a deep frisson of power and excitement ran through her whole being as she felt her mind stretching out towards the flaring orb that lay there just waiting for her touch.

And as she grasped it more firmly, she pulled it towards her watching the strange amorphous mists within the globe start to move, faster and faster, spinning round and round, lit all the time by great, bursting plumes of variegated light as shapes and patterns began to form: weird geometric designs, whole universes and galaxies of stars, great multi-coloured clouds all sparkling with light. Then, quite suddenly, the tormented surface cleared completely, like bubbles from a waterfall into a lake of still water, and Alicia felt her mind soaring away from her body, spinning out of the heavy corpse that trapped it as the power of the Crystal drew her spirit towards it. She felt like a mote of dust in a sunbeam, like a swooping bird, as her soul, freed at last from the confines of its earthly cage, flew her on the wings of the morning into the very heart of the vast, still, pool of liquid light that was forming in the very centre of Lord Roger's crystal Seer Stone.

It was like looking down on the earth from a great height, but with all the power and clarity of a hunting eagle, the whole countryside sweeping past her: hills, rivers, towns and villages; fields, forests, lakes and moorland as Alicia's mind soared over the ground like a bird in a spiralling thermal as it searched for the source of the voice that had called out to her. And all at once she found she was looking at a rough encampment on the edge of a wide clearing, beneath a stand of great trees that rustled softly in the warm night airs that blew around them.

Close beside was a broad stream that flowed past a huge number of horses that were tethered on a series of long rope lines, either stretched between the trees or around hammered stakes right on the edge of the camp. There the ashy remains of a great fire could be clearly seen, now little more than a vast pile of glowing embers with a few flames still flickering within it. And there, gazing up into a sky, hung with stars that winked and sparkled like diamonds, stood a man...while all around him the camp slept. Hundreds of men...hundreds of them, and horses too, all sunk into exhausted slumber; a row of great tilt carts standing upended to one side of the encampment, a handful of guards moving quietly amongst the trees.

He stood beside the fire looking up, his mind wandering, lost amongst the heavenly jewels that flashed and flickered like a million bright candles in the night. Even though the moon was still high, never had she seen so many of them. And as she watched he suddenly turned with open arms and cried out softly: "*Alicia! Alicia?* Where are you?" Looking all around him as he did so. "I'm coming, my darling. I love you, *I love you!*"

Gazing into the depths of the great Crystal, Alicia, her mind swooping like a bird, saw his dear figure standing there as clearly as if she were beside him, a simple cape wrapped round his shoulders, his ring on his finger, his favourite old rope sandals on his feet, the face she knew and loved so much tilted upwards to the sky, his voice so well remembered and so loved.

It was Gui!

And as she recognised him her heart leapt in her breast and almost failed her, the shock making her cry out, tears spilling out of her eyes, her body shaking as if she had a fever, her voice seeming to rise and fall on the wind as she cried out his name, again and again; reaching out to touch his cheek softly as she did so.

Now, there was more movement.

Another man was coming across the clearing, walking with long purposeful strides, and Alicia gasped and gripped the crystal even more firmly, her mind rocked by what she was seeing, for it was L'Eveque! Dear Sir Richard, with his lazy smile and drawling, laconic wit. She was so stunned to see him she almost lost mind contact, the pictures suddenly wavering and wobbling out of focus and she cried out again.

"What in God's name are you doing out here, Gui?" he asked him, amazed. "One of the sentries came and called me to say you were wandering about calling out Alicia's name. He thought you were ill. You gave the poor boy a hell of a fright!"

"It's the owl!"

"What's 'the owl', you silly ass? God knows it's making enough screeching to wake the bloody dead!" he said, looking around for it.

"I thought I heard Alicia's voice, Richard, calling me," Gui said then, breathlessly, clutching his friend's arm. "Truly I did. She sounded so frightened. I couldn't sleep and came out here to look at the stars, watch the fire, look at my ring…I don't know. And suddenly I heard Alicia's voice as close to me as you are now. God's Bones, Richard, I even thought she was actually here! That somehow she had escaped and found us. In fact I actually turned round to hold her…and suddenly that owl flew right by me. *Touched me!"* He exclaimed urgently, pointing to where the bird was still twisting and turning amongst the trees. "*Called to me!* Felt like Alicia's fingers on my cheek…" And he stopped in confusion.

"Gui… dear boy… it's just an owl," His tall friend said to him calmly. "Look, there it goes," he said as the white bird sailed out of the trees on great spread wings as if questing for voles, its sharp '*Kee-Wick! Kee-Wick!*' coming to them ever more faintly.

"You've done too much, my friend. You've just had too little rest and got a touch of the sun as well I expect, and God knows there's been enough of that! Come back with me now," he said draping his long arm over Gui's great shoulders. "And we'll have a stoup of warm cider together with a few of Matthew's herbs in it…and you can get some proper rest. We are not starting out at the crack of dawn today for once, God aid us; and we need you on top form dear boy…Top form!..And in the morning I'll get Matthew to have a look at you. Trouble is, you big lump…you think too much, and you know what 'Thought' did don't you?

"No?"

"'Thought' got it wrong!" And he laughed in his lazy way. "So come on with me and share this cider. It's the last of the really good stuff we brought from Vertou. Narbonne today, Les Monges tomorrow, and if we are going to reach there in good time you are going to need it!"

"The stuff with bee stings in it?"

"Yes, dear boy! Chouchen cider, guaranteed to put hairs on your chest!" he exclaimed with a huge grin. "Been keeping it for a special occasion…and seems to me this is it. Anyone who can turn his Lady into a bloody great owl bloody well needs it! That and a good night's rest will see you right as rain in the morning."

And turning, with arms across each other's shoulders, and with shared laughter…she watched them walk away.

And as they left Alicia's heart cried out in sudden wild distress; her eyes were blinded with tears, her throat swollen with emotion as her whole frame shuddered with the shock of her discovery, and as her spirit cried out once more, a pulsating, keening cry from the very depths of her soul…so the Crystal gave a sudden violent pulse of light and power that burst through her like lightning, flinging her out of the chair and onto the carpeted floor of the Baron's chamber.

Chapter 32...The Company of The White Rose prepares to flee the Castle.

Alicia came-to with a jolt in a sodden heap on the floor, her cream silk over gown clinging to her sweat-soaked body like a second skin, her mind spinning, and she felt sick and confused.

All around her the room was in darkness save for the pools of silver from the full moon that stained the floor like shining mercury. The great globe, now still, was just a giant ball of crystal glass that dimly reflected the looming shadows in the room, standing silently on its stand like a harmless ornament...*So...Gui did not die on the Mary! I knew it! I always knew it! Thank God! He has come to find us, with Richard and dear Father Matthew too, and a whole host of others... Thank God!* And her soul exulted! Where they had all come from she neither knew nor cared...just that they were here! And Gui was alive as she had always believed, and seeking her, and he was close. It was a miracle! But what had Richard said about arriving at the Baron's borders?... 'Narbonne today, Les Monges tomorrow...'

*Sweet Jesus! 'Narbonne today, Les Monges tomorrow...' Tomorrow? That means today!...*And her heart leapt in her breast so that she had to put her hand across it as if to stop it from leaping right out of her trembling body. By this very afternoon Gui and his Command, would be nearby, to rescue her. Her mind was in a panic of apprehension, dizzy with confusion as she leaned panting for breath against the wall, her whole body quivering with emotion as she struggled to gain control over her raging thoughts...*Holy Mary, Mother of God! How can I protect them from the Baron's wiles? He will see everything!...*The Crystal would surely reveal all? Wouldn't it*?...No...No! He cannot know! Not yet. There has been no time for that today, and then he has been with me all evening...*And her head spun with wild thought.

Temporarily exhausted, she slumped down on the chair again,. But how had she been able to see Gui? How had the Crystal worked for her? And would it again? Still trembling, she went over to the huge glass orb in its wooden seat and sitting down, she put her hands on either side of it and with nervous care looked again into its clear crystal depths.

Instantly her hands tingled and the hairs on her arms bristled, the bracelet that Rochine had given her gave off sudden and unaccustomed heat, and at once the orb swirled with colours, like great cumulous clouds tinged by the setting sun. She sat back and took her hands off the glass...and instantly it went opaque, becoming still and clear again as a mountain stream, and her bracelet went cold. The moment she touched it again with both hands it all came back to life, returning to quiescence as soon as she let go. Pausing for thought, she took off the bracelet and again held the glass in both hands.

Nothing!

Look as she would, the great globe remained cold and clear…and dead…*Spirit of the Saints, it is the bracelet! That and some essence of the Baron's spirit perhaps that makes the Crystal glow and come alive? He and I are of the blood! That and some...some other personal 'thing' to join us!...* She did not know, only that Rochine had given the bracelet to her; and that it was one of a pair, the other belonging to her father that he, too, wore all the time! Was that the link? But what about Gui? How could she see him so clearly and how could she know what he was thinking and doing? He had no bracelet that she knew of...*But he has the ring!* The Malwood Emerald, given to Grandmother Philippa, her beautiful de Brocas relative, missing for a generation…and then stunningly returned to Gui on their betrothal night, and which he now wore with such pride at all times.

Was that how de Brocas made things work? With something personal that each person wore? Her bracelet, Gui's ring? Or perhaps it was just something in the blood, as she and Soraya had reasoned?...*But one thing for certain in all this…the Crystal works for me!*

And even as she accepted that, she knew she would have to take it with her, otherwise de Brocas would surely use it to track them down…somehow, she would have to take the Crystal with her!

It had not been in her plan to do so, but now she was certain how it worked, she had no choice. And she looked around her then for something with which to replace its shape beneath its damask cowl, and something in which to wrap it too, now desperately conscious of time passing….*Dear God! That bastard could wake any minute!...*and she looked anxiously towards the further room, knowing that she must leave, and leave now! Before he awoke and noticed her absence from his side and raised the guard…or someone else did.

And if once he captured her no power on earth could ever free her. He'd hold his castle in the teeth of all his enemies; and at the last would kill her rather than ever let her go, especially with her knowledge of the Crystal. This she knew in her heart, just as certainly as she knew that there could never be another man in her life other than the one whom she had so knowingly betrayed, and whom she knew she loved more than life itself…*Pray God Gui will forgive me this night's work…*and she wept again briefly, her vision blurred by tears, too horrified to contemplate a life without him, the more so now she knew that she was carrying his child.

But dashing the tears from her face, and without any further hesitation, she lifted the huge glass ball off its stand, surprised at how light it actually was, wrapped it in the tattered remnants of her dress, replacing it with a round melon from the great fruit dish in the middle of the table, placing the black and gold embroidered shroud on top. And moving silently across the room to the entrance chamber, she thanked God that not only were the great doors that guarded it so well-oiled as to make no noise as they opened, but that Baron Roger had banished his servants and his guards from his apartments. A silent prayer running through her head...*God be with me now. Don't let me fail. Holy Mother aid me, and I will yet get us all safely out of this hellish place!...*And with that she softly opened the double doors just enough for her to slip through, like a ghostly wraith, drifting on silent feet down the winding stairs that would bring her to the wide marble corridor she knew led round to her own apartments.

*

Stealthily, carefully, she descended the broad spiral staircase, her bare feet making no sound on the thickly carpeted white marble treads, her body pressed close against the wall as she went down, clutching the Baron's great Palantir to her chest. And as she neared the bottom, so the light increased, for two flaring torches flamed and sputtered from the iron sconces that lay on either side of the entrance. In daytime there was always at least one guard there, sometimes two, and now she prayed that Xavier Le Brun had not exceeded his master's orders and left even one still standing there.

She had never felt so frightened in her life. Worse even than her flight through the forest!

At last she reached the end, and peered round the edge of the stair wall.

Nothing!

And pausing only for a moment she stepped off the bottom step and into the passage.

It was empty...stretching away into the shadows on either side of her...*Thank God and the Holy Mother!...* And thanking God again that she had been blessed with a good sense of direction, Alicia turned left at the foot of the stairs, away from Rochine's rooms, and with hurried but controlled footsteps she made her way swiftly along the empty corridor, barefooted, the shadows cast by the occasional flambeaux ensconced along the wall leaping and flickering like fell beasts waiting to leap out and devour her, and she was terrified.

Then, when was just fifty paces from safety, she heard the heavy tramp of armoured feet coming towards her, and in quaking terror she pressed herself into a nearby alcove. Desperately praying that whoever it was would keep on pacing past the corridor she was in, and down towards the bailey, she cowered against the wall and shivered with fear, not least because the alcove was barely deep enough to hide her, the very edges of her robe just spilling out onto the cool marble floor.

Next second her heart sank…

"What the fucking hell are we doing up here, Jules?" She heard a hated voice snarl. "I had a nice bit of tail all lined up for tonight…and now that bastard Le Brun has ordered us out. Who the fuck does he think he is?"

"He is the Commander of the Castle Guard, dear cousin," she heard Jules Lagrasse reply with a laugh. "Do you really want to argue with him? He makes the rules, Lucas, and we obey. And we have been ordered to report to him immediately. So…go we must. And anyway, that little tart, Denise Larousse, is anybody's meat. You can have her any day you choose!"

Then she heard them stop, and could feel them looking up the long corridor behind her, her heart hammering in her chest, her mouth dry with fear.

"Which way now, Jules?" She heard Lucas Fabrizan growl. "Didn't you say there was a short cut up there?" And she heard him take two or three steps towards her. "Anything's better than walking bloody miles round this fucking pile of stone and marble."

"You always were a lazy sod!" She heard Jules reply with another laugh. "That way leads to the Baron's apartments as well as to Le Brun's Office chamber, and we are forbidden to use it. You may choose to risk the Lord of Narbonne and Gruissan's anger, cousin…I do not! . There are times for taking short cuts, and times for doing things by the bloody book. And this, you fucking idiot, is a time for doing what we are told! It's really much safer that way. Come on, you miserable bastard. We'll go the proper way for once. Those two bitches we hauled on board the *Morning Star* are along near here. You never know? You might get lucky and find one of them off to the bogs, and get to give her a hand!" And rooting like hogs they turned and walked away.

*

Unable to take a step further for fear she would not be able to walk properly she felt so wobbly, her chest heaving as if she had run round the moat at Castle Malwood, Alicia hugged the great Crystal in her arms and waited until she had stopped shaking. Then, after a few minutes more to calm herself, she peered round the edge of the little alcove she had been hiding in, took a final deep breath and stepped out again.

Hugging the shadows where they lay across her path, and running silently on the soft balls of her feet through the wavering pools of dim light flung out by the torches placed at intervals along the way, she reached her own rooms at last, almost flinging herself into Aquib's arms as she got there. Delighted and relieved to find him massively standing there like the rock of ages, she briefly kissed his hand and with one swift movement raised the latch, pushed the door open, and slipped inside. Closing the door behind her she lay back against it panting, the great glass orb cradled in her arms, revelling in the warm solid feel of the thick oak against her back as she struggled to breathe normally again and control her shaking limbs.

The room was almost in darkness.

Lit only by a single oil lamp and the brightness of the moon, just now sliding behind the battlements, it's harsh light casting shadows everywhere, for a moment no-one moved. Agnes, Soraya and Little Isabelle sat like carved statues of ivory as shocked by her sudden arrival almost as she was at making it.

A split second later the little tableau broke up as Agnes rushed up to her and flung her arms around her.

"Thank God you are back! You've been gone ages…see, the moon is setting. We were despairing of seeing you ever again!"

"*I fell asleep!*" she whispered desperately, pushing further into the room. "I can't believe it. God help me, *I fell asleep*! Or I would have been here much sooner. Quick! Take this from me!" And she held out the bundle she was carrying. "I must get some clothes on. There is not a moment to lose."

"What is it?" Agnes asked uncertainly.

"It is Lord Roger's Crystal!"

"*No!*" Agnes cried out sharply as everyone gasped, Isabelle putting her hand over her mouth in shock. "That thing is evil. Please don't make me, Alicia," she begged, shrinking away, refusing to take it. "I..I cannot!"

"Give it to me, sweetheart," Soraya said urgently, giving Agnes a sharp look of surprise. "You need to get dressed."

"It worked for me, as we thought it might," Alicia said in a rush, handing it into Soraya's outstretched hands with a sigh of gratitude. "I think it's something to do with this bracelet," she added breathlessly, as she slipped off the robe she had been wearing. "I held the thing between my hands and…and, *dear God in Heaven!"* she exclaimed breathlessly. "The damned thing worked! And..and..I..*I saw Gui!*" She burst out almost jumping with excitement, almost laughing at the shocked faces. "I saw him! And heard him. He is alive and Sir Richard and Father Matthew…and a whole host of men with him! Dear God, he's alive! *He's alive!* I can hardly believe it!"

"Where from?" Agnes asked, startled

"From Nantes, I suppose."

"No…the men?" Agnes queried.

"*God's Death, Agnes!*" Alicia snapped, struggling with her underskirt. "I don't know…there seemed to be hundreds of horses, and men, with him. I've no more idea, sweetheart, than you do! But I *do* know exactly where they are…and where they will all be tomorrow." And she paused again as they gaped at her news, adding quietly. "I brought the damned thing with me because I had to!…And I don't suppose he is going to be too pleased when he finds out it's gone, and us with it…and that's putting it mildly! But I just *had* to, or else he will know where Gui is too because of the ring he wears. I have this bracelet," she said, waving her arm in the air. "The one that Rochine gave me in England…the pair to the one her father also has…And Gui has the Malwood Emerald that my grandfather gave to Philippa de Brocas when they married. That's the link!" And with a swift motion she took the great Seer Stone back from Soraya, turned and cast it onto the bed, pulling her tattered dress from around it as she did so, so it rolled briefly and then lay still, innocently winking in the lamplight.

"*Oh, my God!*" Soraya breathed out, hands up to her face, almost panting with fear. "*My God!* It truly *is* his Crystal!" She stammered horrified. "His great Seer Stone that he had from the Emir of Samarkand all those years ago." And with shaking hands she rushed to the bed and reached out to touch its glistening surface, snatching them back again as if she had been burned, while Agnes and Isabelle Soulier hugged each other in terror. "You are right!" She breathed, awed. "He will be enraged beyond belief! Us escaping will be bad enough…but his Crystal? Sweet Jesus, Alicia! How could you dare?"

"It was the only way, I assure you," Alicia went on briskly, catching up a handful of clothes that Agnes, white-faced, handed her, "of making certain that he cannot follow either us, or Gui, anymore! He has some kind of mind-link with us too. I don't really know how it works. Just that it does! I should have taken that damned bracelet off long ago. But Rochine gave it to me and would have noticed instantly if I had not continued to wear it…and she is far too sharp not to have worked out why. But I am sure you are right, Soraya. In the end, it is being of the 'blood' that really does it."

"Where is Sir Gui, and..and all the others?" Agnes asked, her voice shaking.

"They are close to Narbonne, and will be at Les Monges tomorrow," Alicia went on swiftly. "The one place we did not manage to get to. But I *saw* him; *I saw him!* Soraya," she went on, almost panting, shaking the girl by her shoulders as she spoke. "Agnes, my belovèd Gui was there, with all his men. And if Gui was there so too will be your Allan," she added, giving Agnes a swift squeeze as she rushed to change. "I saw him as close as if I were actually beside him! What chance would he and his men have, or us for that matter, if Lord Roger could watch and listen to their..our.. every move?"

"*None!*" Soraya hissed passionately.

"*Exactly!*" Alicia replied swiftly, looking up at her, as she pulled on her boots. "So…I brought it with me. It was a sudden impulse…replaced it with a melon from his fruit dish!" And she suddenly chuckled. "That will give him a mighty shock when he discovers it!"

"Shock? *Shock?*" Soraya shuddered, appalled at the thought. "Shock is far too simple a word for what he will feel! He will be more angry than either you or I can possibly imagine. Incandescent! Dear God, Alicia, but the sooner we are gone from here the better"

"No matter, sweetheart. I know I was right to do so. After all it's only a large ball of glass. We can wrap it carefully and put it in a bag. Izzy can carry it!"

"*Me?*" the child squeaked, her eyes like saucers.

"Yes! You wanted to help?" Alicia said quietly, turning to the young girl by her side. "Well then, you can carry the Baron's Crystal. It is much lighter than it looks, and Agnes can keep with you all the way, she too is armed and will help you if you need it. That will leave me and Soraya with hands free for other things. Najid will go ahead as he did through the forest. Now, please, ladies, are you ready? I am terrified that bastard will awake any moment. First I fell asleep and then I spent far too long in his Crystal room. Is everything ready as we discussed?"

"Yes, Alicia," Soraya said firmly. "Bernard will be waiting for us, with Najid, by the lower staircase. Aquib and Aziz will escort us there as agreed. One ahead and one behind. Najid will come with us to the sally port…and then eel his way back the way we came. God willing, all will be well and we will get clean away!"

"*Insh'a Allah!*" they both said together and suddenly the tension rushed out of them and they laughed.

"By the way," Alicia said quietly, looking up as Agnes tied her wimple, and draped her cloak over her shoulders. "The Cousins are out and about…So

I hope you are both armed?" she added as she heard Agnes' breath whistle through her lips:

"Yes!" Soraya said sharply, showing a long fine-pointed sheathed dagger she had strapped to her thigh. "And I have another for you too, for your boot. But, Sweet Jesus, Alicia," she exclaimed appalled. "Those two bastards? How do you know?"

"They almost ran into me," Alicia replied, slipping the dagger Soraya had given her into its special sheath inside the top of her boot as they both gasped. "On their way to obey a summons from Le Brun. Another thirty paces and they would have caught me. As it was, they turned and went another way. I have never been so afraid as I have been tonight, and the next bit will be little better. There! Finished...now, how do we look?

Throughout their conversation Alicia had been swiftly dressing to match the others so they were all wearing good travelling clothes of soft leather, both dresses and sleeveless jerkins, which they wore over loose cotton chemises, and each with a dark blue woollen cloak to cover their outward garments. With black wimples tied behind their heads, and soft leather boots, they could easily pass as castle wenches from a distance, but up close, the quality of the material would surely give them away. Isabelle was less of a problem as she still had on the clothes in which her brother had brought her up to the castle.

Then finally they were ready, Soraya wrapping the great glass ball in a thick woollen shawl that covered it completely, before putting it into a soft leather draw-bag that she had found at the bottom of a chest. Taking care to put out the lamp that had been burning while they were getting prepared, Alicia stealthily opened the door. And after a few swift words with Aquib outside to make sure the way was clear, one by one they slipped outside, Soraya shutting the door behind them last and turning the key in the lock as she did so.

The die were cast...they were on their way.

Chapter 33...Escape from the Château Grise.

Outside, the long passageway was still empty, but they knew that before long the guard would be coming to replenish the torches along the walls with fresh ones.

Already they were very low, and it was one of the Baron's quirks to maintain full lighting throughout the dark watches of the night. As it was, their dimness helped them considerably, and booted though they were, they were able to make quiet speed along the stone flags, flitting ghost-like from dark to dark as they fled away, Aquib's huge shadow preceding them, Aziz following behind.

Having turned to the right outside their door, they made their way to the first flight of stairs that led downwards towards the base of the great Donjon. From there they'd have to make their way across the open bailey towards the great mass of the curtain wall, and then into the base of the gatehouse tower that contained the narrow sally port Alicia had noticed when she'd first entered the castle.

Steadily they descended through one level after another, Alicia following Aquib with Soraya close beside, Isabella and Agnes sticking to each other like glue as they traversed from one narrow passageway to another. Dodging from doorway to doorway they went, on more than one occasion pressed tightly together in a deeply recessed archway, their hearts hammering and desperately trying to control their breathing, as a file of soldiers passed within feet of them. Once they thought they'd been spotted, but the man was distracted by one of his friends who was in a hurry to go off duty…and never came to investigate fully the sudden flurry of movement that had caught his eye.

And always, at any moment, was the fear that the Lord Baron might awake from his drugged sleep and discover his loss. But, finally they reached the ground floor safely where Bertrand and Najid were waiting for them, and suddenly it was time to say good bye to their two giant guardians.

"This time we must part forever, my Lady," Aquib rumbled in his dark voice. "We had word today that the *Morning Star's* sails have been sighted, and she will be into the harbour tomorrow…and then in a few days, as our Prince said, we will all be gone, taking the Baron with us to Jaffa, as was long ago agreed."

"Oh, Aquib. I don't know how to say 'goodbye' to you," she said with tears in her eyes, and for the first time she threw her arms around the big man who lifted her up as if she had been his own child and held her close.

"You have been the *best* friend and protector that any maid could wish for, or any queen," she said a moment later, after he had put her down…"You and Aziz both," she added, turning towards her other enormous Arab guardian.. "You have always been there for me…for all of us. And I will miss that deep sense of safety you have given me so much, so very much. I had hoped to have met with your Prince just one more time, to thank him for his gift to me of your care and protection, and that of young Najid….for without your strong arms in the forest that morning we would all have been killed But, alas, it is not to be. But, please, be sure to thank *El Nazir al-Jameel-aziz-nidhal*, from his infidel *Nazraani*, the Lady Alicia de Burley, from the bottom of her English heart.

"I..We, owe you our lives, Aquib, and God willing…*Insha'Allah!*…our freedom as well. I cannot thank you enough. I do not know what else to say, my heart is too full." And with tears coursing down her face she flung herself into their arms for the last time. *Allah Akbar! Salaam Alaikum!*" And touching their lips with their fingers and then their foreheads to her, they bowed, turned and softly walked away, their own eyes glistening wetly in the torch light.

*

Moments later, Bertrand, with Najid right behind him on silken feet, was leading them further along the corridor before turning sharply to his left through a low archway, and picking up a flaming torch from an ancient iron sconce by a crudely fashioned stair head, he plunged down a steep, narrow spiral that led to the furthest depths of the keep. Here the air was still and thick, heavy with the scent of age, filth and despair. Halfway down he paused beside a very low recess that was blocked off by a great slab of timber.

"Now listen carefully. Beyond this great chunk of wood is another narrow spiral that runs upwards through the thickness of the walls to another opening just to the left of the main entrance to the Donjon. It isn't used any more, and I only discovered it quite by accident. Once outside you'll find four further steps that lead up to the main bailey. Now keep your heads down and follow me."

To the girls' surprise the great baulk of timber didn't open inwards, but slid sideways into the thickness of the wall on great iron grooves; and following closely behind Bertrand, they began to climb, the scent of pine heavy on the air from the resin in which the torch had been dipped, the smoke making their eyes water.

The filth and detritus of years littered every step.

Great sheaves of spiders' webs festooned every corner, making the girls shudder as they pushed through them; ancient leaves blown in over the years crackled and broke underfoot, and the whole staircase had an evil, unwholesome air about it that made the girls shiver and softly whimper. Then, after what seemed an age, Bertrand stopped before yet another great timber slab. "Right, this is it. Brace yourselves for darkness, for I must first put out this torch, then keep your fingers crossed that this door will slide, otherwise we've had it."

Suddenly the light went out and everything was in deep, suffocating darkness, the air filled with the scent of burnt resin and torch reeds, ancient rot and decay, making them all gasp. Then, after an agonized age of fumbling and grunting, and with a deep groan the door finally moved in its ancient grooves, and the sweet night air flowed in over them. Stepping out into the soft darkness of that summer night they all breathed deeply, before Bertrand turned and dragged the door back into place, the graunching noise of iron on stone sounding frighteningly loud. And they all stood as statues, terrified that they might have been heard by the guards whom they knew were everywhere.

But no-one stirred.

*

Now, out at last from within the mighty stone carapace that had hidden them all, they found themselves crouched down on a small space of stone slabs five feet below the level of the main bailey, some forty paces from the great Forework that rose up to guard the main gateway leading into the Donjon. And with infinite caution they climbed up the few steep steps that lay before them and peered out across the great paved courtyard of the bailey.

Everywhere was a strange mix of bright silverlight and deep shadows as the moon was setting, and at that early hour in the morning the great bailey lay completely deserted. To move out across that wide expanse of stone flagged emptiness seemed absolutely impossible, yet to remain where they were would surely invite detection, for every tower was manned and an extra guard had been detailed to patrol the lower perimeter of the bailey round the base of the keep.

But whatever else they did they must move, and soon!

Suddenly they heard voices coming their way, not the rough surly tones of the common soldiery, but the light ones of women.

"We're in luck," Bertrand whispered. "Those are kitchen slatterns going off duty. Thank God those cloaks of yours have hoods, mine also, and Najid's. We'll wait 'til they've passed and then walk boldly out and join them. The castle is always taking on new girls, so a few more won't look any different. Whatever you do, don't slink or appear furtive. Just behave normally and we might be alright."

With their hearts in their mouths, they did just as he had advised them, every nerve in their bodies urging them to flee. But with arms linked together and chattering brightly they hopped up the last few steps as the women passed them, and tagged on behind the group of eight or so women who had just come past their hiding place as they made their way home. But every step brought them nearer and nearer to the guards who were standing silently before the Donjon's main entrance, and the blaze of orange-yellow light that fell around it from the huge braziers the Baron kept alight throughout the hours of darkness.

*Just as at Malwood…*Alicia was thinking…*Only larger. Pray God they do not spot anything. Surely they will hear my heart thudding!…*And she forced herself to giggle then, digging Agnes in the shoulder at the same time to distract the soldiers as they shuffled past them.

All of them expected a challenge to ring out. But none came, and in a moment they were safely passed. But for them all this was only the beginning of their problems, for though they had got outside the Donjon, they were now actually travelling in the wrong direction.

"We're going the wrong way!" Alicia whispered urgently. "We are going away from the old well, and the sally port is to the left of the main gatehouse as you enter the castle, not to the left of it as you look out!"

"1 know my Lady, but for the time being there's little else we can do."

"Yes there is," Alicia hissed. "We must break out of this gaggle as soon as possiblc. Any moment one of them may turn round and start a conversation. We may be cloaked as they are, but there's no way that we will look like common drabs if once they take a closer look at us…nor will we sound like them either!"

"What do you suggest?" Soraya asked, slowing her walk.

"The next tower we pass, one of us, Isabelle, must stop to adjust her boots, then we can all break off from this group and once she has finished sorting them, we can then saunter casually across the bailey towards the dark shadow that lies opposite, and in the deep corners of every tower. Thank God they are square towers here, and not the new style round ones! This moon may yet do us some good. Then we can shadow hop until we can get to the old well Bertrand told us of."

"Alicia, you're *mad*!" Soraya hissed desperately at her. "Shadow hop? We can't do that! And across that whole open space? They'll spot us immediately! Haven't you noticed how many men there are on those tower tops? The flicker of steel is always there!"

"Don't worry Soraya. The men will only see what they expect to see. A small party of Château drudges going home. Keep chattering, the odd giggle, and keep moving steadily. *Above all you must not run!* Not even if we are challenged! Give them a cheeky answer back...they will love that and will give us no part of their minds. Cheeky maids have been answering back soldiers for generations...and laugh at them. That's normal. Then, once in the shadow of the walls, we can move swiftly right up against the walls themselves where no-one can see us!"

"Holy Mary, Mother of God!" Agnes murmured. "You'll get us all killed!"

"Trust me, Agnes. This is no different from being at home, where I used to do it all the time, remember?"

"But this isn't at home, sweetheart. Oh, Jesus, my heart fails me!"

"Don't be so feeble, Agnes! You know it used to drive Sir Yvo wild that his men never saw or caught me. If you stick to the shadows and keep your body pressed close to the stone you can't be seen by those above you. Not unless they lean right out to do so.

"What about the men on the far side and in the Great Tower?" Bertrand asked.

"Faintheart! As long as we stick close to the walls, the shadows are too deep and they're too far away to see anything clearly. The danger comes when you move. If someone shouts out you must keep absolutely still, as a faun left by its mother or a young leveret!"

"*Faintheart*?" Bertrand whispered, horrified. "You *are* mad, my Lady! Alright," he went on. "But it's just about hair raising enough to work, and I can't think of anything better at the moment. So...let's go!"

Casually, Isabella started to hop and then bent down to adjust her boots, her companions staying with her in a little group, while the rest of the kitchen women moved steadily ahead of them. Then, when they were some twenty yards adrift, they all turned towards the far side of the bailey, and the great slab end of a massive flanking tower that they'd stopped opposite and with a giggle and a burst of quiet chatter they stepped out. Easily, gently they moved, with hearts aquiver and bodies damp with fear...and casually ambled across the open bailey towards the deep shadow that the huge square tower opposite cast across the ground.

Every moment they dreaded a sharp challenge that would bring death amongst them all, while walking out as if they had every right to do so. Desperate not to break into the swiftest possible scuttle that their whole hearts were so urging them to do, they strolled with seeming complete *sang froid*, as if they had no cares in the world, until after what seemed aeons in the open, the tower's great moon-cast shadow at last reached out to hide them. And with a final rush, they were there; stood pressed tight against the cool stone, their breath rasping in their throats and their chests heaving with the sudden release of all their pent-up fear.

Above them the tower soared up into the night sky, the black teeth of its battlements lost against the stars that spread across the velvet darkness arching over their heads. And all the time the clatter of iron feet on hard stone high over their heads, and the glitter of cold steel opposite in the moonlight, was a constant reminder of the danger they were in. None of them had ever felt so exposed before, and at the back of their minds was the terror of discovery and the certain knowledge that at any moment the Baron might awake and find that Alicia and his great Crystal orb had gone!

*

Having got their breath back at last and calmed their nerves a little, it was time to go on, and like formless shadows they moved along the baseline of the castle walls, never forgetting the brilliant whiteness of the moon's light, now at the full, that rippled across the stonework of the castle in silvery waterfalls, bathing everything in its harsh brightness.

The terrifying thing about it was not just the appalling distance between one tower and another, even though they managed to remain in dark shadow most of the time, but every step they took brought them nearer to the great gatehouse and the main entrance to the castle. Here was where the very greatest danger lay, for not only was the area well lit with flaring torches and braziers, but also the guards were constantly being changed to keep everyone fully alert, and there were a lot of them. But worst of all, they had to enter the right hand tower in order to reach the long galleries and deep staircases that would take them down through the walls to the sally port itself.

From there Bertrand and the four women would attempt to make their escape, but first they had to break back into the castle, and there was only one way to do that, as the young squire had explained three days before. And what had sounded feasible then…now looked terrifying when, finally, they reached their last halt, their breathing ragged and their nerves on edge. But until then there had been no challenge, and now they lay back against the great stones of the curtain wall, right in the deepest corner of the last tower, as Bertrand reminded them of what he had in mind.

"Right, there's only one way back inside from here as I said last week, and it will be very risky."

"Go on Bertrand," Alicia said at last. "We've come this far, there's no turning back now. Tell us the worst."

"That old dry well is just the other side of this tower as you know, and it's been out of use for years now, ever since the Great Donjon itself was built. Just below the top there are iron rungs let into the stone-work, put there by the original builders for repair purposes. Fifteen feet down from the top is the entrance to the old water passage I told you of. Probably part of the Roman palace that once stood here."

"Yes we all know about the Roman palace," Alicia said. "We have been in its pool every day since we arrived."

"Right. Now listen," he went on in a soft whisper. "As I told you, when the Château was rebuilt in Baron Thibault's day the water entrance to the passage was blocked off leaving the well dry, but the old passage itself leads to the remains of the Roman hypocaust, and from there is the way into the bottom of the tower. It is very narrow, and without the candles I left down there pitch black. So…I will go first as I know the way. Then you ladies and then Najid.

"I hate being closed in." Isabelle whispered. "It frightens me!"

"Me too, sweetheart," Agnes replied softly, squeezing the young girl's hand. "Just stick close to me and you will be fine, I promise you."

"Dear God, Bertrand. Right beneath the whole building?" Soraya asked him, appalled, now faced with the reality of having to worm her way beneath that whole vast weight of masonry. "Are you sure there's no other way?" She added, her voice a husky shiver.

"Don't be such a *sheep's head*, Soraya," Alicia whispered sharply. "We went over all this before, silly!"

"The Lady Alicia is right!" Bertrand hissed his reply, as Soraya gasped. "Short of going straight up to the guard and asking permission to walk out…this is it!"

"Then we'll just have to try it!" Alicia said, sharply drawing in her breath. "Dear God, we must *all* be mad! Lead on Bertrand; and may God aid us!"

*

So saying, they sidled round the corner of the tower they had been sheltering against, and with their cloaks drawn tightly against them made their way, with all possible stealth, to the raised brick plinth that surrounded the old well head, creeping forward in the deep shadow of the tower that stretched right out to cover the well.

There they cowered down beneath the stone coping of the well itself, not fifty yards from the gatehouse entrance where two more great flambeaux were still flaring, but without a guard in sight, and prayed that no-one would be eagle-eyed enough to spot them.

Across the top was a thick iron grating, and right in the middle was the large square grille, hinged with rusted iron loops onto the main cover, that Bernard had told them about. Crouched down as they were, with their hoods right over their heads and their cloaks covering them completely, they looked no more dangerous than a few great boulders, but someone would have to climb onto the cover and open the hatchway before anyone could climb down.

"Now listen, if we're discovered start screaming! Anything you like, but make it loud, and when the soldiers come say you saw me earlier on and only came to investigate. That way, though I will die, you may be able to save yourselves."

"Rubbish!" Alicia hissed. "If you're found out, then so will we be! How could we possibly explain what we are doing out her at the dead of night?"...*Not to mention the Baron's Crystal!*..."We're all in this together; and I have no intention of allowing you to throw your life away for me, while I go without blamc."

"And the same goes for us too!" Agnes said bravely, giving Isabelle's hand a squeeze.

With that Bertrand and Najid wriggled over the edge and crawled onto the iron cover, crouched over it together like a monstrous bat mantling its wings. The thick metal was cool after the day's heat, and heavily rusted, but by the Grace of God, the hasp that once had held the entrance hatch closed, and had long since rusted through and fallen away when Bertrand had first found it, had still not been replaced, and the grease he had put there, though dry and dusty, was still in place. The thing yet to be discovered was how quickly they could move it.

Struggling round to the far side Bertrand grasped one iron rim and Najid the other and together they heaved at it, gently at first then harder, and with a groan that seemed terrifyingly loud it slowly lifted up. With infinite care that left their muscles screaming for relief they pulled it over and lowered it against the main cover. All this time the shadows from the wall and tower had cloaked their movements, and with the moon setting they were still well hidden, but unless they all managed to clamber down quickly the first hint of dawn would soon be in the sky and that would be deadly.

With a fierce hiss, Bertrand called Alicia over, going first before her and helping her down behind him into the cloaking darkness, guiding her feet until they found the first of the iron rungs that led downwards towards the bottom of the well shaft. Then it was Isabelle's turn, then Agnes's, Soraya's and finally Najid's. Swinging his legs over the edge the little Arab cook lowered his body down into the pit, and with a desperate struggle managed to pull the hatch cover over behind him, but carefully even as he did so it still fell back with a soft *clang!* A noise that sounded like thunder in their ears, and made everyone freeze and draw in their breath, while Najid went hand over hand across the main grid to reach the side-wall of the old well, 'til Soraya grabbed his feet and guided them onto the first of the iron rungs.

Then, just as they were beginning to descend, they heard the sound of voices and the crunch of feet; and to their horror two of the Baron's men came to the very edge of the well and stopped. As soon as they heard them coming they'd all frozen, keeping their heads down to hide the white of their faces, their bodies pressed tightly against the stone as they waited, with their hearts in their mouths, for the instant of discovery. And though one side of the shaft was still brightly moonlit, the other remained in even deeper shadow; and it was in this stygian blackness that all of them were quivering.

One movement, one sound and it would be swiftly over for all of them.

Chapter 34...Beneath the walls of the Château Grise.

"I tell you, I saw someone, or something, crawling across the top of this grating!" And a moment later a man peered over the side and rattled the cover with his hand...his armoured head suddenly silhouetted against the sky. "It was like a giant bat!" And his voice trembled.

There was guttural laughter: "A giant bat? You've been on that gut-rot ale old Chambertin serves off his bottom shelf! Get on, you fool! Fucking bat!" And he laughed. "No-one's been near this place for years. They say it's been closed up for ages, and anyway it's dry."

"All the same, I swear I saw something!"

"Go on then, take a good look. See for yourself, there's nothing down there."

Below them the fugitives held their breath and hugged their trembling bodies even closer to the stone wall and braced themselves for discovery. A casual glance was one thing, but a detailed study could not fail to reveal them. They heard the man move, the scrape of his feet against the stone coping, the rasp of his breath as he heaved himself up onto the grating....then a great shout of anger from somewhere behind them.

"*You two!* What the fucking hell are you two stupid bastards doing there? Come here this instant!" And there was the scrape of the man's feet on the grating as he turned round, followed by the sound of running feet, shouts...and more voices.

"Well, Corp'. This idiot thought he saw something near the old well."

There was a sharp metal '*dink!*' then a yelp of pain, followed by a deep, coarse voice: "Corporal Grevas if you please, you fucking moron, when addressing a superior soldier!" the under-officer growled fiercely, "or I'll give you another sharp '*dink!*' on your thick fucking bonce with my stick."

"Yes, Corporal Grevas. Sir!" Came a loud shout.

"And so I should think, too. You useless crap-head!" And there was another metal '*dink!*' and loud yelp, followed by more noise as the first man finally clambered down off the main grating, followed by the sound of clinking steel as their patrol leader came towards them.

"Listen, you two fucking clowns!" came the dark gravelly rasp. "There have been enough fucking false alarms this night to last me a lifetime. Everyone is starting like frightened rabbits at the first strange thing they see. You," the voice growled. "You're new here, aren't you?"

"Yes Corporal Grevas, I only came in yesterday…"

"Then listen to me, you stupid sod! No-one has been near here for years, and that well is as dry as an old whore's cunt!"

"I told him that!" The man's companion complained. "But he wouldn't listen. Said it was like a great bat!"

"*Like a bat?*" the corporal exclaimed outraged. "Are you fucking mad?" he went on, giving the man's head a mighty buffet that made his helmet clang loudly and there was another yelp of pain.

"A bat indeed! If Commander Le Brun finds out about your little escapade and learns that you left your post above the gatehouse to look for a giant fucking bat, then it'll be double drills and short rations for all of you! And that will mean me as well, you fucking lunatic. Do you want that?"

"No!" came the surly reply.

"No, 'Corporal'! When you address me, you miserable piece of horse shit!" he snarled at him.

"No, Corporal! Sir!" The man snapped back immediately.

"Right! Now, get fucking back to where you belong, before I have the fucking skin off your backs. Go on, *MOVE! Fucking bat!*" Grevas muttered as he stalked after them. "These boys up from the country are mad! Frightened of their own bloody shadows! *Fucking bat indeed!*" And moaning about the quality of the troops that the Baron had recently brought in, he followed his men back to the Gatehouse.

*

As the feet and voices died away Alicia and her little group all gave a huge sigh of relief, Bertrand being the first to move his lips.

"Sweet Lord, but that was close," he said in a hoarse whisper. "Sorry about the language, my Lady. Corporal Grevas never did have much imagination about him!"…*Just as well!*...She thought…*Just one more step…*

"How they didn't see us I just don't know," Soraya breathed from below them in the darkness.

"Anyway they've gone now, so let's move on ourselves. You alright, little one?" Bertrand asked Isabelle, who had been too petrified to move a muscle.

"Yes, thank you, sir," she gasped, her whole body shaking. "I just want to get home!"

"Don't we all?" he replied, quietly. "Don't we all!"

*

Foot by foot they now continued to descend to the bottom of the well, the three girls having to go right past the narrow tunnel opening at the bottom to allow Bertrand to lead the way. Then finally they were all safely within it, pausing while Bertrand struck a flint to light a small piece of tallow candle that he had left there from his last visit. Then, with the young squire in the lead they all set off, all crawling laboriously along on hands and knees in the pitch darkness, with only the faintest glow from Bertrand's candle up ahead to show them they were not alone. Heads constantly scraping along the low brick roof, they leopard-crawled their way forward on elbows and toes, cloaks catching on every bump and projection along the way.

Around them the air was rank and stuffy, seemingly too thick to breathe, and within minutes they were all hot and breathless, the sweat from their bodies adding to the sourness of the air, making their noses wrinkle at the stench and their throats gag on the solid darkness that pressed in on them from all sides. And as they crawled they could hear the sound of rushing water getting nearer, and the ground grew damp beneath them until they came to a solid brick wall down which water was trickling all the time. Beside that was a pile of crumbled brick and ancient rubble, and a great black hole through which the stink of ancient soot and burning still seeped.

"This is the entrance to the old hypocaust I told you of," Bertrand whispered, his voice loud in the tight, confined space in which they found themselves, his tiny candle no more than a distant glow to those at the back. "It is very narrow and twisted, so stick close behind me and keep in touch with each other. I will pass a lit candle end to each of you, and you must follow the chalk arrow marks on each pillar…ignore any other marks you may see. It is a distance…but you can do this, I assure you!"

Crammed into the tunnel they were surrounded by a darkness so deep you could almost feel it, the only light Bertrand's flickering candle, and the weight of earth and stone pressing down on them was palpable, terrifying, and Isabelle was whimpering and struggling to breathe. Choked with the darkness and the thick heavy air that surrounded them, made worse by the stench of age-old fires and furnaces that came from the hole through which they would all have to crawl, all felt frightened and oppressed.

Agnes, sensing Isabelle's distress, held her hand tightly as one by one they crawled over the broken brick work and into the chamber beyond.

Here there were scores of small pillars about two feet high built of thin bricks, and on top of each was a great square tile to take the weight of the paving slabs and concrete on which the palace floor above had long ago been built, and even now, after nearly a thousand years, was largely still in place, though many were cracked and fractured. And in and out between these little pillars they crawled, loopy-loop, like caterpillars in a bulrush stem, as they slithered and humped their bodies amongst them, all following Bertrand's arrows as best they could.

Dear God...how much more of this is there?...Alicia thought, as she brushed her face clear of cobwebs and dirt yet again, spitting to clear her mouth as she did so...*How do miners do their work? This is just ghastly!*...But just then the roof above them changed as they came to where the huge foundation stones of the gatehouse itself had been bedded onto the top of the ancient Roman concrete flooring. Here the pillars had been thickened, and there were small piles of desiccated mortar over which they had to try and force their way, all thinking of the massive weight of masonry that now soared above their heads...and under which they still had to grovel on hands and knees to find the strange stone chamber that Bertrand had discovered. That would lead them to the short flight of steps leading up to it they had come so far to find, and the trap door that lay in the centre of its thick stone flooring.

With a rush they crowded into it at last, panting and struggling to breathe normally, faces and arms scratched and bleeding in many places where they had jagged themselves against the ancient brickwork, their clothes covered in the debris and detritus of centuries, their candle ends guttering, each person desperate not to lose their only source of light before Bertrand could light the little oil lamp he had left behind the last time he had been there.

Terrified of the darkness rushing in upon them, Agnes and Isabelle gasped and cried out as the horror of being crushed beneath the vast weight of the gatehouse tower above them gripped their hearts and shook them to their very souls, until Soraya came and put her arms around them both and eased their terrors.

"Well done," Bertrand murmured softly, looking round them all. "*Well done!* We are now immediately below the lowest chamber of the right hand tower. It is an old store room, as I said, and unless someone has forced the stop I put on the door and filled the whole chamber with great sacks or barrels, we should be able to move the trap and get out of this God-forsaken hole!"

So, while Bertrand and Najid placed their hands on the rough-hewn underside of the trap door, the girls listened intently for any sound of movement above their heads. But there was nothing, and on their signal the two men began to push upwards.

At first nothing seemed to happen, then, with a sudden rush the trap swung upwards and both of them stopped heaving, desperate for it not fly all the way backwards and crash onto the floor, shaking the whole room. So, while Najid held its weight on his shoulders, Bertrand swung himself into the room, lit the small lamp he had left behind, and in its golden light together they lifted the door right back until it lay fully open at last. And after checking all round they leaned down and pulled the others up: Alicia first and Soraya last, with Agnes and little Isabelle and the leather draw bag in the middle, Isabelle's pretty face streaked with tears and her whole body trembling all over. Then, with Najid's help, Bertrand lowered the trap door back down as gently as he could, while everyone looked around them.

*

The room they were in was both dark and empty save for a mass of ancient cobwebs and half a dozen empty and worm-eaten barrels that stood stacked up in one corner. To their immediate right was a short flight of stone stairs with an arched doorway at the top, closed for the time being by a solid oak door with Bertrand's stop still firmly against it. So, for a time, they knelt panting on the floor like dogs after the chase. But they knew time was not on their side and they must move on again as swiftly and quietly as possible.

"Now Bertrand, what next?" Alicia asked him breathlessly, brushing a maze of cobwebs away from her...*Sweet Jesus, how I hate spiders!*

"Well my Lady, we have to get out of here, and then take the gallery that leads away towards the broad spiral that would normally take you all the way up to the wall head. Halfway along that there is a narrow gallery that leads to a long spiral that runs down through the wall to a broad underground chamber, and there, hewn out of the rock and built into the tower's base, is the sally port itself."

"Won't it be guarded?" Soraya asked.

"Bound to be. Xavier Le Brun may be an ignorant savage...but he is not such a fool as to leave so vital an exit undefended. And with your wedding supposed to be later today, there'll be two of them. The last thing the Baron will be wanting is drunken revellers penetrating his defences!"

"Who will they be?" Soraya asked.

"Don't know."

"How do we deal with them?" Isabelle asked, softly.

"Knock them out or kill them. We have no choice."

"What if Natalie's father is there?" Isabelle asked again in her soft voice.

Alicia sighed. "Don't worry, little one. If he's there we'll make sure he is alright."

"And there's no portcullis is there?" Soraya asked, changing the subject. "Only the iron 'yett' thing you told us about, and the door of wood and iron?"

"The yett is fairly easy, and there is no key for that either," Bertrand said with quiet firmness, "only a number of draw bars. I can manage those, and then Najid can put them all back again."

On an impulse, Alicia and Soraya both went to this young man who had helped them so selflessly and flung their arms round him, and he them. So for the space of a dozen heartbeats they clung to one another in a single close knit group, while Agnes, Najid and Isabelle stood by silently and watched, the leather bag Isabelle held fatly swollen by the great Crystal ball still hidden safe within it.

Then they were on their way again, leaving no time for spare thoughts, only immediate action.

Up the short flight of stairs they went, and finding the door mercifully undamaged, it took only a moment to remove the wooden chocks that Bertrand had put there before, and then the door was open and they were off, making sure to leave it closed behind them.

Climbing stairs and scuttling along narrow galleries they made their way as swiftly as they dared; twice hiding in alcoves and garderobe passages from patrols on the way, and once one of the two men who strode past their hiding place actually stood on the edge of Alicia's cloak, so close was he to them. But though it left her badly shaken....*Never been so afraid. Holy Mary aid me! I can hear his breathing and smell his sweat!...*yet they were still at large and now nearing the last part of their escape as, with a final glance all round, Bertrand now led the four of them down the final long set of twisted stairs he had spoken of that led directly to the sally port. Halfway down there was a narrow landing with a foul smelling garderobe just off it, and he left the girls sheltering there with Najid, while he went on down to have a look.

Two minutes later he was back: "There's only one there," Bertrand whispered urgently.

"Thank God for that!" Alicia exclaimed, squeezing Isabelle's hand.

"It's not quite as simple as that." The young man murmured softly, his face white as the others huddled closer to him. "It's Jules Lagrasse! And where he is, that other bastard will not be far behind. There are two helmets hanging up on pegs and a table with a chair and a pack of cards, so somebody must be missing. Lagrasse is drinking ale from a jack."

"*Sweet Jesus, the Cousins!*" Alicia breathed out huskily. "So that's what Le Brun wanted them for earlier…To put them down here on guard…*This just gets worse and worse!*...Well, ill met by moonlight! Those bastards have got it coming to them in some order. Najid?"

"Yes, my La-dy," the little man stammered his reply in his desperately broken Frankish.

"Two men," Alicia whispered slowly, holding up her fingers. "The Cousins, yes?"

"Yes, my La-dy," he said carefully, his eyes suddenly blazing. "I know them! Bad men…Evil men!"

"Yes, Najid! The two from Saint Girons. Kill them!" And she pointed to his khanjar and violently motioned the cutting of a throat, or a stabbing. And once she had seen from a swift nod and a grim smile that he had clearly understood, she mouthed: "We will help. You hide," and she motioned the alcove they were in. "We will draw them up here," and she swayed her body and smiled sweetly at him from beneath her long eyelashes. "Then we will kill them…both! And the earth will be rid of two devils. *Insha' Allah!"*

"*Insha' Allah!* my La-dy!" The little cook replied then, nodding with a beaming smile and patting his khanjar. "*Usama!...Insha' Allah*!" And he gave such an evil grin that Alicia smiled.

"What do we do?" Agnes squeaked.

"Well, one of you will have to lure him away so that Najid and I can deal with him," Bertrand said grimly.

There was a quiet sigh from Soraya and Alicia as they took in what he was saying: "What about that other bastard?" Soraya asked him softly in the darkness.

"We'll just have to take our chance on that," he answered urgently. "We simply don't have the time to wait any longer."

Soraya and Alicia looked at one another and grimaced.

"I'll go," Soraya said. "That sod has been wanting his hands on me this twelve month and more. His eyes will pop out of his head when he sees me. And I've done this kind of thing before with Rochine, so I know it will work, I guarantee it…men are so weak!"

"*No!*" Alicia hissed at her fiercely. "We'll both go. We are in this together, sweetheart, and two are safer than one if he should get difficult. We are both armed, remember? Where do you want him?" she asked the two men, turning towards them.

"Back here, with his back to me if you can manage it, Bernard replied. "We'll lurk in these shadows, near this foul smelling latrine and take him from behind. Izzy and Agnes will have to go further up the stairs to be out of the way and keep a sharp lookout for Fabrizan. He's worse than this one by far!"

"Very well, Bertrand. God be with you. And, Nijad…*usama!*" she added with a grin, turning towards the little Arab cook…*Allah Akbar! Insha'Allah!"* And she smiled.

"Come *on* Alicia!" Soraya urged her, taking her by the hand. "We are wasting time, and time is precious….I'll show you what a 'sheep's head' I am!" she said then with a swift grin into Alicia's startled face. "This time you take your lead from me. We *must* get out of here before Lord Roger wakes up and finds us all gone, and his Crystal with us. 'Sheep's head, indeed!" And with a swift dig into Alicia's ribs, she squeezed her hand and swiftly turned away.

Chapter 35...How Love and Honour paid a dreadful price for freedom.

Keeping their cloaks on, the two girls now pattered softly down the steps to the bottom, where the staircase opened out to reveal a wide barrel-vaulted room flaringly lit by two large sconces that flamed brightly in heavy iron brackets against the wall.

Right between them was the closed iron yett and wooden door of the sally port, and seated next to that, on a wooden bench set against the wall, a table by his side with another chair, a pack of greasy cards, a lamp and a pile of coins, was Jules Lagrasse.

Strongly built, with broad shoulders and dark hair above a sallow face, with big square hands, he looked what he was - a practised, proven fighter - and he was seated, with legs apart, taking a deep pull at a leather jack he held in his hand, the large stoneware jar of ale from which he had just filled it standing uncovered beside him on the stone slabs that lined the floor. His sword, hanging from its baldric, was on a nearby hook, and his dagger was beside him on the table, and as soon as he heard the sound of their steps on the bare flags with which the room was paved he looked up astonished, and lowering the jack he grinned at the two girls, wiping his mouth with the back of his hand as he did so.

"Well, well indeed," he sneered, his eyes lighting up as he saw them approach him. "And what brings you two all the way down here from my Lord Baron's chamber?" he grated at them, standing up slowly and looking them both up and down with his sharp black eyes. "Tired of the Lord and Master and looking for a bit of 'rough' are you?" he said, rubbing his big hands together and spitting into the corner. "What do you want with the likes of Jules Lagrasse?" he asked, linking his fingers together and cracking his knuckles at them, smirking as he did so...*How good that Lucas is not here...he is such a peasant! And I want some fun with these two pretties before we turn them in. I have earned it!...* And his eyes slid lasciviously over their faces and across their breasts and rounded hips with a hot, wolfish look.

"The Lady Alicia and I have been unable to sleep," Soraya lied effortlessly. "It is her wedding day today, and I promised to show her all the special places in the castle. So we have dressed ourselves simply so that no-one would stop us. Commander Le Brun said we could come down here as a special treat...before...before the Lady Alicia's big day." Soraya said lightly. "And anyway, I have been wanting to spend some time with you,

Jules…and..and your cousin Lucas, for some time, so..so we are well met," she lied outrageously, and then giving him a dazzling smile, she pulled her chemise down over her shoulders so the top of her breasts were exposed to his greedy eyes.

"Where is Lucas?" she questioned, unconcernedly, continuing to move closer to him as she spoke, putting her small hands on his chest…*please God he does not turn up just yet!*…"My but you are such a big strong fellow, Jules," she purred, running her hands admiringly over his thick arms and shoulders, "that I'm sure you'll easily manage both of us. The Lady Alicia is not a virgin, you know, Jules," she said with a nod towards Alicia, who blushed furiously at her words…*Why did she have to say that to this ugly brute?*…throwing daggers at Soraya with narrowed blue eyes, while standing just in the shadows behind her, watching her friend sinuously winding her arms around the man as she looked up at him with her huge green eyes. "So there's no blood to prove. And she likes girls too, don't you darling?" she breathed, turning to give a startled Alicia a deep, mouth-watering kiss, caressing her breasts as she did so. "You'd like that wouldn't you, Jules?" She smouldered at him. "You, me and a real Lady…"

The South Frenchman eyed the two of them greedily, flicking his tongue, lizard-like, over his lips as he did so…*My God, but they are a tasty pair, that's for certain. Those tits are lovely!*…he thought, unable to take his eyes off them, his senses reeling and his sound common sense completely fled from his brain: "Lucas was down here, but he has been called away. He won't be back for ages," he said, moving to put his arms around Soraya. "Shame, isn't it? And a rare good job for me it is too. I'm the best."…*and I just can't wait to fuck you, you little bitch. And that other one. She's a rare bit of arse too.* And he smiled…*Fucking marvellous!*

"Of course you are, darling," Soraya said, smiling back as she ran her small hands over his muscled back and shoulders, looking up at him from the corners of her eyes, as good as any street whore. "I like a man who knows what he's doing." And she giggled and shook her head, looking at him from beneath her long lashes, her dark eyes sly with promise. "That really gets me going."…*Sweet Jesus, I hope the lads can handle him. This is not going to be easy!*…And stepping back into the light so that he could see her better, she slipped off her cloak and put his hands on her breasts, closing her eyes and sighing as he pawed at her warm soft body…*Yukkk!*…her head going back and her tongue running over her lips in an apparent ecstasy of desire. Then, taking his hand, she moved delicately away from him, looking over her shoulder at him as she did so.

"Not here," she breathed, licking her lips at him. "I like the darkness, and my friend is not so bold as me. Come on, follow us; I know a place not far from here where we can all be comfortable." And motioning Alicia to go in front of her, she led him across the floor to the stairs...*Like a lamb to the slaughter*...and they began to climb.

Without any hesitation, like an autumn wasp to a jam pot, Jules Lagrasse went with them, unable to believe his luck. Breathing heavily, his loins already rushed with blood, his hot black eyes fixed on the smooth column of Soraya's back and the rounded tightness of her buttocks as they swayed before him, he allowed himself to be drawn away from his post...*That arse is so lovely! Always said I wanted to fuck her rigid!*...And he groaned in appreciation.

In the dark recess halfway up the stairs Bertrand and Najid waited for them in a sweat of apprehension, Bertrand with his long dirk...Najid with his wicked curved, sway-bladed khanjar gripped in his sweaty hands, bodies shaking with nerves. Killing a man in the heat of battle was one thing; doing it in cold blood quite another.

When Alicia passed the opening she stopped, allowing her hood to falloff her head to reveal the true beauty of her face and the warm welcome of her smile, and as Soraya reached her she nodded briefly and turned to block the passage, throwing her shadow across the stairs as she did so. Then, while Jules watched goggle-eyed Alicia bent and kissed Soraya lingeringly on the mouth, her eyes and head flicking back as she did so, before turning her friend round to face him again with a smile.

And taking the man's hands in her own she placed them on Soraya's breasts moving back against the wall to pass behind her as she did so, so that he could see nothing but Soraya's face and body. Then, as he bent forward to kiss her, Bertrand acted: seizing Jules' forehead from behind with one hand while aiming to thrust his knife into his thick neck with the other. But some sixth sense must have warned the man, because even as Bertrand struck, Lagrasse thrust himself backwards so that the flashing blade missed its mark, piercing his shoulder instead of his neck and with a muffled shout the two of them began a desperate struggle on the narrow stairs, while Soraya was dragged backwards over them.

But Najid made no such mistake.

Pulling Bertrand off the struggling, swearing Frenchman, he plunged his great Khanjar deep into his vitals, not once but several times, until his guts were in ribbons and his blood was splashed everywhere...and with a final gasp and rattle Jules Lagrasse was dead, leaving both men panting on their hands and knees covered in his blood.

"Splendour of God, Bertrand. *That was awful!*" Alicia exclaimed, horrified, her clothes and face badged with his blood which had spurted everywhere. "Killing in battle when the blood is hot is one thing, and I have done that: that slaughter in cold blood was truly brutal. But I have no regrets…he deserved to die. Thank you, Najid," she applauded the little Arab cook. "You did well too. Aquib will be proud of you! Now, come on, for God's sake and let us get out of here before that other one returns…he is worse than Lagrasse by far!"

And in moments they were all down in the main chamber studying the wrought iron yett to see where it opened, while Soraya ran back to the bottom step to call up quietly to Agnes and Isabelle: "Come on you two, quickly. It's time to go!"

"*Go where, you fucking bitches?*" A harsh voice spat at them from the stairs, turning them all to stone immediately as if they had seen the Gorgon's head.

"You murdering whores! I will gut you all for what you have done tonight," he said harshly, his feet splashed with his cousin's blood, where he had been forced to step over his body. "Starting with this stupid little slag!" and with Agnes gripped round her throat and Isabelle dragging behind only half conscious from a great buffet he had already given her, Lucas Fabrizan appeared round the corner of the stairway like a fell beast from the Pit, and turning, he blocked the stairway completely.

Next moment he hurled Isabelle down before him onto Bertrand and Najid, still just clutching onto the leather bag she was carrying, sending them both flying, while he turned Agnes in his arms, ripped her chemise off so her breasts were naked, and with both her arms twisted behind her back with one great hand, he held his dagger up to her throat with the other.

"Now, you pair of fucking doxies! You bloody bitches! And those two useless pieces of fucking, human shite with you…you are all coming with me! Back up the stairs to Commander Le Brun and The Lady, and we will see what we will see. *And you two!*" He raged…"*You*, you fucking bastards!" He shouted at the two men, "I will personally gouge the flesh out of your fucking stinking bodies in bloody chunks with a sharpened spoon until you are dead*! Now move!*"

"*No!* My lady," Agnes called out in a stricken voice, while desperately fighting to break free. "*No!* Do not do as he says! He will surely kill me anyway, and even if he does not the Baron is like to have me thrown to the soldiery before selling me. And what will happen to you and Soraya does not bear thinking of. You must go free, my sweeting…for all the reasons that you know so well!" And she began to struggle once more against Lucas's bitter hold around her arms, while crying out: "Go for him! *Go for him!*"

"*Stay back!*" Lucas snarled viciously. "I can manage this fucking little whore," he added hitting Agnes hard with the pommel of his dagger on the side of her head, making her scream. "*Stay back!* I swear to you I will cut her throat unless you obey!"

"Agnes, sweetheart! *Hold still!*" Alicia called back, giving an anguished cry. "I cannot bear to see you slain! Lucas, put her down I beg you and I will come, and the others with me," she said, her voice trembling, the tears starting from her eyes. "You will not be sold, my darling, I swear it. I will marry the Baron before I will let that happen to you and Soraya, or anything else!" Then turning to Lucas she said: "You harm one hair of her head, or me, or any other of the people here and your life will not be worth a single piece of silver!"

But still Agnes struggled against Lucas hold; kicking him and still crying out for Bertrand and Najid to attack him. And before Alicia or any of the others could say or do anything more, with a smile and a grunt of laughter, Lucas Fabrizan thrust his knife into the side of Agnes's neck.

It was a brutal act, as with a violent sweep of his hand he then dragged the sharpened blade across her throat, her hot blood gushing and spurting out of the ghastly wound in scarlet sheets as he held her up, her desperate scream shut off with a vile gargle of sound, before he cast her from him like a broken rag doll, her head almost hacked from her body by his savagery. Then drawing his sword he advanced into the chamber, now a scene of complete chaos and bloody carnage, grunting and laughing at the sight of them all scuttling about in Agnes's blood; and while Alicia leaned stunned with shock against the wall, Soraya and Isabelle huddled screaming in a far corner, Lucas Fabrizan went on the attack.

The room was small, but just wide enough for fighting, and while the South Frenchman strode into the centre, his sword whisking and flickering at them with one hand, his dagger in the other, Bertrand and Najid crowded round the sides, their blades thrust out before them.

Lucas smiled and flicked them aside contemptuously as they circled round him, each diving in and out as they sought to find a way past his guard...*Snap! Snap! Snap!*...the scrape and screech of steel filling the chamber with sparks and the sharp tang of hot metal, like a blacksmith's forge. And all the time Alicia stood like stone against the wall, her face white, shocked to the core by poor Agnes's terrible death, gazing sightless as her dreadfully gored body pumped out its last ounce of blood across the floor, and Soraya cradled Isabelle, her body shaking in her arms, both girls liberally sprayed with Agnes Fitzwalter's hot blood.

But it was an unequal struggle as Lucas knew; one good lunge would see either of his opponents skewered, and he smiled, knowing that time was on his side. Knowing he could end it any time or continue to play with them while they became more and more desperate, or someone came and saw what was going on in the depths of the tower…and then Bertrand made a mistake.

He over-reached himself, got too close, and swift as a striking snake Lucas slipped his left foot forward and thrust his sword into the boy's left shoulder, making him scream and fall to the ground clutching his wound, a spurt of bright blood following Lucas's lightning attack. But even as the Frenchman stepped back he slipped in the great pool of blood that had spread out across the floor from Agnes's murder, falling heavily on his side, and as he did so Najid leapt on him, and in a heartbeat they were both rolling across the floor, bloodied beyond belief and grunting and growling like wild animals.

In moments, however, Lucas was on top of the small Arab, struggle as he might, and bringing his head back he viciously head-butted the little man, banging his head on the flag stones as well as he did so, so that Nijad was hopelessly dazed…but before Lucas Fabrizan could deliver a final smashing blow, Alicia acted.

Horrified by what had happened to Agnes, with Bertrand wounded and Nijad about to be killed, Alicia suddenly sprang into life, and rushing back to where Jules had been sitting she seized the great stoneware jar of ale off the floor, and leaped back to where Lucas and Najid were still struggling. Past Isabelle and Soraya huddled together, terrified for their lives, she ran and pausing briefly to be certain of her aim, she crashed the heavy jar down two-handed, with all her strength, onto Lucas Fabrizan's head as he pulled it back for a final strike at Najid, still pinned beneath him.

And so Lucas Fabrizan too was slain, dying as he had lived amidst violence and bloody murder, for with a disgusting, sodden thump Alicia crushed his skull like a plump water melon in a vile spray of blood, brains and bony fragments, the jar smashing into pieces as she followed through with it onto the solid ground. Ale and blood mixed together in a foul brew that splattered everything, flowing in a disgusting stream of stone shards, human debris and sudden vile stench as his bowels gushed out to fill his blood-boltered clothing.

Pale and fainting, Alicia leaned against the wall retching violently, her head pressed against the rough stone work, her hand across her mouth. A long drool of spittle and vomit hung from her lips and her face was wet with tears, as she gagged and retched against the wall, appalled by the charnel house around her, blood and human mucus splashed everywhere, while Bertrand struggled to drag poor Agnes's body out of the way with his one good arm, and

Najid still lay there amidst the foul mire, stunned by the beating Lucas had given him.

Soraya shook Alicia roughly, wiped her mouth with her sleeve, then slapped her face hard to bring her to her senses.

"Come on Alicia, there isn't time for this!" she hissed violently. "If you hadn't done that he would have killed all of us, for he was more brutal than anyone. Agnes sacrificed her life for us to go free....you and the baby! There is no time to grieve now. We must get out! Come on, and help me with the 'yett' thing Bertrand told us about, and with the door. Remember, Najid has to get back to the bottom of the tower before we are discovered."

Meanwhile, having dragged Najid from under Lucas's body and shaken him back to life, they swiftly had the yett open and were soon struggling with the heavy draw bars across the main door way.

"Come on, give us a hand," Bertrand called out sharply as he and Najid struggled fiercely to free them. "These are stiffer to move than I had thought, and my arm isn't helping. We must get away at once. Any moment someone is bound to come down here. They change the guard regularly and I have no idea how long those two bastards had been here before we arrived!" And he fell back, exhausted.

With a rush the three girls ran to help him, and while Alicia ripped the sleeve off his shirt and used it to bind up his shoulder, Soraya and Isabelle pulled at the lower draw bar that held the door closed, while Najid pulled at the other, both at last sliding away into the stone slots in the walls that were designed to hold them. Pausing only to drag out the coiled rope that lay within the chamber, they grasped the thick wooden handles that were bolted onto the inside of the door itself and dragged the sally port open. Below them, like a yawning chasm, lay the revetted slopes of the Château's great dry ditch...and above them the stars.

The way to freedom lay open at last.

Chapter 36...How the Company of The White Rose was broken.

But this was not the time to enjoy the warm summer airs that blew through the open doorway, and picking up the knotted rope behind him from the floor, Najid flung it down into the darkness.

Then taking up the two torches from the wall bracket inside the room, Bertrand stamped them out in a shower of sparks, and with the smoky fumes swirling round him he took Soraya by the hands and helped her over the edge.

As she disappeared from view Alicia ran to Najid and hugged him briefly, thanking him in the only way she knew by kissing his hands and saying; " *Salaam Alaikum!* Thank you! Thank you!" While he nodded and smiled and handed her to Bertrand to help her over the edge, followed by Isabelle and her leather carry bag.

Having checked that they were both safely on the rope, Bertrand turned then and shook Najid by the hand and then clasped him round the shoulders before turning to grasp the now tautened line with his good arm wrapped around it and, with Najid's help, he walked backwards into the pitch blackness of the castle ditch.

Hand over hand, knot by knot they all steadily descended, the massive walls of the castle seeming to lean over them, their rearing height swaying dizzily above their heads as they lowered themselves into the depths. Then they were at the bottom, huddled together for mutual protection, their faces pressed close together, voices hushed whispers only audible to themselves. Immediately Bertrand gave the rope three sharp tugs and at once it disappeared into the darkness.

They were on their own.

"Are you all alright?" Bertrand murmured, looking round at the three girls.

"Yes, we're fine," Soraya replied. "What about your arm?"

"It'll hold up…It has to!" He exclaimed softly. "How about the Lady Alicia?"

"She'll hold up too, Bertrand," Alicia said quietly, dashing her hands across her face in momentary silence…*Dear God…I cannot believe I have lost her? Oh, Agnes! Agnes!*...Before adding: "I told you. Queens are tougher than you think. Come on now. We cannot stay here. Where to next?"

"The castle ditch falls away here to the far side," Bertrand whispered hurriedly. "About thirty paces, and then in direct line with where we are now is a single white stone. Above that, jutting out from the facings like stepping stones, is a line of corbels that rises diagonally to the top of the fosse, each one striped with white beneath. You can only see them from the bottom, because that is the way they have been painted. I'll go first then you follow."

"Dear Lord, but I'm afraid," Soraya whispered. "Stairs and tunnels are one thing; but this climb is something else again."

"I'm frightened too, my Lady," came a small voice, as Isabelle put her hand in Alicia's.

"Don't worry my love; I'll be right behind you." Alicia murmured softly, giving the girl a quick squeeze. "We are all afraid tonight. Have you got that Crystal safe?"

"Yes, my lady"

"Fine, sweetheart. Now, just don't look down, keep moving, and you'll be up there before you know it!"

Then, reaching for each other's hands in the darkness, they all touched fingers, and were off at a run, crouched down and skirting the many boulders that littered the ground, stumbling over the uneven surface in an agony of bruised shins and scraped finger ends. Never had such a short distance seemed so great, but within minutes they had reached the far side and seconds later Alicia spotted the first white marker stone. In the darkness the rising line of steps were not easy to find, but after a few minutes of desperate fumbling Bertrand was on his way up, clinging to the wall like a spider, his cloak hanging down behind him, masking his movements from any but the sharpest eyes, and even then they'd need to know where to look..

Below him in the great ditch the girls watched his steady progress against the stars, and then they too were climbing. Soraya first, then Isabelle then Alicia; Isabelle, her carry-sack over her shoulders, too terrified of falling to do more than watch her hands, Alicia following immediately behind her to steady her feet as they struggled for a firm purchase.

Across from them the vast bulk of the castle loomed menacingly in the darkness, its near walls now lying in shadow as the moon had set, only the great panoply of stars overhead giving any light. It seemed terrifyingly close and the movement of the guards across its parapets could be clearly seen as they criss-crossed before the braziers that glowed redly from each tower head. The Baron, taking no chances against a surprise attack of some sort, had ordered that stores of readily flammable material should be kept on hand, together with the easy means of lighting them.

Then suddenly they were at the top, and flung themselves down on the dry, bristly earth, hugging it to themselves in an ecstasy of relief and sheer exhaustion, their chests heaving from their exertions, their bodies damp with sweat and fear, before wriggling away from the edge as fast as they could.

Twenty, thirty, forty yards and then they stopped, gasping for breath.

Alicia was the first to speak after they'd all caught their second wind: "Sweet Jesus, we've made it!" she whispered hoarsely. "Dear God! I really didn't believe it was possible. But poor Agnes! *Poor Agnes*!" She cried out softly in distress, her body rocking as she did so. "I cannot believe I have lost her!" And she sobbed quietly into her hands, her body wracked with her grief, while Isabelle and Soraya did their best to comfort her.

"How long have we been gone?" Soraya asked urgently a moment later.

"I've no idea," Alicia replied, lifting her head and snuffling miserably. "I lost all track of time the moment we entered the well."

"No more than an hour. One and a half maybe at the outside." Bertrand whispered back.

"Is that all? It seems we've been on the go for half the night!" Soraya answered amazed.

"No…the moon was only just tilting when we left the Donjon, and now has set. But we cannot linger here. It will get lighter soon and then the dawn will flush up."

"The town is close now, Bertrand," Alicia said, more calmly now her first grief had sped. "We have ridden all around here, so I know."

"Yes, my Lady, straight down the hill," he replied, breathlessly

"Right. First we must put a little more distance between us and the Château," she hissed at him. "Then I'll tell you what must be done next." And getting to their feet they ran, crouched down like frightened partridges, zigzagging as they went 'til they were almost up to the first houses where they went to ground.

"Right Bertrand, my shining young knight," Alicia said. "This is where we must part company with you."

"But my Lady…" he protested vigorously.

"No, Bertrand, don't argue with me, we haven't the time," she said, breathlessly. "The Company of the White Rose is broken, and we must go our own way now. Just listen, I beg you, for you must go at once to your father and tell him all that has happened here. We cannot go with you. Too large a party and we would only slow you up…and speed is of the essence. Steal a horse if necessary, but get there. Tell him that the whole countryside is ready to rise but lacks an experienced leader, and tell him to look out for men with white surcoats that bear a scarlet lion rampant in the centre. Many, many men. More than I could ever have believed possible. And when they come we can clean out this nest of vipers once and for all.

"Those are my men, Bertrand, and two full knights lead them. One of them is my belovèd Gui, The Lord Baron, Sir Gui de Malwood, whom the Baron tried to murder; and a close friend of King Richard of England. The other is his Guard Commander, Sir Richard L'Eveque. They will help you. Take Isabelle with you. She must be gone from here before sunrise, you both must be! The town is no longer safe for her. She can send a message to her brothers once Gui and Sir Richard get here.

"Soraya and I will seek shelter in the town from Guillaume Soulier, his brother Ralph and their friends. I know where to go, and they won't let us down. Gui is close by: Narbonne right now and will be at Les Monges by tonight…at The Golden Cockerel…Armand Chulot."

"I know it well!" he exclaimed softly. "The Baron brought his wife in last night!" Bertrand added, his voice thick with emotion. "Claudine Chulot. He has her in an upper dungeon; to make her husband compliant. Armand will be beside himself for he adores her. Your man should find a ready ally there, I think."

"I did not know. Dear God! Is there no end to his evil? Then tell your father to go there, Bertrand…and take Izzy with you. Do not let her out of your sight; she carries a prize with her, worth more than my weight in gold. Guard her with your life, Bertrand. I charge you with it!"

"Very well, my lady. It shall be as you say."

"Now, Isabelle?" she went on, looking round for the girl.

"Yes, my Lady?"

"You are to go with young Bertrand here, and take the Crystal with you. You must guard it well, the both of you, and on *no* account are you to try and use it! As long as you keep it hidden, he *cannot* find us. Its face will be closed to him and we will all be safe. If the worst comes to the very worst you must destroy it. Otherwise, keep it safe until I can come for it again, or give it to Father Matthew, the Black Monk who travels with my fiancé, Sir Gui de Malwood. Do you understand me? If you should be tempted, it has the power to destroy you both, and with you all of us as well. And remember, the Baron will leave no stone unturned to get it back, me also. So, be warned, little one: his vengeance will be terrible! Now, dear Izzy," she said, looking the young girl directly in the face. "You *must* promise me, you will keep it hidden!"

"I *promise* you, my Lady." she said, rising to her knees. "I will not fail you."

"And you, young Bertrand. You must give me your knightly word to do the same."

“I promise you too,” he said rising to one knee, kissing the hem of her dress as he did so. “And I will do all in my power to keep Isabelle safe as well!”

“Right,” she said, now standing…and lifting them both to their feet she gave them a kiss on each cheek to seal their bargain, Isabelle especially who clung to her fiercely for several moments before stepping aside with tears in her eyes.

“Now, *go*! Don't wait around worrying about us, there isn't time. Any moment our disappearance will be discovered or someone will find those bodies in that awful chamber, and then the fun will really start; but by then, God willing, we'll all be in safe hands at last. And God rest my dear Agnes’s soul; she did not deserve so terrible a death!”

And as she finished speaking Soraya stepped up to the young man who'd helped and risked so much to save them and gave him a great hug and a kiss again on each cheek too, Isabelle likewise. Then, without a backward glance, both youngsters were gone, and the two of them began to hurry towards Gruissan, the first buildings of which were now almost at their shoulders.

Chapter 37...Alicia and Soraya find refuge in the Safe House.

Soon Alicia and Soraya were amongst its streets, so different from the daylight when they would have known their way instantly.

Dark and deserted, the houses pressed closely together with the rank odour of filth and rubbish wafting round their crudely plastered walls. Here and there a dim light gleamed from behind the shuttered windows, and a dog howled from the far side of the town, the sound rising and falling on the soft night airs that brushed their anxious faces.

Hoods pulled over their heads, their thick cloaks wrapped close about them, they ran towards the main square, feet pattering on the roughly cobbled street as they hurried along, the tip-tap sound of their passing echoing softly from the darkened buildings that surrounded them. Continuously looking over their shoulders as they went, frightened of their leaping shadows on the walls and desperate for safety before the hue and cry was raised, they came at last to the main square now lying hushed and still, only the rushing noise of the water from the fountain in the main square breaking the silence.

"Where did Guillaume say you were to go?" Soraya whispered urgently.

"To the house with the blue door opposite the fountain," Alicia replied. "Stanisopoulos's house, remember? The little Greek perfume seller? I only hope to God that someone's awake at such an unearthly hour in the morning. I've no wish to rouse half the town with our knocking."

"Don't they live there then? Guillaume and Ralph Soulier?"

"I don't know, Soraya. Probably not, as it's Stanisopoulos's home and shop by the looks of it. But Guillaume said that if we ever needed help this was the place to reach. Come on, we have no time to lose now!" And dragging her friend by the hand, Alicia hurried across the square, past the fountain that splashed and bubbled there, and so to the only house with a solidly painted door that she could see.

"Are you sure this is the right place? In this strange light it's impossible to tell one colour from another."

"I think it must be. There's no other house with a painted door that I know of, all the others are of rough-hewn timber or crude slats. Quick, you keep a look-out while I go and knock."

So while Soraya stood huddled in her cloak in the shadows, Alicia stepped up to the door and beat an urgent, soft tattoo on its smooth surface, the noise sounding terrifyingly loud in the quiet stillness of the night. And even as she did so, there came the sound of a heavy bell from the castle above them. A deep tolling that went on and on and on, rolling out across the countryside as it called the great Château to arms and instant wakefulness.

Their escape had been discovered at last and the Hue and Cry would be raised against them across the whole sleepy countryside.

With a rush of feet Soraya came to join Alicia, and together now they beat desperately with the flat of their hands at the sullen wood that lay before them. Any minute the great gates of the castle would open and armed, mounted men would pour out to search for them…and the town would be the first place they would surely scour.

"Oh come on, come on." Alicia breathed out desperately as once more she hammered at the door. "Stanisopoulos…answer our plea."

"Thank God. Someone's coming at last." Soraya replied urgently. "I can hear the scrape and shuffle of feet. Quickly, quickly for pity's sake, *hurry*!" she wailed as with barely a creak, the door opened slowly inwards and the dark, slightly bearded, face of a man peered round at them, the light from a flaring torch spilling out from behind him, masking his true features completely. And in the weird morning twilight it was impossible to tell accurately what he was like.

Alicia was just aware of a pair of shrewd eyes glistening from the darkness as they appraised her and her companion, and the voice, when it came, was a soft, sibilant whisper that in ordinary times would have given her real pause for thought, for there was a whiff of hidden malice in its smoothness: "What do you want, my pretties, at such an early hour in the morning? And with the Château calling out so urgent an alarm as well?"

"Shelter, *shelter*! And that right speedily." Alicia replied urgently. "For myself and my friend. Guillaume Soulier gave us your home as a safe refuge in time of trouble. Please let us come in. This place will be swarming with soldiers soon and by then we must be off the street."

Without further ado the man threw open his door and quickly pulled both the girls in, pausing briefly to glance round the square before swiftly shutting it again and bolting it securely. And now, by the light of the flaring torch on the wall, at last they could see more clearly who their rescuer was. Certainly he was not very tall, and the long black robe he was wearing, with its high collar, and hood thrown back onto his bony shoulders, gave him the appearance of greater height and bulk than he actually possessed.

His hands were thin with long, tapering fingers and he had a permanent stoop, brought on through many years of bending over his pestle, mortar and mixing bowls, for though he was not an apothecary, yet his chosen trade required much careful measuring and preparation. His eyes were furtive, dark, almond-shaped pools of secrets that shifted suspiciously from one girl to another, and he had a sharp little pointed beard. Bending forward to pull his cowl over his head before addressing them further, neither girl felt quite sure whether they wanted to trust him or not.

"So, Guillaume sent you to me did he?" he asked, sounding pleased. "Well that is fine and no mistake. Of course, you'll need a secure hiding place. I have a deep cellar that will defy even the most careful search, and when the soldiers have passed on I'll send a message to your friends, then we'll see what can be done."

"What is your name, sir?" Alicia asked quietly. "That I may be certain whom my rescuer is?"

"My name is Stanisopoulos," the little man replied, bowing his head, his eyes darting nervously over them. "Dmitri Stanisopoulos. I am a Greek. A perfume seller from Athens, the only one in Gruissan. The best along this whole coastline and do much business with the Château, especially with the Lady Rochine!"

Alicia and Soraya both started back at the mention of her name, too hurriedly to notice the sudden gleam of interest that flickered across the man's dark olive features, and both clasped each other's hands tightly.

"So, you fear her too?" he said, motioning them to follow him. "As I do also, I assure you," he added, turning to pat Alicia on the arm. "As we all do! But business is business, and one must find it where one can. Come now. Do not be afraid, I will not harm you. Now, quickly, for you must be safely hidden before anyone comes knocking at my door."

And with that the little man turned and scuttled off with his arms upraised like a black scorpion, the two girls following his shuffling figure along a noisome passage that ran through the house to a straight flight of narrow wooden stairs that led sharply downwards, ending at a stout oaken door with a small iron grille let into its hard surface.

Opening it, Stanisopoulos the Greek led the way forward into a fairly large room that was almost completely racked out with rows and rows of jars, phials and great earthenware bottles that clearly contained the many varying ingredients necessary for his wares. Without pausing, he seized hold of one of the racks that lay against the left hand wall of the room and stamping down hard on the stones he gave a mighty heave, and. with a groan of protest the whole shelf space moved slowly outward to reveal a stone trapdoor, set flush with the floor, that had swung open as the shelving was dragged clear.

Taking up a torch that had been burning in the room when they'd entered, the little stooped Athenian called the two women across, and bidding them be careful, began to descend the steep flight of stone steps that fell away into the cool darkness beyond, a rough rope in crude iron stanchions fixed into the wall for them to hang onto as they descended. At the foot of this staircase was the blank face of a very solid-looking door indeed, which when unbolted opened inward to reveal a deep cellar, some thirty foot square, that clearly lay well below the level of the ground. Despite that, the air was quite light and fresh for there were two iron grilles set in the wall high up near the ceiling through which a few stars could just be glimpsed.

A number of padded benches were placed against the walls, with a softly covered couch just off the centre of the room for comfort's sake, with a tall stone pitcher of water beside it and an octagonal table with a number of wooden beakers standing on a tray. In the far corner was a stone sluice that disappeared into the wall and a wide bucket with a wooden lid nearby with a box of rags beside it. Set in iron sconces in the rough stonework were some half a dozen fresh pine torches for light and warmth.

"Now, my ladies, you will be quite safe here 'til the first immediate search is over. You are well below ground level and this place is known to very few indeed. Only I know the mechanism that moves the swinging stone in the floor so even if searchers pull the shelves down around them, it will not activate the spring that holds the trap in place. So have no fear. No idle search will find you out, I promise you."

"You are very kind to risk yourself for us in such a way," Alicia replied. "I hope I will be able to reward you properly at some later date."

"Now don't you worry about that my Lady," he answered her, smiling as his eyes seemed to slither over her body. "I will get my reward, you be sure of that, from being able to serve you and repay a debt I owe to Guillaume Soulier at the same time."...*Now, why do I not wholly trust you, my little Greek friend? There is 'that' about your face that makes me uncertain!*

"So...will you be able to contact him soon?" she asked urgently.

"As soon as maybe," he said, moving to the unlit torches. "But I may have to wait until the searchers have been and gone, and all is quieter than it will be for some time. Now, I'll just light a few of these to chase away the shadows," he said pointing to the torches on the walls. "And then I must leave you. Don't worry about air, there is plenty of ventilation through those grilles up there. You will be fine 'til someone can come and collect you. I will bring you something to eat by and by, but the pitcher is always filled with fresh water and there is a..a bucket and things for your..er..use." he stammered awkwardly. "I do not often have young ladies to visit me, I am afraid. So..er..things are rather primitive down here."

"We will be fine Mr Stanisopoulos," Alicia answered him graciously. "Thank you. But some food would be lovely."

“Very well,” the little man replied, bobbing his head at her. “I will do what I can. Now fare thee well for the time being."

So saying he gave them a sly, toothy smile and backed out of the room, shutting the door behind him. They heard the scrape of his feet on the stairs and the thud as the trap finally closed them in, then silence.

All they could do now was wait.

Chapter 38...How the White Rose of Malwood was bitterly betrayed.

Outside was an appalling scene of noise and turmoil, shouts, screams and curses as the Baron's soldiers searched and ransacked every house in the town: ordering the occupants out into the streets while they turned everything over inside, especially those whom the Baron knew to be the Souliers' friends.

Some were dragged back to the castle to scream out their innocence to Monsieur Gullet, the Lord Baron's torturer, and any who showed defiance were cut down where they stood, before their wives and families, spilling their blood into the street, as house by house Le Brun and his men tore the place apart in their furious search both for the two women who had fled the Château…and for the Baron's Crystal which had disappeared with them.

To say that Lord Roger was incandescent would be to put it mildly, for after the first initial burst of wild fury, an icy rage had settled in his heart that only Alicia's discovery would assuage! Never had such a terrible thing happened to him. Never had Rochine seen her father in such a raging and merciless fury. Never had the Château Grise known such fear as that which stalked its battlements and corridors that dreadful morning.

Upstairs into attics…and down into cellars his soldiers went, shouted on by their sergeants, banging on walls for secret passages and stamping on floors for hidden chambers. But despite the killings and the torture, they found nothing. No-one had heard or seen anything either. It was as if the two young women and the girl had disappeared into thin air, together with Bertrand whom the Baron cursed with chilling violence, even as he sent men to seize the boy's father.

Of course he had the body of one of Alicia's friends, who had plainly been murdered by one of the two cousins who had both been found dead…so all knew from where they must have escaped. But where to…or even how?...as all was found closed up properly behind them, he had no idea.

So he vented his rage on the town and the surrounding countryside until no-one felt safe. Even his daughter felt it wiser to avoid him, as when he was in this kind of mood there was no knowing what he might do…even to her!

*

But of all this Alicia and Soraya remained in ignorance, though they guessed from all the muffled bangs and thuds they heard overhead from time to time during the day; and the screams and cries and angry voices that came down to them from the streets above, and from the burst of violence when a party of the Baron's men came to search the Greek's cellars, that a furious search was surely going on all around them.

Apart from that they remained in solitude, with only their thoughts and each other's company to console them. And it was now that Alicia grieved for Agnes most bitterly. Her lifelong friend and companion of her younger years, who knew her better than anyone…better even than Gui, and was now lost to her forever. And in the end she sobbed herself to sleep in Soraya's arms, feeling too low even to eat the food that the little Greek brought them. She just lay huddled in a corner of the couch they had found there when Stanisopoulos had opened the chamber, too wretched even to look up.

Meanwhile, in the flaring torch light Soraya examined their hideout but found nothing, save a number of ring bolts set firmly in the wall and in the floor that excited a certain amount of interest, but before long she settled down on the couch with Alicia's head in her lap to wait, their warm cloaks wrapped round them against the chill of the cold stone room in which Stanisopoulos had hidden them. They dozed fitfully as the day wore on, while they waited for their release.

Once Stanisopoulos came with a plate of pastries and a small flagon of rough wine, and then again to empty the slop bucket that both girls had been forced to use. But neither time did he stay long, seeming to find it difficult to make conversation with them, until they were both heartily fed up with his stammering and broken half-sentences, and were pleased in the end when he decided to leave them alone.

Eventually Alicia sat up and washed her face, her eyes red from weeping, and looked around her.

"What on earth do you think is going on?" she asked, as the little light that came in from the grilles began to fade. "We have been here for ages! Surely that Greek must have contacted Ralph or Guillaume by now?"

"Well," Soraya replied, "I expect they'll turn this place upside down first, and then when they've drawn a blank they'll move out into the countryside. He did say it might take some time. The Baron will be in a furious temper, and I wouldn't be a Grisian just now for anything. He hates to be thwarted and will strike out at anyone he suspects of treachery. Sadly there'll be a fair few widows come night time, my love, I can assure you."

"Oh, Soraya," Alicia sighed, slipping her arm round the girl's waist, and leaning her head on her shoulder for comfort. "That's just terrible! Not one bit what I expected when I left England with Gui. This whole thing has become a nightmare! Oh, dear God…I wish Gui would come and rescue us!"

"A nightmare is about right, sweetheart. Remember," she added, putting her arms around her friend. "It is not just you and me he seeks, my love. He seeks his Crystal too! That will have hurt him more than anything you could ever say or do. God pity us if ever he should lay his hands on either one of us again! And as for Gui, Alicia? He must be at Les Monges by now. You know him better than I do…would he be likely to rush into battle without first making sure of his ground?"

She sighed and rubbed her eyes. "No! No, Soraya, he wouldn't…and even if he wanted to neither Sir Richard nor Father Matthew would let him…*Oh Gui! Where are you? Come to me! Come to me!...* Just pray that Guillaume comes soon and rescues us. Then we will know."

"Don't you trust him to do his best?"

"Of course I trust him, Soraya. I just want him to *be* here!" she cried out in anguish. "To get us out of this hole in one piece, and then deal with that foul bastard and his whore of a daughter once and for all. And then there's the baby!" she cried out, suddenly cradling her belly. "Oh, Soraya I so want to tell him…not have to remain cooped up underground like two wretched moles, blind to all that is going on around them!" She flung herself down on the couch in frustration. "And what about Guillaume and his friends…and young Izzy too?"

"If they've any sense they'll be as far away from this place as possible!" Soraya answered briskly. "Then go to ground and wait out the storm. I expect that's why we've heard nothing yet. It'll take Stanisopoulos some time to find out where he is, and then if your Gui hasn't arrived he'll surely move us out."

"Do you trust him, Soraya?" she asked, stretching out on the settle and lying back against the cushions.

"Stanisopoulos? I don't know, Alicia. He says he does much work for Rochine at the Château, but I've never seen him before. There's something not very pleasant about him, I must say. Isn't that what you say? 'Beware of Greeks bearing gifts?'

"You found out then? What that means?"

"Bertrand told me the story that day we were with the fishermen. About the Trojan horse! But that could just be his way…Stanisopoulos's. In all honesty, there's not a great deal we can do right now, anyway. I just hope someone comes soon!"

"I didn't like his eyes. They seemed shifty and dishonest to me. But then maybe that's just my Englishness?"

There was a pause then as both girls sat and gazed blankly at the walls around them, both minds far away, lost in thought. Eventually Soraya gave a shudder and put her arms around Alicia...*At least we are together! What would I do without her? But is that Greek safe? Oh God!...Let him come back soon...*

"Alicia, I'm frightened." Soraya said, putting her head on her shoulder. "Suppose he's in league with Rochine? Suppose even now he's sent her a message that we're here in his house, and never contacts Guillaume or Ralph at all?"

"Hey? What's got into you all of a sudden?" Alicia asked, giving her a deep cuddle. "You were the confident one just now."

"I don't know," Soraya mumbled, snuggling into Alicia with a sob. "Just got a sudden attack of the megrims I suppose!"

"Oh, Soraya," Alicia sighed, giving the girl another warm squeeze and pressing her head into the hollow of her neck. "What have I got you in to? You could have stayed safe and sound up at the Château with Isabelle. I could have tied you both up or something...then you would have been fine. Instead of which..."

"Instead of which," Soraya interrupted her, lifting her head and wiping her eyes, "you have removed me from a life of fear and uncertainty in the castle working for Rochine...to a life of fear and uncertainty here with you in this ghastly cellar!" she went on, sitting up and giving Alicia a wobbly smile. "At least here I have the semblance of freedom...if not yet the reality. Don't you worry about me, Alicia. Truly! I'm well out of that place. I promise you. I just pray Rochine doesn't discover our whereabouts. She's worse than the Baron any day. She has a way of doing things that I have no wish to re-discover, I assure you! There are times when I think she is quite mad!"

"She's certainly a very strange lady," Alicia commented, standing up and taking a pace or two. "When I first met her, she was very warm indeed, exceptionally so I might say! Made love to me on the very night of the storm...or tried to."

"Yes! You..you said. I remember being astonished you had managed to resist her. I couldn't!"...And she hung her head.

"She even gave me this amazing bracelet when we first met, then turned completely against me to the point where we became declared enemies."

"Yes - we both saw that on our journey across from Bayonne.

"Well, Alicia," Soraya said, coming across to join her and examining the ornately carved bracelet. "The Lady Rochine has strange powers over people, particularly if they wear something she has given them. As long as you were with her father his power protected you. But now you are on your own anything may happen! "

"Don't frighten me, Soraya. We have enough to worry about without adding unnamed fears as well. But perhaps it would be wise to take it off. I told you I have often meant to, but left it on so as not to alert her to anything. Like you, I have no wish to fall into The Lady's clutches now!"

So saying, Alicia bent to remove the beautifully wrought piece with its finely entwined dragons, but either her wrist had swelled in her nervous excitement or the metal had contracted in some strange way, but try as she might she could not get it over her hand, and all she succeeded in doing was making her flesh red and sore as she tried to force it off. And it was in the middle of this silent struggle, with both girls bent forward in concentration that they heard, at last, the thud of the trap opening, followed by the sound of many feet on hard stone; and with a bang the door was flung open at last and Stanisopoulos came in.

Alicia and Soraya started to their feet in excitement; and then shrank back in horror and alarm for Stanisopoulos was not the only one to enter the room. Hard on his heels came half a dozen well-armed men who filed quickly to left and right of the doorway and then stood silently against the walls ,clearly waiting for their leader to follow. So there was a pause while the two girls, struck dumb with fright, slowly backed away to the far side of the room, as the sound of further treads came clearly to everyone. Then, pausing briefly by the doorway, the Lady Rochine de Brocas stalked in, whip in silk gloved hands, a wicked smile of satisfaction lighting up her face; with Ralph Soulier close behind her, supported by the swarthy renegade Burgundian, Jasper de Rombeau, her personal enforcer.

"So!...I have you both at last!

HISTORICAL NOTE

Firstly a small confession! Alnwick Castle, the home of the Northumbrian Percy family, was actually in the hands of the Bishops of Durham at the time of Gui's arrival up there as a young squire…and not in those of the Percy family at all. They bought it from Anthony Bec, the then Bishop in 1309, and it was after that that the present fantastic fortress was then built. However, the Percy family *were* very much a force to be reckoned with at that time through a very influential marriage. That of Agnes de Percy, Sole heiress to all the estates…which were huge!...to Joscelyn of Louvain, the half-brother to the former Queen of England, Adeliza of Louvain, King Richard's step-grandmother, the widowed second wife of his grandfather, King Henry Ist, who famously died of a surfeit of lampreys in 1135! I hope you will forgive me for that small piece of historical sleight-of-hand?

The Romans are a different matter altogether and produced the greatest civilisation on earth, until the modern era and the British Empire of the 19th Century. They were phenomenal builders, and extraordinary lawgivers. Our entire legal structure came out of Rome, and so did our military structure also. It is no accident that the way the British Army is organised so closely mirrors that of the Romans. After all, until very recent times, an understanding of Latin was a prerequisite for all students in public schools…and by the nineteenth century it was the public schools that largely produced the officers who led our regiments into battle. Hence the Duke of Wellington's reputed quote that 'Waterloo was won on the playing fields of Eton!' The methods and successes of the Roman army were almost imbibed with their mother's milk! The Battles of Cannae and Lake Trasimene are still quoted at Sandhurst. Automatic weapons, aquaducts, great civic buildings, sewers, hydrology and of course…hypocausts.

The construction of a hypocaust is exactly as I have described it. A maze of little pillars of brick and tile, laid on a concrete raft with great overlapping stone tiles laid on top and the concrete floor of the room itself on top of that, often beautifully decorated with the most elaborate mosaic patterns.

The same with the Roman pool as described in the book. There are amazing examples of such work in this country at Lullingstone Villa, and even more marvellous in Cyprus. Breath-taking artistry.

And concrete? Go to Richborough Castle in Kent if you doubt me. Or talk with Adam Hart-Davis. The stuff is still there and it is 1600 years since the Romans left these islands. Sadly there are no Roman aquaducts in existence in the UK…but in southern France, near Nîmes, the Pont du Gard is simply stunning, and that was built around 60BC, nearly a hundred years before the Claudian invasion of AD 43 brought the Romans permanently to our islands.

Something else the Romans had was contraception. The cream that Soraya tells Alicia about in the inn at Trebes was real. Made from the juices of the acacia plant and honey, and used as a plug within the vagina, it nullified the sperm and so prevented pregnancy. Truly they were an admirable people!

While it is true that the great years of the English longbow archer lay in the future when Gui set out to rescue Alicia, its usage was widespread in Wales and the Borders of both England and Scotland, and especially in Cheshire. Strangely the Welsh, from whom we really latched on to its potential, only used the longbow as an ambush weapon! They did not use it in open battle. Edward Ist was the first King to use the longbow in open battle, at the Battle of Selkirk. But Sir Edmund Mortimer used it spectacularly at the Battle of Orwin Bridge in December 1282 to destroy Llewellyn's army of over seven thousand men. He was the last *true* Prince of Wales and his death on that day, December 11th, led directly to the fall of Wales.

There were longbow archers with Richard's army in Palestine, but not in large numbers. The crossbow was his weapon of choice and he was deadly with it, as he showed at the siege of Acre. And raw recruits could be taught to us it quite quickly and easily…like muskets when they appeared five hundred years later. But as a weapon of war, the longbow was unprecedented. Twelve arrows a minute from a really competent archer, and with an effective range of 250 yards, it was devastating…as de Courcy discovered at Saint Jean D'Angély and Sir Jules at Castelnaudary…and the French later at Crécy, Poitiers and Agincourt!

Oh…and the tale of an arrow piercing a man's thigh, his saddle and his horse is absolutely true. Only it happened to one of William de Braose's mounted men-at-arms during Edward's wars in Wales. In fact de Braose goes on to say that the same Welsh bowman then pinned the same soldier, in the same way, through his other leg!

Cider! Well, Cider in Brittany makes its appearance officially in the 13th century…but the Saxons were wassailing their apple trees long before William turned up, so I have our chaps happily drinking it a hundred years earlier…not least because they already were cheerfully downing it in Normandy and in England. Chouchen Cider is real, it has honey in it and, in Gui's day, certainly was 'beefed' up with bee stings! Sadly today that is no longer the case…'elf an' safety have seen to that!

And finally a word on dildos! As Rochine found out for herself when her great-great-grandfather unearthed the Greek and Roman vases when building his castle…and verified by the many artefacts and paintings discovered more recently in Pompeii…sex toys have been around for a very long time. Now made in plastic, then made in leather and used in exactly the manner you would expect them to be…and Rome produced the best!

Aristophanes made much use of them in his comedy 'Lysistrata', written in 411BC, about a wife who forces the Greeks to stop making war by persuading every woman, including those who sold their bodies for sex, to stop allowing any man to make love to them…hence much use of dildos. And there was a thoroughly scurrilous poem doing the rounds in London in 1673, called '*Signor Dildo*', and published in November of that year by John Wilmot just at the time that Charles II's brother, James…later King James II…was considering marriage with the Catholic Italian Princess Maria of Modena, which is both witty and amusing. Purists would call it common doggerel, but I leave you to find it at your leisure…if not pleasure!

And S&M has been around long before '*Fifty Shades*' tweaked so much interest from so many people, or the Marquis de Sade gave his name to the whole practice of sexual enjoyment from pain!

Book IV...THE LION AND THE WHITE ROSE TRIUMPHANT.

Chapter 1...The lady has the White Rose of Malwood in her power at last.

Dressed in a long flowing loose dress of red satin cut low across her breasts, with her dark hair braided up on top of her head and lightly flicking her ebony-handled silken lash, the Lady Rochine de Brocas smiled brilliantly at her cousin and at Soraya, both white-faced with shock, their eyes huge with sudden terror, while Stanisopoulos gestured with his hand at the two women: "Here they are, my Lady, just as I told you!"

"You have done well my friend," Rochine said softly with her warmest smile. "And will be well rewarded too. Now leave us, and see to the other arrangements that I spoke of." And with a final, sliding glance around him the little Greek perfumier left, his dark eyes lingering on the two girls as he closed the door behind him, leaving Ralph Soulier to slouch against it, his face alight with victory, while de Rombeau's men stood back from the walls as they watched the drama unfold before them.

"Well, well!" Rochine exclaimed softly, after a pause, her green cat's eyes glittering in the torch light as she sauntered towards the two girls, now huddled together against the back of the cellar room, their arms tightly round each other.

"Just look who we have here?" she cooed softly, pleased beyond all measure as she looked them both over with a sardonic smile and a lifted eyebrow. "If it isn't two little damsels in distress?" And walking forward she chucked Soraya and Alicia under their chins, running the very tips of her nails down their cheeks, her eyes sparkling with pleasure. "Come from young Ralph to seek help from dear old Stanisopoulos, the little perfume seller? Tch! Tch!" She exclaimed softly with a low chuckle. "Whatever would Papa say now if he were here?"

And turning gently on her heels, she beckoned with her fingers to the dark-haired Burgundian who had been standing behind her.

"Jasper, my dear man," she went on, her voice almost a delicious purr of expectation. "Whatever should we do with these two lovelies for whom my father, in his so blessèd wisdom, is even now tearing the countryside apart with such persistent fury?" And with a cruel smile she turned back to flick each girl gently across the shoulder with the silken lash that tipped her ebony-handled whip; while her personal enforcer, the Burgundian mercenary, Jasper de Rombeau, stalked from the shadows of the open doorway into the middle of the room.

Above medium height and powerfully built with broad shoulders and heavy thighs, he had jet black hair that hung lankly to his shoulders in greasy strands, and small dark eyes placed close together that glittered in the torchlight. He reminded Alicia of the great black rats that she used to see from time to time around the tithe barn at Malwood. And now clothed in thick black leather stitched all over with heavy chain mail, the unmistakeable black boar insignia on emerald green of de Brocas fixed to his left shoulder, he looked even more so now. Indeed with so much black leather beneath his armour, and with sword and long dagger at his waist he was the very harbinger of evil intent, and the hard look on his face made both girls recoil in fear and distaste.

But most terrifying of all, across his shoulder he was carrying the great metal tipped scourge of Monsieur Gullet, Lord Roger's executioner.

While Soraya knew him of old, Alicia had never encountered him before, but she knew him at once for what he was and cowered away from him as he advanced into the middle of the room. Whatever else Rochine might have come for, rescue and reconciliation were not remotely in her mind...*Dear God aid us! Oh Gui! Where are you now?...*Clearly her cousin was bent on vengeance.

"I think, my Lady," de Rombeau said, his voice dark, his humour sardonic. "That these two naughty ladies need a damn good thrashing!" And in two swift, violent movements he whirled the great scourge around his head and flensed the nearest walls with terrifying force, forwards and back again, tearing chunks of plaster and ancient mortar out of both, and making the two girls scream with fear as he did so. Then, stepping back, he flicked the scourge back over his shoulder and laughed.

Too horrified to move and numb with shock, Alicia and Soraya could only stare at him with sheer terror in their eyes.

"Hmm, Jasper," Rochine said, turning towards him with a smile. "You are probably right, and you are experienced in these matters, I know. But that 'toy' of yours would leave them mauled beyond repair...and me unsatisfied." And she swayed gently away from him, a curious smile on her lovely face. "I have a different plan to teach them a lesson they will never forget!"

And in that instant, the Lady Rochine's whole posture and attitude changed. Gone was the sauntering, affected manner of her entrance, and with a swift turn she stalked towards where both girls were standing and let loose a tirade of fury.

"*So!*" she raged at them. "You thought to escape, did you? Thought you'd just run off into the night and find your little friends the Souliers? 'The house opposite the fountain with the blue painted door', if my information is correct?" she snarled, watching Alicia's face closely…and as she saw the shock of her statement register in the other girl's eyes she smiled.

"You little fool!" she sneered disdainfully, moving towards Alicia as she spoke. "Did you think I wouldn't know? This place crawls with my informers. Very little moves in Gruissan that I don't know about…but most stupid of all, you picked the wrong house!" And she laughed, the cheerful sound totally at odds with both time and place. "Almost any other householder would have helped you, cousin…but you came to my friendly little Greek, Stanisopoulos, instead!" And throwing back her head she laughed delightedly, her eyes sparkling with malice.

"You thought he was a friend of the Souliers. But in fact he has hated them for ever, and takes every possible chance to thwart them whenever and however he can! Guillaume believes he is a friend. And so he is…*my* friend!" She raged at them again, in another complete change of mood and speech. "He told you, you would be safe…and so you shall…safe with *me!*" And she laughed at the richness of her planning and the completeness of her victory.

"But Ralph Soulier?" Alicia managed to gasp out at last. "He is against the Baron, like his brother…" Her voice tailed away as she gaped at the enormity of his betrayal.

"Against my father?" her cousin laughed, dismissively. "Against Papa? *Ralph Soulier?*" she repeated, throwing her head back again and laughing uproariously.

"Dear Ralphy? He has been in my pay for *years*. He *hates* his brother as much as Stanisopoulos does!" She sneered at Alicia, her eyes darting over at Ralph's leering face. "But he likes my gold and longs to be the important one in the family. The one to make the decisions, the one that all the others look up to! He has been plotting to destroy his precious brother for ages…and now he has seized his chance to do so! He has served me well, and I always reward those who serve me."

"You traitor!" Alicia screamed at Ralph in dismay. "You saw me take your sister under my care, yet all the time you intended just to destroy your family. And for what?" she spat out at him. "This creature's money? For power? You disgust me!"

"Ho, the little bitch has teeth has she?" Rochine queried, laughing at Alicia's fury, flicking her switch from side to side as she spoke. "Come,

Ralph," she gestured, "and savour some part of your reward. Gaston!" she called over her shoulder. "Have two of your men hold this creature and let us see what she is made of!"

Even as she spoke, de Rombeau jerked his hands at two of his men, and before Alicia could move, they had seized her arms and shoulders and lifted her almost onto her toes in such a grip that any movement made her cry out, and using their thighs and calves they forced her legs apart.

"*No! No! You cannot do this to me!*"

"Yes I can, cousin!" Rochine snarled into Alicia's horrified face. "You thought to escape, didn't you?" Rochine hissed, coming right up to the helpless girl, Alicia cringing away from her as far as she could. Then handing her switch to one of de Rombeau's men, she plucked a knife from the man's belt as she passed, and seizing Alicia's kirtle in her hands, with one swift movement she ripped the sharpened blade through the rough material, through her under skirt and chemise, tearing the slashed material from her cousin's trembling body and so stripped her naked before them all.

"You thought you could bed my father and then just slip away unnoticed? Leave him sleeping unawares and then steal his Crystal? You little fool!!" She snarled, gripping Alicia's shocked face in her free hand and shaking it roughly. "How do you think you got out so easily, and with so many guards around?" And she threw back her head and laughed delightedly at the utter dismay that filled Alicia's face, and at the way she looked this way and that in complete turmoil.

"Oh...I don't know all that you did; nor how you reached your final goal...the sally port chamber is like a slaughter house. And how you slew the Cousins is beyond my reckoning! But I know enough. I told you that I knew this castle better than anyone alive.

"I watched you with my father, you little whore!" she spat at her. "Watched him fuck you until you didn't know whether you were coming or going," she added coarsely. "He's good, my dear Papa, isn't he? Ravaged you until you flew up into the stars, did he? Oh yes! I heard you both cry out. Watched you shake your pretty titties at him," she went on , smacking Alicia's naked breasts hard with her open hand at every word, making her cousin fling her head back and gasp through gritted teeth at every blow.

"But never again! I thought I could learn to share him with you, my so sweet cousin...you little bitch! *But I cannot*!" she screamed at her, flecks of spittle flying from her mouth. "Then I saw you leave your room with this...this *disgusting* animal," she said spewing the words out in Soraya's direction, "and that stupid girl, Isabelle, with the leather bag over her shoulder, and your pathetic little friend, that Agnes...and I knew you would come here.

Long before Stanisopoulos's message reached me, I knew! To the house with the painted door? The 'safe house' that Guillaume told you of? Yes?" And she laughed as the colour drained out of Alicia's face as the true horror of her situation struck home. "But it is *my* safe house, you fool!" she exclaimed again. "*My safe house!*" she screamed at her, and she hit her again one more time and walked away. " Now…take her Ralph, as I promised," she said over her shoulder. "She's all yours… just don't mark her!"

Alicia screamed and struggled desperately, like a butterfly in a spider's web. "*No! No!*"

"You can scream all you like, Alicia," she went on as her cousin cried out again in fear and horror. "No-one can hear you down here. There is no-one to help you now,"

And stepping away from Alicia, she let Ralph Soulier have his fill of her beauty, her long smooth legs and alabaster skin, jutting breasts still flushed and marked with the beating they'd just been given, the nipples bursting out of their swollen areolas, the girl's face white with shock and anger, helpless in the grip de Rombeau's men had on her. While all the time Alicia watched Ralph through slitted eyes, her face tight with disgust, her body shaking, her mind braced for his first touch…*I hate you, you ignorant bastard. Hate you! Hate you! You traitor! Just try to kiss me and I will punish you beyond your wildest nightmares!…Oh, dear God, help me! Help me!…*And stepping up, Ralph hit her breasts again, making her cry out in sudden pain and shock. "Where is my sister, you whore?" He snarled, foam from his mouth spattering her face as he struck her breasts again. "What have you done to her?"

"Done to her?" Alicia gasped, the pain of his assault rushing through her.

"Yes! Done to her. You and that filthy bitch over there," he gestured crudely at Soraya. "The Lady tells me you have murdered her…"

"Murdered her? Isabelle?" Alicia cried out, stunned by the wickedness of it.

"Don't lie to me, you bitch!" He shouted, striking her face this time with his open hand. "You persuaded her to help you in your pathetic escape and then murdered her! Her clothes have been found beyond the town covered in blood. But of my sister there is no sign!"

"We have done nothing to your sister, you *dolt!*" Alicia screamed back at him, squirming desperately against the hands of the men holding her, her eyes blurred with tears, her face stinging from his attack. "Except save her from your clutches, you ignorant beast!" And she spat at him. "That must be the blood of the men we killed by the sally port, you fool! Not your precious sister, you disgusting peasant!" She sneered at him.

"Oh, 'beast' am I? 'Dolt'? Disgusting 'peasant'?" He raged at her, striking her face again and again until her cheeks were badged with blood from her mouth and nose; her head snapping violently from side to side as he did so. "*You fucking whore*! You piece of vile English shite! With your smart voice and ladylike ways," he mocked her. "I'll show you what kind of beast I really am!" And shouting at de Rombeau's men: "Hold her open, you fucking idiots!" Ralph Soulier thrust his fingers deeply into Alicia's loins, twisting them inside her as he did so, making her scream out in torment, "*No! No!*" Her whole body leaping and squirming in the soldiers' grip as he plundered her, like a great fish on an iron gaff, her breasts bouncing and pushing out at him as he viciously raped her with his calloused fingers.

"Dripping!" he said triumphantly as he thrust his fingers roughly in and out of her loins. "The slut *loved* her smacking!" He shouted out to Rochine de Brocas, and grabbing Alicia's face with his other hand he forced his tongue into her mouth, slathering her with it until she could hardly breathe, while de Rombeau's men laughed at her agonised cries as they held her upright, her legs forced open so his fingers could continue to pump her; while he ate her face with slobbering lips, and Soraya screamed out and wept into her hands, unable to watch Alicia's torture.

Violated to her very core, twisting her body to try and free herself of the hated fingers as they deeply probed her, the stench of his breath washing over her, Alicia almost gagged on his tongue, thrust so boldly into her very throat. But she was ready for that, and sucking his tongue deep into her mouth…*Now I have you, you bastard!*...she gave him the punishment she had thought of moments before, and with one mighty clench of her jaws, her eyes bulging in her face with the effort, the Lady Alicia de Burley drove her teeth crunching through the vile thick, rubbery flesh that filled her mouth and with a final toss of her head she bit his tongue off almost to its roots!

This story is continued in Book IV:
The Lion and the White Rose Triumphant.

Glossary

Abigail	An 'abigail' is the generic name for a young female servant, but most 'abigails' often became highly valued close personal servants.
An 'Alien' House	For monks, often a Priory, where the 'Mother House' for those who lived there was overseas. 'Alien' Houses paid no taxes to the Crown and Henry V suppressed them all by Act of Parliament in 1414.
Apollo	The Roman and Olympian god of light and of the sun, who drove his flaming chariot across the sky. Synonymous with Helios, an earlier Titan god of the sun and his brother Hyperion, the Titan god of Light….whom the Celts called Lugh.
Ashlar	Blocks of smoothly worked stone, every face a flat perpendicular.
Aurora	The Roman goddess of the dawn and herald of the sun.
Bailey (The)	This was the courtyard, sometimes huge and often down to pasture, that lay within the encircling walls of a castle. By the time of this story the usual castle Motte was being replaced by a massive stone Keep…London, Dover, Rochester…sometimes called a Donjon and, because of the Crusades, being built round instead of square…like Windsor, Orford and York.
Bailiff	A man appointed by a lord to work with his Steward to manage an estate. He comes midway between both, and had wide powers to fine and punish the Manor workers.
Baldric	The belt that carries a sword and dagger.
Ballista	Roman style stone throwing machine, could also fire a heavy iron-headed bolt, a torsion machine worked by ratcheted arms and twisted animal sinews. Could fire a 20lb weight 3/400yards.
Bears	There were bears in the great forests of England right up to the Conquest and beyond, but not by the time Alicia fled into the Forest! However there *are* wild brown bears still in the Pyrenees, similar to the grizzly bear from the Rocky Mountains.

Black monks Because of what they wore; the Benedictines, the most influential Monastic Order of the Middle Ages.

Betrothal In the Middle Ages a 'Betrothal'…what today we call an 'Engagement', was like a marriage. Blessed by a priest and accompanied by serious promises, you could *not* then marry anyone else without first formally being cleansed of your vows. Very serious stuff!

Bilges The very bottom of a ship, below the lowest deck cover, where loose water from leaks, rain or sea can collect and then be pumped or bailed out.

Blazon The heraldic beast, or device, worn by a knight with its heraldic background.

Bliaut Long over gown, often pleated, worn by both men and women. Very popular for generations and made of every material known in those days.

Borel folk Illiterate country workers.

Brigandine A tough leather coat studded with metal plates, where the plates are *underneath* the jacket, not on top like a byrnie.

Bulwarks The sides of a ship above the deck, as opposed to 'bulkheads' which are dividing partitions below deck.

Buss An exceptionally large cargo ship of the time. Bigger than a cog and deeper.

Byrnie A tough leather coat to which metal plates, scale armour or chain mail has been fixed. Sometimes just thick boiled leather with loose chain mail on top.

Cable A 'cable' is taken from the length of an anchor cable in the days of sail, usually 100 fathoms. Six feet to a fathom; so, 600ft in imperial measurement, about 200 yards. Officially one tenth of a nautical mile!

Cabochon Gemstones were not 'cut' as such in those days, they were shaped and polished. The cutting wheel was not invented until the late 1400's, and truc faceted stones, as we know them today, not until after 1914.

Cadge A square wooden frame for carrying hooded birds of prey. It is carried on long straps over the shoulders by a hawking assistant walking in the middle of it. Not used on horseback.

Cambric A light-weight material made from Egyptian cotton and used for making fine shirts, or night gowns.

Candia	Candia, the modern city of Heraklion, on Crete. The whole island was then an outpost of Venice and famed for its slave trade. Candia was seized by the Ottoman Turks in 1669 after a sixteen year siege. The longest siege in history!
Cantle	The high back to a medieval saddle.
Casque	The round dome-topped helmet that came in around this time, sometimes with a nasal protector, sometimes with a perforated faceplate when it was known as a 'salt cellar'.
Chain Mail	The most usual form of body defence at this time. Best chain mail was a mass of individual iron rings individually riveted and interlocked one around another, weighed around 80lbs and covered the wearer from head to foot. In these times the hood, and the mittens, were an integral part of the whole suit, and it took two men to help put it on and pull it off.
Chausses	Trousers, usually leather, like the 'chaps' worn by cowboys, but could be any favoured material. Often overstitched with chain mail, and covered by a long hauberk.
Chemise	An under shirt, or blouse, could be of almost any material to suit the wearer, the occasion and the purse. Worn by both sexes. Sometimes took the place of a girl's shift or nightdress.
Christian mail	This was much thicker and heavier than Eastern mail, and Syrian arrows could not pierce it!
'Clack' of wine	A large swallow or good mouthful of wine.
Collops	A cut of meat, usually venison but can be beef or lamb.
Crenellations	The proper name for 'battlements'. The crenel is the gap between the merlons…the upright 'teeth' that make up the battlements. Any knight wishing to turn his earth and timber castle into a stone one had first to get a 'Licence to Crenellate' from the King. Any castle built without Royal authority was illegal…adulterine!...and could be destroyed.
Curtain wall	That stretch of battlemented wall that lies - hangs - like a curtain, between one tower and another around a castle.
Curtilage	The land that surrounded the home or castle or farmstead, with its immediate outbuildings. Still used by solicitors in conveyancing.

Cyclas A knight's long over dress, only ever worn over armour, that carried his blazon, usually of white material...but could be coloured.

Demesne The home farm.

Destrier A trained war horse, or charger…hugely expensive. Cross between a Shire and a heavy hunter. Now an extinct breed.

Devil Wind Today this is called 'La Tramontane' and blows violently from the north-west down the Pyrenees towards the Mediterranean, sometimes with torrential rain. It howls and rages and can drive people mad, hence its name!

Diana Roman goddess of the moon and hunting: her twin brother, Apollo, tricked her into shooting her lover Orion in the head while escaping from a giant scorpion. Her father, Zeus/Jupiter, could not make him immortal, but put him in the sky alongside her, so she could be still be with him every night. Ahhhh! Bless!

Djinns Muslim spirits of fire, we call them geniis, made famous by Aladdin! Can be really evil, and always tricksy, Can assume human form, often hideous and sometimes found in lamps and bottles!

Drudges Menial servants, usually women, who worked in the kitchens or about the castle, doing manual labour.

Doucets The testicles of a deer: quite a delicacy when cooked in a garlic and white wine sauce.

Doxy A low born mistress, or woman of uncertain morals, often found in ale-houses…what today might be called a 'tart' or a 'slag'. One up from being a whore!

Ermine The white body and black tail of a stoat in its winter colours; very exclusive and very expensive. Used for the edges of valuable clothes, even a lining, and as a decorative background for a knight's blazon: still worn today in full House of Lords regalia.

Fetlocks The lovely long hairy bits above and around a horse's hooves

Fewmets The droppings of any hunted game animal, but especially of deer as in this case.

Flambeaux Flaring beacons in an iron basket on an iron stand, very much like a giant torch.

Friars Also wandering monks but in brown habits. Often chaplains to Great Houses. Think 'Friar Tuck'!

Furlong A measurement of land, still used in horse racing today. One eighth of a mile - 220yards. A cricket pitch is one tenth of a furlong

Gambeson Like a thick eiderdown…a tough leather coat, split to the waist between the legs for ease of movement, stuffed with wool and stitched all over in pockets to maintain conformity. Usually worn under a knight's chainmail armour to protect him from the battering effect of weapons in combat.

Garderobe A loo. Great fun to find when out 'Castling'!

Gralloch The gutting of a deer after a kill, usually done immediately by hanging the beast up from a tree. The lights and offal were given to the hounds.

Great Helm A close fitted barrel helmet made of hammered iron, or steel if you could afford it, with slits for the eyes and perforated for breathing. Padded with wool and straw and fitted almost to the shoulders. Secured by a strap under the chin and sometimes connected to the waist by a chain. Many crusaders had a cross shaped piece of iron/steel across the front and over the back of it for additional strength: could be domed or flat.

Greek Fire Truly a horrendous weapon, and remains a real mystery even today. Modern chemists believe it was a form of napalm, probably petrol-based, with pine resin and maybe sulphur added: but no-one's quite sure. Water spread it and it could only be extinguished with sand, vinegar or old urine! The Moslems tried to replicate it but were unable to perfect it. Theirs was known as 'Arab Fire' and seems not to have been nearly so explosive as true 'Greek fire'.

Grey monks The Franciscans, wanderers and teachers, named after St Francis of Assisi, the patron saint of all animals.

Guerdon A reward to a knight for his courage and his chivalry from a lady as a symbol of her love before going into battle, or at a tournament, and signalled by the gift of a piece of silk placed around the end of his lance…to be reclaimed afterwards.

Hauberk	A knight's jacket, or whole coat, of chain-mail or overlapping scale armour, sometimes loose and worn over a gambeson; sometimes stitched or riveted to a tough leather jacket/coat…and by the time of our story reaching to the ground if the knight could afford it.
Heater shield	Shaped like the bottom of an iron. Easier to use than the kite shaped shield of earlier years: came into fashion about this time.
Herne the Hunter	Mythical god of the forests, probably Celtic.
Jack	Leather 'Jacks' were the tankards of the Middle Ages, and hugely popular everywhere. Only in England were they made waterproof!
Kist	A large wooden chest, for clothes or armour, often strengthened with iron or brass, and often with domed tops to ward off the rain! In the case of the Royal Treasury…literally filled with gold and silver coins!
Marchpane	What we call marzipan. Name changed in the 19th century.
Meinie/meisnie	A knight's personal armed followers, his own household troops. Took oath of their Lord and were paid and maintained by him. They wore his blazon.
Mie	Your lover: could be used to a much cherished child.
Mistral (Le)	Violent cold wind that blows down the Rhône valley from the Alps into the Mediterranean basin, and can cause sudden ferocious storms. Napoleon passed a law that excused 'crimes of passion' if committed when the Mistral had blown for more than three days!
Liripipe	A long tail of material attached to a hood that acted like a scarf in foul weather.
Lure	An essential falconry item for recovering a bird: usually the wings of a wood pigeon, because the grey and white feathers flicker when it is swung, or some other game bird. Sometimes fixed to a small piece of wood and then to a long cord that can be whirled round and round to attract the falcon/hawk, with a tasty lump of meat tied on its back to reward the bird when it has been successfully 'lured'.
Lymer	A scent hound, like a bloodhound, but wholly different in shape from today.

Mangonel Light medieval artillery. A siege weapon, sometimes like a giant crossbow on wheels, sometimes with an upright bar against which a throwing arm could strike instead of a bow. Could throw a 50lb missile 300/400yds.

Mantling What a bird of prey does to protect its kill, by drawing its shoulders…its wings right over the prey object. Bats do the same thing.

Medium Usually a woman through whom spirits can be heard and even seen when in a trance.

Merlons The upright 'teeth' that make up the battlements of a castle.

Meurtrières Murder holes in the roof of a castle gateway passage through which boiling oil or any kind of missile could be poured or hurled upon an enemy below.

Nemesis Traditionally the daughter of Zeus and the distributer of fortune and retribution, neither good nor bad necessarily, but each in due proportion to what was deserved. Often seen as the implacable distributer of Divine retribution against hubris…human arrogance before the gods!

Orphrey Beautifully intricate embroidery, often with gold and silver thread, very expensive and very popular at this time.

Ouches Great brooches of intricately worked gold and precious stones mostly used to pin a cloak to the shoulders.

Outremer This word literally means…'Beyond the sea'…and could apply to anywhere beyond the borders of one's own country; but by the time of this story had come to signify the Holy Land. The King could not make his barons fight 'Outremer'. Fighting 'beyond the sea' had to be voluntary.

Palantir A Seer Stone, a great crystal ball used by anyone of sufficient intellect and mental power to view things from afar, sometimes through a Medium. Made famous by the Dark Lord of '*Lord of the Rings*'…and by gypsy fortune tellers!

Palfrey A light riding horse, usually ridden by women, or a knight wishing to spare his destrier on long journeys. Different from a rouncey.

Paynims	A very medieval word for a heathen, a pagan, or any kind of Moslem infidel.
Pommel	The high front of a medieval saddle, or the weighted handle-end of a sword, iron or steel, sometimes with a fancy jewel set into it.
Poniard	A dagger with a fine pointed blade.
Quillons	The metal cross piece at the top of a sword or dagger: could be chased…incised… with gold or silver.
Rache hound	Like a modern fox hound.
Revetted	Lined with shaped stone…most often a castle ditch, or moat.
Rouncey	A breed of Spanish horse that was most popular at this time as a 'maid-of-all-work'. About fifteen hands, so not a large animal, but sturdy and strong in work.
Sabatons	Steel boots that could be worn to protect the feet.
Sanglier	The wild boar, big and dangerous, especially around mating in the autumn, or if cornered…or sows with shoats at heel who feel threatened, and will defend their young with extreme vigour! A large male can weigh over 600lbs and have six inch tushes, often curled, razor sharp and deadly.
Sarcenet	A thick silk material used for lining garments.
Sendal	The finest of silk material used as a lady's light over gown or negligée. Almost transparent, like Soraya's yashmak.
Sconces	Wall fittings for holding a torch, or a big candle. The torches themselves were usually made of long bundles of reeds, or strips of unseasoned soft wood, usually pine, tightly bound together and dipped in pine resin; could come in a portable metal holder.
Scorpion	Similar to a small mangonel sometimes with a sling: a torsion weapon, using twisted animal sinews.
Seneschal/Steward	A hugely important post on any great estate, or in the kingdom; usually a member of the knightly class, like Sir James at Malwood, often a family member on a big estate, who 'ran' everything in the absence of his Lord, or alongside his lord if he was at home.
Sheets	In sailing, 'sheets' are ropes for handling sails or spars.

Sherbet or Sharbat A deliciously refreshing drink made with fresh fruit and spices, very popular in the Middle East where alcohol remains forbidden: even better with ice.

Shoats Young wild boar; prettily striped in ochre, chocolate and cream for the first six months or so.

Sounder A group of wild boar, usually sows, young males and babies. Adult males are much more solitary except at mating time in the autumn.

Sumpter A horse used especially for carrying goods in boxes or wicker panniers carried on either side on a special frame called a 'crook'. Like the rouncey, not a big horse, but strong in work. What today would be called a 'pack horse'

Talbot A very large pure white scenting dog for hunting game, now extinct. The heraldic beast of the Earls of Shrewsbury: like a big dalmatian…but with a heavier jaw and without the spots. Norman, very popular with the Conqueror, who is said to have brought them with him.

Thews The mighty muscles in any fighting man's strong arms and thighs!

Times of Day Matins: Midnight; Lauds: Cockcrow…3/4.00am; Prime: 6.00am; Terce: 9.00am; Sext: Noon; None: 3.00pm; Vespers: 6/7.00pm; Compline: 9.00pm.

Trebuchet The heavy artillery of the medieval world. A huge stone throwing machine that could hurl a 300lb stone, or a dead horse, over quarter of a mile! An enormous timber construction worked by a vast counterweight, with a throwing arm the size of a tall pine tree with a sling on the end. Monstrous and accurate. The best example of a full size working trebuchet is at Warwick Castle…and they have never tested theirs to the limit!

Trencher A large, thick piece of stale bread that served as a plate on which your meaty meal could be served. A good 'trencher man' was one who finished off his meal by also eating his 'plate', having already eaten everything else!

Trumpet sleeves Long deep sleeves, sometimes almost to the ground and often trimmed with ermine. The sleeve hangs down from the upper arm, which itself is usually tightly sleeved by an undergarment called a chemise…what we would call a shirt or blouse.

Tushes A wild boar's fighting tusks…See '**Sanglier**'.

Vassals In the Middle Ages a vassal was anyone holding land from, or owing allegiance to, someone else: peasants were vassals of knights; who were vassals of barons and earls…who were vassals of kings who, in turn…technically…were vassals of the Pope, who ultimately sanctified his Kingship, and the Pope was/*is* a vassal of God! All of which led to terrible rows between kings and the Church as to which was the greater, and whom should pay homage to whom! Led to Thomas Becket's murder in 1170.

Verderers Technically they were what today would be called 'gamekeepers', with all the skills with birds, animals and habitat that that implies, but in the Middle Ages they were also Officers of the Law; and given tough powers of life or death over poachers!

Vexin (The) This was a small buffer 'state' between Normandy and the lands ruled directly by the Kings of France. 'The Vexin' was really hot property, and caused huge problems between the Kings of England and the Kings of France…hence Alicia's bitter comment!

White Monks The Cistercians because they wore white habits. The greatest breeders of sheep and cattle in the Middle Ages, and noted for their ale and their wine making. Sprang out of the Benedictines in 1098. Tintern, Fountains and Rivaux for example.

Wimple This was usually a very simply made woman's headdress held in place with a fillet of precious metal, or a different piece of material. Not the hugely elaborate headgear that came into fashion in the fifteenth century!

Withers A horse's shoulders.

Wolves Typical European timber wolf…and were a real menace in the Middle Ages, especially if the winter was cruel, forcing them to seek food from the farms and villages….so very much a part of Gui and Alicia's life in the Forest in 1190. The last British wolf was shot in Scotland in 1680, and extinct throughout the British Isles by the late 1700s.

Zeus — The Olympian King of the Gods, whom the Romans called Jupiter or Jove.

VERY SIMPLE HERALDRY

Blazon — The whole coat-of-arms, including any heraldic beast on its field.

Colours — Azure: blue; Gules: red; Vert: green; Sable: black; Purpure: purple

Fields — Background colours, metals or furs on which the principal device of each family is painted.

Furs — Ermine: white with black tails…the stoat in winter colours.

Vair: Squirrel, uniquely patterned and usually in alternate colours. Either fur can be used as a whole field.

Metals — Gold: or; Silver: argent. These also double as yellow and white fields

Heraldic Beasts — Too many to mention. I have used several, including dragons: here are the four principals from the story:

Lion Rampant…upright on his back feet, forward facing, paws up…De Malwood.

Lion Rampant-Gardant…upright on his back feet, paws up but looking at you…Richard L'Eveque

Stag's Head Erased…just the antlered head of a stag looking at you…De Burley

Boar's Head Erased: Just the tushed head of a wild boar looking forward and upwards…De Brocas

Beasts Armed — Claws, teeth and tushes all coloured or metalled differently from the main beast: EG: 'armed gules'…all the 'bits' appropriate to the beast described on the blazon but coloured red. Stags are 'attired' not 'armed'.

Langued — Tongues coloured or metalled different from the main beast.